FACING EVIL

ALSO BY KYLIE BRANT

FACING EVIL

THE CIRCLE OF EVIL TRILOGY, BOOK 3

KYLIE BRANT

THOMAS & MERCER

Published by Thomas & Mercer, Seattle

www.apub.com

Amazon, the Amazon logo, and Thomas & Mercer are trademarks of Amazon.com, Inc., or its affiliates.

ISBN-13: 9781477829851
ISBN-10: 1477829857

Cover design by Marc J. Cohen

Printed in the United States of America

For Bri, our soon-to-be newest member of the family. Given the number of years you've been exposed to this crew, you can never claim you didn't know what you were getting into!

Welcome to the family!

Two Days Earlier

The killer briskly worked the duct tape over her captive's bound wrists, threaded the ends through the car's steering wheel, and wrapped it around several times. "You don't remember me—I can tell."

The retired social worker couldn't speak. The length of tape across her mouth made it impossible. But she shook her head, her eyes wide and terrified.

"You broke up my family twenty years ago. Took my son away." Satisfied with her handiwork, she glanced at her victim. "Still nothing? Probably can't keep count of the families you destroyed. Nosy bitch. It took me eight years to track him down to the shitty foster home you had him stashed in. But he was never right after that. Damaged his mind when you took him away from his mother. Now he's dead, and you're going to pay for that."

She left the victim struggling to free herself and went to the bushes at the mouth of the overgrown driveway nearby. The gas can she'd stashed there last night sloshed as she walked back to the vehicle. Taking her time, she unscrewed the cap, then opened the driver's door, waiting for the delicious moment when her victim realized her fate.

The social worker's screams were muffled, but her frenzy was satisfying. The killer methodically doused the front seat of the car, smiling as she tipped the can so the fluid ran over the woman's hair. Down her face. Dousing her frumpy flowered blouse and baggy denim capris. Streaming down the woman's spider-veined legs and pooling around feet encased in a pair of blindingly white tennis shoes.

After shaking out the last few drops, the killer tossed the now-empty can onto the seat beside her captive and leaned in to turn on the ignition. Her victim was shrieking behind the tape, the guttural sound raw and primitive. "Got your attention now, don't I? Didn't listen worth a shit when you took Sonny away from me, though. Bet you don't even remember recommending that my parental rights be terminated, because I didn't deserve to ever see my son again." She smiled, straightening to pull a pack of matches from her pocket. "Time for you to get what *you* deserve."

She scraped the wooden match along the side of the box until it flared, then held it out for her victim to see. With a flick of her thumb, she sent the match tumbling through the air to land in the woman's lap.

The killer watched with fascination as the flames leaped to life. Jesus, it was fast. The blouse ignited first, shooting greedy little fingers of flame in all directions. For a moment she was sorry she'd gagged the older woman. The screams were always so very satisfying. She listened to them sometimes in her dreams, echoing and throbbing inside her, haunting reminders of her own screams all those years ago when she'd been helpless. Hopeless.

But not for a long time. Never again.

The heat from the conflagration inside the car soon forced her to retreat several feet. The social worker's hair was on fire now, and the killer chuckled at the sight. Like Bozo the Clown, only with a ring of fire instead of that wreath of red hair. Waving gaily, she turned and bent to retrieve the license plates and the screwdriver she'd used to remove them before walking away from the abandoned building site and down the road. Her vehicle was a couple of miles away. She'd be long gone before anyone figured out where the smoke was coming from.

She and her partner had planned for every contingency. Overplanned, maybe, but lack of trust would do that. And she was following their plan to a T. With a few of her own variations. She was capable of multitasking. And there were scores that needed settling.

The sun seared through her, although it was only midmorning. July in Iowa. Why the hell hadn't she left here a long time ago? She wouldn't be sorry to leave this fucking state behind when the time came.

But that time wasn't quite yet.

Her son was dead. The memory squeezed her chest. Her poor Sonny. He'd been kinda sweet as a little kid. Not all crazy like he'd been once he'd grown up. There were people directly responsible for the crazy. One of them was dying right now. The men who had hurt him way back then would all pay. It was just a bonus that death excited her. And coupling it with revenge was every bit as fulfilling as she'd remembered.

The heat sent nasty little trickles of sweat down her spine as she walked. The trickles had become a river before she turned up the overgrown grassy driveway and made her way through a grove of trees surrounding a blackened shell of a farmhouse. Detouring toward the sagging and gaping front steps, she dropped the license plates from the social worker's car in one of the yawning cracks before continuing to the back. Rounding the rotting home, she beelined for the car she'd left behind an old shed a hundred yards from the house. The thought of the air-conditioning that awaited her in the vehicle was welcome. The sound coming from the closed trunk, however, was not.

"Hot enough in there, Curt?" she asked conversationally, pitching her voice over the sound of the banging and muffled curses. "I think you've got a little preview of hell coming to you. Nothing less than you deserve for the way you abused my poor Sonny."

Slipping into the car, the killer turned on the ignition and was greeted by a blast of tepid air from the vents. After backing carefully down the rutted drive, she turned onto the ribbon of gravel, her mind already focusing on the list she kept in her head. Not everyone on it would be as easy to pick off as the dumbass social worker and Curt. And the ones who had caused Sonny's death would be the most challenging. The fucking cop who had followed Sonny to her place, forcing her to leave her dying boy and go on the run. And the shrink who had worked with the cops. The bitch had probably read Sonny's demented mind like a psychotic dot-to-dot. Worse, she'd distracted Vance from their strategy.

The killer smiled, reached in her purse with gloved hands to flip open a pair of sunglasses, and slipped them onto her nose. Those two required something special.

And her plan for their end was nothing short of brilliant.

Michael Frasier waved irritably at a fly and peered at his smartphone. Lingering over his morning coffee to peruse Craigslist was a daily ritual. Most people didn't realize how often you could find free stuff on there, posted by people who just wanted someone to haul it away. He'd gotten his couch that way, and a decent entertainment center.

He'd also cased a few places worthy of a later return, which had turned out even more profitable. People stupid enough to invite strangers to their personal addresses were, in Michael's considered opinion, fucktards who deserved whatever they got.

Elbows propped on the diner's cracked counter, he skimmed the day's offerings, following links and opening pictures. Finally deeming the listings uninteresting, he switched his attention to the personal ads, which, if less fruitful, were always entertaining.

A familiar heading jumped out at him. *Dark Fantasies.* The ad had appeared a couple of weeks ago. He wondered how many others found it as intriguing as he did.

Females in Des Moines area looking for tough, undomesticated males to make our rape fantasies come true. Thorough and anonymous screening process. Stringent rules applied to ensure safe, legal, titillating pleasure. The phone number that followed wasn't local.

Frasier lifted his cheap coffee mug to his lips and sipped, gaze still glued to the ad. He wasn't exactly sure what *titillating* meant, but it sounded dirty. The whole thing had to be too good to be true. Some sort of police sting maybe? But they wouldn't waste their time on what went on between consenting adults. Which meant it was legit, leaving him to question what kind of women would post something like this to strangers.

He pondered that as he drained the cup and set it back on the counter, sending a commanding look toward the tight-lipped owner lurking at the far end of the scratched Formica. He and that dried-up old bitch had an ongoing battle, but they'd come to terms weeks ago. She wouldn't hassle him about his habit of coming in and paying a dollar fifty for constant coffee refills if he was out of there before the lunch crowd started. In return, he wouldn't slash the tires on that piece-of-shit car she drove every day. Silently the old bat brought a fresh pot over and set it down in front of him before sidling away again.

The women he came into contact with at the bars he hung out at wouldn't have to put an ad in the paper. Most of the guys they were acquainted with would be all too happy to drill them any way they wanted it and a few ways they didn't. Which meant the women who'd posted this ad were different. They weren't whores, strippers, or addicts, and they didn't know the kind of men who didn't give a shit about dating and could do them hard and dirty and then walk away. *Anonymous.* Because the females placing the ad couldn't afford to have people know what they were up to?

He brooded over his coffee. Bored housewives maybe. Or some broads with important jobs who'd blown their way to the top and now couldn't afford to have people know how kinky they really were.

He blew at the steam rolling off the coffee before taking a cautious sip. With six months left on his parole, Frasier couldn't afford to screw up and get sent back to Anamosa. But there was no way his candy-ass parole officer could find out he'd called a number in the personals, for chrissakes. No harm in that. And if there was a woman out there just dying to take it rough and hard . . . His smile had the woman behind the counter retreating a step.

Well, then they were a perfect match.

Chapter I

A raucous trio of crows wheeled across the summer sky, their cries splitting the reverend's final prayers for everlasting peace to be granted to Emily Stallsmith.

Division of Criminal Investigation special agent Cam Prescott surveyed the crowd at Des Moines's Bethel Cemetery and wondered how many of the five-hundred-plus people packed inside its gates actually knew the deceased. From the looks of things, a full quarter of the mob was media. Sadly, Stallsmith would always be best known as the seventh victim of the Cornbelt Killers.

It was inevitable that some airhead national news anchor would come up with a nickname for the trio that had robbed, raped, tortured, and killed at least fourteen women. Just the thought of the cheesy moniker put a frown on Cam's face as he scanned the crowd.

Seeing his expression, Sophie murmured, "Do you think Vickie Baxter is here?"

"If she is, the cameras we mounted will pick her up." Agents were scattered throughout the crowd, all of them armed with photos of Baxter. Cam slanted a glance at the woman by his side. "You don't believe she'd come, even if she's still in the vicinity."

She looked pensive. "I don't have reason to, no. She lacks the ego of Mason Vance. The mental illness of her son. Sonny Baxter was the one to fixate on the victims after he'd killed them. His mother is much more calculating. As soon as they were dead, I think the victims ceased to exist for her."

It would be hard to discount her words, even if he wanted to. Dr. Sophia Channing was the forensic psychologist who had worked with DCI on the case almost from the beginning. She'd narrowly avoided becoming another victim when she'd been kidnapped by Mason Vance nearly six weeks earlier. It was Sophie who had predicted the second killer's mental instability, even before they'd had the evidence of it.

Ice skittered down his spine at the memory of how close she'd come to dying at Vance's hands. He'd almost lost her then. That thought was never very far from his mind. And although the bruises on her refined features had faded and she no longer wore the splint on her wrist, he knew there'd be less-visible scars from the ordeal that persisted.

He'd experienced for himself just how long the effects of traumatic stress could linger. And while she was a psychologist, it was a helluva lot different counseling patients with PTSD than it was grappling with it yourself.

Recognizing that made him cautious, even as a primitive sense of protectiveness had him keeping her close. They'd known each other professionally for years. Had first been lovers for twelve glorious days in May. She'd kicked him to the curb shortly before this case had brought them back together again, platonically this time. At least at first.

The idea of platonic had been blown to bits the moment he'd learned a madman had kidnapped her. Somehow Sophie had ignited a hunger in him that he'd yet to assuage. He was beginning to believe he never would.

She leaned into him a bit, tipping her face up to his. "Vance is in jail awaiting trial. Sonny Baxter is dead. And his mother had every reason to flee the state. There's nothing left here for her except eventual capture. I know it's second nature for you to be suspicious, but two out of three of the killers are accounted for. You can start to breathe a little easier anytime now."

Cam eyed her. She had a discomfiting ability to read his mind at times, a quality that could make him more than a bit uneasy. But in this case she was spot-on. Vance was currently in Polk County lockup awaiting trial for the rape, torture, and murder of at least six women. Sonny Baxter was dead, at his mother's hand. Vickie Baxter—the woman who had donned victim three's identity and been known to them as Rhonda Klaussen—was at large.

His team was still putting together the extent of the woman's role in the crimes. What they now knew was that she and her son had been killing long before Mason Vance came on the scene. "I'll relax as soon as Baxter is in a cell like Vance." He returned his gaze to the cluster around the open grave. Some people on the fringes of the scene began to drift away.

Sophie said, "I want to speak to Kevin Stallsmith before we leave." He nodded, and they began to make their way toward the graveside. The widower was surrounded by sympathetic well-wishers, and they waited for several minutes before the man spotted them and excused himself, heading toward Sophie.

"Dr. Channing." Stallsmith halted in front of her. The heat had turned his square face below the blond crew cut slightly pink. "Thank you for coming." His sidelong glance might have been meant to include Cam in the pleasantry, but it was difficult to tell. Neither of their two meetings had been under the best of circumstances. "I appreciated the note. Your words . . . they helped. Thank you."

The expression on the man's face was so rawly emotional as he took Sophie's hand that Cam had to look away. He lacked her ease with wading through the stickier human sentiments. A moment passed, and Stallsmith cleared his throat. "I wanted to thank you, too, Agent." Cam met the man's gaze. "If you hadn't solved this thing, I would always have wondered . . ."

Shaking his proffered hand, Cam said, "I'm sorry. It wasn't the news we wanted to deliver, but at least it's closure."

"Yeah." Stallsmith tried a smile. Didn't quite pull it off. "I guess that's something."

They stepped aside to make way for others wanting to speak to the widower and turned to walk slowly back to where Cam had parked the vehicle. The radio clipped to his belt remained silent. Which meant there had been no visual of Vickie Baxter. He wasn't really surprised. Nothing about this case had been simple so far.

He slipped his hand around Sophie's waist, ready to support her if she stumbled on the uneven grass in those death-defying stilts she called sandals. They were the same pale yellow as the suit she wore, and with her matching purse and halo of gilded hair she looked, he thought, like a walking sunbeam. "Briefing is tomorrow at eight. Are you ready with the profile on Baxter?"

"I have a *preliminary* one ready." Her inflection was unmistakable.

He knew that tone. "It's an evolving document. I get that." He'd heard the phrase from her often enough. Maybe there'd been a time when he'd grown impatient with the distinction, but his investigations evolved, too. As more information came in, the direction of their manpower was reshaped, refocused.

But that didn't mean he couldn't rib her about the meticulous way she approached her work. "So if Baxter doesn't show up here today, I think you can add a new aspect to the profile. She's phobic. Doesn't mind putting people in the ground, but she's got a fear of cemeteries. What do they call that?"

The sharp poke of her elbow to his ribs was too precisely placed to be accidental. "Coimetrophobia? If that's true, I can relate. I have an overwhelming fear of smart-asses myself."

Cam smiled. A year ago—hell, even a few months ago—he would never have suspected the endlessly fascinating facets that existed beneath Sophie's polished professional facade.

He'd certainly never suspected he'd find them so alluring.

She dug in her purse for a pair of tortoiseshell sunglasses and slipped them on. "The Department of Human Services' files on Sonny Baxter after he was removed from the home as a child added a few details. Other than that, facts about Vickie's life were sketchy. The warrant that granted access to the DHS case from *her* child-hood provided critical details for the profile. I'm still going through the information."

"We'll have even more answers when we're finally able to inter-view Courtney Van Wheton." With Sophie's help the other woman had escaped Vance only to lie in a coma for weeks afterward. Three days ago he'd been alerted that Van Wheton had regained conscious-ness, but her mental state so far had been deemed too precarious for interviews.

Cam scanned the fringe of the crowd near the gates of the cem-etery for one of his agents. Caught the eye of a man in a dark suit with thinning black hair and a long, taciturn face standing next to a tall redhead whose gaze was glued to her cell phone. Agents Tommy Franks and Jenna Turner. He steered Sophie toward them.

"No word on a sighting?"

Cam shook his head in response to Tommy's question. "It's still possible that the cameras will catch something as the crowd dis-perses." But he wasn't holding out much hope. It had been a long shot to bank on Baxter being the sort of killer who got off on seeing her victim laid to rest. But with dwindling leads on the woman's whereabouts, it had been a chance worth taking. He was all too aware that since they'd missed her by minutes after she'd killed her deranged son two weeks ago, her trail had grown increasingly cold.

And despite Sophie's earlier assurance, he'd never be satisfied with two out of three of the Cornbelt Killers in hand.

"Well, here's something that might be of interest." Jenna finally looked up from the screen of her cell. "You've had me watching the intrastate crime feed, and Ellen Webster's name just popped up."

Cam frowned, flipping through mental files as he tried to place the name. A moment later it hit him. "Sonny Baxter's social worker. The one that placed him in foster care when he was a kid. She's retired now, right? What'd she do, swipe the pot at weekly bingo?"

"She was the victim, not the perpetrator. The Boone County Sheriff responded to a vehicular fire seven miles south of Perry a couple days ago. There were no plates on the car, but the vehicle had cooled sufficiently to allow them to identify the VIN number today."

Cam's interest sharpened. Sheriff Beckett Maxwell of the neighboring county had been working with DCI since the case began. The first bodies found had been buried atop vaults in several of the area's rural cemeteries. Before the team had discovered the role Vickie Baxter had played in the killings, she'd been housed—at taxpayer expense—in a small home in Maxwell's county.

"That poor woman." He felt the slight shudder that went through Sophie's frame. "Was it a car accident?"

Jenna impatiently reached up to tuck her hair behind her ear as her gaze returned to the screen of her phone. "Not a lot of details on here. Apparently the state arson investigator had a look, and the death has been ruled a homicide."

"I can't think of a more horrible way to—" Sophie broke off then, catching the three agents contemplating her. "You're wondering if Vickie Baxter could be responsible."

"We're nowhere close to that conclusion." The response was automatic. Cam was circling the thought, but he wouldn't embrace it without evidence. "We need to get the particulars of the case from Beckett. Webster would have presided over hundreds of cases in her career with child services. Vickie Baxter would have been only one in a long line of people who would have a grudge against the woman."

"It would be well outside this killer's MO," Jenna offered doubtfully.

"We know Baxter has killed nonritualistically before," Sophie reminded them. "The body you found in that old cistern at the farmhouse where she'd been living is evidence of that." Gladys Stewart, the owner of the farm, had been shot with the same weapon found in a kitchen cupboard at the farmhouse. The lab had delivered the ballistics report only yesterday. The gun had borne Vickie Baxter's latents. "And what are the chances that another disgruntled former family member experienced an emotional trigger at precisely the same time that Vickie did?"

"Trigger?" Cam's cell rang, and he glanced down at the screen. He looked up again to give Tommy a headshake. This call would have nothing to do with the cameras they had posted around the cemetery. He stepped aside to answer the call, his attention half on Sophie's response.

"The death of her son. Regardless of what she subjected him to as a child, there was still a bond. Somehow they reunited after he'd been in the foster care system for years. And the timing of Webster's death is suspicious. She's been retired—what? Two, three years? Her murder is too coincidental . . ."

The speaker on the phone had all Cam's attention now. He listened, a sense of increasing urgency feeding his irritation. "Two days ago? And you're just calling me now?" The forthcoming explanation was only partially mollifying. "I'm going to want to see for myself. No, don't bother. I'll come to you."

Slipping the cell back in his pocket he turned to address the group. "The Homeland team at Des Moines airport say they've got a sighting of Baxter on their surveillance feed from Saturday."

Franks muttered an obscenity. "So a lot of good it's done us to monitor midwestern airports, train and bus stations for the last two weeks."

"My thought exactly." He narrowed a look at the man. "I'm going to leave you to supervise the facial recognition setup here. Take the cameras back to headquarters and get a couple agents to help go over the feed." His smile was grim. "Apparently Baxter can slip in places and never be noticed."

Switching his attention to Jenna, he said, "We'll cover all bases. Head over to Boone County and get everything Beckett has on that fire. I'll get Boggs on putting a canvass together for Webster's address." Corbin Boggs had returned to light duty this week after being shot by Sonny Baxter when the man had tried to execute Sophie in her apartment. Even though he'd worn a vest, the agent had sustained injuries that had taken a couple of weeks to recover from.

"What do you want me to focus on?"

In response to Sophie's question, he took her by the elbow and guided her toward the entrance of the cemetery. "Maybe you can teach me some meditation techniques on the way to the airport. I'm going to need something to avoid getting slapped with an assault charge when I talk to the idiot who let Vickie Baxter slip through our fingers."

———

The Homeland Security Airport Unit was formed after 9/11 and staffed by officers of the Des Moines Police Department. Cam frequently worked with DMPD in the course of a case, most recently on this one, usually with far greater success than at the moment.

"You're sure?" His question was quiet. Maybe too quiet. The fortysomething officer he was addressing had a gleam of perspiration above his lip that wasn't a result of the lack of air-conditioning in the surveillance room.

"Yes, Agent Prescott, I am. You can watch the interior security streams yourself. I've downloaded copies and emailed them to you. Our focus has been on apprehension, and Vickie Baxter never stepped foot inside the airport. She certainly didn't buy a ticket and fly out of here. Every airline agent in our facility has her likeness on their computer and took second and third looks at women traveling alone, just like you ordered."

"She wouldn't necessarily have traveled alone," Sophie put in. At Cam's cocked brow, she shrugged. "Given the manhunt for her, she'd not only have tried to disguise her appearance but also alter the impression she'd present. Most likely she'd have found a man to travel with to give the illusion of a couple rather than a single woman."

Her words had Reams, the security officer, taking out a handkerchief to wipe his upper lip. "Regardless she was never picked up on feed inside the airport. Just outside it at ground transportation. I've combined the sightings from all the exterior cameras she appears on into one sequence."

He picked up the remote and pointed it at one TV in the double row of monitors. The short clip replayed again. A ball cap was pulled low over her face, and her long hair was back in a ponytail, but there was no mistaking Baxter. The film jerked at intervals, presumably where Reams had spliced feed from two different cameras together. Silently they watched her disembark from a shuttle with a handful of other people and approach the ground transportation area alone, where she hailed a taxi. The entire sequence took less than two minutes.

"Where did the shuttle come from?"

Reams reached for the bottle of water in front of him and drank before responding. "Long-term parking. We've got two lots across the highway a couple blocks from here. Shuttle service runs twenty-four seven. I've talked to the driver on duty at the time, and his name is on the report." He indicated a slim sheaf of papers on the corner of his desk that Cam had yet to look at. "Unfortunately he sees a lot of people and can't place Baxter."

"Could she have come from a different area and walked to the shuttle service?" Sophie put in. "Maybe the return rental lot."

Reams shook his head doggedly. "She didn't rent a car here in the last two weeks. She wasn't in the airport, and I double-checked the surveillance stream near the rental areas myself."

"She could have rented it prior to the alert we sent out on her," Cam pointed out without much conviction. Baxter had owned a truck under the name Rhonda Klaussen, the alias she'd used for years. It was possible she'd kept another vehicle under a different name, stashed elsewhere. Nothing had ever shown up on the BOLO they'd put out on the truck. That could mean she had a place to hide it. Although if she'd wanted to get rid of it, she could have left it unlocked in an inner Des Moines neighborhood where it'd be certain to end up in a chop shop.

"I can check the interior surveillance feed from before the time we received the alert." Reams spoke quickly, eager to make up for failing to scrupulously monitor the exterior security. "How far back you want me to go?"

"I've used those long-term lots myself," Sophie murmured. She aimed a slight smile in the other man's direction. "You must have some system in place that checks the cars in and out, so you can tell how much to charge a person for parking. Maybe even with license numbers as identifiers."

Cam's mouth quirked. He'd said it before; Sophie would make a helluva cop. She'd protested that assertion once, claiming she was a coward at heart. He knew for a fact that was bull. It had required fortitude and brains to outsmart Mason Vance, and she'd done exactly that. The woman had more guts beneath that polished exterior than she gave herself credit for.

"Exactly. The lots are inventoried by license plates along with arrival dates and times." Reams looked from one of them to the other. "I can call ABM for the information if you want."

Cam's chair scraped as he rose from it. "I'll have a look myself." He took the report from the officer's desktop and allowed Sophie to precede him to the door.

"You sure?" Reams called after them. "Neither lot is shaded at all. It's going to be hotter than hell out there."

Three of them, counting the parking cashier on duty, were a tight squeeze in the parking booth. A square box fan hung on the wall and lackadaisically stirred the hot air inside. The attendant, a college-age girl with a fondness for facial piercings, was obediently writing down the license numbers of all cars that had entered the lot two days ago. Cam was taking a picture of each plate number with his cell and sending the attachments to Brody Robbins, the newbie DCI agent on the task force. It would be his job to run them through the Department of Motor Vehicles for owner names.

"Do you have a record of vehicles parked here on the day in question that may have already left the lot?"

"Sure, but there won't be many," the attendant said in response to Sophie's question without lifting her gaze from her task. "I mean, the reason they call this long-term parking is that it's, y'know, long-term. Most people just here for a day or two would pay the fee to be closer to the airport."

"We'll still want to check," Cam affirmed, finishing his task. Sweat trickled down his neck beneath the collared shirt and suit coat. He cast a look at the fan desultorily pushing the air around. "Fan doesn't provide much help in this heat."

"Air-conditioning is broke," the girl said disgustedly, shoving a limp strand of hair away from her face. "I turned it on more because of the stench than anything else. Smells like something crawled into the weeds around here and died. It was bad yesterday, but it's way worse today."

Cam stilled. "Did you notify anyone?"

The girl shrugged a meaty shoulder. "Lots of drivers mentioned it to me, like I wouldn't have noticed it myself. We get skunks around here sometimes. Maybe it's that."

His cell rang. "You got a hit on this plate." Robbins reeled off the number. "Twenty twelve Chevy Malibu. Green. Registered in the name of Kent and Heidi Flaugher. Stolen out of a Walgreens parking lot three days ago. Mrs. Flaugher said she just ran in for a moment, left the car running to keep it cool. It was gone when she came out of the store."

"Thanks." Cam disconnected and returned the phone to his pocket. Stabbing an index finger at the plate number on the list she'd prepared, he repeated the make and model for the attendant, following up with, "Where will I find that vehicle?"

The girl took her time turning to the monitor in front of her and punching the plate number in. "Lot two, southeast corner. Careful, though. That's the area the skunk smell is coming from."

He waited for Sophie to join him in his vehicle before he nosed it down the row of cars in the direction the girl had indicated. After parking behind the Malibu, he threw open the door and got out, shedding his suit coat and leaving it on the seat.

"Dear Lord." With a grimace of distaste, Sophie dug in her purse for a Kleenex tissue to press against her nose. "That's no skunk."

"Not even close." A familiar feeling of dread tightening his gut, Cam popped the trunk of his vehicle and dug around inside until he found a crowbar.

He crossed back to the Malibu. As telling as the smell of putrefaction was, the faint buzzing inside the trunk was even more so. "Maybe you should wait in the car."

Sophie ignored his suggestion, coming to stand beside him. He knew better than to waste time arguing with her and instead spent the energy on the crowbar. It took a minute of determined prying to raise the lid, and as it did he stepped aside, one sleeve to his face. It was little protection from the overwhelming stench of decay.

"Oh, dear God." Sophie's voice behind him was horrified. His vision was impeded for a moment by the swarm of insects he'd disturbed.

But there was no mistaking the bloated, unmoving body inside as being all too human.

⁓

Franklin J. Paulsen III had enjoyed moderate success as a trial lawyer. With offices in West Des Moines and Ankeny, he managed a combined staff of sixty. He had a home in the gated Des Moines neighborhood of Glen Oaks, a membership at its exclusive country club, and a townhouse in Florida. Thrice divorced, he'd been wily enough to engineer prenups for each, so he'd extricated himself from wedded bliss with slippery ease.

Despite his many accomplishments, he hadn't yet reached the professional heights of Marcella Rosen or Antonio Cavanaugh, two of his fiercest competitors. He lacked Marcella's old money and Antonio's over-the-top, attention-getting behavior, both of which garnered a lot of business and press that otherwise might have come Franklin's way. He'd long maintained that all it would take was one high-profile case to cement his place in the upper echelons of Iowa's legal community.

Mason Vance provided that case.

Whether the man was guilty or innocent was beside the point. If it went to trial—and Franklin would make sure it did—the national media attention would more than make up for the fact that he was working the case pro bono. This was the biggest crime story in Iowa's history. There'd be interviews, magazine spreads, and very possibly a TV documentary. All of which would elevate Franklin's career to the lofty status he deserved.

That Vance was an alleged monster didn't enter into the equation. Even monsters deserved their shot at justice.

He allowed himself to fantasize about the possibilities as he parked his car at Manor Oaks and walked up the pebbled, hydrangea-flanked walk to the double carved-oak doors. Franklin came each evening promptly at six. Mother would be back from dinner and was usually alert for an hour or so before the bedtime routine would begin. By seven he'd be on his way to dine at Lucca with a nubile, young, blonde attorney looking to switch firms. He didn't necessarily have a place in his offices for another lawyer, but Franklin prided himself on keeping an open mind. And based on their previous date, the young attorney excelled at blowing that mind.

He signed in at the front desk just inside the door and read through the daily notes collected by the staff about Mother's day. The bills for the place were astronomical, but the real guarantee of quality care was his daily personal visits. It was hard to cut corners with a family member checking in every day.

"I didn't realize you'd be joining us this evening, since you sent your assistant to check on your mother," the receptionist said chattily. She'd swung her chair from the front desk to the computer screen on an adjoining counter.

Franklin's gaze flew to the plump middle-aged receptionist. "Pardon me?"

"Ms. Mason?" The older woman got up to lean over the desk and tap a business card that had been paper clipped to the top of the notes. The card he hadn't even noticed since it bore his business logo. "She arrived about fifteen minutes ago. She's with your mother now."

Her words flowed over him as he stared hard at the name embossed on the business card. With his firm's logo on it.

Vanecia Mason.

The woman lowered her voice, the pleasant smile on her pudgy face not altogether masking the note of censure in her tone. "We appreciate that you're a busy man, Mr. Paulsen, but perhaps a phone call would be in order the next time you send one of your colleagues to our home. In the interest of security."

Her words were lost behind him as he turned away and almost ran to Mother's room. It had been carefully selected, and he paid a premium price for one not too close to the dining room racket, yet close enough to the social activities so as not to discourage Mother from joining in. He burst through the door of her room, chest heaving more from fear than exertion.

The space was large and private, boasting a set of triple windows that overlooked a serene courtyard. It was furnished with some carefully selected items from Mother's home. Her prized rocker. The dresser that had belonged to her parents. A specially ordered queen-size Sleep Number bed with elevate options.

A woman standing over Mother's small form in the bed held a large pillow in her hands. As she raised it and leaned toward Mother's head, a flare of pure panic jolted through Franklin.

"Get away from her! What are you doing?"

"Vanecia Mason" turned her head and shot him a smile over her shoulder. "Hey, Frankie. About time you showed up. Just thought your mother looked a little uncomfortable. I was going to add another pillow."

After hurrying across the room, he snatched it from her hand, sending a frantic look at the sleeping woman in the bed. Mother's frail chest rose and fell with reassuring regularity.

"What are you doing here? Our deal was to meet in the parking lot. You are never to come inside. Ever. I was very clear about that."

"Vanecia Mason" crossed her arms and looked amused. "Careful you don't pee yourself, Frankie. Were you under the impression that you were the one making the rules here? That's pretty stupid, even for a lawyer. I need to talk to Mason. Put a call through."

Momentarily mollified that his mother was fine for the time being, Franklin put a finger to his necktie and loosened it a fraction. There was a fleeting instant in which he wondered if he'd gotten himself in too deep.

One had to be determinedly unobservant not to guess the identity of the woman he'd met with here a few times at the behest of his client. Her image had been splashed all over the news for weeks. Tall and big-boned but lean, the way—he thought with a hint of fear—a hungry tigress would be. The sedate gray suit and pumps were at odds with the same air of hardness he saw every time he made the mistake of looking directly into his client's eyes.

"This . . . arrangement is going to have to change." What was meant as an order came out in a stammer when that hazel focus landed on him. "I have my professional reputation to worry about." But he knew he had much more than that to be concerned with. If anyone suspected he had dealings with the Cornbelt Killer still at large, his law license hung in the balance.

Alleged killer, he reminded himself. The distinction didn't allay his nerves.

When he felt his blood pressure rise at the thought of his exposure, he comforted himself with the fact that no one had recognized her at the desk of the rest home today. So how could he have been expected to make the identification?

His excitement over landing this client had blinded him to reality for too long. He could admit that now, when he was in too deep to extricate himself. Franklin had excellent sources at the Polk County jail and so knew for a fact that Mason Vance had interviewed both Marcella Rosen and Antonio Cavanaugh before settling on him. His good fortune had blinded him to some of the red flags raised in the time since he'd taken Vance on as a client.

Like facilitating occasional phone calls from his "fiancée."

"This will be the last time we'll meet like this." The bravado he'd summoned died a rapid death when she stared unblinkingly at him. "I'm not going to risk my license on this case. From now on, it's by the book."

The woman's smile turned his blood to ice. "Sure. Mason will understand. In the meantime I hope you don't mind me continuing to visit your mother. I think she really took a liking to me before her nap." The threat was clear.

"Franklin?" His mother picked that moment to wake. "Who's this woman? This isn't one of the nurses. What's she doing here?"

He stepped up to the bed, took his mother's hand, and said soothingly, "She's just leaving, Mother. Please excuse us."

He grasped the younger woman's elbow and escorted her out of the room as he pulled his cell phone from his pocket with his free hand. Polk County jail was on speed dial. As Baxter smirked with amusement, he requested an urgent call with his client and prepared to wait the several minutes it would take for them to bring Vance to the phone.

"I'm going to have a talk with security here and let them know you aren't to be let in the door again."

"No, Frankie, you're not." Her eyes went steely. "And here's why. Security cameras would show that you and I have had several conversations over the last couple weeks on the grounds here. Wouldn't take anything at all to tip off the cops to take a look at them. After, of course, I have a friend slip in and arrange a little accident for dear ol' Mom." She gave a smile of mock sympathy. "Bones that age break so easily, don't they? Like dry kindling. It'd be a shame for her to shatter a hip or pelvis just because you're being shortsighted."

His bowels turned to ice. The specifics of the case against Mason Vance were all too familiar to him. And he was beginning to believe everything the news reports had said about this woman, as well.

With a flash of understanding, he realized why Vance had summoned one after another of his colleagues to the jail. Not just to evaluate their legal expertise, as Franklin had assumed. But to allow this woman the opportunity to assess each for possible vulnerabilities.

And his mother was his.

When the familiar voice came on the line, he handed the cell wordlessly to the woman who was certainly Vickie Baxter. And while he walked back to his mother's room, his mind frantically whirled with ideas to get out of this mess.

Nothing occurred. And Franklin couldn't help but be reminded that all the people Vance and Baxter had set their sights on had ended up dead.

Chapter 2

Boone County Sheriff Beckett Maxwell declined to speak from the front of the DCI conference room, instead electing to stand beside his chair. "State fire marshal made the official call that the fire was a homicide. He says unless the victim figured out a way to bathe in accelerant and bind herself to the steering wheel, she had help. The autopsy isn't scheduled for a couple days, but calls to Ellen Webster's number have gone unanswered. When I contacted the DMPD, I discovered her daughter had reported the woman missing last night."

"Results of the department's interview with the daughter and canvass of Webster's friends and neighbors should be completed today," Agent Jenna Turner volunteered as Beckett reseated himself in the chair next to her. The way he jostled the agent as he made himself comfortable didn't escape Sophia's eye. Nor did she miss Jenna's irritation as she moved infinitesimally away.

Sophia hid a smile. Cam hadn't done Jenna a favor by pairing her with Maxwell yesterday. The sheriff was attractive, amiable, and likely all too used to female attention. Jenna's lack thereof would be construed as a personal challenge.

"You working on dental records?" Cam asked.

Beckett nodded. "The daughter gave us Webster's dentist's contact information. It won't take long to be certain."

Sophia's earlier flash of amusement faded as she thought of the unknown relative anxiously waiting for word of the test results. Some families of the victims of the Cornbelt Killers had waited years for the last tenuous thread of hope to be snapped. Neither scenario would be easy.

Cam turned his attention to the group gathered in the room. "We got a hit on the latents on the corpse in the trunk at the Des Moines airport yesterday, and an identification has already been made."

Sophia listened to Cam from her seat in the front row. The group was smaller than it had been a few weeks ago when the task force was newly formed. With Mason Vance jailed, Sonny Baxter dead, and Rhonda Klaussen, aka Vickie Baxter, presumed to be fleeing the state, the DCI brass had lost no time reallocating resources. There were now only four agents assigned solely to the case, with others utilized on an as-needed basis.

As much as she wanted to believe more manpower wouldn't be necessary, Sophia knew that Cam's next words were going to send that hope up in flames.

"Curtis Traer. Fifty years old. Has a sheet spreading over the last two decades, but only did time once—three years for aggravated assault." A mug shot of the man found in the trunk was displayed on the overhead screen. "He's been out for a couple years, although his probation officer indicates he's had chronic unemployment issues. Currently living with his sister, who claims a woman came to the door looking for him last week and left a number for him to call. Three nights ago when the sister got home from work, Traer was nowhere to be found. We've got DMPD officers canvassing the neighborhood now. But the sister tentatively ID'd Vickie Baxter as the woman who came to her door. She denied ever seeing her before or hearing her brother speak of her."

"Baxter's got brass balls—for sure," Maxwell muttered.

Cam sent them a grim smile. "That's becoming apparent. Last night Agent Turner and Dr. Channing also had an opportunity to speak with Courtney Van Wheton for a short time in her hospital room. From what Van Wheton said, it was clear that Baxter was a participant in her initial torture before being ordered away from the barn by Vance. Van Wheton was able to put to rest any remaining questions we might have had about the extent of Baxter's involvement. We can now narrow our focus to what's keeping the woman in the area. So I'll turn this over to Dr. Channing."

Sophia rose and joined Cam at the front of the room. Special Agent in Charge Maria Gonzalez and Major Crime Unit Assistant Director Paul Miller were present but not the agency director himself. Yet another indication that this case had been formally moved off the front burner. She imagined Cam would consider the lessened scrutiny a good thing, except when it came to resources.

Sophia took a moment to retrieve her notes from her briefcase, hoping that her sleepless night didn't show on her face as starkly as her mirror that morning had attested. When the call came from the hospital early yesterday evening that Courtney Van Wheton was asking for her, Cam had elected to stay with the crime scene team in the parking lot and dispatched Sophia and Jenna for the initial interview. He'd believed, and Sophia had concurred, that the former victim would be more comfortable initially talking about her ordeal to females.

The interview had been necessarily brief, the disclosures harrowing. But it had been long enough to unlock the door to memories of Sophia's time as Vance's prisoner. When it had proven impossible to sleep, she'd gotten up and worked on filling in details on the profile.

But even then sneaky, terrifying reminders of her captivity had persisted. Her reaction to the memories seemed like cowardice. Sophia hadn't suffered what Van Wheton had at Vance's hands. Not even close. And yet . . .

Her fingers trembled slightly as she opened the profile she'd retrieved. "Courtney Van Wheton told us that she saw Vickie Baxter once, when she first awoke in the abandoned barn Vance was using to confine his victims. She said Baxter suggested torture techniques to use on her and actively participated in the acts. When Baxter professed her desire to help Vance rape the woman, he ordered her away to deal with her 'crazy-ass kid.' The two had a short argument before Baxter stormed off, leaving Van Wheton alone in the barn with Vance."

Alone. A mental image flashed across her mind. A vast cavernous space, its darkness splintered by fingers of daylight filtering through the cracks in the walls. She felt again the wash of despair she'd experienced while there and took a moment to fortify herself before continuing. "Lab results confirm that Baxter's prints were found in the first cell inside the door where Vance had confined Van Wheton." As he had countless others, given that there had been matches to latents from several of the identified victims.

The first stall had been occupied by Courtney. Sophia had been secured in a cell at the other end of the barn, her vision obscured by the wooden slat sides and the stone wall behind her. She'd had no idea that she hadn't been the only victim in that barn. Until it was too late.

"Vance also shared details of his plans for Van Wheton's death when he finished with her." He'd enjoyed doing that, Sophia recalled. It had fed his godlike ego to strike terror in the hearts of his victims. Certainly he'd been successful with her. "When pressed she indicated that he hadn't threatened to kill her himself, though; he'd just said that she'd die. Which is in keeping with my own experience with him. I think that underscores our conclusion that Sonny Baxter was charged with the actual murder of these victims, at least these latest ones."

"A claim I'm sure we'll hear from Vance's defense," Cam inserted wryly.

She nodded. "Before the doctor shooed us away, Van Wheton was able to identify photos of Mason Vance, Sonny Baxter, and Vickie Baxter." A murmur swept through the room, and Sophia unconsciously reached for the bottle of water Cam had left on the table before her. Drank to soothe a throat suddenly parched. The hovering doctor had dismissed them at the first signs of Van Wheton's upset. Sophia sincerely hoped that Jenna had not been able to discern how eager she'd been to leave the hospital.

That could have been me. The thought hammered at her, sending haunting echoes careening through her system. If her own abduction had been planned with Vickie Baxter's involvement, instead of being an act of rage by Vance, she had no doubt she would have shared Van Wheton's fate. Or worse. As it was, Mason Vance had been infuriated when her profile on him had been released to the public. His ego had demanded revenge, so he'd kidnapped Sophia. The decision eventually led to his capture.

But she was constantly reminded of how easily it could have turned out differently.

Steadier, she set the bottle down deliberately and began again. "What Van Wheton was able to share helped solidify some of what we know about Vickie Baxter. Her childhood DHS case file revealed that she was removed from her father's care because of longtime physical and sexual abuse. A paternal aunt took her in after parental rights were terminated. That aunt lived two miles south of where Ellen Webster's charred remains were found."

She saw Cam's head swivel toward her. There hadn't been time to share that particular detail with him this morning. He'd left for work shortly after she'd slipped back into their bed, falling into a fitful slumber. Somehow delving further into Baxter's tawdry life had given her some much-needed emotional distance after Van Wheton had brought memories of Sophia's captivity hurtling back.

"So she has an anchor in the area, too."

She sent a sidelong glance at Cam, affirming his understanding. "She was born in Oelwein, but there's usually something that keeps a killer returning to a certain spot. For Vance the connection was the summers he'd spent at his grandfather's farm north of Ankeny. For Baxter, it may turn out to be the time she spent living with her aunt and uncle. She left at age eighteen, but when Baxter was twenty, the relatives who took her in were killed in a house fire. The investigative case file notes that a man verified her location that night in Des Moines."

"Vickie is a puppet master when it comes to men," Jenna noted. "It would have been no problem for her to find one willing to provide her with an alibi. In return for sexual favors, of course."

"It's unlikely we'll ever know if the man providing her an alibi was lying," Sophia agreed. "But her DHS file indicates that while she was in her aunt's care, on at least two occasions, men named her as an accomplice to a string of robberies and burglaries in downtown Des Moines. Since there was no evidence of her involvement, no charges were filed. But she had a pattern of acting out sexually with older men during her teens, no doubt due to her own sexual abuse and torture at the hands of her father." Every intact deceased victim they'd found bore a number burned into the skin on their shoulder blades with the tip of a lit cigar. Vickie's number was one.

"The interviews done when she was a child disclosed a trauma experience almost textbook in the development of her pathology. Victims of incest may experience guilt, shame, distrust of others, self-hate, depression, low self-esteem, or later revictimization."

"Since she turned into a murdering psychopath, I'd say none of the above," offered Franks. Sophia glanced his way. The senior agent rarely said much, but she knew he didn't hold forensic profiles in particularly high regard. He wasn't alone in his attitude; in her role as a nationally recognized forensic profiler, she'd met similar attitudes from law enforcement. Some from cops much more verbal about their opinions.

"Or maybe she's all of the above." She tempered her disagreement with a smile. "It doesn't excuse her actions. It just helps us understand her better. The data kept by her caseworker offers a rare insight into Vickie's evolution into a killer. Teenage rebellion, sexual acting out, bullying and assault complaints from school. The incidents taken in totality paint a young woman determined never to be a victim again. And somewhere along the way she began to experience pleasure in victimizing others. That sense of satisfaction, once experienced, likely consumed her."

"And how does knowing that lead to her capture?" Cam asked bluntly.

Sophia smiled inwardly. There had been a time when the man had shared Franks's attitude about her assistance on cases. He'd thawed, but he remained a bottom-line cop. Profiles were useless if they couldn't assist in directing the investigation.

"It helps us predict her actions." Driven to move, Sophia began to pace. "Something is keeping her in the area when common sense would dictate she get far away. Is it a great love for Mason Vance? I doubt she's capable of the emotion, at least not as we'd recognize it. This is a woman who physically abused her own young son. Who allowed men to sexually assault him, according to Sonny Baxter's DHS file. She has a history of manipulating men, and I imagine she utilized Vance to implement the scheme to rob and rape wealthy women." With a nod toward Cam, she added, "She had a willing partner in that, as his cell mate told us Vance had expressed a similar plan while in prison. Those two finding each other was incredibly bad luck for our victims."

"Why did she need Vance?" As usual the rookie agent Brody Robbins flushed when he dared to ask a question. But gamely he barreled on. "She's killed alone. We have recent proof of that. And she had Sonny to do it for her before she shot him."

"Sonny was also the one who stalked the women and eventually kidnapped them to bring them to his mother and Vance," Jenna noted. "Not all the victims we found can be attributed to Vance, because the timeline doesn't fit."

It was a valid point. There were also the three sets of unidentified skeletal remains that had been pulled from the Raccoon River at the state medical examiner's office awaiting aging. And this was exactly where the profile was transported beyond the evidence and reached into expert conclusion territory.

"I suspect that Sonny was a disappointment to his mother in that regard." It felt strange to experience a pang of empathy for the dead killer. "His psychosis was too involved for him to be reliable. Vickie Baxter was likely motivated by a need to make other women experience what she herself had gone through as a child. Rape. Torture. Helplessness. Becoming predator rather than prey made her feel strong. Sonny was sick but in a far different way than she is. When he couldn't enact the crimes in the manner that she found sexually satisfying, she looked for someone who could."

Sophia could feel the gaze Cam drilled into her. "You're saying she's the mastermind. She was the one calling the shots."

The room abruptly stilled. Nodding, Sophia returned to the table and reached for the water again before remembering that it wasn't hers. She could feel heat rising in her cheeks, an involuntary reaction she'd never been able to master. "Vickie would have attempted to use Vance to help fulfill her needs. She would have had her hands full with him. He was vicious in his own right. And his temper made him unpredictable."

A phantom pain throbbed in her jaw at the memory of the stinging blow Vance had delivered the first time she'd provoked him to anger. Aware of Cam's gaze on her, Sophia struggled to mask her expression.

"Regardless, something is keeping Vickie here. Her motivations are simple. If the burned corpse turns out to be Ellen Webster, there's not a doubt in my mind that Baxter killed her. And if she did, it's not much of a stretch to believe that the man in the trunk was a revenge killing, too. Maybe someone who did her wrong years ago. Perhaps even someone who had assaulted Sonny when he was young."

"It takes a special kind of twisted thinking to blame the men she invited to rape her son," Franks muttered.

"Yes. And if revenge is her motivation, there's no telling how wide she'll aim." Sophia paused a beat while she scanned the room. "She may even target members of this team."

"I volunteer to be bait," Beckett Maxwell drawled. "Just dangle me out there and see what she does. If she gets to me before you all do, well"—he jerked a thumb at Jenna sitting next to him—"Red can deliver my eulogy. She always has the sweetest things to say."

The Boone County sheriff's words earned a laugh, lightening the mood.

Jenna cocked her head to consider the man beside her. "We can coat your naked hide with jam and hope to draw her like an ant."

"There you go again, honey, coming up with ideas to get my clothes off. Don't want to keep breaking your heart, but no means no."

From Jenna's narrowed green eyes, it was clear that Maxwell was wandering into dangerous territory.

"What'd you guys do all day yesterday, anyway?" Boggs wanted to know.

Beckett doubled over, wincing while Jenna placed the heel of her pump squarely on his toe and ground it. "In a supreme act of self-restraint, I managed not to strangle him. I can't promise the same for today."

Sophia smiled, although she noted that SAC Gonzalez and MCU Assistant Director Miller weren't joining in the levity. "That's one idea, anyway. But I don't think you're going to have to worry about drawing her out. It would be a mistake to underestimate Vickie Baxter. She's twisted but lacks her son's psychosis. And she isn't driven by ego, as Vance was. It appears that she's been moving around the area freely."

"So revenge is keeping her in the vicinity?" Cam sounded unconvinced. "If that's the case, she could have taken it many times over. She's lived around here for years. Why now?"

Sophia reached into her file folder and brought out a photo. "Because of him." All eyes turned toward the picture of Sonny Baxter. "His death triggered something inside her. Remorse maybe. She could be seeking vengeance on his behalf. It doesn't make sense to us. She was the one who shot him minutes before you tracked him to her house. But in her mind that makes you responsible, not her."

"So she's not sticking around because of Vance?"

"That's also possible," Sophie answered Franks's question. "Not because of the man personally. But if there was something else, something left undone . . . maybe one last score or plans left unresolved . . . Whatever it is, if she's staying for Vance, it's because he's a stepping-stone to something she wants." She swiveled her head to regard Cam. "But there's no way she can get to him."

Cam caught the eye of SAC Gonzalez and shook his head. "We've got him in a solitary cell. His lawyer's been filing motions, but soon I expect a trial date to be set. Polk County jail is on high alert while he's there. His visitors are restricted to only his lawyer, and he'll be well guarded at all times. Baxter would have to be hallucinating to believe she could get him out on her own."

Just the mention of Vance escaping had dread circling. "She's wily enough to have eluded capture this long. After killing Stewart she managed to collect the cash rent on the woman's farm for two years by forging a power of attorney and posing as the woman's niece."

"Netting nearly four hundred thousand bucks," Franks inserted disgustedly.

Nodding, Sophia added, "Regardless of whose idea that was, it was Baxter that played the role. And no one suspected a thing. Not the renters or the bank. Stewart's death and body disposal is proof that Vickie can be every bit as brutal as Vance."

She began to slide pages back into the folder, suddenly spent. It would be tempting to credit her exhaustion to last night's lack of sleep. It was the subject matter, however, that was mostly to blame.

Cam was alert to the slightest sign that she hadn't recovered emotionally from her time as Vance's prisoner. As a psychologist she wouldn't dream of claiming otherwise. There was a difference, she'd insisted repeatedly in conversations with him, between still dealing with the effects and being an asset to this case. The two weren't necessarily mutually exclusive.

But visceral responses lingered, and she was going to have to learn to cope with them. Because she could ill afford more nights like the last one every time mention was made of her kidnapper.

"Beckett, the tip line has yielded a few calls from your county. You want to check them out?"

The sheriff nodded. "We'll take care of them."

She listened with half an ear as Cam handed out assignments to the agents gathered. Then waited another few minutes for him to finish a short conversation with Gonzalez. When the SAC moved away, Sophia crossed to Cam. "Unless you have other plans for me,

I'm heading to Boone County. I made an appointment to speak with a former neighbor of Baxter's. She lived down the road from Vickie's aunt and uncle, the Coates."

"The ones who took her in when she was a teenager. Still no cooperation from the cousins?"

In addition to caring for a teenage Vickie Baxter, Mary and Allen Coates had had three children, the youngest of whom died in the fire that killed the parents. There had been a boy and girl closer to Vickie's age at the time that had been away at college when the fire occurred. Sophia had reached the son, who had proven unwilling to discuss his murderous relative. She'd managed to extract a promise that he'd talk to his sister about submitting to phone interviews before he'd hung up. Given his attitude, she had doubts whether that conversation would ever take place.

"Not yet." She walked with him to the table where he'd left his materials and watched him shovel the case files back into a battered briefcase. She made a mental note that a new briefcase might be a functional, if not particularly impressive, birthday gift for him in a couple of months.

Then caught her breath. Because despite everything that had occurred in the past few weeks, thoughts of a future for the two of them were tantalizingly persistent. In those heady few days during their initial affair, everything she thought she'd known about herself had been upended. She'd felt too much, much too fast. Cam Prescott had shredded her usual cautious approach, and he represented the exact opposite of the safe choices she prided herself on making.

Safe. Her kidnapping had proven the folly of her prudent approach to life. Nothing and no one was ever really safe. Life was tenuous, and joy should be embraced. Including what she felt for Cam.

While unsure of his feelings, she was all too aware that he didn't trust her to know her own mind in that regard. As if her harrowing kidnap and escape from Vance had somehow turned her into an emotional cripple. His reaction would be infuriating if she didn't realize it stemmed from concern for her.

"Okay." He took his phone out, checked some notes on it. "Give me a half hour to return some phone calls, and I can take you."

"I have a vehicle, an address, and GPS. I can handle it. Stay here." They fell in step together as they headed toward the conference room door. "I know you have a million details to tend to." With the possible connection to Webster's murder, the hundreds of threads that comprised an investigation were about to become even more tangled. She wondered for a moment if he'd talked at all to Gonzalez about more manpower for the team.

"I'm an expert at multitasking." He didn't smile, but the creases beside his mouth deepened for an instant. "Just this morning I made the coffee while checking the box scores."

"Which accounts for me having to dump the pot and make a new one." They were in the hallway now heading toward his office. "I'm serious. I'll just go on my own, and then I have to go to my office later to confer with Dr. Redlow." In addition to her forensic consulting business, Sophia maintained a private practice. The man had been handling her clients during this case. She was working on transitioning back, at least part-time until the case was resolved. Or she would be, she thought with an inward sigh, if Cam would drop his hovering.

"Beckett could take you to the interview if he's heading back to his office."

"And then what? I fly home?" She lifted her palms, waggled the fingers. "Look, Ma, two hands. I have a car. A driver's license. With Vance in jail and Sonny Baxter dead, I no longer require

37

round-the-clock protection." A fact she was exceedingly grateful for. "You can't be two places at once. You need to be here." She pointed at his office door, which they had paused in front of. "I, however, do not. I can check in with you later. You know, much as your agents will be doing as they go about the tasks you just gave them."

He said nothing as he leaned forward to open the door to his office and waved an arm, ushering her inside. She didn't make the mistake of misconstruing his silence for agreement. With an inward sigh, she preceded him into the space, then turned to face him, already mentally bolstering her argument.

All thoughts flew out of her head a moment later when he closed the door behind him with a well-placed backward kick and then whirled her around to press her against it, fitting his mouth to hers.

Her bones went immediately to water. Unconsciously her hands glided up to wrap around his shoulders, her questing fingers delving into his short-cropped dark hair. She returned his kiss, her lips parting to accept his tongue for a sensual battle. There was a hint of frustration in his kiss and a leashed hunger that she recognized. Cam Prescott excelled at control.

Which just made those moments when he lost that famed restraint so memorable. When his response was raw. Primitive. Unchecked. And completely devastating.

He lifted his head a fraction, and a part of her mourned. "Missed that this morning."

"You missed more than that by going to work early," she teased, tipping her head back to look up at him. "I made bacon. Ate every last slice myself."

"You have a mean streak." He gave her butt a pinch before releasing her. "People don't suspect it with that whole angel-face thing you've got going on, but it's there. It's your forgetfulness that has me most worried right now, though."

And that quickly, that neatly, they were back to the conversation they'd started in the interview room. His single-minded focus wasn't reserved for just his job. And while she was often warmed by his concern on her behalf, recognizing the genuine fear that had first ignited it, she'd discovered that it could be . . . confining.

"We all need to be cautious, but unless you expect me to believe that your fright of Vickie Baxter is going to keep you at headquarters, cowering under your desk—"

His snort was its own answer. "Well then." Sophia went up on tiptoe to brush another kiss against his mouth. Lingered when his arm tightened around her waist. She was breathless by the time he lifted his head, her thinking more than a little bit muzzy.

"I want hourly updates." It was gratifying to note that his tone had gone raspy. "Texts are fine, but *hourly*. Keep your phone on. I want to know where you're heading and when you get there. I'm serious about this, Sophie." His eyes were dark with emotion. "I'm not taking chances with your safety. Like you said earlier, it would be a mistake to underestimate Vickie Baxter. Same goes for you. If your gut is right, she's killed twice more in the last few days. She's escalating because she figures she's got nothing to lose. Either way makes her dangerous. I accepted the risks of this job when I took it. But I'm not risking you again."

~

Karen Denholt peered at Sophia from her wheelchair through glasses as thick as telescopes. At seventy-five the woman looked a decade older, no doubt due to the MS that had ravaged her limbs. But given her rapid-fire conversation since Sophia had first entered her apartment at the Perry Assisted Living Center, her mind was far more agile than her body.

"When I heard Vickie Baxter's name on the news, I knew it had to be Mary and Allen's niece." The woman wheeled around to a pitcher of lemonade she had sitting on the coffee table and poured two glasses. "Common enough name, probably, but that girl . . . I knew even back then that she was meaner than a rattlesnake. Not a grateful bone in her body for her relatives taking her in like that. Mary didn't have a thing to do with that no-good brother of hers until he went to prison, landing the girl on her doorstep."

Sophia leaned forward to accept the glass the woman held out for her. Sipped from it while Denholt poured herself another, her gaze sweeping the small area. Framed photographs adorned most of the available wall space. More were scattered on the entertainment center and end tables. "Were you close with the Coates family?"

"We were neighbors for over twenty years. Our farms were just a mile or so apart. My husband and Allen used to help each other out, repairing equipment and what not. There was a time Mary and I used to have coffee together when we could spare an hour or so." The woman went silent after that, her mouth tight. "That changed after Vickie. Just about everything changed after she came."

"It was a difficult transition?"

Denholt blew out a breath. "There was no transition. Plopping that girl down in Mary and Allen's family was like setting a bomb off in the house. In the entire area, truth be told. Mary tried to do her Christian duty by Vickie, and Lord, you had to feel for what the girl's father did to her. But sometimes good intentions aren't enough. There was something broken in that girl. You couldn't help her. She wouldn't allow it."

"The Coates followed through with the counseling recommendations for her?" Vickie Baxter's DHS file had yielded directions for the girl's care. When Denholt's head bobbed, her stiffly sprayed iron-gray hair didn't move a fraction.

"Mary was always meeting with this social worker or that counselor. But she couldn't do a thing with Vickie. She'd drive her all the way to Des Moines once a week to see some fancy psychologist, and Vickie would walk into the building, through it, and out the back door. Then she'd disappear for hours, leaving the family to fret. So Mary wised up and started going into the building with the girl, sitting in the waiting room. And Vickie would just sit in the shrink's office and never say a word. All that money down the drain. The girl wouldn't help herself. Mary couldn't be held accountable for that, could she?"

"It sounds like a difficult time for the family while she was there." Recalling the surviving Coates children's reluctance to speak to her, Sophia asked, "How did Vickie's presence in the household affect Mary and Allen's kids?

Karen Denholt's lips pressed together so tightly they almost disappeared. "It was drama all the time. Vickie was sneaky. She'd steal from Caty and then deny it. Walk around naked in front of Jon and then claim he'd gotten fresh with her. Treated Sally just awful, and her just a little kid at the time. Skipped school as often as she went, but it was the same thing there when she bothered to go. She was always one to create havoc, whether it was cozying up to another girl's boyfriend or even to a teacher."

A thought occurred to Sophia then. "Where did she go?" At the woman's puzzled look, she said, "When she skipped school. Did she have friends, a car, money?"

"Friends." The word sounded like an obscenity. And not for the first time Sophia was struck by the fact that Denholt's dislike for Baxter seemed personal. "There are always boys willing to take up with a girl like Vickie Baxter. Even good kids. She had a way of figuring out everyone's weak spot and then homing in on it."

"So when she wasn't in school she was with a boy?"

The woman jerked a shoulder. "It's likely. Although a small group of them would hang out sometimes. Smoke marijuana and drink, from what I heard."

"Where would that happen?"

"Sometimes they'd gather in an old abandoned corncrib that's since been torn down. Willard Montrose owned the property. It was on Triumph Avenue just a few miles from my home. When Montrose found out that kids were using his place to hook school, he got some neighborhood men to help him bulldoze the structure. He was afraid one of them would get hurt there and he'd be liable. Place was ready to fall down as it was."

Her words resonated. "Triumph Avenue. You're sure?" Triumph Avenue was the name of the road Ellen Webster's burned corpse had been found on.

"Of course I'm sure. Willard farmed eighty acres right around that spot. He didn't have any kids that age, of course. His were grown. The corncrib was just a handy place to hang out and raise heck. Until, of course, Vickie got herself pregnant."

A curious choice of words, given that Sophia had yet to meet any woman who had accomplished that feat on her own. Vickie would have been about seventeen when Sonny was conceived. "Did the Coates learn who the father was?"

The other woman grimaced, took a long drink from her glass. "Vickie wasn't saying, or maybe she just didn't know. But there was talk, most of it ugly. And untrue."

There was something there, something the woman wasn't saying. Sophia picked her way carefully. "That's the nature of gossip, isn't it? Hurtful and unhelpful. I'm sure it was a very trying time for the family." When the woman only looked away, she tried another tack. "And, of course, those unfairly named in the gossip."

"You have no idea." Karen's voice was bitter. She took a big gulp from her glass as if wishing it held something stronger. "There was talk naming Cal Patten, the gym teacher, as the father. He was fifty if he was a day back then. Reverend Minskel was even accused. Not to mention every young man in the area within a decade of her age."

"Someone in your family?" It wasn't even a guess. The woman's white knuckles gripping the glass were a telltale sign.

"My son, Bobby. He was much older than Vickie. Twenty-three. He was a bookworm. Never dated much. He worked at the school for a while as a custodian." She took another drink and then set the sweating glass down on a magazine lying atop the table. "It wasn't true, of course. But that didn't stop people from repeating it. Even Karen had the nerve to ask . . ." Her throat worked. "Bobby swore to us that he'd never . . . Well. That was a long time ago. Things got strained between us and the Coateses, so we started avoiding Mary and Allen after that." Regret deepened the creases on her face. "Always thought there'd be time later to repair our friendship."

"But then the fire happened." Sophia used her thumb to make a design in the condensation on her glass, her attention riveted on the older woman. "And that got people talking again."

"Heard all kinds of craziness. Milt, my late husband, said a deputy told him it started when a space heater fell over onto the couch. They thought maybe the cat knocked it over. Never believed it myself," the older woman said with a sniff. "Sure, those old farm-houses were drafty, but Allen Coates—rest his soul—was stingier than a coon with corn. I never knew him to have the thermostat set above sixty-eight in the house all winter."

Interesting. "So it would be unlikely that he would have a space heater."

Snorting, Karen reached for her glass again. Drank. "Other folks didn't seem to think much about it, but it never made sense to me. Why would the only space heater in the house be downstairs when the family slept upstairs? And it just so happened that the batteries in every single smoke alarm in the place were dead. Always struck me as mighty convenient."

It was becomingly abundantly clear that Karen wasn't above fueling the rumor mill herself. "I always said I wouldn't put anything past Vickie Baxter. Spiteful little witch even then. Milt said I was too hard on the girl, even after what she put our family through, but I told him"—her nod was certain—"mark my words. That girl is capable of anything. And the papers for the last few weeks have proved me right."

A chill chased over Sophia's skin. Baxter was indeed evil. But had she been capable of such an act at age twenty? Most serial killers evolved over several years. Even decades. "The fire wasn't designated as arson. And I believe Vickie Baxter had someone who swore they were together the night it happened."

"I'm sure she did," Karen said with an eye roll. "And I'd lay odds it was a male saying it. Vickie had a way with men, even back then. I never really suspected she snuck back out here and burned her aunt's house down . . . until I read the papers. Maybe she started killing long before you all know."

Sophia recalled Courtney Van Wheton's words. That Vickie had been in the cell participating in the torture.

They already knew what the woman was capable of. Cam's team had excavated six bodies from rural cemeteries. Three more sets of bones were found encased in weighted-down body bags in the Raccoon River. Another four bodies were discovered in shallow graves on the riverbank. And even with the staggering body count, it was certain that all Baxter's victims hadn't yet been discovered. One of them had borne the number sixteen.

The number one had been burned on Vickie Baxter's shoulder blade. Her son bore number two. Sonny had been taken away from her when he was nine. Her parental rights were later severed. Sophia didn't know how the woman had managed to escape jail time for the brutality she'd inflicted on her little boy, but she was beginning to realize that perhaps she'd been the one underestimating Vickie all along.

Maybe the act of setting the house on fire had marked the beginning of Vickie's evolution into a serial murderer.

"I'm still in touch with some of my old friends from when we lived on the farm. I hear the Coates kids haven't been back since the funeral. Both live in California now. Don't know what ever became of the old place. Guess they rent the property out."

Reading fatigue on Karen's face, Sophia asked her for the names of former neighbors that would have gone to school with Vickie. She rose then, collecting her purse. "I appreciate your time, Mrs. Denholt. I know these weren't happy memories for you."

"Lots of time to think, sitting in this chair," the woman murmured, her gaze traveling around the sunny living room. "It would be too easy to wallow in regrets. That's why I try to surround myself with happy memories."

Smiling, Sophia walked up to a cluster of pictures on the wall nearest the front door. "Your family?"

Karen wheeled behind her. "These are older ones of us, when the kids were younger. Milt looks stern there, but he was actually quite a jokester. Used to drive me crazy sometimes, the trouble that man had being serious. Cancer took him almost ten years ago now. I moved off the farm shortly after. The kids' graduation pictures are on the outside. Susan's there on the left. Rhonda is the dark-haired one, and Bobby on the right. He's the youngest."

Sophia spent some time admiring the photos. The girls bore the middle part and long straight hair that was a 1970s giveaway. She lingered longer on Bobby's picture.

He had the vaguely unformed features of a young man on the brink of adulthood. The wire-rim glasses and sandy-colored hair were nondescript. His looked like thousands of other senior pictures. Anonymous. Unmemorable.

Saying her good-byes, Sophia went out the door. The heat wrapped her in its sweaty fist. She hurried to her vehicle parked at the curb, even knowing the air-conditioning would take far too long to cool the car.

Gingerly, she got in and turned on the ignition. Mothers had a tendency to rush to their children's defense, but if what Karen had said was true, things had been unpleasant indeed for Bobby Denholt. The kind of vicious rumors she mentioned would have been devastating for a shy, bookish young man.

But not as devastating as knowing you'd fathered Sonny Baxter.

Chapter 3

When an incoming text sounded on Cam's cell, he reached for it without tearing his gaze from the large map tacked to the wall of his office. Updates came in regularly from his team, some demanding his attention, others simply keeping him apprised of progress. Or lack thereof.

He glanced down at the screen, his mouth quirking for a moment when he read the message. *Survived my appointment with Denholt life and limbs intact.* He shook his head. And Sophie claimed *he* was the smart-ass. Her next words, however, had his amusement vanishing. *Going to take a look at the old Coates farm site.*

His reaction was immediate and visceral. And, even he realized, more than a little illogical. He didn't want her anywhere near that place, near *any place* that was affiliated with Vickie Baxter. At least not alone.

Realizing the response stemmed more from the personal than the rational made him pause before framing a reply. He was living with the woman. Sure, he'd told himself her safety had been the reason for their close proximity. After Vance had snatched her out of her shower and Sonny had later broken in to assassinate her, Cam had wanted to keep her as close as possible.

But those threats were over. Repairs on her condo had been finished for days. She hadn't mentioned moving back home, and he sure as hell wasn't about to suggest it. He still wanted her near. And he couldn't pretend his reasons were only safety related.

It might have been this case that had brought her back into his life, but it was far more that had her back in his bed. And if he couldn't believe her professions of love—was afraid she couldn't possibly be healed enough to utter them—he sure as hell wasn't ready to blow this thing.

His fingers were poised on the texting keys, waiting until he could frame a restrained reply. He knew better now how Sophie worked. What it took for her to compile a profile and construct a pattern of behavior. To crawl inside sick psychotic minds and link their pasts and presents in a way that might predict the future. She considered it a bonus when she could walk in the criminals' footsteps. Go where they went. See what they saw. It helped, she said, put herself in their heads. God help her.

Your limbs won't be intact if you turn an ankle at the farm, he finally wrote. He was being stupid. It was broad daylight and hotter than hell. He didn't know whether the place had been repaired or razed. Either way, it was doubtful she'd have reason to linger. There couldn't be a whole helluva lot to see there.

Satisfied, he set the cell down and returned his attention to the wall map. DMPD was managing the tip line Cam had set up to handle calls reporting possible sightings and information about Vickie Baxter for the last two weeks. The volume of calls was staggering, and they peaked again with every new mention of the woman in the media. A few days earlier the family of one of Vance's victims, Cassie Wright Urban, had offered a $50,000 reward for a tip leading to Baxter's arrest. That had taken the volume of calls from unmanageable to absolutely impossible.

Picking through the information gleaned from the calls was like looking for a fish in the ocean. First came the crackpots, then those sniffing for a reward. Throw in dozens of "tips" from vengeful exes wanting to make life difficult for a former spouse or significant other, add several disgruntled neighbors, and then sift through all of them for the few stemming from genuinely concerned citizens. It was a recipe for failure, but the tips couldn't be ignored. Somewhere in that mass of calls, he had to believe, was a genuine sighting of the woman. Maybe a lead that would blow this thing wide open.

His method was simple. Red and blue pushpins—one color correlated to each week—delineated the area for every sighting reported. They were coupled with a second purple pin if it was a "stationary" sighting—a neighbor, an ex, a clerk in a store who bore a resemblance to Vickie Baxter. Impaled on each pin was a number correlating to the tip it represented.

Cam propped a hip on his desk, arms folded, and sent a narrowed look at the map. The most promising tips had been checked out. Then they'd considered the locations where there were clusters of sightings. Canvasses required significant manpower, and that particular technique hadn't panned out. He was getting less and less assistance from the Des Moines Police Department for the task, and he really couldn't blame them. Resources were tight everywhere. He needed a new strategy.

A knock sounded at his door, and Tommy Franks stuck his head in. "Busy?"

"As you can see, I'm practicing for the ballet. Show's in a few hours."

Ignoring the sarcasm, the agent came the rest of the way in and folded himself into a chair. "Yeah, I can see you in tights and one of those—what do you call them?—tutu things."

"It's my legs." He worked his shoulders tiredly. "You're not the first to notice them."

"Don't let the compliment go to your head. I'm half-blind from looking over the feeds from the cemetery."

"Nothing?" Given the other man's demeanor, it wasn't a question.

"Unless she's some kind of master of disguises, she wasn't there."

It wasn't surprising, but the dead end added to the leads they'd been following that hadn't panned out. A week ago—hell, up to a few days ago—Cam had suspected it meant that Baxter had left the area. The recent sighting of her at the airport, however, said otherwise. His gaze drifted back to the map. And the answer to her whereabouts might be right in front of him.

Franks strolled over to peer at the scattering of pins. "Looks random."

"Tell me about it." Cam stared at it broodingly. "But she's here. We know that. She's moving freely around the area. Someone's seen her. Maybe even reported it. There's got to be a different way to narrow down the leads." The tips had been fed into a database and could be coordinated according to different parameters—addresses where the suspect had been seen, stores, streets, and so on. "I've been focusing on similar locations, but when you factor out the tips that didn't hold up to further scrutiny, that's been a wash."

"So where's she staying?" Unconsciously Tommy mimicked Cam's stance, crossing his arms across his chest. "What's safest? Not with a friend, even if she has one she hasn't murdered yet. Risk is too great that someone would turn her in for the reward."

"Sonny had a house rented in his name. We know she isn't there. She hasn't returned to Vance's home in Alleman or to the Stewart farmhouse she was staying at near Perry. Maybe there's a safe house somewhere. A place they kept just in case they needed to lay low."

"She'd stand out in one of the smaller surrounding towns." Franks settled into the familiar rhythm. They'd often bounced ideas off each other, one playing devil's advocate for the other. "Des Moines metro area offers more anonymity."

"But a stationary spot still brings scrutiny. There are neighbors, unless she's at another farm or acreage."

"There's no property owned in any of their names." Vance had been staying in his grandfather's residence while the old man resided in a nursing home. Sonny's house had been rented, and Baxter had murdered the old woman who owned the farmhouse she'd been living in when they'd first caught up with her. "Can't see them going for something that permanent."

"That leaves renting, leasing, or . . ."

"A motel," the two men said simultaneously.

"Any of those three possibilities still doesn't account for the randomness of the tip reports." Franks pressed the heels of both palms against his eyes. Rubbed. "We've got nothing to link the sightings for us. Most of the tips place her at different locations simultaneously. So we're back to where we started." He lowered his eyes, caught Cam's gaze fixed on him. "What?"

"Stationary. Staying in one spot is stupid. Vickie Baxter is a lot of things. Dumb isn't one of them. Sure, it makes sense if she's hiding out in a rural, secluded area. And if she is, we're going to be damn lucky to find her. But if she's not . . ." He rounded the desk, sat down at the computer. "She's active again. Damn active if she's responsible for both Webster's and Traer's deaths. She's on the move. Scouting their whereabouts. Learning their routines. That takes time. Both were living in Des Moines. That puts her here for the interval it took to plan and pull off their kidnappings."

He started typing commands into the database. "Motels are perfect. Anonymous. People coming and going all the time, with the added benefit of many of the occupants not being local."

"We sent Baxter's picture out to every bed-and-breakfast and motel in a hundred-mile area," Franks pointed out, but he was intrigued enough to round Cam's desk and stand behind him as he typed.

"Which hopefully gave the employees a heads-up, but what about the guests? To them Vickie Baxter is just another face in an anonymous setting. And for hotel workers who see hundreds of guests a day, she might not stand out, either."

"Maybe." Tommy leaned in closer to look at the screen. "Especially if she's transient. Doesn't stay in one place for too long, and if someone does call a tip in, it's too late. She's already gone. But every time she checks into a new motel, she runs the greatest risk of being recognized."

As the results of the new search command scrolled down the screen Cam felt his initial surge of interest begin to dissipate. "Out of nearly a thousand tips we've got thirteen reports coming from all different motels. Is she going to a new one every night?"

"Some of the sightings were called in on the same day. A motel guest made all but one. Maybe that's what Baxter was counting on. The time it takes to check out the reports. The people are gone. Out of town, most likely. Makes the follow-up tedious." Nothing about Franks's tone sounded optimistic. "Where are we on your request to Gonzalez to get the team fully staffed again?"

"She's working on it. Patrick and Samuels might be available by tomorrow." Cam turned to look at the other agent for a moment. Then he reached for his phone again.

"You've got a better idea?"

"I'm about to trade my firstborn to DMPD for some uniforms to help with this."

"You don't have a firstborn," Franks pointed out. He straightened and wandered back to the wall map.

"I've been thinking of getting a dog. Maybe they'll settle for pick of the litter. Rodriguez." He switched verbal gears seamlessly as the lieutenant answered. "We might have something but need some manpower . . . Wait. Will you wait? I think I can make it worth your while . . ."

⸻

Sophia hadn't expected to find much at the site of the Coates farm. Old rubble from the home, perhaps. Or a new ranch-style home sitting where the farmhouse had once stood. But she was surprised to discover a blackened shell of a decaying house. Tall weeds choked its foundation. Windows were boarded over. Porch steps were cracked or missing completely, and what once had been a porch railing now looked like a gap-toothed grin.

Getting out of the car, she tipped her head up and shaded her eyes above her sunglasses. The chimney that had once graced the south side of the home seemed to be tilting. The entire structure had a definite lean to it. She couldn't help but wonder why the Coateses' surviving son and daughter hadn't had the remains torn down. She wondered if it had anything to do with their unwillingness to talk to her. Maybe they hadn't dealt with their parents' deaths, even after all these years.

She scanned her surroundings. Thigh-high corn crowded the fencerows on three sides. Outbuildings dotted the area, all in varying states of disrepair but untouched by the fire that had ravaged the home. A rush of excitement filled her. It was rare for her to work a case in real time. Most often she was called in to consult from afar, relying on case notes and law enforcement logs to write her profiles. When she did travel to locations, there wasn't usually time to spare revisiting a suspect's past. She depended on histories and demographics to develop the profiling framework. This opportunity was oddly satisfying.

Picking her way carefully, she circled the dilapidated house. For whatever time Vickie Baxter had spent here all those years ago, the place had been part of the woman's life. It had marked her in some way. She wondered if Vickie had marked it in return. If she had been responsible for the fire that had killed Mary and Allen Coates and their youngest daughter. If the hollowed-out shell of a house stood in silent testimony of the evil that had been wrought there.

The skin on her arms prickled. She doubted it would ever be known whether Vickie Baxter was responsible for the fire. But Sophia thought it was entirely possible that she had been. The abuse the woman had suffered from childhood at her father's hands would have significantly impacted a normal person's capacity to trust. To form attachments. According to Denholt, Baxter hadn't cooperated with the therapy that represented her best chance to heal.

Perhaps even at that young age it had been too late for her. And much too late for her future victims.

All too aware that her heeled sandals weren't the best footwear on the uneven ground, Sophia moved cautiously through the tangled weeds. The damage the house had sustained would be mostly inside. Denholt had told her that Mary and Allen's bedroom had been the closest to the stairway upstairs. Even if they had awakened once the flames had rushed up the steps, they would have had to leap from the upper windows to safety.

In her line of work she regularly immersed herself in the unbelievably cruel acts people inflicted on one another. Had Vickie Baxter been capable of arson and murder at the age of twenty? Her son had been taken away only a few years later, after years of savage abuse. Somehow she'd managed to escape punishment for it, leveling the blame on the men in her life. But the story Sonny Baxter had told his social worker was far different.

Giving one last long look at the house before turning for her car, Sophia thought it entirely possible that the woman's evolution to serial predator had started sooner even than the fire that had destroyed this home.

It had begun with the torture enacted on her own young son.

⌒

She listened for the sound of tires crunching over gravel to fade. To disappear completely. Only then did Vickie Baxter raise one of the cracked and warped exterior doors that led to the cellar's entrance and run in a crouch to the corner of the house to look at the departing vehicle. A black Prius. It turned left at the drive onto the dusty gravel road and was soon lost in a cloud of dust.

Seeing the vehicle cemented her certainty about the identity of her unwanted guest. Even through the crack in the storm cellar door, the glimpse she'd gotten of the bitch had been enough. Dr. Sophia Channing.

She could have ended it right there. It would have been so easy. Once the bitch walked by, she could have thrown open the door and blown her fucking head off. But she had something better in store for Channing. The shrink would get everything she had coming to her. And first she'd play an unwitting part in Vickie's plans.

Stay or go? Torn, she shielded her eyes as she gazed down the ribbon of gravel, half expecting a plume of dust heralding the cops' arrival. What else would have brought Channing here if she hadn't been looking for Vickie?

The answer came in a snippet from the past.

A shrink's office. One in an endless string that her aunt had dragged her to. A male this time. He'd been annoyingly difficult to manipulate, so she'd stopped talking to him altogether. But that hadn't stopped *him* from talking.

You have to open up about your past, Vickie. I can't help you if you don't. Take me there. Help me understand.

Channing didn't know shit about her, and that's why she'd come. The realization had her lowering the weapon she clutched. Sliding the safety back in place. If there was one thing Vickie knew, it was how shrinks worked. Channing hadn't suspected Vickie was here. Couldn't have seen her car parked behind one of the old wooden sheds.

The cunt shrink had been trying to get a clearer picture of her past. Amused, she released a chuckle and turned to the crumbling stone steps leading to the dark cellar. She bent and picked up her Maglite.

Good fucking luck with that. The only thing a charred, deteriorating, crappy farmhouse could tell her about Vickie Baxter was that she'd had a lot to learn at twenty.

She'd meant to burn the fucking place to the ground.

With the aid of the flashlight, she made her way back into the cellar. There was a gaping hole in part of the floorboards overhead from where the fire had eaten away at the living room floor. She liked to picture dear old auntie screaming as the flames melted the flesh from her bones. It'd be disappointing to think that they'd gotten off easy by dying of smoke inhalation.

When Vickie rounded the corner into the cellar, the woman there flinched away from the bright beam of light. "You got ten minutes to eat and drink." Ripping the duct tape carelessly from her face, she warned, "If you start screeching again, you'll go hungry."

But the fight had streamed out of the woman. Awkwardly she reached out with her bound hands to bring the bottled water to her lips and gulped greedily. After a few moments, she lowered the bottle. "What are you going to do with him? He needs food and drink, too. You can't just—"

"Shut the fuck up and eat. You've got eight more minutes."

"But he—"

"Is not your problem. Guess you're not hungry." Vickie kicked the bag of fast food away with one foot and set down the light to pick up the roll of duct tape at her feet. Roughly she wound a length of tape around the female's head again and over her mouth. Maybe she had Aunt Mary on the mind, but this woman was starting to sound just like the old bitch had. Constantly telling her what to do. "Bet you'll be ready to eat tomorrow."

Ignoring the muffled sounds the woman was making, Vickie picked up the Maglite again and picked her way through the debris-strewn stone floor toward her other victim. Taking the knife from her pocket, she bent toward the figure, smiling as he frantically rolled as far away as his bonds would allow. She sliced through the tape securing his ankles. "You and me are taking a little trip, pal." Grabbing him by the shirt, she stuck her face close to his. "You do something stupid, and I slit your throat and leave you here for the spiders to eat." After hauling him to his feet, she nudged him toward the cellar steps.

Snapping off the flashlight, she left it on the top step before moving into the bright sunlight, squinting. She pulled her victim to a stop until she could be sure there was no one in sight. The place was deserted. The windbreak planted decades earlier still provided an effective screen.

She'd have to return to shut the cellar doors and refasten the padlock she'd bought for the rusted hasp. But first she needed to control the victim. She dug in her pocket for the fob with her keys and pressed the button that raised the trunk's lid. Giving him a push that sent him sprawling against the bumper, she ordered, "Get in."

~

"I told you on the phone earlier, we're very careful with our guest information." The manager of Saxony Suites brushed back his limp blond hair and pursed his too-full lips. "But if you want to just leave a picture, I'll try to make sure that my employees see it. I don't want you to waste your time."

Cam's temper was dangerously frayed. "Waste of time" was an exact descriptor for the hours spent so far chasing down this lead. They had only checked out five of the thirteen motels on the list, even with the help of the two uniforms Rodriguez had grudgingly assigned, after extorting Cam's fifty-yard-line Hawkeyes tickets for the biggest game of the fall season. His mood had started out surly and had progressively worsened.

This was the only motel where it had been an employee making the report. But the others had to be checked out, as well. Even if it had been a guest calling the tip line, it was possible workers there would recognize Baxter's picture. It was a tedious job.

There was management to go through and employees to round up. Although a few had recognized the photo and sketches Agent Jenna Turner had done depicting Baxter, none could be certain whether it was from the motel or from TV.

The result was far more "maybes" than he'd feared, and nothing solid to go on. Cam's patience was thinning accordingly.

"You have an employee by the name of Alison Jaye, right?" The woman had called the tip line a week ago, but the responding officer had been unable to contact her. "Is she working today?"

With a long-suffering sigh, the manager led them back to his cramped office and plucked a schedule book from a teetering stack on his desk. Flipping to find today's date, he ran his finger down an employee list. "Yes. She's here. Alison runs the housekeeping unit, so you'll find her in her office or on a floor, checking on the cleaning progress."

"Call her." Tommy Franks's tone brooked no opposition.

"I'll be glad to direct you to her—"

Reaching across the desk, Cam picked up the receiver of the phone and handed it to the man. "Call her."

Lips pressed together, the manager obeyed. His voice, when he spoke to the woman, was peeved. Once he'd hung up, Cam said, "Now I want to talk to those employees you have on duty. We'll use your office. Bring them here in shifts."

The manager's face flushed. "As I said earlier, that's not necessary. I can show them the picture myself."

"Every motel in the area was faxed a picture of the suspect two weeks ago. Did you show it to your employees then?" Cam paused, watched the man squirm. "Exactly. Start calling your people in."

Moments after the manager left the room, a young woman appeared in the doorway and looked around. "I'm Alison Jaye. I see you got rid of Attila for the moment. We'd better make this quick."

The two agents exchanged a look as the slight woman moved swiftly into the office. Young, vivacious, with a wealth of light-brown hair and eyes that looked permanently amused—the woman was the manager's polar opposite.

"Attila?" Cam asked.

"The day manager. Donald Huncombe. Attila the Hun. Believe me—work with him a day and you'll get the analogy."

"I think we got a taste. DCI, Agents Franks and Prescott." Cam made the introductions. "You made a phone call a week ago to our tip hotline regarding a possible sighting of this woman." He held up a picture of Vickie Baxter. Unlike Huncombe, she stepped forward and took the photo, studied it carefully.

"Yes, that's the woman I saw. Room one-oh-eight. Four of my maids called in sick that day. *Four.* Day from hell. So I was pitching in, helping clean the rooms." She handed back the picture and rounded the desk to sink into the manager's chair. "Sorry. Don't want to be rude, but I never get a minute to sit on this job. So . . ." Her gaze was bright, bouncing from Cam to Tommy and back again. "No offense, but you took your time following up."

"I believe an officer contacted you a couple times but was unable to reach you."

She frowned at Cam, tapped her fingers on the desk. "Really? I'm usually . . ." Her face cleared. "I was in and out. Took a couple days off here and there because—this will come as no surprise to anyone but Attila—I'm interviewing for different jobs. Also my cell is currently residing at the bottom of the Saylorville reservoir in a freak tubing incident and I just got it replaced. So my fault." She made a face. "Anyway, there isn't much more to tell you. I saw her the day I called. I cleaned room one-oh-eight, spoke to this woman briefly, and went on my way. It was only that one time. But at dinner that night I saw the news and thought, hey, long shot, but the pic they were showing looked a lot like her."

"What did she say when you spoke to her?" Cam wanted to know.

Alison screwed up her brow. "I'm not going to remember the exact words, but something to the effect that she wanted no housekeeping services. At all. Said the room wasn't to be touched and she'd call for towels when she needed them." She shrugged. "We make note of special requests on the master schedule and act accordingly. That one stood out because, hey, makes less work. You know?"

Interest flickered. "Is the woman still here?"

Alison hid a yawn behind one balled-up fist. "Sorry. Double shift. Another reason to love Attila. I have no idea about reservations. That's not my gig. All I know is I still have the request on my schedule. If she's checked out, no one's told me. I use a software program that keeps track of everything. Each time the room is cleaned and by whom, special requirements. Staff is supposed to keep track of any and all requests they fill. They don't always, but they're supposed to. Helps me improve customer satisfaction if I can be sure they're fulfilled in a timely manner. Not to mention tracking employee work production."

"A software program." A spurt of adrenaline kick-started in his veins. "So you could check the last time a call came in from room one-oh-eight asking for towel service?"

"Maybe. If it was documented the way it was supposed to be, yeah, I could."

"I need that information."

Huncombe's voice could be heard in the hallway, and she leaped from his chair, jostling the desk as she did so. Eyes wide, she watched the stack of file folders and books begin to sway. "Oh, shit." She made a wild grab in vain. As if in slow motion, the pile toppled to the floor.

The manager picked that exact moment to walk in the door, then stopped, mouth open when he saw the mess. He aimed a narrowed look at the woman. "Alison! Are you responsible for this?"

Cam stepped between them. "Sorry. I must have brushed the pile as I went by."

Alison sailed to the door as Cam crouched next to Huncombe to help gather up the mess. She paused in the doorway, blew them a kiss, and scurried away. Cam felt a twinge of amusement. A sense of humor was probably a must working with the man.

"It's fine. I can get this." The manager stood, his arms bulging with folders. "I've summoned the bellhops first. If you could be quick, I'd like them back on the job as soon as possible."

Franks headed out the door, leaving Cam to deal with the manager. "I need the name of the guest in room one-oh-eight on this date." He glanced down at his notes and recited the date of Jaye's call to the tip line. "How long did the guest stay, was she alone, payment information . . ."

Huncombe was shaking his head, the folders and books hugged tightly to his chest. "We protect our guests' privacy. You'll need a warrant for that."

"That won't be a problem." He was already digging into his pocket for his cell phone, having decided that Gonzalez could expedite the task better than he could. It went without saying the process would take longer than he wanted. Judges didn't exactly sit by their phones waiting to respond. "We'll continue this conversation in front of room one-oh-eight."

"What?" Huncombe dumped the mess on his desk and rushed after Cam as he headed out the door. "I don't think that will be necessary."

"Yeah, it is. I may not be able to get into the room until the warrant comes through, but no one else will be allowed in, either."

Michael Frasier was on his second overpriced beer and already pissed off. This whole rape fantasy ad he'd answered was starting to be a pain in the ass. First was the list of questions he'd had to answer about his background. Then the demand for medical records proving he was STD-free. He'd almost said fuck it then, but the cash for the doctor visit had been messengered over to his place as promised. He could have taken the money to the casino and forgotten the whole thing, but he couldn't forget it. Dammit, the more he'd heard about this deal, the sweeter it had sounded. An entire night playing out his own rape fantasies with an anonymous willing woman? There wasn't a guy with a dick who'd walk away from that.

Which was why he was sitting outside Legends on Court Avenue, an area of town that boasted scarce parking, trendy restaurants, and pricey drinks and was frequented by people who tended to stare at a guy with prison tats on his knuckles sitting alone at a table in the far corner of the terrace.

He pegged the woman as the one he was waiting for as soon as she stepped through the door. She wore a big, floppy, black hat, sundress, and huge shades. Something about her suggested she wasn't entirely comfortable in the dress and heels she wore. She scanned the outdoor patio area for a couple of seconds before heading toward him.

Frasier looked her over as she approached. Bigger than he liked but not overweight. He'd never gone for the cows, even at closing time. Just because he'd been in prison didn't mean he couldn't have standards. She had decent-size tits, and from what he could make out her ass would definitely do. He felt himself begin to harden. Maybe this hadn't been a complete waste of his time after all.

The woman sat down, and they were silent for a moment while he felt her checking him out from behind the shades. When she spoke her voice was brisk. "Do you have the test results? And your ID?"

He pulled the rolled-up envelope from his back jeans pocket and tossed it over to her. Then yanked out his wallet, flipped it open to his driver's license, and slid it across the table to her. His earlier annoyance began to return. He'd already given the woman on the phone his name and address, and he'd bet money a background check had been run. This was worse than applying for a damn job to get his parole officer off his back.

He finished his beer while the woman looked at his lab results. She surprised him when she reached into her purse and withdrew a white envelope very much like the one he'd handed her and gave it to him. "My friend's lab results. Safety first."

He stared at her, not opening the envelope. "Your friend's?"

The woman shook her head at the approaching waitress, and the server veered off course, leaving them to their solitude in the corner. "It's sort of a bucket list for a few of us. Each chooses a man to make one friend's ah . . . sexual fantasy come true. You'll do for her. I think you'll do just fine." She nodded to the envelope he still hadn't opened. "Inside you'll also find her name, home and business addresses, and a list of what she's into sexually. Feel free to spice things up with your own ideas, the rougher the better. My friend has a hard time finding men who aren't afraid to do whatever it takes to satisfy her."

"Maybe she hasn't looked in the right places."

"Oh, I think we can agree on that." She gave a silent laugh. "Your approach is up to you. She wants it realistic. So either you snatch her off the street or you find a way to enter her business or townhouse." The woman fingered the trio of bright-red bracelets on one wrist. "She's got a boyfriend she's been staying with recently and a security system at home, so keep that in mind. The money included is for any . . . toys you might want to bring along. I stuck in a business card for where you can buy that stuff."

Obviously finished, she rose and stuffed the papers he'd given her into her large purse. "The timing is up to you, but if you wait too long, I'll figure you're not following through and make the arrangements with someone else." She smirked. "There are several guys interested, as you can imagine."

"Oh, I'm interested." And not totally disappointed that the target of this little role-play wasn't the woman in front of him. She didn't look like the type to submit easily.

"Good." Something about the smile she gave him had the hair rising on Frasier's nape. "I want my friend to get everything she deserves. Don't disappoint us." With that she turned and made her way through the collection of patio tables and chairs on the terrace.

He didn't bother to watch her go. Tearing open the envelope she'd left behind, he gave a cursory glance to what looked like lab results attesting the patient was disease-free. Then he shook out the other items the woman had mentioned. His brows rose when he saw the hundred-dollar bill inside and the business card for the Pleasure Emporium. He'd heard of the place but had never been inside. Not much call for props when most of his hookups were whores or women too drunk to even recall it the next day.

There was a folded note included with a list of instructions. Because he'd never been fond of rules, he skipped over most of it after noting the "safe word" was *squeaky*. Frasier snorted. Women and their games. But his ire faded when he read the description of what his target was looking for. Jesus, she must be a twisted little piece. No wonder she couldn't get what she wanted from most guys.

Fortunately, Michael Frasier was not most guys. He could fulfill every wish on this list all night long, and he wouldn't need the help of medication, either. He was also imaginative enough to throw in a few other acts that might teach her a thing or two.

He shifted uncomfortably. Just thinking about it had his cock straining against his jeans. There was one more item in the envelope. He shook it out and held it up, squinting at it in the fading light. Printed on eight-by-eleven paper, it was a digital picture of a petite blonde taken as she walked down a street. Full length, it showed her whole body. On the short side but with enough curves to make him anxious to strip her out of the skirt and heels she wore and get down to business. His gaze fell to the name at the bottom of the picture.

Sophia Channing.

Classy name for a classy piece of ass. She looked like a woman used to getting whatever she wanted.

He shoved the papers back in the envelope and drained the rest of his beer. In this case, he was just the man to oblige her.

Lavontae Cross was 270 pounds of solid flesh. A mountain of a man, he had full sleeves of tattoos depicting an ongoing battle between dragons and demons. He'd gained steady employment at seventeen as a leg breaker for a bookie in the East Village. He'd graduated to security at Sid's Pleasure Palace, protecting strippers from the attentions of inebriated patrons. No one mourned the renovation of Des Moines's east side as much as he did.

For the last four years he'd been employed by Rico Cervantes, who ran a profitable heroin and Oxy supply business catering to upscale professionals in downtown Des Moines. The dealer was unique in that he allowed credit. His rationale was simple: his clients were known to him, gainfully employed, and all had much to lose if they were outed for their habit. There was still the occasional customer, however, who abused Rico's good nature. And when that happened, Lavontae stepped in. He was presently in Polk County jail for puncturing the eardrum of a recalcitrant client with an antique ice pick.

He hadn't made bail because of Rico's displeasure with him. Not only had Lavontae been caught; he hadn't retrieved the money owed.

Besides Lavontae's, the only solitary cell was one directly across from him in the opposite corner. The man occupying it had muscle-bound shoulders and a gleaming white head. Everyone in lockup knew who he was and what he'd done. And they all had something to say about it.

But not Lavontae. The two hadn't exchanged a word the entire time they'd been there. A man who had accomplished what Mason Vance had deserved a little respect. A little deference. Not because of what he'd done—Lavontae didn't hold with rape—but for what he'd accomplished. The TV news claimed the man had raked in more than $300,000 kidnapping those women and forcing them to make hefty withdrawals from their bank accounts.

Lavontae appreciated a businessman. One like Mason Vance. Like Rico. While Lavontae had the brawn, the other men had the know-how.

Vance also had enviable aim. Nearly every time he came back from a talk with his lawyer—who had generously offered to represent Lavontae for free—within an hour a tightly folded fifty-dollar bill would come sailing through the bars of Lavontae's cell. Not a word had ever been exchanged between them, but nothing built loyalty like a steady stream of Grants.

People like them didn't need words. Lavontae knew that when the time came, he'd have a role to play.

Chapter 4

Sophia looked up at the slight noise, ears straining. Hearing nothing further, she resumed reading, mentally berating herself.

It was easy to trace the source of her residual jumpiness, she admitted. It was a by-product of her stop at the old Coates place. But the visit had been useful, as it had sparked something for her. When she'd gotten to the office, she'd done far less work than she'd intended checking on the progress of her patients. One of her colleagues, Dr. Redlow, had taken over her client list during the time she'd been on the Cornbelt Killers case. It'd been two weeks since they'd discovered Sonny Baxter's body and learned the woman they'd thought was Rhonda Klaussen was really Vickie Baxter. It was assumed the woman had disappeared. A few days ago Sophia thought it was time to start resuming some of her client appointments.

Of course, that was before they'd discovered that Vickie was still in the area. And had resumed killing again. So today the task of tweaking Baxter's profile had consumed her.

Other profiles she'd completed for previous cases were stored on her laptop, but the textbooks she wanted to consult were kept in the small research library in the suite she shared with three other psychologists. They all had their own receiving areas and offices, with the library a common hub in the center. Each of their individual spaces radiated from it like spokes.

As a rule the building was fairly quiet, although there were always the usual business sounds to be heard. Phones. Voices in the hallway. The sound of clients coming and going.

Which didn't explain her startling at every little creak or rustle. Frustrated with herself, she reread the paragraph she'd been trying to focus on.

As a female serial murderer, Vickie Baxter had already achieved a relatively rare status. She shared the female predator commonalities of childhood abuse and her later abuse of children, her own son. Although there wasn't a comprehensive work of interviews with female serial killers, it was known that they were somewhat more likely than males to work with partners. When they acted alone, their crimes most frequently involved children and the infirm or monetary gain.

Sophia looked at the profiling framework she'd developed for the woman. Baxter was even more unique for being a female sexual predator. The short interview with Van Wheton had cemented that theory. From a clinical standpoint, the woman was a treasure trove for forensic psychology.

Giving up on reading for a moment, Sophia leaned back in her chair. Stretched. The one time she'd met Baxter the woman was still posing as Rhonda Klaussen. Although Cam was suspicious, they'd had no way to know at first that she wasn't another of Vance's victims, as she'd claimed. As Klaussen she'd been a consummate actress, and Sophia had found her credible. How much of the personality she'd shown had been pretense and how much real? If she could just figure that much, she'd be well on her way to—

A clatter in the hallway had Sophia's heart leaping to her throat. Leaving her work on the table, she went to her adjoining reception space and looked out the front door. Paul, one of the night janitors, waved at her from down the hall. Feeling foolish, she gave a weak wave in return and ducked back into her suite again.

Okay. It was time to stop kidding herself. Clearly staying past office hours had been a huge error in judgment. She hadn't come in until midafternoon and it was now—

She checked the clock above her absent secretary's desk—after seven.

She winced. Her last communication with Cam had been a couple of hours earlier when he'd texted a terse summary of the motel lead they were following up on. Clearly he was still immersed in that, or he would have reached out and nagged her about her whereabouts.

Sophia went back to the library and put away the reference material she'd been using. The space was accessible from both of her colleagues' suites, as well, but there was no door to the hallway. She gathered up her profile notes and the cell she'd taken with her. Heading back to her office space, she flipped the light off before closing the door behind her.

After stuffing her files into her briefcase, she collected her purse, pausing to send Cam a text message saying she was on her way home before dropping the phone into it. Then she locked up her office and walked swiftly to the building's back entrance. The office space available in the building was affordable and perfect for her needs. The parking was less so. The clients used the side facing the street, while the occupants of the building used the smaller lot in back.

Her heels clicked lightly on the blacktop as she dug in her purse for her keys and used the fob to unlock the driver's door. The furnace-like heat inside the vehicle slapped at her as she slid cautiously into the driver's seat. Although she was appreciative of the seat-warming features in winter, leather seats in Iowa summers weren't a benefit.

Sophia checked the rearview mirror as she began backing up. There were only a handful of vehicles in the lot at this hour. Most sane people would have gone home a couple of hours ago.

She thought she heard a rustle and braked. Listened. Heard nothing but faint traffic sounds.

Seriously. Irritated with herself, she resumed backing up. Sophia had infinite patience with a client dealing with the aftereffects of a traumatic event. She'd suggest coping techniques. Relaxation measures. Ways to avoid triggers. She was far less tolerant of her own state. Maybe she needed to take some of her own advice when she got home and—

She caught a flash of movement in the rearview mirror and jerked the car to a halt. Her head whipped around to look behind her. Just in time to see a man in a face mask rise from his crouched position in the hatchback to lunge over the backseat toward her.

⁓

Donald Huncombe wrung his hands as Cam watched the DCI crime scene team working in the motel room. "This is just horrible for business. How soon will your people be out of here? We're full on RAGBRAI's overnight stop in Des Moines this week. If word of your presence here gets out . . ."

Reaching for patience he was far from feeling, Cam tried to reassure the man. "We'll be gone long before then." RAGBRAI, an annual weeklong bicycle ride across Iowa, had more than ten thousand bikers descending on different towns each night in their trek across the state. The stops were a boon for local businesses, a pain in the ass for law enforcement. "Our presence here today isn't going to be made public. You should have nothing to worry about."

The radio clipped to the man's belt buzzed then, and thankfully he hurried off to deal with another matter, brushing by SAC Gonzalez as she came down the hallway to join Cam.

"Making friends?"

He blew out a breath and returned his attention to the criminalists' progress.

"Motel rooms make crappy scenes," Gonzalez muttered, half turning to follow his gaze.

Ordinarily Cam would agree. They'd find hundreds of prints here, and likely unrelated stains and fibers. But he had no reason to believe this room was a crime scene, and he wasn't trying to identify an UNSUB. All he needed was forensic verification that Baxter had been here. Since they already had her prints on file, a match could be relatively simple.

"She registered one week ago for an extended stay. This motel offers a reduced rate for a twenty-eight-day reservation." The warrant Maria obtained for them had opened up the registration information, and those details had jostled the memory of one of the reservation clerks, although she'd been shaky on the photo ID of Baxter. "Extended-stay requests are infrequent enough that a front desk clerk recalled it. Said the woman had mentioned being in and out of town on business all month."

"And then she made arrangements to ban housekeeping from the room by requesting towel service on an as-needed basis," Maria mused, her dark eyes shrewd. "Any idea when she last made the request?"

"The housekeeping software shows two days ago." Mentally Cam blessed Alison Jaye for being so organized. "They were told to leave the towels in front of the door."

"And the door had a Do Not Disturb on its handle."

"If this is Baxter's room and she had anything to hide, it's gone now," Cam countered. "Likely she wanted to keep her exposure to a minimum." He and Maria had frequently partnered on cases before he'd taken a multiagency task force assignment. The assignment had proven to be longer and more harrowing than he'd expected. During his time away from the agency, Maria had been promoted to special agent in charge, a position she deserved. Her promotion hadn't dulled the instincts he'd valued when they worked together. But administrative politics sometimes trumped investigative instincts. It was a compromise she'd been willing to make. Cam wouldn't have been so accepting.

She had made swift work of the warrants today, so he was in the mood to be expansive. Hotel reservations meant credit cards, and tracing the one Baxter had used to check in had taken another warrant. It was also potentially their best lead so far. His hunch told him the woman wouldn't be careless enough to leave a trail that could so easily be traced. But no one could cover all their tracks. He was counting on that.

"We made a list of the motels in the metro area that offer extended stays, which unfortunately is a lot of them." Cam and Maria watched the activity in the room from the hall through the doorway. "But when we cross-checked those with the tip line database of reported sightings, we can narrow it down to five others. Gives us a place to start."

"All the extended-stay motels will need to be notified."

His reaction to the obvious statement was an arch of the brow. He owed her for the warrants, so a little diplomacy was justified. "I've got Jenna and Brody on it. But this is going to take manpower, Maria. I'll need Patrick's and Samuels's returns to be full-time. And depending on how this shakes out, I may need more agents. DMPD is as strapped for manpower as we are."

She tapped her lips, thought a moment. "Beachum and Loring are on that child murder case in Ames. But when it looks like we're getting close, I'll give you everyone I can spare." Her expression went grim, and he noticed again the threads of silver in her dark hair and the creases on her face that hadn't been there just a few years ago. "I want this bitch caught, Cam." Her tone was as fierce as her expression. "Media pressure and political bullshit aside, I want her brought down. She's a drag on humanity, and she needs to be put in a cage for the rest of her life."

He considered her. "You always said women were the more vicious of the genders."

"Damn straight." She stepped aside when one of the criminalists walked out with the bagged linens. "But we're the smartest, too. So catching her isn't going to be easy."

"Maybe not." His voice was as hard as hers. "But it sure in hell is going to be satisfying."

Sophia screamed. A short burst of sound, but the echoes of the shriek careened through her, reverberating through her system. She stomped on the brake, her fingers scrambling for the button to unlock her door. Felt the kiss of a cool steel blade against the side of her throat. Stilled.

"Oh, no you don't, bitch. Stay put. Get this tin can moving."

She tried to think through the roar in her head. Her heart was jackhammering in her chest. A thread of cold fear traced down her spine. She needed to think. To *move*. But paralysis had gripped her limbs.

Not again not again oh God oh God oh God . . .

The flashback rolled over her like a mental tidal wave. Of Vance pulling her out of the shower, overpowering her easily. Feeling helpless. Hopeless.

"Please." Sophia moistened her lips. "You can have the car."

"I'm gonna take me a ride on something a little racier than this piece of shit." She felt his breath on her nape and shivered. Vance's face swam before her again. She gave herself a mental shake to dislodge it. Not Vance. He was in jail. Who then was this? "I got some nasty surprises for you, bitch. Hope you cleared your schedule." She closed her eyes and shuddered when the blade slid up to her earlobe and down again. "What I got planned for you will take a few days. Now drive. You make a move for the door and I cut your throat."

"All right." She released a breath and eased up on the brake. Sophia was calmer now. Steadier. The lot was empty except for the cars she'd noted earlier. Traffic on the street flanking it was light. "You'll have to tell me where to go." She kept her right hand on the wheel. Her left crept toward the pocket at the bottom of the door.

"Turn left out of the lot. I got lots more directions for you. You're going to—" The blade pressed threateningly against her neck. "Get both fucking hands on the wheel, or I slice you open like a pig."

"I need a tissue." Her fingers scrambled inside the small area in a mad search. She found what she was seeking and took a deep breath. "I'm so scared . . ." She turned suddenly and brought up the small canister she'd been seeking, spraying the pepper spray directly into his eyes.

"Fuck fuck fuck!"

She fumbled with her seat belt release and unlocked the door, half falling from the vehicle. The car kept moving slowly. Out of the lot. Across a lane of traffic. Sophia slipped off her shoes, stumbled to a run, expecting the maniac with the knife to jump from her car and come for her at any moment.

She'd gotten only a few steps when she saw the taxi bearing down on the vehicle. There was a loud crunch and the shriek of grinding metal as it hit her Prius broadside.

—

Cam burst into the DMPD interview room and stopped short when he saw Sophie at the table with a plainclothes detective. The uniform accompanying him had assured him she was unharmed, but he'd needed to see that for himself. He took visual inventory as he moved into the room, ignoring the detective.

"Sir, you'll need to leave. You're not authorized—"

"Prescott. DCI." Cam badged him without taking his eyes from Sophie. "Someone heard her name on the scanner and contacted me." Satisfied for the moment that she was uninjured, he spared the man a glance. "I didn't get any details."

"It's all right. I'm fine."

The detective, a balding man with the seamed face and tired eyes of a veteran, spoke over Sophie. "DCI have an interest in an attempted rape?"

Cam went still as the words washed over him. *Rape.* Fear tangled in his gut with something much more visceral. Primitive. "I have an interest in this one. She's mine." It took a moment to realize what he'd said, and he backtracked. "That is . . . Dr. Channing is working on the Cornbelt Killers case with us."

"Detective Sam Udall." The man looked interested. "Any chance this assault is related to the case?"

"It's doubtful." After reaching inside his suit jacket, Cam withdrew his card from the inner pocket and handed it to the detective. "We do know Vickie Baxter is still in the area, and that she's killed again. The Traer case? Detective Manning is liaison on it. That said, I'd appreciate being kept up-to-date on this."

"Not a problem." Udall returned his attention to the notebook on the table before him. "Dr. Channing, I just have a few more questions. Any idea how this guy got in your vehicle?"

"He was in your car?" Cam sank into a chair next to her. Took her hand beneath the table. Squeezed it reassuringly. She sent him a small smile before answering.

"None. I always lock it, even at home. And it *was* locked before I got into it." There was the slightest quaver in her voice. Udall might not notice it, but Cam did. And it scraped something inside him. Unconsciously he balled his other fist.

"He was in the hatchback. Probably under the tarp." Her Prius had a protective covering there to be used over luggage or other items hauled. "I don't know. I didn't notice him. I was in a hurry to get home."

"Did you see his face?"

She shook her head. "He was wearing a face mask. When I caught a glimpse of movement in the rearview mirror, he lunged over the backseat. And then he was behind me the whole time, with the knife." She winced and tugged at her hand. Only then did Cam realize how tight his grip had become. Loosening his fingers, he brushed his thumb over the back of her hand soothingly.

But there was no soothing the bubbling rage that was spreading through his veins. *A knife. Jesus.*

"He never took the mask off?"

"No. He still had it on when I turned and pepper sprayed him. Then I threw open the car door and started running."

"You pepper sprayed him." His chest eased infinitesimally, and he bumped her shoulder with his approvingly. "Nice job. With that lipstick vial?" She'd balked at his talk of teaching her to shoot, and with her wrist still tender from the sprain she'd gotten escaping from Vance, it was going to be a while before that was an option, anyway. So he'd bought her several vials of police-strength pepper spray. Had been blown away when she'd shown him the pink capsule of spray on her key chain that he'd always thought was a lipstick.

"No. I knew I wasn't going to be able to free it, so I dug in the side pocket of the door for one you'd put there."

After she'd come into protective custody at his place, he'd planted the damn things around the home and cars like land mines, and she'd laughed when he'd shown her a map he'd drawn of where to find them. He was grateful for his foresight now, but she'd been lucky. Damn lucky. And the trouble with luck was it had a habit of running out.

"Have you questioned him yet?"

Udall shook his head in response to Cam's question. "He's being treated for minor injuries at the hospital first. When Dr. Channing jumped from the car, it was still in reverse." A smile deepened the creases on the man's face. "Gotta put this one down to poetic justice. The perp was blinded in the car while it continued to roll into the street and got smacked by a cab. Then when the guy did manage to get out of the vehicle and attempt to run, the cabdriver tackled him, thinking he was trying to flee the scene of an accident because he didn't have insurance. Kept him there until a cop arrived." He let out a chuckle. "Karma's a bitch."

"You get an ID?"

Udall pushed a file folder across the table. After flipping it open, Cam studied the mug shot inside. "He's got a sheet."

"Aggravated assault, fraud, domestic violence . . . This guy's been around the block a few times. We're going to send him around again."

Cam handed the mug shot photo to Sophie while he scanned the arrest summary. "Dennis Leslie." He glanced at her. "Recognize the face or name?"

"Not at all." She looked at Udall. "How do you think he got into my car?"

"Responding officer didn't find any broken glass or tools for illegal entry like a slim jim. Other than that, we've got a gang of pretty sophisticated car thieves working the area who can actually clone the RFID in car fobs. This guy, though"—the detective reached over to thump Leslie's picture—"is no rocket scientist. I can't see him having the know-how. Sometimes I've heard of them hiding as a Prius pulls up and then just as the driver is getting out, unlatching the hatch before it's locked."

Cam's brows skimmed upward. "Be a pretty hot wait today."

"Or he somehow got your keys."

For a moment her mask of composure cracked, and Cam glimpsed a flare of panic. "I had them in my purse, in my desk. Usually I lock the drawer, but I was alone there today."

"Did you see anyone? Talk to anybody else?" Udall asked.

"A colleague of mine. Dr. Redlow." Her hand in Cam's trembled just slightly. "I stepped next door to his office, and we spoke briefly. Most of the time I spent in the library, which is attached to my reception area."

Udall exchanged a look with Cam. "I'll know more when I talk to Leslie. At this rate, it probably won't be until tomorrow."

Aware of the slump in Sophie's shoulders, Cam said, "Is she about done here tonight?"

"I think so." Udall dug a card out of his pocket and handed it to her. "Dr. Channing, give us a call if anything else occurs to you. Otherwise, I'll be in touch."

"All right." Sophie took the card, looked around, and then gave a little laugh. "It just occurred to me I don't have my purse."

"It's at the front desk," the detective assured her. His chair scraped the floor as he pushed it back and rose. "Responding officer got it out of your car before it was towed."

She winced at that as she stood. "I guess I'll need a ride home tonight. And for the foreseeable future."

"No problem. I can have one of the uniforms . . ." The detective looked at Cam and amended his words. "Something tells me Agent Prescott's got it from here."

"I do." To Sophie Cam said, "Why don't you go on ahead and collect your things. I'll be along." The look she shot him told him she knew exactly what he was up to, but she headed out the door alone.

When she was gone, Cam switched his focus to the detective. "Any chance I can sit in on the interview?"

The man's faded brown eyes were shrewd. "For professional reasons? Or personal?"

Cam's smile was sharklike. "Let's call it both."

Udall lifted a shoulder as they both followed Sophie out the door. "I'll give you a heads-up when I get it scheduled. I'm guessing Leslie will be lawyered up before he even hits the cell."

"He was caught in the act. He's going to need more than a lawyer to make this go away," Cam said grimly. "He's going to need a damn magician."

⁓

"How long will it take for the credit card company to come through with the information on Baxter's card?"

Cam slid a glance across the car's darkened interior toward Sophia. "We don't have to talk about the case now."

Touched by the concern she heard in his voice, she reached over to rest her hand lightly on his arm. She could feel the muscles clenched tightly there. And realized she wasn't the only one affected by her recent ordeal. "It's okay. It'll distract me."

He was silent for a few moments, as if unconvinced. Finally he said, "The information should come through tomorrow. The card was issued in the name of Greta Talbot. Address is a PO box in Ames. We've already filed a warrant request with the credit card company."

"I thought maybe it might match one of the victims we've identified. But I suppose you've already run the name."

"Yeah, I did. There's no record of a Greta Talbot in the state or federal databases for missing persons. But the magnetic strip on the back of credit cards carries all kinds of personal information. Maybe we'll hit something with the phone number and home address. It's a long shot," he added, "but it's something."

Mulling that over, she said, "So now what? You void her key so she has to go to the front desk so they can alert you? Or place an agent in the room until she comes back?"

Cam passed a livestock semi and took the exit leading to his home. The smell would have given away the truck's cargo, even without the squealing that split the air. "You're on the right track. Voiding her key might tip her off, but I left Boggs there for the time being to rig up our own surveillance camera. Feed will come directly to my computer."

"She almost certainly would use more than one motel." Sophia leaned her head against the headrest, exhaustion sweeping over her. "She's too careful to do otherwise. And if she's using motels, that makes it less likely that she has a safe house somewhere, doesn't it?"

"Maybe." His tone was noncommittal. Cam had never been one to draw speedy conclusions. A faint smile curved her lips. He was the king of empirical evidence. Her smile faded as she recalled that his difficulty accepting things at face value splashed over to his personal life, as well. And he still didn't seem quite convinced that her feelings for him were of the lasting variety.

Understandable, perhaps. It had been she who'd called it quits in May when they'd started the affair that had represented a huge variation from her usual cautious choices. She'd been a coward then, she admitted with a mental sigh. Running from something that had hit her way too hard and way too fast.

They had that in common. She pressed a hand to her mouth to stifle a yawn. Both of them were wary of any aspect of their lives outside their control. Which seemed supremely ironic given her brushes with danger in the last month. It was as if the fates were trying to show her how little control she really had.

She was content to finish the ride in silence, his companionship comforting in the confines of the car. Following him into the house, she set her purse on the counter and slipped off her sandals. And then she stood, gripping the back of a breakfast stool. Sleep held no temptation for her. After the day she'd had, it was a given that dreaming would be vivid and nightmarish. Another woman might relax with a long hot bath, but Sophia had never been a soaker. And since Vance had snatched her naked, dripping, and terrified from the shower stall weeks ago, a hot shower was the last thing that would ease the tension from the day.

Cam disappeared into the bedroom and returned without suit jacket or weapon holster. He went to the kitchen and after a few moments pressed a too-full glass of wine into her hand.

"I'm not sure this is a good idea," she began.

"I am." Taking her free hand, he led her to the recliner, sat, and then drew her down into his lap. "Drink. All of it. It'll relax you."

Obediently she sipped. "Not like that," he chided. "Didn't you ever have chugging contests in college?" He lifted a finger to tip the glass to her lips. "A real drink."

She drank again, more deeply this time. And when he only cocked a brow once she'd lowered the glass, she took another drink. And then another. "Somehow I think you and I had very different college experiences."

"I don't doubt it. Someday I'll explain to you the charms of a keg stand."

Under his watchful gaze she drained the glass. A sacrilegious way to treat her favorite pinot noir. But she couldn't deny that the pleasant warmth spreading through her veins wasn't going a long way toward relaxing her.

When he set her now-empty glass on the end table and drew up her foot to massage it, he accomplished what neither a long bath nor hot shower could have. Boneless, she snuggled against his chest. The light from the adjoining kitchen spilled into the front of the room, but they sat in shadows.

His thumb rubbed rhythmically across the ball of her foot. "I can't imagine how traumatic that was for you today." The words were a husky rumble. "On top of what you went through with Vance . . . How bad were the flashbacks?"

"They were there," Sophia admitted. "I was jumpy all day. From speaking to Courtney last night. And then seeing the place where Vickie spent a few years. I strongly suspect she set the fire that killed her relatives. I know it will probably never be proven," she added, stemming his response. "But it fits with what Karen Denholt told me about her behavior at the time. With the profile I've constructed. That would make the Coates family her first victims."

"But she didn't burn numbers to mark them."

"No." She thought for a few moments. Lucy Benally, a Polk County medical examiner, and forensic anthropologist Gavin Connerly had been working to age the remains of the discovered victims. They were still waiting for the final results. But they already knew some of the bodies predated the entry of Vance to the killing trio. He'd been incarcerated in Nebraska at the time of some of the preliminary estimates of victim deaths. So either Baxter had had another male accomplice prior to Vance, or she and Sonny were responsible for the others.

"The corpse of Gladys Stewart didn't bear a number. Neither did that of Curt Traer. They didn't warrant them. Only the victims that were sexually and physically assaulted in a manner similar to what Vickie went through were part of that . . . sequence, I guess you'd call it. She only numbers them if the kills reflect her signature."

He switched his ministrations to her other foot. "This is the last thing you need to be thinking about right now. Sleep might be your best distraction. Tomorrow is time enough to deal with it."

But the turn the conversation had taken didn't summon a spiral of nerves. And the reason for that had less to do with the wine she'd consumed and more with the man she was curled up against. "I was terrified," she admitted quietly. "More so because of the memories of almost being Vance's victim. At first it was like in those dreams. You know, the ones where you're in danger but can't scream or run or think."

He tipped her chin up with one crooked finger. "But you did. Even with a knife to your throat, you showed brains and courage." Releasing her, he traced a light finger over the long, ugly scratch that was a testament to what she'd gone through that day. "You don't lack guts, Sophie. You need to give yourself more credit."

"That's what I held on to while I was going over my statement with Udall." She could admit it now, surrounded by him, the sound of his heart thudding reassuringly in her ears. "I'd been so annoyed with myself for being spooked the whole time I was at the office. Every little noise rattled me. I fought through the fear and acted. Knowing that . . . It helps."

She didn't try to fool herself into believing it would completely counter the nightmares or assuage the guilt she felt over Courtney Van Wheton. But battling a past trauma required tools and forti-tude. Realizing she'd been able to use her wits to escape what Leslie had in store for her today provided her with both.

Sitting with him like this brought comfort. There had been a time when she would have been afraid to lean on the man—on any man—in case the moment came when his support wasn't there. She'd hedged her emotional bets by restricting what she'd offered to other men, in an effort to shield herself from the possibility of future pain. She'd done that all her life, even with her ex-husband, and he with her. She could see it so clearly now in hindsight. Other than her career path, every choice she'd ever made had been dutiful. Safe. *Boring.*

Cam Prescott could never be described by either of those words. Which made loving him an unprecedented risk. She shifted position to twine her arms around his neck.

It had taken the events of the last few weeks for her to realize that some risks were worth taking.

Sophia cupped his face in her hands and brought it closer. And when her lips closed over his, it felt like coming home.

His reluctance was easy to taste. Though his mouth moved under hers, there was no answering pressure. She could sense his restraint, which was summoned by a misguided need to protect. But it wasn't his protection she needed tonight. Sophia set out to prove that to him.

Taking his bottom lip between her teeth, she worried it not quite gently as she lowered a hand to unknot his tie. She traced the seam of his mouth with the tip of her tongue, enjoying the opportunity to take the lead. To break through his famed control. Free it.

As she turned her attention to the buttons on his shirt, she plunged her tongue between his lips and went in search of his. His mouth twisted against hers, and she smiled as she slipped her hand inside his shirt. His heartbeat was no longer steady. Not quite calm.

The wine-induced warmth in her veins changed temperature. Became little balls of heat that snapped through her bloodstream and spread throughout her body. She slid her hand over the portion of his chest that she'd bared and felt a sudden uncharacteristic need to have him naked. Immediately.

Later that need might embarrass her, but right now it made her desperate. Without releasing his mouth, Sophia wiggled around to change positions until her knees straddled his hips. Impatient, she paused long enough to allow him to tug her jacket down her arms before resuming the task of freeing his shirt from the waistband and unbuttoning it completely.

Only then did she release his mouth to map his chest with her lips. With her tongue she traced the line where bone bisected muscle, creating intriguing hollows and angles that tempted her to linger. She sipped from one of them, tasted the salty musk of his skin, and the flavor ignited her pulse. Powered her quest.

One of his arms banded around her back, and she felt him dragging the zipper down on her dress. He hooked a finger in the bodice, urging the garment over her shoulders. Reluctantly, she raised her head to pull her arms free of it. Only when her bra came with it did she realize he'd unhooked it, as well. With his help she was bare to the waist.

Her gaze caught his, and she hissed in a breath. Not so collected now. Desire had dampened his brow beneath the short-cropped dark hair and had turned his pale-brown eyes nearly gold. He bent forward, arching her over his arm, the position offering her breasts to his mouth. And then he feasted.

Colors wheeled behind her closed eyes. He lashed her nipple with his tongue before drawing strongly from it. Her hands went to his head. Clasped tightly to pull him closer. The deep pulls on her flesh reverberated to her core. Called to something within her that was both primal and feminine. She gasped when she felt a slight sting as his teeth scraped her.

Her need to watch his restraint slip was forgotten as she was caught in the silken web she'd started spinning. Instead of seducing, she was seduced. He switched his attention to her other breast while hitching her dress up around her hips. Unerringly his hand found her mound, moist beneath her silk panties, and rubbed gently. Her hips arched beneath his touch, and she leaned forward to kiss him again. Accepting the hungry thrust of his tongue, she sucked it eagerly.

The heel of his palm pressed firmly against her mound, while he teased her clitoris with the pad of his thumb. Circling, rubbing, brushing. Teasing strokes designed to shred thought. Escalate need. All the nerves, all the fear and chaos of the day coalesced into one burning ball of heat that tightened viciously with each light touch. The silk that separated them became slick with her dampness, and she abruptly resented even that slight barrier between them.

He straightened in the chair, the position pressing her bared breasts to his naked chest. The feel of flesh against flesh was a purely carnal pleasure. Her hips ground against his hand, seeking a firmer pressure, and the world narrowed to this moment. This man.

There was a slight smile on his face as he watched her, a primitive stamp of male satisfaction. The expression reminded her of her earlier mission, and she struggled to gather the remnants of reason. It wasn't enough to lose her mind, her sanity with him. She wanted him just as greedy. Just as desperate.

She shifted away slightly, although the loss of contact had her senses screaming. Just enough to give her the space she needed to undo his belt. Unfasten his pants. And when she found him, thick and straining behind the cotton of his shorts, a semblance of control returned.

The breath hissed from his lips when she freed him, took his heavy shaft in her hand. Tightened. She stroked his length, leisurely at first. Then more quickly. Timing her pace with the growing tightness in his jaw. The glitter in his eyes. The muffled curse he uttered.

His hands reached beneath her dress, and there was a slight sound of ripping fabric as her panties were torn away. She didn't need his urging to rise slightly and fit the crown of his erection to her moist folds, the welcome pressure an unbearable sensual relief.

With a slowness designed to drive them both a bit crazy, she lowered herself on him a fraction at a time, pausing to catch her breath as her body adjusted to each small movement. Her eyes were open but glazed. His face blurred. But her tactile senses were tingling, exquisitely sensitive.

Inch by inch she took him until he was sheathed inside her, the stretched fullness teetering between pleasure and discomfort. He tipped the balance by unerringly finding the tight cluster of nerves that still throbbed from his previous ministration and began massaging in slow, expertly soft circles.

Her body melted against his, and the need to move built. She lifted carefully, lowered to take more of him, then lifted again. His fingers curled into her hips, flexing but allowing her to set the pace.

She blinked away the haze of desire, wanting . . . *needing* to see him. His neck was arched, pressed against the chair, and every muscle in his chest was taut with tension. But still he let her set the rhythm. Leaning forward, she pressed her lips against his as her hips rocked. Faster now. Control was lost to the most basic of elemental needs. And when she moaned his name, something seemed to snap inside him, and the animal was unleashed.

He wrapped the fingers of his other hand in her hair. Her head lolled under the pressure of his mouth, tongue, and teeth warring with hers. With the other hand he held her hips steady as he surged upward inside her, jackhammering into her in a series of constant inexorable thrusts that drove him deeper. Then deeper still.

She couldn't breathe. Couldn't think. Only feel. They were sealed together, hips, chest, mouths. And still it wasn't close enough. Every movement of his hips had her body pulsing in pleasure but seeking more. Seeking an ultimate, intimate explosion.

He tore his lips away to take her nipple in his mouth as he yanked her hips down to meet each frantic lunge from his. She raced for something shimmering just out of reach, her breath coming in quick sobbing bursts. *"Sophie!"* Her name on his lips was raw. Guttural. The sound of it, coupled with the final powerful thrust inside her summoned her climax. Sensation slammed into her, ever-widening eddies of pleasure pulsing through her.

Limp, she lay weakly against his chest, the thunderous sound of his heartbeat in her ears. She was only distantly aware that they were still partially clothed. Only half-stripped, she was still laid bare.

"I love you." The words were whispered achingly against his damp chest.

He tipped her chin for a languorous, thorough kiss. And although she was aware of his lack of verbal response, she understood the fear that drove it. Someday soon, she vowed as he shifted her limp body to cradle her in his arms, he'd learn to trust her words. He strode to the bedroom, laid her on the bed, and followed her down on it. He'd learn to believe they didn't stem from trauma or fear.

In an incongruous twist it had been her ordeal with Vance that had taught her to put fear—at least the emotional kind—behind her. As she pushed the shirt off his broad shoulders, she was certain that she could teach him to do the same.

Chapter 5

Cam stood before the closet, one tie in each hand, peering at them closely. "Are these stripes black? Or navy?"

Sophie strolled over and slipped her hand through his elbow. "You've got one of each there. Which color are you looking for?"

"Black."

She tapped the darker one. "There you go, then. But I don't know why you want to wear a tie with black stripes when you're wearing navy pants."

He looked down at his trousers. "Are you sure? They look black."

Rolling her eyes, she went on tiptoe and kissed his ear. "You have no idea how much your fashion impairment pains me. Maybe I could put little Garanimals tags on your clothes so you can mix and match your outfits."

Returning the black tie to the closet, he threaded the navy tie—in this light the stripes looked *black*—through the collar of his white shirt. "I don't wear outfits. I'm not a girl. And what the hell is a Garanimal?"

"A line of children's clothes. Each piece has an animal tag so the kids can mix and match easily. I can put little pandas on your blacks and giraffes on your navies. You'll never mix them up again."

"Why do I need tags if I've got you?" She'd wandered back to the dresser and was using the attached mirror to apply her lipstick. It hit him then that as neat as she was, there were signs of her everywhere in his condo. Her toiletries in the bathroom. Her favorite coffee creamer in the kitchen. Clothes hanging in the guest room closet.

There'd been a time in the not-too-distant past when the realization would have sent him backpedaling. He had it on good authority—if that's what you could call ex-girlfriends—that he was a master at emotional distance.

But instead of that familiar thread of alarm he was accustomed to, he found the sight of her things in his place oddly satisfying. They lent it an air of permanence that he'd never sought before. Hadn't believed he wanted.

His fingers jerked as he knotted the tie. He was a long way from thinking he *did* want it. And even if he decided he did, it was way too soon to expect Sophie to reach that conclusion. She'd been through too much recently. Trauma left scars, not all on the outside. He'd battled PTSD himself and knew that for a fact. She was in no condition to be making plans for the future.

And that suited him. His hands went clumsy, and he mangled the knot. Started over. It suited him fine. She was in his life. His home. His bed. It was enough. It was more than enough. She needed time. They both did before she could be certain of her feelings. And yeah, hell, he knew it hurt her when he questioned her professions of love.

She just couldn't know how much he wanted to believe them.

"Are you trying to strangle yourself? Let me do it." Dropping her lipstick into yet another purse she went to him and batted his hands out of the way. Making quick work of the knot, she tightened it, gave it a pat.

His hand snaked around her waist, hauled her closer. "You're pretty handy to have around."

She fluttered her eyelashes. "Sweet-talker. You can keep it up, but I'm still not making you bacon."

"Pancakes would be faster," he agreed, his attention successfully diverted. He bent down for a quick kiss. "But it'll have to be fast. I want to get an early start this morning."

"If memory serves, you already got an early start this morning."

Ducking from his embrace, she directed the teasing words over her shoulder. A surge of remembered satisfaction filled him. "Yeah, we did. Maybe I should make *you* pancakes."

He watched as she deftly transferred the contents of her purse to the one she'd selected. One that matched the slim-fitting sleeveless dress with matching jacket she wore. He'd never had much interest in the female art of what she called accessorizing, so it was difficult to explain his newfound fascination. Sophie favored what he'd call fruity colors that no real guy would be able to identify. There was probably a Crayola name for the pinkish-orange suit she was wearing right now. But the overall effect was polished. Professional but feminine.

She caught his eyes on her in the mirror. "What?"

Stalking toward her, his hands went to his tie. Loosened it. "Maybe we could forget the pancakes."

"Not a chance." Laughing, she dodged when he made a grab for her. "After I just got you dressed? We don't have time."

"I can make the—" The sound of his cell ringing made him a liar. Cam looked around the room, remembered he'd left it in the kitchen. He headed to the door. "Grab me a suit coat to match, will you?"

"Sure. Should I make that a panda or a giraffe?"

His mouth quirked. Either he was rubbing off on her or she had always had untapped smart-ass tendencies. "I'm a guy. Let's go with a crocodile."

By the time she'd brought his jacket to him, his amusement had long since faded. "Right. I appreciate the call." He glanced up, taking the garment she handed him. "No, I can arrange that. Thanks."

He disconnected and shrugged into the jacket, dropping the cell in its pocket. "Detective Udall. Leslie hasn't lawyered up, but he's being a pain, demanding to talk to someone. Since he seems primed for it, Udall is going in early to interview him."

"And you're going to be there?"

"I'm going to make sure that piece of shit is off the street for good." He took two quick steps, cupped her face in his palms. "He's not going to hurt you again, Sophie. I'll make damn sure of it."

Her hands came up to clasp his wrists, and when his mouth pressed against hers, lightly this time, her lips parted. He couldn't identify where this need to protect the woman came from. Couldn't control the urge. Any more than he could control the need that started firing through his veins from just a kiss.

He lifted his mouth, rested his forehead against hers. He could do with a little of that famed emotional distance right now. "I have to go. Do you want me to drop you at headquarters on the way?" Even with that scumbag Leslie behind bars, he wasn't going to allow her back in her office. Not until he found out for sure what had gone down yesterday. They definitely needed to take a look at her security there.

"I'm going to be a little while here calling garages for estimates." He dropped his hands, and she stepped away. "Then I have to arrange for a rental for a few weeks." A frown marred her brow. "Or maybe a new purchase, depending on what the estimates are. I'll be in after that. It might take a couple hours."

He'd dealt with more than his share of auto body shops, and he was willing to bet she was underestimating the amount of time it would take. He crossed to the front door, strangely reluctant to leave her behind. "Keep the doors locked. Reset the—"

"Alarm after you leave. Yes, Daddy."

He turned. Eyed her soberly. "I think it's only fair to warn you that my feelings toward you are distinctly unpaternal."

Her lips curved slightly in a secretive, feminine smile. "Well, I certainly hope so. I wouldn't think of offering my father . . . Garanimals tags."

———

Dennis Leslie looked slightly the worse for wear after spending the last few hours in Polk County jail. The slender man's dark-brown hair was standing up in tufts all over his head, and he sported a day's growth of whiskers. His red and watery eyes were probably an after effect from the pepper spray Sophie had used on him. Cam couldn't tell if the bruise on his temple resulted from the car being hit, or if he'd managed to piss off a cell mate. He found himself hoping it was the latter.

The man coughed into his sleeve. "That shit she sprayed me with is in my lungs, man. My eyes are still burning. Can I get permanent damage from this? Because if I do, I'm suing that broad. Is that stuff even legal?"

Detective Udall exchanged a look with Cam. "There's nothing like the taste of irony in the morning." Returning his attention to the suspect, he said, "Mr. Leslie. You were found in the victim's car, with a face mask and a knife. We have both the victim's account, and that of the taxi driver. Based on witness statements, you're looking at a charge of attempted forcible rape. And I'm not going to lie." The detective's tone was jovial. "It's a slam dunk. I love arrests that are slam dunks."

Leslie shook his finger at him. "See, that's where you're wrong. That's why I'm here of my own free will, no lawyer or nothing. 'Cuz this thing, it's not what it seems."

"Do I have you on record as denying the services of an attorney, Mr. Leslie?"

"Bastards are useless, anyway." The man slapped the table for emphasis. "First thing we do, we kill all the lawyers. Am I right?" He looked from Udall to Cam. "That's from Shakespeare. Most people don't know that. Who knew they even had lawyers back then?"

"How did you get into the victim's car?" It was Udall's case. Cam sat silently while the man worked it.

"Let's stop calling her a victim, okay?" Leslie blinked rapidly. "There was no crime, so there's no victim. Channing was in on the whole thing." The expressions on their faces had him nodding smugly. "See what I mean? Things are different than they seem on the surface. She wanted this. Planned it all out. I was just supposed to make it realistic. I mean, guys like us, we'd just go to a motel and have ourselves a fuck fest, am I right? But chicks." He gave a fatalistic shrug. "They like their games."

The accusation had Cam smoldering. But years of experience kept him from reaching across the table and choking the lying little bastard.

"Dr. Channing. So you knew your target?"

"Target's another one of them—what do you call—charged words. You don't want to believe me." His head swiveled from one of them to the other. "I can see that. A classy piece like that? No way a scumbag like me is getting near her. But here's something you gotta consider." He leaned forward, lowered his voice confidingly. "Those high-society broads? Secret sluts. They have this position. People think they're one thing, so they can't really act how they want, see? So they have to get it on the down low with guys who can really deliver the goods and who they don't have to worry about bumping into at a board meeting the next day."

Cam spoke for the first time. "You might want to get a psych consult on this one."

"Think I'm lying? Think I'm crazy?" The man's hand went to his heart in a gesture of innocence. "I've got proof. How's that for ya? I mean, I shoulda known this gig was too good to be true, but this Channing is so hot for it she put an ad on Craigslist." He slapped the table again, leaned back. "Believe that shit? So I answer it, right? I mean, what guy would pass up a chance like that? I meet with her—"

"You met previously with Dr. Channing?" Udall put in.

"No. Not her. The other one. Her friend."

A cold snake of dread was coiling in Cam's stomach. "Did the friend have a name?"

Leslie shrugged. "Didn't say. Didn't ask. First I call the number in the ad; then she calls back. We talk. Then we meet. She gave me all the details. It's a club, like. Bunch of women who want to get their rocks off, and each of them finds a guy to do one of the others. This broad was setting things up for Channing." He chuckled. "Lots of pain. That's what she said Channing wanted. She's one of them . . . maso . . . masa . . ."

"Masochists?"

The man snapped his fingers at the detective's word. "Yeah, she said Channing was into that whole scene. Getting tied up and hurt and fucked hard. Gets turned on by pain, and the fantasy part was making it seem like rape. That's what the ad said. Like I told you." He spread his hands. "There was no victim. Channing was in on the whole thing."

"How long ago did you see the ad?"

With a quick jerk of his shoulders, Leslie said, "Two and a half weeks ago, maybe. I didn't answer it right away. Not for a couple days."

"Did you make a copy of it?" Cam asked.

The man looked confused. "Why would I? Don't need one anyway, 'cuz it's still there. Least it was yesterday."

Everything inside him stilled. The implications of the man's words were chilling. "Do you remember what the ad was called?"

"Rape . . . something about . . . rape fantasies. Something like that."

He took the cell from his pocket and brought up Craigslist. It took less than a minute for him to find the ad. "Was it this one?" He turned the cell to show the other man.

Leslie read slowly, his lips moving. Finally he nodded. "That's it. Only one I've seen posted like that, so I'd remember."

"When did you meet with her?"

Pursing his lips, he said, "I figure a couple weeks ago."

"And it never occurred to you that the victim might not know a damn thing about it." Udall's tone wasn't jovial now. It was whiplash sharp. "You never thought, hey, wait a minute. Maybe this total stranger is setting someone up, and I'm the dupe dumb enough to commit a sexual crime for her."

Leslie gave a violent headshake. "Nope. And you know how I know it was for real? She gave me a copy of Channing's medical records. You know, saying she's clean and all. I'm not gonna lie. I wasn't happy about having to get tests run. I told the broad, I said, I keep my junk clean. A guy's not careful, shit down there could fall off. Those STDs are nasty. But she said it was a deal breaker, plus she gave me the cash, so . . ." His shrug said the rest. "I still got it. The whole envelope of stuff. It's at my apartment."

Cam went to the photo gallery on his phone, found the picture he was looking for. He held it up for the other man. "Have you seen this woman before?"

Leslie leaned forward again. "Maybe. Sorta looks like the friend. She had on this big hat and shades, but could be her."

"Did she say anything else? Anything you haven't told us?"

He jerked a shoulder. "That's it, mostly. She did say she wanted this to be perfect, 'cuz of Channing being a friend of this woman's son. Said her kid was where he was today 'cuz of her, so follow the directions exact."

The dread in his gut was roiling now. A hot frothing tide.

She may even target members of this team.

The fact that Sophie had predicted the possibility made the whole thing even worse. He caught the detective's eye. Nodded imperceptibly toward the door. When he got up, Udall followed him, leaving Leslie to wail plaintively behind them, "Hey, where you going? I told you everything, guys, just like it happened. You gotta—"

The door closed on the last of his words.

"One of our agents is a forensic sketch artist," Cam told the detective. Jenna Turner served in that capacity for the agency, and her talents had been used frequently on this case. "She's heading into town to do work with a witness in conjunction with a murder in Boone County. She can stop by here, work with Leslie on a sketch of the woman he met with." If nothing else, it would give them another drawing of a persona Baxter had used recently in case Gonzalez wanted to make it public.

"You think she's the woman in the picture you showed him from your cell?" The older man's eyes were alight with interest. "One of the Cornbelt Killers?"

For once Cam didn't wince at the nickname. He had far more sobering things to think about. "Vickie Baxter, yeah. I never thought . . . Never occurred to me last night how she could be involved in this except that she's very good at manipulating men." His gaze went to the closed door behind them. "How long do you think you can keep him off the street?"

"With his record, the prosecutor's office will probably still file charges. I don't figure the scumbag in there can make bail, but you never know." The detective rubbed his neck. "Could have a kind-hearted granny who thinks he's next in line for canonization. It will get ugly for Channing if this thing goes to trial," he warned. "Defense attorney is going to argue lack of intent on his client's part and jump all over Leslie's 'evidence' that she knew about it. Want my jaded opinion? If his story checks out like he claims? Best-case scenario, the DA's going to cut a deal, and he goes away for a few months. Worst-case . . ."

"A judge lets him walk." Broodingly, Cam contemplated the closed door behind them.

Udall cleared his throat. "Almost don't want to bring this up, but you realize that dirtball in there may not be the biggest threat to Channing right now."

Cam had already recognized the ramifications of that ad. "Yeah. No telling how many men read that listing."

Rape. Pain. The fury in his veins mingled with a wash of stark, arctic fear. Damn Baxter's black heart. Sophie might have escaped the fate Vance had in store for her. But the other woman had come up with a highly effective way to guarantee a constant threat from men willing to fulfill it.

$\sim$

The doorbell rang, startling Sophia. She glanced at the clock as she hurriedly picked up her purse and briefcase. The cab service was fifteen minutes early. The fates must have decided she was due for some pleasant surprises for a change.

Before disengaging the alarm, she looked out the Judas hole and saw nothing. No one. Not a yellow taxi at the curb or, she changed positions slightly, in her driveway. Nothing but . . . Her gaze lowered.

After disengaging the security, she opened the door. "Hi."

The boy couldn't be more than six or so, with sandy-blond hair and solemn hazel eyes. She'd never seen him before, but she wasn't all that familiar with Cam's neighborhood.

"Can you help me?" Because he looked as though he was on the verge of tears, she crouched to his level and smiled encouragingly. "I'm looking for my cat."

"A cat, huh. What's its name?"

"Whiskers. He's a girl."

She nodded solemnly. "Good to know. What color is Whiskers?"

"Black and white. With a white front paw and white right here." He patted himself on the chest.

"I wish I could help you, buddy. But I haven't seen a cat. If I do, though, I'll let you know. What's your name?"

He hesitated. Then said, "Adam. I live over there." He pointed down the street.

Something in the boy's wistful expression had her softening even further. If she caught a glimpse of the animal, Cam would undoubtedly be able to track down the boy's parents.

"I hope you find your cat."

The boy nodded, shifting from one leg to another. Then he clutched himself in an unmistakable sign of distress. "I have to go to the bathroom."

Amused, she said, "You better head home then."

He squirmed. Hesitated. "I'm not gonna make it."

Sophia hesitated, a sliver of caution threading through her. She scanned the street in front of the house again and finally nodded. "Okay. You can use ours." After unlocking the screen, she held the door wide to allow him to enter and led him through the room and down the hall to the guest bath. Then she returned to her stance at the door, as much to watch for the cab as make sure she could hail any concerned parent who might be in search of the child.

She was no expert on child rearing, but she couldn't imagine letting a six-year-old have the run of the neighborhood without supervision.

"Can I have a glass of water?"

The cab was heading down the street, slowing in front of the condo. "I can get you a bottle of water to take with you, okay?" She dashed into the kitchen and grabbed a small bottle from the refrigerator and returned to the room. Adam hadn't moved. The room shrank him somehow, making him seem small and forlorn. "You can take this with you. But I really have to go." She smiled to soften her dismissal. "Maybe Whiskers will come home on her own."

She loosened the cap on the bottle and handed it to him before leading him to the door. Opening it, she allowed him out, reset the alarm, and then followed him onto the front porch, pulling the door shut behind her.

"Maybe I'll see you again."

His eyes were wide and too solemn for his age. "I hope so. You're nice."

They parted then, and, as Sophia walked to the waiting cab, she watched the boy trudge down the street in the direction he'd indicated his house was.

The driver got out and walked around the car to open the back door for her. Although the weatherman had promised a respite from the brutally hot temperatures, she couldn't detect a noticeable improvement. The air-conditioning in the cab would be welcome.

Catching sight of a vehicle parked down the street, she paused. The nondescript tan sedan was familiar. She'd seen it in the neighborhood before. Once she'd caught sight of a man in the front seat, but it appeared to be empty this time.

Despite the temperatures, a chill crawled over her skin. Given that this was a residential neighborhood, there was any number of reasonable explanations for the vehicle to be parked between two driveways in the middle of the morning. And none had to do with Vickie Baxter or Dennis Leslie.

But that didn't stop her from looking at the license plate and memorizing the number before she got in the cab. The driver closed the door and rounded the vehicle to get in the front as she buckled her seat belt. Sophia gave him the address of the rental place she'd made arrangements with, and they waited for a minute as he punched the information into his GPS.

As the cab backed out of the drive, she gave one more look at the tan car before checking on Adam's progress. The boy had already passed the house where she thought he'd indicated he lived. She could detect a dejected slump to his little shoulders. *Poor little guy.*

She really hoped he found his cat.

He walked a couple of blocks, turning down one street. Up another. He wanted to run, but he knew she was around somewhere. Watching. Then she'd catch him. And then it would get really, really bad. He shivered despite the heat. 'Cuz she was really bad. A monster. Only not the kind in ghost stories or in movies. She was real. And that was so much worse.

The black car pulled up by him and slowed, the window going down. "Get in."

The boy stopped. Unsure. "Do I have to ride in the trunk again?"

"Not here, dummy. Jesus, there could be people around. Get in the backseat."

He climbed in and buckled the seat belt. "Can I go home now?"

"Shut the fuck up about that. I'm tired of hearing it. Did you do everything I told you?"

She stared at him through the rearview mirror. He shrank back against the seat. He knew her eyes behind the big sunglasses would be hard and mean. "Yes."

"Where'd you put it?"

Thinking about what he'd done had tears stinging his eyes. He blinked them away. Crying made her mad. And even meaner. "I stuck it under the table. The one in front of the couch."

"Good boy."

For a minute he wondered if she'd lied to him. She'd said the little square thing she'd given him would let her listen to what the people in the home were saying. But that didn't make sense. Who cared what they talked about?

Maybe it was a bomb. The thought made his chest hurt. Maybe it would explode and kill the lady he'd talked to. "Don't hurt her," he blurted out. "She was nice."

Her mouth twisted. "People aren't always what they seem, kid. It's her fault my son is dead. Hers and her cop boyfriend. She's a murderous bitch."

He looked out the window so she wouldn't see his face. Because he didn't believe her. Not a bit. The lady had been nice, but this woman . . . She was bad and hurt people. And that made her a monster.

They whizzed by cars and bikers on trails along the street. Past businesses and malls, full of people. None of them could help him. None of them could know what the monster had done, because if they did, then things would be worse. People would die. That's what she'd said when she'd squeezed his arms so hard that they were sore and bruised afterward. And he believed her. No one could help him.

And he couldn't help the nice lady, either.

Chapter 6

Sophia stuck her head inside the morgue suite, surprised to see only one person inside standing at the counter, gazing fixedly into a microscope. The blond ponytail made him instantly recognizable.

"How long is Berkeley going to let you milk this whole getting shot thing?" she wondered aloud. Gavin Connerly looked over his shoulder, then straightened and turned, a broad smile splitting his face. "Sophia. Good to see you. In answer to your question, not much longer. For some reason they're insisting I need to be back on the job in a couple weeks to get ready for fall semester. That gives you ample time to pack, though. At least I'm assuming you've come to take me up on my offer to run off together."

As Sophia laughed, Lucy Benally, one of the state medical examiners, walked in through another door. "Bad form to make the offer to multiple women at once, Connerly," she advised. "We tend to compare notes."

Sophia's mental brows soared at the implication. If Gavin had suggested to Lucy that she move back to California with him, it wouldn't have been done jokingly. Somehow the forensic anthropologist who'd come to consult on this task force had gotten through the medical examiner's prickly exterior. Even the woman's normally caustic tongue was mellowed with him. Relatively.

She supposed that was a natural enough reaction to having a crazed gunman shoot the only man Lucy had allowed close enough to care for and then kidnap her, leaving Gavin to bleed out on Lucy's kitchen floor. Sonny Baxter was dead now and would never answer for what he'd put Lucy or Gavin through.

Which made it all the more imperative that Vickie Baxter was brought to justice. Sonny's mental illness had led to him targeting Lucy, but he'd been his mother's pawn in all other ways. Even when it came to kidnapping and murdering the victims.

"Where's Super-Agent?"

She smiled, amused. "I'm supposed to meet Cam here. I must be early." Lucy and Cam had a verbally caustic relationship. Sometimes she thought he had her accompany him on morgue visits in an effort to defuse Lucy's acerbity. Sophia suspected every male of a certain age received the same treatment. The fact that Gavin had plowed through Lucy's iron guard was telling, indeed.

All eyes turned to the door when it opened. Cam stepped in, his gaze immediately zeroing in on Sophia. And the flare of heat she detected in his eyes made something inside her go molten.

"Get a rental all right?"

"I've had my fill of dealing with all things vehicle related for a while." She said nothing more. While Lucy was a friend, she wasn't quite ready to rehash the details of yesterday's ordeal. She looked at Gavin. "I'm assuming we're here because you and Lucy have performed some magic on the remains taken out of the Raccoon River and the mass grave found on its banks."

The ME went to the wall to lower a screen and then plugged her computer into a projector. She typed a few commands and a PowerPoint presentation appeared on the pull-down screen. "Aging bones is never precise but Gavin and I agree—"

"That phrase alone is worthy of note," Gavin inserted jokingly.

"That the remains retrieved from the water did not predate some found on the riverbank, at least not by much." Ignoring Gavin's comment, she flipped to the next slide, which bore fourteen numbers corresponding with the bodies that had been found at the dump sites. There was a date next to each, and those that had been identified through DNA testing were coupled with names. Bodies found with the number intact on their skin had that numeral in parentheses.

Solidifying the timeline for the victims' deaths would help nail down the sequence in which they had died. Sophia studied the slide carefully. Some of the remains had been skeletal. On a couple of others there hadn't been enough skin remaining for a number to be found, although there was evidence of burns in the bone.

Sophia counted quickly. There were still six without identifiers. She couldn't imagine a more awful situation for family members than to go to their graves never knowing what had happened to their loved one. The detective on Emily Stallsmith's case hadn't even been certain she hadn't left voluntarily.

As her husband had said at the cemetery, closure was at least something.

"Fourteen victims in all," Sophia said evenly. Objectivity was imperative in her line of work. But sometimes difficult to summon. "Vickie Baxter bears a one and Sonny a two. Seven occur during the time Vance was in prison the first time, so we can credit the Baxters with all those found on the riverbank or in the water. Except for number sixteen."

"Maybe all the bodies first went to the cave," Gavin said. "There Sonny . . . uh . . . *enjoyed* them for a while before he gave them a final disposal. Could be he would have found a final resting place for number sixteen atop a vault in a freshly dug grave like he had the previous six when he was done with her."

"Since Sonny Baxter was seen sexually assaulting her corpse, it's obvious why she hadn't been buried yet." Cam's voice was absent as he moved closer to the screen, squinting at it thoughtfully. "But carrying a corpse in that Ziegler box and gurney down through the woods and down that steep incline to the clearing and then back up would be a lot of work. And pointless, when he had a disposal site right there. No, he would have dumped her there. In the mass grave or in the river. The question is why did he revert to his original disposal method?"

"Because it suited his purpose." Though the other three had drawn closer to the screen, Sophia remained rooted in place. As if her physical distance would equate with an emotional one. "Always the paraphilia is about the offender. His wants. His needs. Remember the last victim was embalmed, where the prior six hadn't been." Through the course of the investigation they'd learned that Sonny Baxter had once worked in a funeral home. "I think the question is were the other bodies found in and near the Raccoon River embalmed?"

Lucy turned to beam a smile at her. "Give the lady a gold star. We can't be positive, of course, about the three in body bags found in the river."

"Two of the bags smelled strongly of formaldehyde, though," Gavin put in. "And every body in the mass grave there was embalmed."

"Fascinating," she murmured, her mind racing.

"Not actually the word I'd use to describe a killer with necrophiliac tendencies, but to each their own."

Sophia smiled at Gavin's words. "I meant from a psychological standpoint. From what we know of Sonny Baxter, he was his mother's tool, but the disposal was left to him, endowing him with a measure of power. He then chose a method that allowed him to indulge his paraphilia for a longer amount of time."

"He said something like that before he kidnapped me," Lucy recalled. Gavin closed the distance between them. Gave her hand a squeeze. "That they could love him longer when they were embalmed."

"But then Vance came along, and I'm betting Sonny's only bit of control was taken away. Now he wasn't just taking orders from Vickie but Mason Vance, as well. Maybe it was even Vance's idea to dispose of the six bodies in the cemeteries."

"So embalming victim sixteen was Sonny's way of reexerting control." Cam's face was set in grim lines. He balled his fists, shoved them into his suit coat pockets.

"I think you're partially right." Involuntarily Sophia drew closer to the screen. "Insofar as it meant he could indulge his fetish again. That need would have been paramount over any other. When he was discovered, it was because he had fixated on the last victim."

Her gaze flew to her friend's. He'd fixated on Lucy, as well. Had shot Gavin, kidnapped the woman. Had things happened differently, the medical examiner could have shared the fates of the unfortunate women designated by the numerals on the screen.

"The aging of the rest of the remains helps with the sequence. It supports some of our conclusions." Cam moved away from the others. Paced a bit. "We now can be certain Vickie and Sonny killed ritualistically seven on their own over the course of nine years, and when Vance came on the scene, there were seven more victims in less than two years."

"Sonny disappeared out of foster care when he was seventeen. This timeline means his mother had him start helping with killings within two years." Sophia rested a hand on an empty metal gurney beside her, before snatching it back, recalling what the gurney was used for. "She got pregnant with him when *she* was seventeen. I suspect she was responsible for the fire that killed her relatives when she was three years older." She caught Cam's swift glance. "That leaves a span of sixteen years in her life in which she likely evolved ritualistically. Maybe she role-played, engaged in BDSM." And maybe she killed, for profit or thrill. But however she'd spent the time, her development into a serial murderer had been progressing.

"This helps, thanks." Cam's words addressed both Gavin and Lucy. Then he grinned at the other man. "Guess this means you'll be taking your souvenir bullet hole back to California to show off to your friends."

Gavin's teeth flashed. "And most visitors leave Iowa in the summer with nothing but a bag of sweet corn to remember their stay."

Lucy flipped her dark braid over her shoulder with an agitated movement. "I'll email the report to you, Prescott. Let me know if you have any more questions. I've got an autopsy scheduled in ten minutes. If you guys want to talk over good times, use the hallway." She stalked out the door she'd entered through.

Seeing the surprised expression on the men's faces, Sophia shook her head. Guys, she decided as she started after her friend, could be decidedly obtuse.

She caught up with Lucy in her office, where Lucy was staring fixedly at a computer monitor. "I left Cam and Gavin tied to gurneys but need your help with the oscillating saw."

Lucy gave a snort of laughter. "Don't tempt me." She whirled around in the computer chair to face Sophia. "But even I realize my tolerance for dumb, stoic male humor is short these days."

"Gavin almost died," Sophia said gently, going farther into the room. "You have a right to be a little sensitive on the subject."

"There's that," the woman agreed broodingly. "Plus . . . he's leaving. And he's asked me to go with him."

"I'd gleaned that much." She drew up another chair and sank into it. "Are you considering it?"

"See, that's the thing." Lucy stabbed a finger in Sophia's direction. "I'm tempted. How am *I* tempted? I don't do permanent.

Never have. Never wanted to. This has to be chalked up to, I don't know, some sort of guilt or something. Sonny Baxter came after me. Gavin never would have been shot if he hadn't come tearing after me after I left his motel room. I'm the reason he almost died."

"I'm not unfamiliar with the weight guilt can bring to bear." Sophia's chair squeaked when she settled more comfortably into it. "That first night Vance came for me in the barn . . . He was in a rage because the profile I'd done on him had been released to the public. He started beating me. I knew he meant to rape me." The deep, fathomless darkness of Lucy's gaze invited confidences. And this was one that still haunted. "I tricked him into agreeing to let me write another one. One he could release to the media. After a short interview, he left me to write it." Buying valuable time, she'd thought at the time; the familiar vise of remorse gripped her. "Moments later he began assaulting Courtney Van Wheton in another stall. I had no idea there was another victim in that barn with me. But if I hadn't put him off, she would have been spared that night."

"Well, sure, since you're blessed with omniscience, you should have known she was there," scoffed Lucy. "You realize that's not logical, right?"

"Have you had any luck trumping emotion with logic?" she queried.

"Point taken." The other woman drummed her fingers on the desk in front of her. "Jesus, look at us. We're ridiculous." Her glare dared Sophia to dispute it.

"Maybe the key is to focus on how you felt about Gavin before he was shot. Sure, those feelings may have deepened by now over the last couple weeks. I happen to know you spent a lot of time by his side in the hospital. Had him convalescing at your home. But before all that . . . Did you have feelings for him then?"

"I figure you know I did." The other woman heaved a sigh. "But he realizes I come with a neon, blinking caution sign. He's asking too much. Maybe we can try a long-distance relationship first. See how that goes."

Sophia hid a smile. Something told her Gavin had asked for far more than he expected to get just to win this concession. "Conventional wisdom would say that surviving a traumatizing event could cloud judgment. But I'm learning that it can help you focus on what's really important." And somehow she'd convince Cam of that, she thought. That a trauma in her past couldn't be allowed to dictate their future.

"You're right. And we so should be having this conversation over wine."

"Next time," she promised. "Right now we should probably get back to the autopsy suite and untie the guys from the gurneys."

Franklin Paulsen replaced files in the Italian leather briefcase and snapped the lid shut. "I've reached the end of my stall tactics. Our last hearing will be within the week." There was no visible reaction from the man sitting across the table from him. Just the flat pale-blue stare that turned the attorney's bowels to ice.

"I thought you'd have more for me."

The words were fraught with meaning. Innocuous in case anyone overheard. There was no one else in the small room used for attorney–client conversations. But a guard was posted outside and kept watch through the glass at all times. Franklin was increasingly grateful for that.

"I've done enough for you." The memory of the orders he'd followed so far made his heart race. "You wanted pro bono services for your friend inside; I offered them. You requested that both his and your hearings be on the same day, and I arranged that. But things will be strictly by the book from now on. It's important that nothing be allowed to jeopardize your case."

"You should reconsider."

The attorney's palms went damp. The physical response angered him. He wasn't the one locked up and who would—despite Franklin's very robust defense—likely die behind bars. Franklin walked in and out of here freely.

And his mother had been safely moved to another facility, a fact that she complained of bitterly. He'd promised that she could go back someday. Once the danger was over. Once this man and his accomplice were both imprisoned for good.

"I'm not going to reconsider." He said the words crisply, making sure he kept his back to the door. He'd always suspected some of those guards were adept at lipreading. "I'm a respectable attorney. All of my dealings have been and will always be above the law."

The law, thankfully, could be obscured and confounded by an adept lawyer. And everyone had different standards of legal. He'd passed money to his client each time he was here, but giving Vance the capsules "Vanecia Mason" had given him was a risk he wasn't going to take. And now that the couple had no leverage against him—now that Mother was safe and Franklin had hired security for himself—he was in control of the situation.

He pushed his chair back from the table and rose. "Here's a little piece of advice, Mr. Vance." He couldn't keep the triumph from sounding in his words. "Not everyone can be bent to your will. Violence is no match for wits."

He turned and gestured to the guard, who unlocked the door. It wouldn't be opened until a second guard had joined the first so Vance could be secured and taken back to his cell.

"Guard," he heard Vance shout as he walked through the door. "I need to make a phone call."

Franklin's step faltered before he stiffened his spine and marched on. The precautions he'd taken meant he had nothing to fear. Mason Vance had taught him a valuable lesson. It was important to be safety conscious when taking on high-profile criminal cases. It was just as important not to overestimate the power and reach the criminal had.

He whistled a bit as he walked to his car, his step jubilant. He doubted either Marcella Rosen or Antonio Cavanaugh could claim to have backed down the most notorious killer in Iowa's history and lived to tell about it.

It was a shame, he thought, giving his keys a jaunty toss and recapturing them, that no one could ever hear the story.

———

"I need to catch you up on a few things, and I don't know the next time I'll get the chance today." Cam steered Sophie toward the vinyl-upholstered furniture in the lobby just inside the entrance. The state morgue shared the building with the state crime lab and had recently scored a new facility.

"All right." She sank gracefully into one of the chairs and cocked her head, waiting for him.

Shit. He'd rather stab himself in the eye with a fork than tell her what he'd learned that day from Dennis Leslie. On the other hand, if she somehow found out about it from another source, she just might be the one wielding the utensil. He sat beside her and told her the gist of the interview, glossing over details in a manner that—so sue him—she'd probably call sugarcoating.

And the shocked, sick comprehension on her face was like taking a hard right jab to the solar plexus.

"The ad is still running," she repeated in a numbed voice. One hand went to the bracelet on the opposite wrist, fidgeted with the silver links there. "Meaning Leslie might not be the only one. There could be an unknown number of men Vickie Baxter talked to about this. Dozens even."

He took her hand in his, hating that he'd put that look on her face. Knowing she'd detest him more if he'd tried to keep the news from her. He'd learned that particular fact about her the hard way. She didn't like to be coddled from the truth. Even when it was brutal. "We're getting an injunction to get the ad taken off Craigslist." He didn't tell her how lengthy a process that might be. "Maria talked about going public with the story. Not with names," he added hastily when her gaze flew to his in alarm. "Just a general local warning for people to watch out for."

"Reporters would never be satisfied with that."

The lady saw too much. Which was why honesty was always best with her. "No," he admitted. His thumb brushed the top of her hand. "And I don't want them digging. So I convinced her it'd be best to place another ad with a title linking to the original, cautioning people that the first one is a scam."

She drew in a deep breath. Released it slowly. "All right. I'll have to be hypervigilant. I get that. Oh." Her blue eyes widened. "Have you ever noticed a tan sedan in the neighborhood? I've seen it twice now, both times parked close to your place. It was there again this morning."

He knew exactly what car she was talking about, and the fact that Sophie had noticed it, too, meant someone wasn't doing their job very damn well. He dutifully wrote down the license number, promised to check it out. Then saw the concern on her face and couldn't prevent a mental sigh. Like the lady needed even more dumped on her plate.

"I'll check to make sure, but it's probably the feds."

From her expression he could tell she'd completely forgotten the old multiagency task force that wouldn't stay closed. It had risen from his past, determined to suck him back in. "They've been watching your place? Because of the threat from the cartel?"

Pablo Moreno, head of the Mexican Sinaloa cartel, wanted whoever had orchestrated the raid that had crippled his operation a couple of years ago. But Cam knew the federal interest in him likely had more to do with his recent contact from Matthew Baldwin.

Matt. The man who should have been scooped up with the rest of Moreno's people in the raid. The man who had slipped away because Cam had made sure he wasn't there when the doors were kicked in.

Every action had a consequence. And Matt finding him was Cam's.

"Like I said, I'll double-check." And chew someone's ass for being obvious enough in their surveillance that Sophie had picked up on it. "But it offers an extra layer of protection, which is why it's safer for you to live at my place."

"I can't figure out why you're not writing romantic ballads. Seriously. Come live with me. In my home. It's safer there," she crooned with a passable country twang.

He was grateful to see humor chase away her worry, even if it was at his expense. "I have it on good authority that I excel at sweet nothings. Maybe when I retire I'll go to work for Hallmark." With that he stood and drew her to her feet. "So in that vein . . . You can ride with me, and I'll send someone for your rental. I don't want to let you out of my sight."

❦

The boy was obediently silent as he accompanied the woman into the motel. He kept his head down, just the way she'd told him. But when she stopped and opened a door, waved him inside, his shoes turned to concrete.

He looked through the door. Didn't move. "I want to go back to the basement."

With a quick look both ways down the hallway, the woman grabbed him by his shirt and shoved him inside. Then she shut the door. Locked it.

She aimed a kick at him, but he dodged out of the way. "One thing you gotta learn, kid, is to keep your fucking mouth shut. You're not going back there. This is better. What's your fucking problem, anyway?"

When she stared at him like that, with mean scrunched into her face, it was hard to answer. He retreated slowly until he could feel the wall at his back. "That lady down there. She needs food. And something to drink, too. You have to go back there. When you do, you can take me." It had been dark there. Damp. Spiders had crawled on him. Just the memory of it had him shivering. But he still would rather be there with the other lady who had been taken just like him than here in this motel room alone with the monster.

She stared hard at him, and he felt his bladder grow tight. Then, giving a bark of laughter, she passed him to go to the TV. "You know, for a minute there you reminded me of my son when he was your age. Never knew when to shut up, either. But he learned." She lifted the remote and turned on the flat-screen TV, went to the menu. "You like cartoons? I'll set it to Cartoon Network or something. Sonny always liked that."

A new Tom and Jerry cartoon came on, and he craned his neck to see the screen better. She stripped one of the bedspreads off the mattress. "Get on the bed. Not that one, dumbass," she snapped when he started toward the one that was still made. "This one."

Slowly he crawled up on the bed. Scooted up to the pillows.

Her heavy purse hit the mattress beside him, and she started digging in it. When she came up with a roll of duct tape, he shrank against the pillows. She grabbed his hand. Wrapped one end of the tape around his wrist.

"Hope you got enough to eat and drink in the car, 'cuz I've got stuff to do and I'm not dragging you around. You can sleep and watch TV the whole time I'm gone. Most kids would die to be in your place right now."

"When can I go home? You said if I helped you—"

The stinging slap brought tears to his eyes. They trickled down his cheeks. His shoulders shook with the effort it took not to cry out loud.

"Forgot what a pain in the ass kids were," she muttered furiously and stuck a piece of tape over his mouth before tying his ankles together. By the time she was done, he was sitting up against the pillows, with lengths of tape securing his legs and one wrist secured to the bed frame. One wrist was tethered to the other but left loose enough for him to move it.

She dropped the tape in her bag, bringing out a cell phone and the newspaper she'd bought. She propped the paper on his lap, then aimed the phone at him. "Say cheese." She snapped several pictures. The way she had yesterday. And the day before. He knew enough now not to ask what she was going to do with them.

"Okay, I'm gonna leave the wastebasket by the bed in case you gotta pee. I'll be back later." She dragged the table with the lamp well away from the bed and looked around, her hands on her hips. "Well, what the hell." Going to the door, she peered through the peephole before cracking the door an inch to look up and down the hallway. Then she hung a sign on the doorknob, shut it, and secured the safety latch.

A jolt of fear shot through the boy when he thought she meant to stay there with him. But she didn't look at him as she crossed the room to the window. A minute later she was gone.

Tom and Jerry took turns chasing each other in circles on the TV. The monster was like that. But she caught the people she chased. And they were afraid to run again, even when they weren't tied up.

He hoped the monster was going to go feed the lady in the basement. But maybe that lady was like him. Maybe she didn't care about eating or drinking.

As long as the monster didn't come back.

———

Agent Jenna Turner walked briskly down the hallways of Polk County jail, sending a jaundiced glance toward the man who fell in step with her. "Maxwell. What are you doing here?"

"Caught a ride with one of my deputies. He's got court today." Although she made no effort to slow down, he kept up with her easily, a fact she found irritating. Of course, nearly everything about Boone County Sheriff Beckett Maxwell irritated her.

He was too . . . sure of himself, she decided, as he opened the door for her and she walked into the brutal bright sun. Too attractive, too easygoing with that aw-shucks manner that she strongly suspected was a facade. The man was well respected by his law enforcement peers, which meant he was more than competent at his job.

Which was too bad, Jenna thought as she reached into her purse and took out her sunglasses. After shaking them open, she perched them on her nose as she headed for her car. It'd be so much easier to ignore an incompetent cop. Easier still if he sported jowls and a paunch.

"Cam said you were heading over to do the sketch for that witness in the Ellen Webster case." He took her elbow, eased her back as a driver shot out of his parking space without sparing a glance for pedestrians. "I'd like to go along. Talk to the woman myself."

Jenna stared at him shrewdly. "You've got the report from the DMPD officers who did the canvass. What else do you think you'll learn from her?"

"It's what I think *you* might learn from her." He cast her a sideways glance. "The dental records confirm that my crispy critter was Ellen Webster. Hillary Carlson has been pretty vague about the woman who took her car out the morning she was murdered. If you manage to jog her memory during the sketch, I want to be there to follow up."

She opened her mouth. Shut it again. Jenna was perfectly capable of conducting an interview, but that skill functioned separately from her role as forensic artist. Not to mention that the Webster murder was his case. It might turn out to be entwined in the one the task force was working on, but he was still the principal investigator on it.

"Questioning has to wait until after the sketch is finished," she finally replied, leading the way to the agency vehicle and unlocking it, leaving him to get in the passenger seat. "And you can't be in the room. The environment needs to be completely nonthreatening in order to get the best results."

"Did I ever tell you I have a thing for bossy women?" he said conversationally, drawing his seat belt together. "Especially redheads. They're my Kryptonite."

The engine roared to life, and she backed out carefully. "Lucky they're in such short supply, then." And lucky for her that she had no such weaknesses. Especially in the form of Mr. Tall, Dark, and Pretty sitting beside her.

She was going to do her damnedest to keep it that way.

—

"Yes, that's her. That's the woman I saw." Hillary Carlson peered closely at the sketch. "You've drawn her exactly. That's so interesting . . . I wasn't even sure I remembered that much about her."

Jenna flashed the woman a smile and began piling the photo reference books in her briefcase. "Our mind stores information that our conscious isn't even aware of. The details were all there. You just needed help recalling them." With time and proper technique, a good forensic artist could extract those details from witnesses. Perfect them.

And after more than two hours, the product was eerily similar to other photos and sketches they had of Vickie Baxter. "There's a sheriff outside who would like to ask you a couple more questions, if you can spare another minute or two."

The older woman looked at her watch. "Goodness, we worked clear through the afternoon. I'm supposed to meet my daughter for an early dinner in a half hour."

"I'm sure he'll be quick," Jenna pressed when she sensed the other woman wavering. "Five minutes, I promise."

"Well . . ." She took the lack of another protest as agreement and texted Beckett. She'd make sure he was swift. Although if Jenna was any judge of character, the perfectly coiffed, plump, fiftyish woman's objections were going to melt away once she caught sight of the sheriff.

Her prediction was verified when he gave a light knock, then entered the apartment. Hillary's eyes widened, and Jenna gave a mental shrug. At least, she rationalized as she settled in to wait, Jenna wasn't the only female Beckett Maxwell affected.

Fifteen minutes later the sheriff was still asking questions, which Hillary was happily answering. "I couldn't be sure before. I mean, I barely could recall what the woman looked like, so how could I remember if I'd seen her prior to that morning? But the sketch helped jog my memory. That's the lady I saw getting in the car with Ellen Webster that morning in the parking garage at our apartment building. I thought it was odd at the time, because she got in the backseat instead of sitting right next to Ellen."

"But you were distracted, you said."

She aimed a smile at Beckett. "That's right. I was having an argument with my daughter on the phone. Not that we fight, but the girl can be so stubborn! So my mind wasn't really on Ellen. I just waved and continued to my car. Oh." Hillary stopped as if a thought had just hit. "That woman might have been the last one to see Ellen alive."

Of that, Jenna thought, they could be pretty sure.

"And you saw the stranger before that day." Smoothly Beckett steered Hillary back to the point at hand.

The woman gave a vigorous nod, sipped from her bottled water. She'd insisted on providing each of them with one, a burst of belated graciousness. "At least once before. Three weeks ago. Maybe two and a half." Her furrowed brow didn't seem to help improve her memory, so she smoothed it. Shrugged. "She was sitting in a vehicle in the visitor section of the parking garage when I went to get my car. I noticed her because it was the only car in the section. And I remember thinking, 'Oh, I wonder who has a guest?' Most of us know one another in the building. At least to wave at. And that's all I remember. I'm not sure how it could be helpful."

Jenna wasn't sure, either. But it was clear from Beckett's thoughtful expression that he was hearing more in the words than she was. So she stemmed her impatience until they were back in the car. Headed back to the Iowa State Patrol post where zone one DCI agents were stationed before saying, "So Vickie Baxter stalked Ellen Webster. That's hardly surprising in the face of what we know about her. She'd need to learn the woman's routine to best figure out how to accost her."

"We got a positive ID from Carlson, so we can be pretty sure it was Baxter who last saw Webster alive." He'd adjusted the lever on his seat on the trip over, and now he had his long legs stretched as much as the space allowed, with the back slightly inclined. It added to his overall manner of indolence, but she wasn't fooled. There had been strategy guiding his questions. She just didn't know where it was heading. "So we know more than we did this morning."

"I got that much from the sketch." Her voice was droll. "What'd you get, Maxwell?"

"You mean other than the pleasure of your company? A timeline."

"A timeline."

She pulled to a stop at a red light and tapped her fingers lightly on the wheel. "Of when Baxter focused on Webster?"

"You're sharp, Red." He adjusted his glasses and put his arms behind his head. "I've always said it."

"It was after Vance's arrest. Although we can't tell how many times Baxter trailed Webster that we *don't* know about."

His teeth gleamed. "Exactly. I know Prescott likes things nailed down before he considers them, but we work differently. He likes to wait until he can click every proven piece of evidence into place to get the bigger picture. Me, I look at an investigation like soup. Drop this detail in, then that; stir it up. What do you have? Take something out—replace it with something else . . ." He shrugged. "Just the way I process things."

"A food analogy. Of course." Jenna accelerated as the light changed, amused in spite of herself. "So what kind of soup were you making back there?"

But there was no answering humor in his voice. "Mason Vance was apprehended over five weeks ago. Vickie Baxter, the woman known to us up until then as Rhonda Klaussen disappeared two weeks ago. In the last week she's committed two murders. Now we know she set her sights on Sophia and Webster at least two and a half weeks ago."

Jenna's head swiveled to look at him for an instant. "What?" His shoulder jerked. "I'm in the loop."

Apparently. She'd heard just the bare bones of the Dennis Leslie incident before going downtown to do the sketch with him that morning. It had taken supreme self-control not to beat the little weasel with her briefcase.

Her exit was coming up. Switching lanes in preparation, she said, "You're going somewhere with this. Let's hear it."

"My point is that Baxter seems focused on revenge. And all her moves toward that end occurred post-Vance being locked up."

She still didn't get it. "So? Sophia mentioned a trigger. Her son's death. Oh." Realization hit.

"Yeah, oh. She started plotting revenge before she killed Sonny. I was reading the updated case bulletin that Cam put out this afternoon while you were busy with Carlson." He clutched the armrest as she zoomed off the exit. Jenna grinned. To his credit, Beckett didn't make a crack about it. "They found a second motel where she's registered, by the way." He smiled when she arrowed a surprised look at him. "Check your email. Different name, different credit card number. Issue date on the first card was six months ago."

Jenna was connecting the dots. "So it was applied for well before Vance's capture."

If he noticed that she was speeding, he had the grace not to mention it. "Two motels so far. At least two different cards. The warrant on the first card went through. Valid cards, false identity. Everything matches a real Greta Talbot living in Chattanooga except for the mailing address and phone number. That Greta said she'd been in Des Moines just last year and had her purse stolen."

Slick, Jenna thought as she passed a white cargo van filled with teenagers. She'd worked a fraud case just last year, and it had been an eye-opener. For a couple hundred bucks you could buy a machine that would read the personal information off the magnetic strip on the back of a card. Plug it into a computer, and the info showed up on the screen. Use that information to fill out some credit card applications, and very soon one had valid cards in hand. No worry about the lost or stolen cards being deactivated.

Of course, the crooks ran up the bill to its max before discarding it.

"That took weeks of planning. Months probably."

"Who knows?" Beckett adjusted his seat back slightly. "Maybe that was part of their gig, in addition to kidnapping wealthy women and draining their bank accounts. The point is they had the cards. Maybe as part of their scam. Or . . ."

"Or maybe they had a contingency plan."

"Exactly." Beckett took off his sunglasses to clean them, sending his profile into sharp Adonis-like relief. "So me, I'm questioning the timeline. Baxter's been pretty busy with details, but you know what else takes time? Planning. How is she going to get at Webster? At Traer? Sophia? What are the options and pros and cons of each? Revenge is a factor, but when you add up everything that had to be put in place in a short amount of time, some of it had to have been planned ahead."

"Great. Now we just have to figure out which is which."

"There's more." Beckett's face was grim. "Those leads from the tip line I helped check out? Most of them went nowhere. Except for maybe one. Remember when Vickie Baxter was posing as Gladys Stewart's relative?"

Jenna remembered. Baxter had killed the elderly woman and then managed to convince everyone Stewart was in a nursing home while Baxter collected the rent payments for the elderly woman's farm. "Hard to forget."

"Talked just this morning to a guy who worked a grain elevator in Fraser. He claims Baxter visited the co-op and talked to him about purchasing ammonium nitrate."

Jenna stilled. "That's the stuff they used in the Oklahoma City bombing."

"It is. It's also a fairly common farm fertilizer. At least it was. It's very heavily regulated these days. Some places don't even sell it anymore. He told her their co-op didn't, and that was the end of it." His cell pinged. Beckett took it out to read the incoming text and then pocketed it again.

"You don't think . . . When was this?"

"The guy couldn't be exactly sure of the day, but he does remember that it was the same day he saw the first news release about the bodies being found on top of burial vaults in rural cemeteries. He admits he should have reported Baxter's inquiry to his boss, since he didn't know the woman. But it went clear out of his head because he was watching that newscast."

She clenched her fingers on the steering wheel as she absorbed the implications. "But there is nothing in Vance's or Baxter's backgrounds that indicated either of them has any familiarity with explosives."

Beckett's face was unsmiling. "Again, timeline. Up until that point, they operated in the dark. No one had ever linked those victims' disappearances until Cam caught this case."

"So they were spooked enough to start making some plans in case we got too close." Suddenly chilled, Jenna reached over to turn down the air-conditioning. "Guess we should count ourselves lucky that Vance didn't manage to booby-trap that barn he kept his victims in. Or his house." Members of the task force had entered both.

"Yeah." His voice brooding, Beckett turned to the window. "So I'm full circle on this, back to the evidence of their planning." He turned his head to look at Jenna again. "Baxter's the one still left, and she's gone after a lot of people so far."

A vise tightened in her chest. She could have finished the thought in tandem with Beckett. "It makes you wonder what she has in store for Cam."

—

It had been a long time since Franklin Paulsen had prayed, but he was doing so now, head bowed and hands clasped tightly in his lap. Ever since he'd gotten the call from the nursing home about Mother being rushed to the ER, he'd been calling on every deity he could think of.

None of them were answering.

She'd been unconscious when the nursing home had called 911, and enough time had passed for them to perform surgery, had that been necessary. He'd been assured her condition had been stabilized, but no one had yet explained what that condition was or what had caused it.

There was a nagging fear in the back of his mind that he didn't want to listen to. She'd been eighty-four on her last birthday. Old people had health issues. It didn't have anything to do with him.

It couldn't.

"Mr. Paulsen?" He looked up when his name was called and then rose to approach the nurse standing near the desk. "The doctor is ready to talk to you now."

She led him to a tiny room off the waiting room, where he stood for a couple of minutes until a woman wearing a lab coat and stethoscope over neon-green scrubs entered.

"I'm Dr. Sisson." Her handshake was firm. "I want to assure you that your mother is going to be all right. But she did give us a scare."

"What happened? What was wrong with her? Was it her heart again?" As an attorney he was a man used to finding answers. Or having someone find them for him.

"No, not her heart. Let's sit down." The doctor gave him a faint smile as she sank into one of the seats. "It's been a long day. Your mother's lab results verified my suspicions about her condition. She became dangerously hypoglycemic. How long has she been diabetic?"

Relief warred with confusion. "Diabetic? She doesn't have diabetes." He shook his head impatiently when the woman opened her mouth to speak again. "I know my mother's health history like the back of my hand. I'll give you the number of her regular doctor. He'll tell you the same thing."

The woman frowned. "Her blood sugar numbers, coupled with what looks like a fresh injection site—"

"The only medication Mother takes is for osteoporosis and her heart," he said firmly. Now that the crisis was over, Franklin was anxious to get to Mother's side. He would make sure her regular internist visited her tomorrow. "No shots. Which is a good thing, since she detests shots."

Her voice troubled, the doctor said, "Mr. Paulsen, I can't think of anything else that would have sent your mother's numbers that low, that fast. And there definitely is a puncture area in her arm. I think we need to do a bit more investigating."

He stilled. And the tiny little fear that he hadn't wanted to acknowledge grew. "What are you suggesting?"

"Medication mix-ups happen far more often than we'd like to think." Her tone was careful. "I would suggest that you start by speaking to your mother's caretakers about possible answers for your mother's episode today."

There was more, but Franklin didn't hear it. Guilt spiked through him. Because he knew that the answers he needed to get from the new nursing home had nothing to do with medication mix-ups.

And everything to do with who had been allowed in his mother's room.

Once the doctor had left, Franklin took out his cell. Fingers trembling, he keyed in a number he'd promised himself he would never call.

"Frankie. Tell me—how is dear ol' Ma feeling?"

Just the sound of "Vanecia Mason's" voice was enough to have him quaking. "You're a demon. You have no soul."

"And you're an idiot for needing proof of that. Make no mistake, Frankie, it was *you* that almost got your mother killed. Are you calling to tell me that I'm going to need to make another trip? Because next time you'll be calling from the funeral home."

"Tomorrow morning." He'd give the damn capsules to Vance and hope to God the man was planning a suicide. "First thing—I promise."

"Hope I can trust you to keep your promises, Frankie." The woman's voice was menacing. "Because I've already shown that I keep mine."

When Vickie Baxter disconnected, she made two calls. A male answered each time and to both she said only a single word. "Tomorrow."

Chapter 7

Cam's office had taken on the appearance of a war room. Two huge maps hung on the wall, each punctuated with a multicolored array of pins. Another wall was covered with white paper, a timeline of sorts filled with the details of all the homicides since the case started, short profiles on the trio of killers, and item points for the confirmed sightings. Included was the information Beckett and Jenna had discovered today.

Two laptops sat on a table pushed against one wall running the surveillance feed from the two motel rooms Baxter had booked under false identities. A fax machine was next to them. Another table held folders and notebooks filled with computer printouts of every detail of the investigation so far.

The effect was overwhelming, Sophia decided, even for someone as well versed as she was in the case. But for Cam it seemed to represent pieces to the same puzzle. One of those five-thousand-piece ones where all the pieces were nearly the same color. The most difficult part about the investigation wasn't a lack of leads, she mused, but deciding which new bit of information was relevant and how.

Jenna was manning the feed at the computer while tracking down the real Maxine LaCoste, the name on the credit card Baxter had used at the second motel where they'd discovered her registered. Sophia and Cam had been on scene at the Comfort Motel until he had to head back for meetings with SAC Gonzalez and Major Crime Unit Assistant Director Miller. Interspersed with those briefings he was on his cell with motel managers and credit card companies, while directing the agents still checking for more motel registrations.

One thing she'd never be able to accuse him of was an inability to multitask.

He strode back into his office now, carrying three bottles of water, and handed each of them one. After twisting off the cap of the third, he took a long swallow before lowering it to ask, "Come up with anything of interest?"

"Zilch on the motel surveillance." Jenna looked up from her laptop. "I haven't been able to find any evidence that Greta Talbot and Maxine LaCoste knew each other, and neither could identify the photo I sent of Baxter. What they did have in common was they'd both visited Iowa in the last eighteen months and had their purses stolen."

He slanted Sophia a glance. "Neither of the names popped for you?"

She shook her head. She'd been focusing on Baxter's classmates during the time she spent with the Coates family. It hadn't been difficult to find contact information for most of them. The district's website had a page for alumni, she supposed to make it easier to plan for reunions.

"I haven't gotten a response yet to many of the email inquiries I sent, but most of the ones I talked to remember Vickie. None of them fondly. All say they haven't seen her or heard from her since she left school."

She'd managed to speak with Cal Patten, Reverend Minskel, and Bobby Denholt. But her efforts were in vain. All had denied having contact with Baxter. "I made a call to both of the Coates children again. Left messages." Messages she doubted very much they'd answer. She wondered for the first time if their reticence had less to do with unresolved grief and more to do with fear of Baxter. They had, after all, lived with Vickie for a time. They might know all too intimately what she was capable of.

"I've sent a memo about Baxter's alias to all law enforcement in the surrounding area." Cam took one more swig of the bottle and went to his desk, sat down at his computer to check his email. "Both motels where she registered require photo ID in addition to a credit card. It goes to figure she has driver's licenses in every false identity she's assumed. Likely a passport, too."

"Then you can contact places in the area where passports are issued," Sophia suggested, then stopped when she saw Jenna shaking her head.

Cam was engrossed in something on his computer screen. "Good thought, but the IDs will be fake. Licenses and passports."

Jenna put in, "We helped bust a ring in Chicago two years ago that was supplying fake Iowa licenses to college students. I mean, flooding the campuses. It was getting to be a real problem."

"Let me guess," Sophia put in drolly. "Students weren't purchasing them so they could vote."

"ID means alcohol-purchasing power. We shut that ring down, but you can bet some other enterprising outfit has sprung up to take its place."

"For the right price, fake IDs and passports can be had online. Some pretty good forgeries. Totally anonymous." Cam's voice broke off, and he peered more closely at the computer. "Here it is."

"Here what is?" Jenna got up from her seat to cross to his desk. Sophia joined her.

"Maybe Vickie Baxter's first mistake." He hit a command, and a moment later the printer started whirring. Another moment and it spit out several sheets of paper.

"The credit card in the name of Greta Talbot was only opened four months ago. No purchases made with it. But Maxine LaCoste... that account was opened last year. And there's a transaction history."

Jenna strode to the copier and snatched the copied sheets from it. Sophia bent slightly to read over Cam's shoulder. "This seems careless," she murmured. "She's never careless."

"Not really." There was a note of suppressed excitement in his voice. "What's the point of having the false cards if you can't use them instead of wasting cash? See here . . . She racked up a couple thousand in expenses eight months ago and made minimal payments online to satisfy the requirements."

"Online?" Jenna was shuffling the papers back to the top sheet with account information on it. "We can get Cybercrimes on it. Maybe we can get an IP address."

"Call Campbell. He'll let you know what's involved in the process." The tall, lanky Cybercrime agent was a genius with all things technology related. Cam scrolled back to recent transactions, and Sophia saw immediately what had elicited his excitement. "Phil's Pawn and Jewelry. Not exactly a name guaranteeing quality."

"Not everyone has your sensibilities." He was already rising and heading toward Jenna, who handed him the copies. "You can make another copy to show to Cybercrimes." Cam paused at the doorway, turned back to cock an eyebrow at Sophia. "You're with me on this one."

"I am?" She collected her purse and joined him. "I don't know anything about pawnshops."

"We're about to expand your education." He held the door open for her and allowed her to precede him out. "The first thing you need to know is that pawnshops sell things a lot more interesting than jewelry."

Phil's was a popular place. Cam stepped into the store after Sophia and scanned the area. Three customers and a burly clerk were crowded into the store. Every inch of the cramped space was used to showcase Phil's wares. A jewelry counter for rings, necklaces, and watches. Used power tools and small electronics. A couple of large smart TVs. Vacuum cleaners. Sports memorabilia.

And guns. A whole case of them. He made a point of lingering over the showcase. Phil, if that's who the bearded man behind the counter was, had made him for law enforcement the instant he'd walked through the door. The man was less certain what to think of Sophie. It was obvious from the way his gaze kept following them while he had a discussion with the customer at the counter over the worth of a digital camera he was trying to pawn.

"Just a minute," he told the man he was waiting on. After disappearing into the back, he returned a moment later with a woman, who took his place at the counter. The clerk bypassed the next two customers and stopped next to Cam.

"Help you?"

Cam flashed his DCI credentials. "DCI special agent Cam Prescott. I'd like to talk to you about a purchase made here two and a half weeks ago."

"We're a busy place." The man's lips were almost completely hidden by the reddish beard that hung to the base of his neck. "Not going to be able to remember any one purchase." His voice was pitched deliberately low. But the shop was too small to ensure privacy, and he seemed to know it. One of the customers started edging nonchalantly toward the door. After opening it, he sidled out. The action didn't escape Phil's attention.

Cam took a tri-folded sheet from the breast pocket of his suit coat and shook it out to show the man. Phil gave the photo a cursory glance and shook his head. "Don't know her. And I'm not going to recognize everyone who may have come in here."

"Maybe this will jog your memory." He handed the man the credit card page listing the sale from his store.

He gave the sheet back. The man's denim-clad beefy shoulders jerked up and down once. "Can't tell anything from that."

"That's why you need to go through your records," Cam explained patiently. "I want a match for what was purchased with this credit card."

Phil smiled for the first time since they entered his store. "We both know that's gonna take a warrant. Since you don't have one, get the hell out and don't come back until you do." The words were spoken loudly, for the benefit of his remaining customers.

"Somehow I thought you'd say that." Cam looked around for Sophie. Found her gazing in awe at the array of mounted moose, deer, and bear heads on the wall. "Agent Channing." She turned, cocked her head quizzically. "This shop is closed for business until further notice. Clear it."

"You can't do that!" This from the woman behind the counter.

"I'm afraid we can, ma'am." Sophie addressed the customers. "You gentlemen will have to leave. It's possible the store will reopen. At some point." Both of them shot a look at Cam and scurried out the door.

"What the hell do you think you're doing?" Phil folded his arms across his chest. "I know my rights. You can't just come in here and—"

"I can and did. You want me to get a warrant. Until that warrant arrives, I have the authority to prevent you from any activity that I believe might sabotage our investigation. That includes possibly destroying files or tampering with evidence."

"This is bullshit." Phil turned his head and addressed the woman. "Get Radner on the phone. My attorney," he explained for Cam's benefit. "By the end of the day, he'll have your ass and your badge."

"Be sure and tell him that the warrant will include all your bills of sale for the past year, and the federal documentation of all gun sales for the same period. Any violations we find will, of course, be turned over to ATF."

The woman behind the counter paused in the middle of keying in the number. Looked from her cell phone to Phil.

The man hesitated a moment. Then shrugged. "Let me see that credit card statement again."

He looked it over much more carefully this time, and then went to the back again. Cam's hand crept inside his suit jacket. Hovered over the butt of his weapon. But when Phil reappeared he was carrying a laptop. He set it on the counter. Painstakingly typed in the number correlating with the bill of sale number on the credit card statement.

"Okay," he said after a moment. "Says here she bought two paintings. A flat-screen TV and a used laptop." He turned the computer around for Cam to see the screen. When Cam only looked at him, he said, "Go ahead and look. It's all documented right there."

"I can't figure out if you're incredibly stupid or just stubborn. I'm guessing the former." Taking his cell phone from his pocket, Cam pressed the key to speed-dial Jenna. "Fill out a warrant for Phil's Pawn and Jewelry," he said evenly, then recited the address. "Take some time with it. We want a thorough search of the premises, including computerized record keeping, bills of sale, firearm documentation—"

"All right. I can help."

"Shut the hell up, Mandi."

"You shut up, Phil. Idiot." The woman behind the counter looked to Sophie for support. "Maybe some mistakes were made." She reached up a hand to shove a strand of dirty-blonde hair behind her ear. "If we give you the answers you want about that lady that came in here, you'll leave us alone?"

"That depends on the sort of information you have to share, ma'am."

Sophie's noncommittal answer nearly had Cam grinning. She could deny it all she wanted, but her time spent with law enforcement was definitely rubbing off on her.

"Okay." Mandi rubbed her palms down her jeans-clad thighs. "So we had this guy working for us. Roger Dutton. Just part-time, you understand. He waited on this woman, like you said. And without us knowing about it, he sold her some firearms and ammunition."

"Jesus, you and Dutton are going to land me in federal prison," Phil moaned, rubbing the back of his neck. "Listen, the guy falsified the bill of sale, and I could tell right away it was bullshit when I went over it the next day. I canned him on the spot."

"And didn't report it," Cam said evenly.

"Think I don't know I could lose my license for this? He had strict orders not to sell any weapons at all when I wasn't here. Moron thought I wouldn't notice three of my best guns gone from the case? I should have beaten the shit out of him while I was at it. You know what he risked my license over? Bitch gave him some cash under the table and a blow job." He slapped his hands on the counter in disgust. "For that alone he should have his ass kicked."

"Tell him the rest," Mandi whispered in a loud undertone. Phil gave her a warning look, but the woman was adamant. "We recognized the name on the photo because she was in here before. When both Phil and I were working. It was about six weeks ago, maybe. And that time she was asking Phil what he knew about explosives."

—

"You can't ignore this." Jenna was pacing Cam's office in an unusual show of agitation. "Two witnesses who can tie her to an interest in bombs or potentially explosive material." She took a second to glance at the surveillance feeds on the computer screens as she paced by. Continued her rant without missing a beat. "Beckett was right earlier today. You have to look at the timeline. What does it tell us about what Baxter and Vance were thinking? What they were planning and when?"

Cam raised his brows. "You and Maxwell must have had quite the conversation today."

"We did." She stopped. "That's not the point." The agent turned to Sophia for help. "Don't let him change the subject."

Her throat tight, Sophia said, "I mentioned the possibility that Baxter might target members of the task force. We know now what she had planned for me. But you. . . You were—are—the face of the investigation. We've spent a lot of time talking about the killings, the motivations, but we haven't spent enough time thinking about what must have gone on between the three killers when you tied the victims together. Were they panicked? Did the discovery cause a rift between them, or did it draw them even more tightly together? What steps did they take to avoid discovery?"

"Our focus was exactly where it needed to be to solve the case." Cam's voice was maddeningly even as he propped his feet up on his desk while he went through the texts from his agents. "We can't waste our time on what-ifs. We have to go where the evidence leads us."

"You're not obtuse." His narrowed gaze caught hers when she uttered the words. She read the irritation there. The warning. She ignored both. "If you're downplaying this because you think it worries me, too late. I'm worried. She started looking for explosives after your name was released as lead investigator on the case. They may have planned it to take you out."

"I'm not downplaying it." His gaze encompassed both of them. "Baxter's queries about explosives tell us more about what she and Vance are capable of than anything else. Did they ever acquire them? There's no way for us to be sure. So we'll be careful, all of us. But I doubt very much Baxter would be dumb enough to try to wire my car while it sits in the DCI lot. Or at a scene. And my home is secure."

Of course it was. Sophia recalled their conversation from that morning. Federal agents were watching it. Her chest eased a bit, even though she was well aware that explosives could be deadly in many forms, not just as car bombs. But this interagency task force from two years ago that had arisen again meant constant surveillance on his whereabouts. Digital and physical surveillance on his home. One probably couldn't hope for better protection than that.

"There's nothing in either Baxter's or Vance's backgrounds to indicate they have a familiarity with explosives." She would cling to that fact when worry threatened to consume her. "But the developmental arc of serial criminals include new behaviors as they evolve and change. They'll adapt to their new reality or environment." She paused a beat. "Or to a new threat. It would be a mistake not to take that into consideration."

"I am."

Finally, Jenna blew out of breath. "Yeah, okay. No use hammering on it." She went back to the computers and dropped into a chair in front of them. "Cam's too much of a professional to—ha ha—blow this off."

"The charms of cop humor," Sophia said darkly as she plopped with much less grace than usual into one of the chairs in front of the desk, "have always been lost on me." His cell rang then. When he answered it, the alertness in his face had Sophia getting to her feet. She was already turned toward the door when Cam made the announcement.

"We've got a positive ID on a third motel Baxter registered at."

The one-story, whitewashed, cement building had seen better days. Vickie sat in a shaded corner in the rutted lot behind the structure and waited. At half past five, a woman she'd noticed before came out of the back of the structure, standing in the doorway for a moment, still talking to someone inside. Then she pulled the door closed, shut the screen carefully, and made her way to an older blue Honda parked next to the structure. She didn't spare a glance in the direction of Vickie's vehicle. Gravel spit from beneath her tires as she drove away, obviously in a hurry.

Putting her car into drive, Vickie did a slow loop around the building to assure herself that no one but the owner was inside. Then she went around to the back again, this time pulling up right next to the lone vehicle left there, a dinged and dented midsize sedan.

She got out, threw a quick look around, and then, hefting her purse over her shoulder, walked quickly to the door. Let herself in.

The man she was looking for was hunched over a desktop computer. He was thinner than she remembered, with a bald patch on the back of his head and stooped shoulders. He jolted in the chair as he heard a sound behind him, blacking out the screen with a quick, practiced move of the mouse. But not before she'd glimpsed the images that had so enthralled him.

"Greg." Her lips curled as he whirled in the chair to face her. "I see your interests haven't changed."

Greg Davis went still, like a rabbit faced with a lion that was crouched and ready to pounce. "Vickie." The word ended on a squeak. He cleared his throat. Moistened his lips nervously. "It's been a while."

"That it has." She moved around the room, taking inventory. The room looked to serve a dual role as storeroom and office, with metal shelves hemming in the desk he sat at, each overflowing with books, equipment, and dog and cat food. "But you saw Sonny more recently, didn't you? And you were always far more interested in him than you were in me. At least when he was a kid."

He had the brains to look nervous. He was practically peeing himself.

"That was all so long ago. I've changed." He tried for a smile. Couldn't pull it off. "We've all changed."

"Let's see how much you've changed, Greg." She unzipped her oversize purse with one hand, gestured to the computer with the other. "Show me what you were looking at when I came in."

A small sound escaped him, and somehow without moving he seemed to shrink in the chair. "Nothing. Veterinary training videos. That's all."

"Uh-huh." She took a gun from her bag and aimed it at him. "Show me."

His shoulders slumping, his hand moved to the mouse. Clicked. The screen was filled with images of men engaged in sex acts with young boys. "All I do is look anymore—I promise. I told Sonny that the last time he was here. I *helped* him! Every time he came to me, I helped. I gave him the drugs he wanted. And when he got hurt a couple weeks ago, I patched him up." Tears were leaking from his eyes. "I repaid my debt."

A slow burn ignited in her chest. She didn't know when he might have patched up Sonny, but the paralytic . . . Yeah, it had been her idea to send Sonny to collect something they could use to subdue the women they had kidnapped. And Davis had owed them. Had owed Sonny most of all for the way that he'd used him as a boy.

But that didn't repay his debt to her son. Not even close.

"Then you won't mind helping again. I need another drug. Something strong enough to use on a large animal." She smiled thinly as his head whipped around to meet her gaze. He knew, of course he did, what type of large "animal" she was referring to. "I want something that will kill it. But not quickly. I don't mind if it suffers. In fact, I prefer it."

"I don't have anything like that," he said quickly. "You should go. Your face is all over the news. There have to be cops looking for you everywhere, and I don't want them coming—" His voice broke off abruptly when she waved the weapon threateningly.

"Don't try to bullshit me, Greg. I know you work with both farm animals and pets, so I figure you've got some Micotil. I want it in a thirty cc disposable syringe, fourteen-gauge needle." She pressed the gun against the side of his throat, traced it down the cord there to where the pulse was beating madly. "Get me that, and I'm on my way."

He tried to stare her down, ended up looking away. "I forgot you used to be a nurse's assistant. That would be more than you'd use on a thousand-pound cow. Overdose like that is going to cause nausea, dizziness, chest pain, limb numbness . . . Left untreated the . . . animal . . . would certainly die."

Pathetic little puke of a man. He'd once had a sense of imagination and taste for kink that had interested her for a while, though. In the end, however, he had disappointed her. Most men did.

"That fits with my research." She moved away, noting the quick flash of relief in his expression when the gun was off his throat. Leaning a hip against the desk, she gestured with the weapon, pointing it meaningfully at his crotch. "I'm guessing you have it around here somewhere. And that you would be delighted to get it for me."

Perspiration beaded his high forehead, highlighting flecks of dandruff clinging to the thinning hair there. "Ah . . . let me think. Maybe . . ." He swallowed hard. "Come to think of it, I do keep Micotil on hand to treat bovine respiratory disease."

"I thought you would." She followed him to a connecting hallway that led to a small surgical suite. The small hall had floor-to-ceiling shelving on both sides, and he turned to one and dug through the boxes and supplies, muttering. Then he stopped, withdrew a box and a plastic-wrapped syringe.

"Here." He shoved both at her, but Vickie made no move to take them.

"Back in the office. You can fill it up for me." Her smile was thin as he preceded her to the back room where she'd found him.

He swallowed hard. "Administer a single subcutaneous dose of one-point-five to three milliliters of Micotil per hundred pounds of body weight. This is way more than you need." He reseated himself and removed the protective cap from the amber bottle and carefully stuck the one-and-a-half-inch steel needle into the rubber center of the top, expelling the air from the syringe before filling it.

She reached past him as he was tapping the syringe to rid it of air bubbles to click on the mouse, bringing up the screenful of images again. "There." She snatched the syringe from him, recapped the needle. "I'll let you get back to your kiddie porn." When he just looked at the floor, she demanded, "Look at it! How many boys just like my Sonny did you rape like that?"

He started weeping in earnest. "You told me to! You said it was what you wanted—"

Vickie slammed the weapon against his head, knocking him to the floor. "It's your fault he turned out like he did, crazy like he was at the end. Your fault he's dead." He curled up on the floor, sobbing like a three-year-old having a meltdown, and she looked at him with disgust. At least Curt put up a fight. Davis wasn't even making this satisfying. *Sniveling little prick.*

Pressing a knee to his back, she placed the gun against his temple. "Don't move a muscle." He stilled obediently, except for the involuntary quivering of his body. "You're getting off easy. I'd like to shoot your balls off and shove them down your throat."

He tried to squirm away, in belated realization of what she was about to do, but she'd already flicked the cap off the needle and jabbed it deep into his ass. Pressed the plunger.

"No!" He came alive at the first prick of the needle, trying to roll away, one hand frantically fighting hers as he wrestled for the syringe. Then he began bucking beneath her, wild jerky movements. He managed to knock her off balance, and she landed hard on the floor. His fingers closed around the syringe still sticking from his bony left cheek.

And then he stilled. Davis's breathing was already labored. His eyes were open but glazed. Vickie was impressed. "One drug that lives up to its billing." She got up to empty the contents of the syringe into him, before drawing it out carefully.

This stuff just might come in handy later. She grabbed the rest of the bottle and dropped it in her purse. Searched for the needle's cap on the floor. Found it beneath Davis's shoe. "Thanks for the help, Greg. I'll just be taking this stuff with me. No use making it easy for them. Let them have to work to figure out what you got injected with."

Rising, she put the gun back into her purse and swung it over her shoulder. The syringe she'd place in the glove compartment for now. With her luck she'd jab herself searching for her cell phone.

"You know what's best about this whole thing, Greg?" Was he still breathing? She couldn't tell. Didn't care enough to check. "The first thing someone will notice when they find you, other than your corpse, of course, is what's on your computer screen. Everyone's going to know what a pervert you always were. Maybe they'll even agree that you got exactly what you had coming to you."

Chapter 8

I s it just me, or is this beginning to feel like déjà vu?" Sophie's words were spoken around a yawn. It was after nine, and they were just now heading home. Cam made sure to avoid the vicinity of Fleur Drive and George Flagg Parkway. The streets flanked Water Works Park and Gray's Lake, where thousands of the RAGBRAI riders were camping. Getting caught up in the detours for bike traffic would slow their progress to a snail's pace.

"It's getting better. This motel actually produced the registration information without a warrant." Cam was at the point where he appreciated any time saved. "With luck we'll have the credit card information tomorrow morning." He'd been tempted to swing into a fast-food place on his way home. Had he been alone, he would have. But the woman sitting in the seat beside him had caused him to reconsider.

It was late, but there was something to be said for fixing a simple meal at home. Putting their feet up. Maybe grabbing a beer. And just taking some time to forget about this case long enough to enjoy being alone together.

Warmth curled through his belly at the thought. Every minute they could steal from the investigation was golden. He was going to make sure they counted.

"Rose Macomber." Sophie stretched her hands over her head. Arched her back. "Do you think the third identity Baxter used will turn out to be a visitor to Iowa who got her purse stolen, too?"

"No. Given the law of averages, I'd say the real Rose Macomber is likely from the area."

"And who do you think was responsible? Sonny Baxter, Vance, or Vickie?"

He had to admit he'd never given it much thought. "It could have been any of them. You can buy identities off the Internet. People steal the cards, try to max them out before they get canceled, and then sell them to others who are doing identity theft."

"That's a possibility." Sophie's voice was pensive as they pulled into the drive at his condo, paused for the moment it took the automatic garage door to rise, then drove into the garage. "But I think Vickie is capable of it. Look how easily she stole the car she used to kidnap Traer. It makes me wonder if she made a living by theft before she started killing. We know she manipulated men into stealing for her when she was still in high school."

He shut off the ignition of the car and pressed the button so the overhead door would descend. "We're going in the house now. And we're not going to think about this case."

Something in his voice must have alerted her. He heard the smile in her voice as she answered. "Oh? What are we going to think about?"

"This." He leaned over and brushed his lips over hers. Settled in to increase the pressure. His hand slipped behind her head to cup her nape, and he let himself just sink into the softness that was Sophie.

Each time was familiar but different. The taste of her. The scent. It was never exactly the same. And maybe that was why he couldn't get enough. His tongue pressed her lips open, went in search of hers. And that first sweet tangle of lips and teeth and tongue swept his mind clean.

It couldn't be hotter each time. The craving deeper. But the reality defied logic. She made a mockery of all he'd thought he'd known, what had always been. Previous experience didn't matter because with Sophie everything was unique. It was all uncharted territory with her. And he no longer let that alarm him.

Her arms twined around his neck, and she turned more fully into him. He tore his mouth away to string a necklace of kisses along her jaw, and she gave a little sigh. "You know, I think this is a first."

He nuzzled the soft spot beneath her ear, pleased when she shivered. "There's something wrong with your memory, baby. This is definitely not our first time."

"No, I . . ." She arched her throat when he went in search of all the places there he could find her pulse beating beneath skin. "I mean . . . I don't think I've ever necked in a car before."

That had him raising his head. "You've got to be kidding. Never?"

"I don't think so, no."

"How is that even possible? No making out in the backseat? No hot-and-heavy petting while your parents flicked the porch lights on and off?"

She gave his chest a little shove. "Now that sounds like the voice of experience."

Cam grinned. There had been damn few good memories in his formative years, but those experiences numbered within them. "Let me guess. Prearranged dates by your parents, with a boy walking you to your door, giving you a chaste kiss on the forehead under the watchful eye of your father." She'd told him enough about the rigid confines of her childhood that he could be pretty sure he was correct. Although come to think of it, if he had a daughter who looked like Sophie, he'd be overprotective, too.

"That's it exactly." She nibbled at his chin, rubbing her lips over the growth of whiskers there. "If I hadn't gone away to college, I would never have gotten laid."

That surprised a laugh from him. She could still do that. Take him unaware. The phrase, so at odds with her usual precise speech, had him hopelessly, helplessly enchanted. "Sweetheart, looking like you do, the only wonder is that you made it to college before losing your virginity."

"So." She rubbed her lips over his. "Are you going to remedy that egregious void in my experience and show me how you came by your disgracefully vast experience with girls in the backseat?"

He was tempted for a moment. More than tempted. Then he gave her a last hard kiss and set her firmly away. "Actually car sex is overrated. I do my best work inside."

"Is that right?"

"It is." They got out of the car and headed for the entrance to the house. "I'll be glad to exhibit my skills to you as soon as you feed me."

"Once again, showing exactly where I stand," she teased. He found the key, fitted it into the door lock, and pushed it open. "There's bacon. Pancakes. Various other food items. Then me. No wait, I forgot about the Cubs. And the Hawkeyes. It's a long list. I'm not sure where I fit in."

He caught her fingers, drew her toward him. Then closed his arms around her waist and pulled her closer. "At the top, Soph." And his voice was no longer teasing. "When it comes to my priorities, you're at the top."

This time their kiss was flavored with unspoken promise. He threaded his fingers in her long hair, and earlier plans were forgotten. He touched her, and everything else spun away. She was a dangerous distraction, but there was a limit to his professional focus. This time, this moment, he wanted to immerse everything he was into her.

Her fingers were nimble on his shirt, pulling it from the waist of his pants. Unbuttoning it. Her purse hit the floor when he pushed her jacket down her slender arms and buried his lips at the smooth skin of her shoulder. Muscle whispered beneath flesh, calling to something primitive in him. Something he was determined to unleash until they were both satiated.

He cupped her face in both his hands, brushed his thumbs across the smooth skin, awash in a welter of feeling that should have scared the hell out of him. But not this time. Not with this woman.

His mouth was lowering to hers again when the ring of the doorbell split the darkness.

She jerked a bit in his arms, startled, and for a brief instinctive minute his arms closed reflexively around her. Then logic returned. Followed by temper. Whoever was at the door, Cam thought grimly as he released Sophie and stalked toward it, better be wearing a cup.

He turned on the porch light and took a look through the Judas hole. Then, mouth flattening, he flicked the light off again and disengaged the alarm. Pulled the door open to look at the man he would have just as soon never have seen again.

"Harlow."

"Cam." FBI agent Del Harlow put his hand out. Allowed it to drop to his side when Cam ignored it. "We need to talk." He tilted his head to look beyond Cam. "Ms. Channing probably needs to hear this, too." The man's booming voice echoed a bit in the small foyer.

"It's *Dr.* Channing." Cam didn't make a move to open the door wider. "And I can't think of one good reason to involve her."

"Well, since I'm here, I'm involved." Sophie took the decision out of his hands by walking to the door. Subtly elbowing him aside.

"Agent Harlow. Come in." Grudgingly Cam moved away to let the man enter. Looked through the door outside in both directions. "Where's your car?"

"Another agent dropped me off."

Sophie turned on the lamps in the living room. "Can I get you anything? Coffee? Water?"

"I wouldn't say no to coffee if you have decaf."

Cam didn't move. Didn't offer the man a chair. And didn't give a damn that he was acting like a dick. "You could have come to DCI offices," he told him. "Better yet, called and made an appointment."

Harlow slipped his hands in his pockets and considered him. The man was dark-haired, tall, with a swarthy complexion. He'd probably considered himself hot shit with women at one time, but a fondness for steak and Jameson had thickened his girth. Softened his jawline. Cam had it on good authority by people who should know that Harlow was considered a damn fine agent.

It was just too bad that the man was also an unprincipled prick.

"Way I hear it, you're in the middle of a hot case. The Cornbelt Killers, right? You pick off the last of the lot fairly quickly and your reputation is golden." The man wandered past him, dropped down in Cam's favorite leather recliner. "How's the case going, anyway?"

"It's going."

"You're a talkative guy." Harlow accepted the mug Sophie brought him and included her in his comment. "He always this chatty?"

"It's been a long day." She sank down on the couch, putting two mugs on the table in front of it. After a moment, Cam sat down next to her.

"You got news?"

"The arrangements for the operation in Southern California are nearly complete." As if he'd had a trying day himself, Harlow used the lever on the side of the chair to prop his feet up. Sighed a little.

"Moreno is planning a takeover of a rival cartel. He's rebuilt some in the time since the task force gutted his operation. But he's really overextending himself to pull off this takeover. He'll replenish what he lost from the raid if he's successful. If he isn't . . ." The agent's smile was thin. "The Ramos cartel will have accomplished our job for us."

"Only if they manage to take out Moreno." Cam reached for the coffee he didn't want and drank. Christ, that multiagency task force he'd worked on for nearly two years refused to die. He'd been approached for it because of his earlier work for DNE, the narcotics division that paralleled DCI. A contact he'd made during that time would ease his infiltration into the Sinaloa cartel, which was one of the most powerful drug-trafficking syndicates in the world.

What was supposed to be an assignment lasting months had stretched nearly two years. And his FBI contact, Del Harlow, was the lone link he'd had to his other life. He'd relied on the man to share strategy and intel, as well as messages to and from his mother. Harlow had declined to share the news about Cam's mom's heart attack. Cam hadn't heard about it until he was back in the States, while he was being debriefed. His mother had survived, thankfully.

But any trust that had once existed between him and Harlow had been shattered. Every time he looked at the man, he had an overwhelming urge to put a fist in his face.

Harlow raised his mug to his lips, watching Cam carefully over its rim. "You and Baldwin in contact?"

Here, at last, was the reason for the agent's visit. Cam cradled his own mug, returned the agent's stare. "Why would we be?"

Matthew Baldwin epitomized the reason Cam had gotten out of undercover work in the first place. Too long in deep cover had black and white blurring into a muddy shade of gray.

The result was Matt Baldwin.

"He met with you two weeks ago. Not the feds, you."

"But he agreed to work with the feds in return for his family's guaranteed safety." Sophie was sitting very still beside him. He'd told her most of the story when Baldwin first made contact. Her mind would be busy right now, reading nuances, dissecting every tone and inflection. She knew about the friendship that had sprung up between Matt and him. Knew that when the whole bust was about to go down, Cam had made sure Matt was elsewhere.

Every action had a consequence. Moreno sending Baldwin to kill Cam was his.

"This sting . . . The whole thing hinges on us trusting the word of a known scumbag."

Cam sipped from the coffee. Wondered why it was that every time Sophie touched the machine, the brew tasted better. "If Baldwin wanted to kill me, I'd have been dead a month ago. Offing me would have cemented his position in Moreno's upper echelon of lieutenants. So when he says Moreno is holding his wife and daughter until he finds the informant, I believe him. He had everything to gain by killing me when he tracked me here. Everything to lose by crossing Moreno while the man holds Gabriella and Zoe. No one has more at risk if this operation goes wrong than Matt."

"You would know." Harlow's tone was meaningful. "From what I hear, you and he were buddies during the operation."

Everything inside him went still. But he'd survived life immersed in a Mexican cartel. When a thoughtless word or slip meant the difference between life and a slow brutal death. Dodging a verbal grenade lobbed by Harlow was child's play. "Survival undercover depends on building relationships. Establishing connections. It's how you get information, and it helps you keep from getting a bullet in the brain. So, yeah. He and I were friendly. Like I was with some of the others. What's your point?"

Sophie laced her fingers with his. And the slight contact eased a measure of tension.

Harlow shrugged. "Just an observation. He managed to be absent when the bust went down."

Cam drank, wishing for the jolt caffeine would have given him. He was too damned tired to play cat and mouse with the man. "Maybe sometime you and I can sit down, go through your case files. That'd be a real education to read about all those FBI busts that went off perfectly, without a hitch." The man couldn't know that Cam had made sure Matt wouldn't be there. He was fishing. And damn close to the truth.

"Touchy." The FBI agent looked at Sophie. "He always this sensitive?"

"Apparently," she said coolly, "just with you."

"Apparently." He regarded Cam silently for a moment. "It's important that Baldwin is getting his orders and all his information from one source. We don't want to send mixed messages. The success of the upcoming operation depends on it."

Cam's gut tightened at the thought of his involvement in the sting they were planning. Symptoms of the PTSD from his ordeal last time had faded. But he didn't kid himself that they'd completely disappeared. Not when a random nightmare could still yank him from sleep, sweating and shaking.

"Since my ass depends on the success of the upcoming operation, you appear to be preaching to the choir."

"Okay." Harlow drained his mug, leaned forward to set it on the coffee table. "I just had to be sure. We suspect he might be communicating with someone, but we can't prove it. Maybe we're paranoid. We just can't afford to take any chances this time around. There's too much riding on the success of the bust."

Including, Cam figured, Harlow's career ambitions. "What'd you discover about the license plate I texted you? The one Sophie has seen twice on the street near here?"

"Dr. Channing's very observant." The smile the man aimed at Sophie was as insincere as his words. "It was one of ours." He got up to leave. "You'll be relieved to know we haven't noted any suspect activity in the area. With the exception of your little friend"—he nodded in Sophie's direction—"all has been quiet."

Cam looked at her quizzically as they both stood. "You have a little friend?"

"A neighborhood boy came by looking for his cat."

They followed Harlow to the door. He had one hand on the doorknob before turning back to them. But his words were addressed to Sophie. "Baldwin got to Cam the first time by approaching you. It's important if he does contact you to get in touch with us immediately."

With that he pulled open the door and walked out into the darkness. Cam closed the door behind him with barely restrained force. Reset the alarm.

"Well." She went back to the table and picked up the empty mugs. Carried them to the kitchen. "He's every bit as pleasant as you mentioned. Why would he think Matt might contact me?"

"In an operation as big as they're planning, they attempt to isolate the informant. Close off all outside communication to try and control his exposure. They don't trust Baldwin, but they're willing to use him to make the bust." And Cam had reason to know Matt didn't trust the feds either to follow through on their promise of immunity. With good reason. "Harlow isn't worried about you. This was a veiled warning to me."

She sent him a shocked look. "To you? Why?"

He shrugged. Went to the kitchen and started taking the makings for sandwiches out of the refrigerator. He didn't bother with the beer. His plans for a couple of relaxing hours before sleep had just been shot to hell.

"He wants to be the one doling out any information that gets shared. Maybe he's afraid Baldwin and I will compare notes. Adjust the eventual plan."

Which proved, Cam thought as Sophie came to help him in the kitchen, that the agent had better instincts than he would have given him credit for. Because that's exactly what he and Matt were doing.

———

"You're up early." Sophie leaned a shoulder against the doorjamb of the bathroom, looking surprisingly alert given the hour. But of the two of them, she was definitely the morning person.

Cam ran an appreciative gaze over her form, clad in a flimsy thigh-length robe. "I got notice a couple hours ago about some explosives that detonated at Water Works Park."

"Oh my God." Horror threaded her words. "All those bicyclists camped there . . . were there injuries?"

He swiped at his chest and shoulders with a towel before carelessly wrapping it around his hips. "Yeah, but I don't have the specifics. Just that DMPD got an anonymous tip after the first one detonated, claiming there were others set to go off in the park and along University Avenue, the scheduled bicyclist route out of the city." He could only imagine the logistics required to evacuate the park and then reroute thousands of bicyclists. Even with the help of neighboring suburbs' departments, the police and emergency resources would be severely strained. "Hard to sleep after hearing that."

"Harder still for you not to be in the middle of it."

He arrowed a glance at her as he picked up his shaver. She saw too much sometimes. "DCI assistance hasn't been requested." The agency became involved only at the formal request of other state law enforcement entities. "My team has enough on its plate right now. If help is needed, Maria would allocate other agents." He started the electric razor and spoke over it before drawing it along his jawline. "All of which doesn't explain why you're up so early."

He surveyed her face carefully, but saw only concern in her expression. Not the telltale signs of a sleepless night. She still had them, too often. And Leslie's attack would likely worsen the condition.

"I just got a call from Bobby Denholt while you were in the shower."

He turned off the razor for a moment. "The neighbor of the Coateses. The son that got caught up in the paternity gossip over Baxter's pregnancy. Okay."

She stepped inside the room to prop her hips against the bathroom counter. "Yesterday I spoke to several people who knew Baxter back then, and, like the rest of those I talked to, he denied having any contact with her since she left home."

"And less than twenty-four hours later he wants to talk." Intrigued, Cam considered the timing. "Something tells me he has a guilty conscience."

"Let's hope. Guilty consciences loosen lips." She moved over a little to give him a few inches of space. "He wants to see us before his first appointment. Which is at seven."

"Traffic is going to be a nightmare," he warned. "With RAGBRAI riders and the emergency response teams, things are going to be a mess." Not to mention the news crews that would be mobbing the area.

"I know." She glanced at the bathroom clock. "That means we'll have to leave faster than humanly possible." She pushed away from the counter and hurried out of the room.

Cam resumed shaving, mentally figuring the best course to take south to Indianola. He'd have to discover how the bicyclists had been rerouted, so he could avoid the area. He'd had Sophie's car delivered to the DCI offices but hadn't seen the point of both of them driving home and then back. If it wasn't safe there, surrounded by DCI agents and State Patrol officers, it wasn't safe anywhere.

Not that he would have allowed her to make the trip without him. With all hell breaking loose on the Baxter case and the entire city, the safest place for Sophie was at his side.

———

Sophia looked past Dr. Denholt to the open office door directly across the hall. She'd suspected that Cam's presence would have a chilling effect on the man, and Cam had already nixed letting her meet with him alone. This was their compromise, and neither of the men seemed particularly happy about it.

"I was glad to hear from you, Dr. Denholt." The man kept sending suspicious glances toward Cam, despite her assurances that the DCI agent was there only to ensure her safety.

"You can call me Bobby." His smile was fleeting. "Mom said she'd talked to you."

"She explained about the circumstances that destroyed your parents' friendships with the Coateses."

Denholt looked away. He'd gone from the unformed nondescript boy in the senior portrait to an undistinguished man in his late forties. Thin, with graying hair and glasses, he was fading into midlife. There were three pictures on his desk. One of him with his mother, another with his siblings, and a third of a sunset over water. If he had ever married and had a family, there was no evidence of it here.

"What you asked me yesterday." He still wasn't looking at her. Instead he seemed intensely focused on brushing a piece of lint from his slacks. "I didn't tell you everything."

Excitement thrummed through her veins. But her voice reflected only polite interest. "You mean about Vickie contacting you?"

Nodding, his fingers clutched the tops of his thigh convulsively. "It's been years. More than a decade at least. But Vickie did call me, three different times."

"How long ago did the calls start?" There was very little known about the woman's life from the time she left her relatives' home and the time the bodies began showing up. Any light he could shed on those years could possibly be useful for the profile.

"The first time was"—he reached up to rub his nose—"let me think. Fifteen years ago, I believe. I had just started my own business."

Comprehension dawned. "She asked for money?"

His voice was miserable. "I didn't have it. I tried to explain to her that I was strapped myself. I paid for graduate school on my own, and my first job out of school didn't pay much. I had to get help buying this place. But she . . . You had to know Vickie. She had a way of making people do what she wanted."

Sophia was fairly certain that she could predict how the conversation had gone. "Did she mention her son?"

"She said . . . She claimed he was mine. That I hadn't paid a dime of support all those years, and she lost custody of him because she was broke. That it was my fault, and she was going to make sure my mother knew it."

Recalling Karen Denholt's bitter defense of her son, Sophia could imagine just how frantic he was to keep the threat from going any further. "Could the baby have been yours?"

"I don't . . ." He looked away. Swallowed hard. "It was only that once. I couldn't believe it myself at the time. I was still living at home, working for the school. I'd see her sometimes in the hallways there. She never even acknowledged me. Then on a night our parents were playing cards together at the Coateses' place, the rest of my family went along. I stayed home because I had a cold. And she showed up at the door."

Sophia could imagine the rest. Where some teenage girls were femme fatales, collecting male affection like fireflies in a jar, Vickie would have been more manipulative, even at that age. "But there was never a paternity test."

He shook his head. "Not that I know of. Certainly I never took one. I had to take out a payday loan so I could give her a couple thousand dollars. She came back for more twice after that, claiming she was using the cash for lawyers to fight DHS."

"She never fought for custody," Sophia said gently. "She didn't show up for the custody hearings at all."

Biting his lip, he nodded. "I figured I was getting scammed. I mean, she was with a lot of guys back then. *A lot.* There was probably no way for her to be sure, and she never asked for a blood sample or anything like that. So that last time, I said that was it. I wanted a picture of the boy, at least. Something that I could look at and maybe see . . . if he at least looked like me."

The confession was just a little heartbreaking. Bobby Denholt had likely been easy prey for Vickie Baxter. Even as a grown man, Sophia doubted his confidence with women.

And maybe for a man without a family or prospects for one . . . Maybe a part of him had wanted to believe what she was telling him, even when deep down he knew how implausible her story was. "And that was the last time you saw her?"

"She knew I meant it. My mother had believed me all those years ago." He had the grace to look a little ashamed. "And she had despised Vickie. There was no way she'd believe her over me. Vickie never came back."

She'd run that well dry, Sophia corrected silently. And then she'd moved on, looking for a fresh mark.

Unzipping her purse, she reached inside it for a card. Handed it to him. "I doubt you'll hear from her after all this time. But if you do, it's very important that you contact Agent Prescott at DCI. You've seen her name on the news."

He looked slightly sick. "Her name. And her son's." Slowly he took the card from her. Withdrew his wallet and carefully tucked it inside. "Tell me, Dr. Channing." His brown eyes appeared enlarged and slightly myopic behind the glasses. "You worked on this case with the DCI. You would have seen him. The boy. Sonny."

Comprehension dawned, filtered with compassion. In truth, all Sophia had ever seen of Sonny Baxter were the death photos. But she knew what the man was asking. "I don't notice a resemblance. He doesn't look much like Vickie, either. I imagine that Sonny Baxter takes after his father in looks."

She'd expected to see relief in his expression. She just hadn't thought it would be mixed with disappointment.

"Good. That's good." He rose, then didn't seem to know what to do from there. "It haunted me when I started hearing about . . . things he'd done. I really never believed Vickie when she claimed I was the father, but there was always that fear."

"I understand completely," she said gently. "I appreciate you telling me this, Dr. Denholt. I know what it cost you. Emotionally." He gave a jerky nod, and she turned to join Cam.

Leaving behind her a man torn between the fear that he'd fathered a monster and disappointment that he hadn't been a father at all.

―

Polk County Jail was located between Ankeny and Des Moines. Those inmates due for court hearings were transported to the old jail downtown to be closer to the courthouse and then returned to the newer facility.

There were currently a dozen men in the cells, passing the time sleeping or bullshitting with each other about topics ranging from sports to women.

Vance had been put in a cell across from Lavontae's. There was an empty cell next to the other man's, but Lavontae had two neighbors in the one nearest his who were currently squabbling about which of them had banged hotter pussy.

Same shit, different day. At Polk County Jail Lavontae frequently got fed up enough that he had to threaten to knock some heads together just to get some fucking peace. It was almost the highlight of his days. Broke up the monotony.

Something came skittering into his cell. Lavontae looked down at the folded-up bill. That Vance could sling those things like tiny flying saucers right through the bars. He bent to pick it up, looked over at the man, grinning broadly. Vance was on the edge of his bunk, staring fixedly at him.

And Lavontae knew it was showtime.

He turned to the next cell and sent the flying bill through the bars. It took the occupants a moment to figure out what it was. None of them, Lavontae figured, would ever work for NASA. But belatedly two of them dove for the money, fists and curses flying as they fought for possession.

Lavontae's voice sounded over the ruckus. "Bitches, bring me that bill. You know it's mine."

The man who had eye gouged his cell mate and come up with the Grant gave Lavontae a long look. Decided he liked breathing. "Yeah, sure. Here you go." He came over to pass the bill between the bars, and Lavontae grabbed the inmate by the neck of his loose orange jumpsuit and used his considerable strength to slam him repeatedly against the bars.

The inmates erupted in cheers. Items clattered against the bars, and in a burst of enthusiasm more fights broke out. By the time the jailers came pounding into the area, and Lavontae dropped his opponent to the ground, the other man's face was unrecognizable and he was barely conscious.

He went back to his bunk and stretched out, watching the proceedings with interest. The uninjured man next to him was secured, and a medical officer was allowed into the cell. After a couple of moments, the man looked up at a jailer. "Call an ambulance. He's lost some teeth, and his facial injuries need to be x-rayed." Then his gaze went to the cell across from Lavontae's. "What the hell is wrong with him?"

Mason Vance was on the floor, his body jerking uncontrollably, his mouth frothing, eyes rolling in his head.

"Get two ambulances," the medical officer shouted.

Lavontae grinned in delight. Yes, sir. He sure did admire those with know-how.

Chapter 9

We hit pay dirt again on the Rose Macomber credit card." Cam was standing behind his desk looking at his computer screen. Agent Samuels had just spelled Agent Patrick on the surveillance videos on the laptops. One of the screens had been split to show the camera feed at the third hotel.

"Baxter used this one before?" Sophia looked up from her laptop on which she was transcribing the notes from that morning.

"As recently as yesterday. One hundred dollars at the Walmart on Stagecoach Drive in West Des Moines. And"—his voice took on a note of suppressed excitement—"eighty-seven dollars at the neighboring gas station."

Samuels gave a slow, satisfied smile. "Gas station means surveillance camera."

"And by reviewing the footage we might discover what she's driving." Cam nearly sprinted to the door. "I'm taking Franks with me. Soph, staying or going?"

As if there was even a choice. She stood and slipped her laptop into her briefcase and joined him at the door. And wondered as she followed him if the noose was finally beginning to tighten around Vickie Baxter.

———

After the prisoner was handcuffed to the metal stretcher, EMTs Daniel Adams and Rusty Simmons lifted the gurney into the back of the ambulance with a well-practiced move before crawling in after it. Daniel expertly fitted the oxygen mask over the man's face, while the other EMT started the IV.

Rusty looked up when the driver got in. "Hansen? What are you doing? You've got the other vehicle."

The driver shrugged. "Pavlovich wanted to trade. I don't know what his problem is." An FBI agent opened up the front passenger door and climbed in. "Police escort behind this vehicle and the second." He looked back to check on the prisoner. "You guys ready to roll?"

"Give us a minute here," Rusty said, but Hansen had already put the vehicle in gear to lurch ahead of the other ambulance. "When did that guy become such a prick?" he asked the other EMT.

But Daniel Adams was busy checking the prisoner's vitals. His hands shook as the man on the gurney opened his eyes. Looked straight into his. Fingers fumbling, Adams reached into his shirt. Brought out the TASER and turned it on Rusty at the same time that Hansen reached over and stunned the agent. Both the wounded men yelped. The fed slumped forward against his seat belt, and Hansen reached over to grab him by his shirt. Pull him upright.

"Oh fuck, oh fuck," Adams moaned. He backed away from the gurney. Kept the stun gun pointed at his partner, who was still writhing on the floor of the ambulance. "Did you disable the tracking system?"

"Why the hell do you think we're in this one? Hang on." Hansen hung back until the lead police escort car was through the light before speeding up and taking a hard right, barreling down the side street.

"Turn off the siren!" Adams screamed.

The order was lost as an ear-deafening explosion sounded behind them. The force of it jolted the vehicle forward, causing it to teeter on one side precariously as it was pelted by debris. Hansen pulled hard at the wheel, and it righted itself even as he floored the accelerator.

"Get these fucking cuffs off me." Mason Vance sat up on the gurney, yanking the IV and mask off. "Do it now!"

Adams shoved his hand in his pocket. Drew out the keys that had been in the box with the TASER and a prepaid cell phone that had been delivered after the first contact had been made. The texts with attached pictures of Henry. Tied up in a trunk. Looking small and helpless. Like a child whose father had failed to keep him safe.

He wiped away the tears streaming down his face and obeyed Vance's command. His hands shook as he unlocked the cuffs securing him to the side of the gurney and then the shackles on his legs. "Henry. I did everything she said—now tell me where to find him."

"What . . . what . . ." The FBI agent was struggling to speak, then was thrown to the side when Hansen took another right down an alley not open for traffic. The mirrors scraped the buildings as they passed through it, the vehicle bouncing over downed garbage cans.

Vance grabbed the TASER from Adams and leaned forward to stun the fed again. A long steady stream of fifty thousand volts.

"Stop!" Adams shoved his arm. "You'll kill him."

"That's the point, asshole." The man then shot another stream into the other EMT. The ambulance jumped a curb, careened to the left, sirens sounding close behind. Too close. Daniel looked behind him. The windows were tinted, but a flash of strobe could be seen between buildings to the back and left of them.

They sped down the streets, slamming from one side of the vehicle to the other as Hansen took a series of sharp turns. Finally,

Daniel was thrown violently against the wall as the driver turned sharply again. The ambulance came to a shuddering, screeching halt with an overhead door descending behind them.

"What . . ." Adams moistened his lips. His ears were still ringing. "What do we do now?"

"Shut the fuck up and wait." Minutes crawled by. Five. Ten. Then there was a bang on the double back doors of the vehicle. Vance tried to open them, but they must have been damaged in the blast. He kicked at the doors from the inside as the banging outside them continued. Then they were pulled open, and a woman stood framed in them. And when she spoke, Adams heard the horrible haunting voice from those phone calls.

"Hey, Mase," she said to the prisoner. "How was your ride?"

~

"There she is." Special Agent Tommy Franks stepped aside to allow Sophia closer to the computer screen in the gas station's office. She peered closely at the surprisingly clear digital feed.

Vickie Baxter was shown clearly at pump three putting the gas nozzle into a midsize dark-brown sedan. She climbed back in her car for the duration, likely to escape the heat. Six minutes ticked by on the digital clock showing on the DVR feed before she got back out, unhitched the hose, and paid at the pump with her credit card. All of them drew closer to the screen as she drove away.

"AO . . . or was it AC . . . Replay it," Cam ordered. Tommy did so. Three times before Cam gave up. He looked at the gas station manager, a young man barely out of high school. "Which cameras would give us views of the car as it approached and left?"

"Six and four," he said immediately. They all parted to allow him to the computer, where he tapped in some commands and brought up a screen split into a dozen camera shots. He zeroed in on number six. They watched as the car drove up to the pump. The screen clearly showed the entire number. A Missouri plate. ACX1207.

Sophia drew in a breath as Cam gave Tommy an enthusiastic thump on the shoulder. This was it. The biggest break in the case since Baxter had escaped minutes before Cam's team had reached the farmhouse where she'd been staying. As much as the woman had seemed to be on the move, surely police would spot it once an alert was issued on the vehicle.

"It looks like a twenty fourteen Impala. Maybe a twenty thirteen," Tommy corrected himself.

"Can we get a screenshot of the car?" Cam asked the manager. "Two or three different angles."

"No problem." The young man's fingers flew over the keyboard. A moment later the printer in the corner of the office began to whir. Cam's cell rang, and he took a few steps away from the group to answer it.

"They've got pretty sweet equipment in here," the young man said. "And we need it, too. You wouldn't believe how many people think they can get away with driving off without paying. It's a real problem."

"Where? Who's in pursuit? Goddammit. I'll be there." He disconnected. The expression on his face had a pool of dread forming in Sophia's stomach. It turned to ice with his next words.

"Mason Vance escaped this morning. Law enforcement lost sight of the vehicle."

"Get zip ties on these assholes and gag 'em." Obediently Vickie dropped the crowbar and started digging in the oversize bag she carried while Vance checked out the place she'd rented four weeks ago.

The warehouse had seen better days. The windows had been broken out and replaced with plywood that was then painted a dark color. The wood was splintered, the paint peeling.

But no one from the outside would be able to see in, either.

In preparation for the ambulance's arrival, Vickie had set up a couple of battery-operated LED spotlights around the area. Their brightness, and the shine of the headlights, was the only thing that split the gloom in the large interior.

Mason walked back to the vehicle, a hand held to one ear. "Fucking explosion. I'm lucky to still have my hearing."

"You're here, aren't you? And the cops following you aren't." She was still shaking from the experience. She'd had the explosive in a backpack near the curb, nearly hidden by a parked car. This time it hadn't been possible to use a bomb with a timer. She'd had to wait down the block with the detonator, but the timing had been critical. Once she'd seen the ambulance clear the corner, she'd triggered the remote and run for the warehouse without looking back at the resulting chaos.

"Did you bring everything?" Vickie was finishing securing the EMTs in the back. "The rest of it's in a pack over there. Jesus, why don't you take care of a couple of these guys?"

"I'll handle the fed." Mason Vance rounded the vehicle to yank open the front passenger door. The agent was still jerking uncontrollably from that last blast he'd given him. "He looks like I did when I took those fucking capsules you gave Paulsen. What the hell were they anyway?"

"Your get-out-of-jail-free card," she snapped.

Vance searched the agent, relieved him of his weapon. "Fucking pussy." He brought up his arm to hold the TASER against the man's neck. The fed's eyes rolled wildly, but he couldn't even move away. The long jolt of electricity Mason gave him had him slumping forward. Completely still.

He went around to the other side, dragged the driver out of the ambulance. "My wife. My wife, Lisa," the man stammered, as Vance hauled him around to the back and shoved him inside the vehicle. "Please. She said she'd let Lisa go. I didn't report it. I did everything she asked. Please."

"Yeah, we'll let her go," Vickie said with a frown at Vance. "The kid, too. As soon as we leave here, you'll all be found, eventually. There's an office here in the back. I'll leave a note there about where to find both of them."

Vance gave a nasty laugh, and Vickie secured the driver, before crawling up front to get the keys. Then she jumped out of the vehicle with the bag and closed the doors, tossing the keys to Vance.

"You get everything we talked about? You didn't forget nothing?"

"I got everything. I *did* everything." God, she'd forgotten what an asshole Mase could be. "While you've been laying on your ass all day for the last several weeks, I've been taking care of things." He didn't need to know that she'd added to the original plan. That was her business. "You didn't leave me enough cash to get all this done, either. I had to use some of my own, and that's fucking bullshit. You're paying me back from your cut."

Mason grabbed her by the hair, hauled her close. "No, what's fucking bullshit is having to listen to you bitching and moaning the minute I finally get out of that hellhole." He shoved her, hard enough to send her sprawling, knocking over one of the spotlights so its glare was directed beyond them.

He looked past her. "What the fuck." He strode over, and defensively she rolled away, but not quickly enough. His kick still caught her on the hip. "You only brought one goddamned set of wheels?"

She struggled to her feet. Dusted herself off. She could already feel the pain radiating through her body. On a level no one else could ever understand, it felt good. Normal. Life was pain. Vickie never felt more alive than when she was giving or receiving it.

"The idea was two motorcycles. By splitting up we divide their attention. You stupid, stupid bitch. Can't follow simple directions."

"Fuck you." Her punch in the gut caught him unaware, and the breath whooshed out of him. "There's a little thing called money, but you don't want to hear about how much all these details cost. I've got a car. I traded the truck under the table to some guy in Missouri for it. They're only going to be expecting to see one person on the cycle, anyway. Most guys get busted out of jail might say thank you." She didn't bother to tell him that had he had his own set of wheels, she couldn't be sure where he'd decide to go when they got out of here. This way, together on one bike, she still controlled the situation.

"Still mean as a swamp rat, aren't you? I'll give you that one." He rubbed his stomach where she'd hit him, but she didn't kid herself. He'd make her pay for it later. "Got my clothes? I'm sure the hell not leaving here wearing this fucking jumpsuit."

"In here."

He grabbed the bag still in her hand and pulled out the jeans and shirt she'd brought. "I gotta piss. This place have a bathroom?"

"Maybe we could head to the Ritz so you can have a fucking spa day." Her voice was caustic. "Just take a leak in the corner, for God's sake, change your clothes, and let's get this thing done."

She could hear the trickle of urine hitting cement as she turned her back and walked over to the backpack she'd brought when she'd arrived in the middle of the night.

"Okay." Vance came trailing over. "Where's the other stuff you brought?"

She went to the backpack and dug around in it. Handed him a weapon.

"A SIG. Nice." He dropped the fed's gun into the backpack and pulled up his shirt to jam the SIG in his waistband next to a stun gun he'd stashed there. She hoped he'd blow something off, just to teach him a lesson. "Everything go off as planned at Water Works Park?"

She smirked, wishing she could have hung around to watch the panic she'd set in motion. "It's all over the news. One of the bombs detonated at four thirty. Sent a dozen bicyclists to the hospital. Injured a bunch more. They'll be looking for more explosives for hours." The details she gave in her anonymous 911 call would make sure of that.

He grunted. "The smaller one you set off for the police escort nearly took us out with it. Don't be bitching about your expenses. I paid out the ass for those explosives. Spent lots of time learning how to use them, too. Not to mention teaching you."

"There's one left in the pack." No use telling him she'd saved another at the motel. Her plans for it were none of his business. Her nape itched. She could almost feel the press of cops in the area. "Hurry up. Let's get the fuck out of here."

"Relax." He lifted the bundle of tightly wrapped explosives from the backpack and went to the ambulance. "This will only take a few minutes."

***

The area south of Martin Luther King Parkway had seen only sporadic efforts at urban renewal. On good days the neighborhood had an aura of shabby decay. But today, around the perimeter of the search area, it looked like a war zone.

The streets were closed to traffic, clogged with law enforcement. Cam had left his car there, too, with a very shaken Sophie inside. Until he knew what the risk level was, she was far safer in a locked vehicle surrounded by uniformed officers intent on keeping the gawkers away.

Because Mason Vance was on the loose again. There was an ulcerated burn in his gut. The man had kidnapped Sophie. Had planned to rape, torture, and kill her the way he had the other victims. She rarely spoke of the emotional aftereffects that were a result of her ordeal, but he knew they were there. Had held her when she woke from a dream, a scream on her lips, her body trembling. He noticed the way she had to steel her spine sometimes just to enter the shower.

The certainty of Vance's continued incarceration had been the one thing she could count on to ward off the haunting memories.

And now that certainty was gone.

With Tommy Franks at his side, he made his way toward the cluster of DMPD and Polk County sheriff personnel that seemed to be directing the search, flashing his badge to any uniform that tried to halt their progress. He recognized Polk County sheriff Dusten Jackson, who held a rolled-up map in his hand, but Cam didn't know all the men with him.

"Prescott." Jackson broke midsentence at their approach. "You must have sprouted wings after I called." Briefly he made introductions. "Captain Mark Tibbitts, DMPD watch commander; Lieutenant Cal Ellis, Metro STAR tactical commander; my chief deputy, Tanner Ott . . ."

"The others I know." Cam nodded at FBI agent Mila Sparks and US Marshal Hank Krieger. "DCI special agents Cam Prescott and Tommy Franks. We arrested Vance."

"We followed the case," Tibbitts said. Tiny twin images of Cam were reflected in the man's mirrored glasses when he looked at him. "Hell of a thing. This escape was orchestrated. He had help."

Jackson nodded grimly, his gaze going to the officers searching door to door. "We think one of the other inmates was paid off to start a distraction. When the medical officer responded, he noticed Vance having a seizure. The officer followed protocol, applying first aid while an ambulance was summoned. Two ambulances—" The man broke off as his cell pinged, and he read a text from it. Then he continued on with the thought. "The distraction I mentioned? Another inmate required medical care, as well. Because Vance is a federal prisoner, FBI agent Mike Simms accompanied him. We had two escort vehicles. Ambulance went off route and when the police vehicle followed"—his jaw tightened—"an explosive took the car out. The officers were seriously injured. The street behind the emergency vehicle was impassable. By the time the second escort car got down the next street, the ambulance was no longer in sight."

"Vance and Baxter orchestrated this whole thing. The RAGBRAI explosives and now this." Cam was stunned at the level of sophistication the two had managed. The planning.

"The sheriff didn't recall anything in the Cornbelt Killings case file that indicated Vance and Baxter were familiar with explosives," Krieger put in.

Sheriff Jackson had been peripherally involved in the case since some of the bodies were discovered in his jurisdiction. Which likely explained his showing up in person to this scene. "Explosives weren't part of their signature, no," Cam replied. "But we have gotten reports that the two had been trying to get their hands on some in the last few months. Didn't find evidence that they'd acquired any, but a bulletin was sent out about their inquiries."

"Looks like they succeeded." Mila Sparks's mouth was flattened to a thin line. "But they had help inside that ambulance. Had to."

"The driver was either in on it or coerced," Franks agreed. "And at least one of the EMTs." "We just identified the vehicle Baxter's been driving and sent out a statewide BOLO on it. Iowa State Patrol is providing two planes to aid in the surveillance. I'll direct one to assist in this search." Cam looked around the group. "You have a bomb squad on scene?"

"As you can imagine, we're stretched pretty thin there." Jackson's meaning was clear. "We've got a few men from one unit at work on the scene where they took out the escort vehicle." The Des Moines area had two local assets for such incidents, the state Fire Marshal Division and DMPD. "But we have units coming from Cedar Rapids and Council Bluffs to assist."

Jackson unrolled the map he still held across the trunk of his cruiser. "You can see in red the intended route for emergency vehicles to the medical center. The ambulance veered off here." He jabbed an index finger at an intersection that was highlighted in yellow.

"So the lead escort car would need to make a U-turn, and by the time the rear one responded, the bomb had been detonated." Cam studied the map. With the destruction to the street, the ambulance had gotten a valuable lead.

"What's the X refer to?"

"Last visual of the vehicle." Ellis, the Metro STAR commander took over. "And these circles"—he indicated four areas on the map—"are where we have marksmen located." The men would be situated atop buildings in the search area reporting intel back to command, Cam knew. "DMPD is doing a canvass of the apartments in case the fugitive has taken shelter in one of them. But the ambulance has to be in one of four warehouses we don't have visual into."

Cam traced the dotted black circle designating the search area, then glanced up to scan the street before him. The neighborhood they'd be focusing on was a two-block square still gripped in urban neglect. Warehouses crowded against abandoned buildings and dilapidated tenements. The bright neon sign of an occasional bar dotted the street, but the sidewalks were oddly deserted.

Or maybe that wasn't so odd. Residents in the area had limited eyesight and memories when it came to talking to the police.

"Sounds like our next order of business"—Cam looked at the others in the group—"is to get visual into those boarded-up buildings." This was where Metro STAR would excel.

And every resource was going to be needed to bring a quick end to Vance's escape attempt.

———

Vance was taking forever. Vickie suspected he didn't know what the fuck he was doing. She didn't care how much he thought he'd learned about explosives. It wasn't exactly like learning to ride a bike. After coming this far, she didn't want to get blown up by a dumbass with a bomb.

Everything to this point had gone off without a hitch. Because *she'd* been in charge, she thought. But now that the deal was done, nerves were scrambling up her spine. She'd taken pains to change her appearance when she'd needed to move around the city, but here she felt trapped. Jumpy. It came from knowing the goddamned cops were all over the area searching for Vance. The plan they'd come up with months ago in case one of them was caught suddenly seemed riddled with flaws.

The end result would be worth it, though. Once they pooled the money they'd stashed away, they could set up in another location while they figured out a new operation. Sonny wouldn't be around to help this time. A pang struck her. Maybe she'd hang on to the kid. Henry. If she taught him right, he'd learn to be better help than Sonny ever was. Smarter, without the crazy that had made her son so unpredictable.

The back and front sides of the building had once been lined with large metal overhead doors. A few were still operational. Others had been boarded over. There was also a regular exit to the alley in the back next to the office. She went to it now. Unlocked the dead bolts and eased it open.

The alley was empty, with the exception of a drunk sleeping it off on a pile of garbage next to a dumpster. She watched the street that ran past the alley's end. Saw a cop cruiser go by, no lights, no siren. But no other cars passed. *Shit.* Likely they had the area barricaded already.

She ducked inside again, went back to where she'd left her things. Vance was still busy, so she took out her phone. Earlier in the week she'd slipped in here just to make sure she could get cell phone reception in the old warehouse. She'd been half amazed when she could. Fucking technology was unbelievable.

Scrolling through the channels on the police scanner app she'd downloaded, Vickie found nothing that pertained to them. There was plenty, however, about the RAGBRAI bombing. She chuckled. As much as she hated handling the damn explosives, they'd been a pretty good diversion so far.

"What are you doing?"

She jumped a foot. Jesus, she was nervous. Turning, she glared at the man grinning at her. "Asshole. I'm checking the police scanner. Haven't found a thing about your escape. Thought maybe we could listen to the cops' search."

Since there was no point to it, she slipped the cell into her backpack. Then she took out the map she'd prepared.

"Here." Thrusting it at him, she buckled the pack. "Better learn where the fuck we're headed to."

Vance studied the map much too briefly and then jammed it into a pocket in his jeans. He went to one of the helmets she had next to the cycle. Put it on. When he spoke next, his voice was muffled, even with the visor up. "They're probably keeping it off the radios in case we're listening. Which we are."

Vickie rolled up the bag, which was now half-empty. It was a tight fit in the backpack. She struggled to get the pack over her shoulders, and then secured it with a strap around her waist. "You done with everything?" She reached for the second helmet and put it on, tucking her hair beneath it.

He laughed, low and ugly. "I'm not going to be the one who's *done* once those back doors to the ambulance open. But yeah. Ready to roll." He picked up the two overhead garage door openers, which still sat next to the motorcycle. "Which of these opens the back one?"

Jesus. There were times she really wondered how the man walked and talked without help. "The one with the word *back* written on it in Magic Marker."

He shot her a look. "Haven't missed your smart mouth at all, Vick. But I missed all the time I put in teaching you when to shut it."

Sizzles of excitement popped through her veins, and her nerves faded. Some of those times with Vance had been memorable, when he didn't get carried away. "Maybe later you can give me a refresher. For now"—she waited for him to get on the cycle and then settled on it behind him—"gimme the opener." She aimed it at the lone door that worked on the back wall and it creaked slowly upward. When they were out she'd close it again. No use making things easy for the cops. "Let's move out."

⁓

"I was beginning to believe you had intentions of leaving me in the car all day."

Cam slanted Sophia a glance. "No use you standing around in the heat until I figured out what the situation was."

Until he'd assessed the threat, he meant. She hadn't needed to run the air conditioner much while she waited, because the thought of Mason Vance on the loose with Vickie Baxter again had chilled her to the bone.

As they walked Cam filled her in on what he'd learned so far. "Maria's on her way," he finished. "Sheriff's office, DMPD, and SWAT are already represented. I'm figuring it's only a matter of time until Assistant Director Miller shows up with city brass in tow. I want everyone brought up-to-date about the killers before then because once the suits start flooding the scene, things go downhill quickly."

The leaders would then need to spend more of their time pacifying and explaining than strategizing. Sophia's step quickened. Cam was right. Every minute was vital.

"We've isolated the abandoned buildings in the area, and Tommy is chasing down the property ownership." As if realizing he was outdistancing her with his stride, Cam slowed his pace. "We've got Metro STAR members using three-dimensional imaging devices on those buildings that lack interior visual access. We'll know soon if the ambulance is in the area."

"Any word from the personnel at the motels?" On their way to the scene Cam had lost no time placing an agent in each of the motel rooms they'd tracked to Baxter.

He shook his head as they walked up to the tight knot of law enforcement members watching a SWAT member work the block, affixing the audio set to the building and listening for sound inside. When he introduced Sophia, Jackson immediately asked, "Dr. Channing, based on the profiles you've developed for Vance and Baxter, can you predict their next move?"

It was her least favorite sort of query, and exactly the kind of question she was asked most in situations like these. "Always the offenders are going to behave in the way that best meets their needs, which right now would be to evade police. I would be concerned about the hostages in the ambulance. Once they've served their purpose . . ."

Mila Sparks's face went ashen, making Sophia regret her words.

"Mike Simms is in that ambulance. One of my colleagues."

Tibbitts turned to look at her. "Are we sure Baxter would be on-site?"

"Almost certainly." There was no question in her mind. "She has likely spent the time since Vance's arrest arranging all the details for his escape. And they probably planned for such an eventuality prior to his capture."

"So they'd have a place to go to already set up."

"Yes." The heat index wasn't as high as yesterday, but it was still hot enough to have Sophia's temples dampening. "I think it will be one of the motel rooms she's booked. It sounds like she's been using them on a rotating basis, and I can't figure a reason for that if she has some other safe spot to use."

Doubtfully, Sparks said, "Seems more likely they'd just take off. Try to get out of the area. Leave the state."

"I don't doubt that they will. But first . . . There's a reason Baxter has done all this for Vance, and it isn't her undying love for him. They have unfinished business to tend to together. That will come first."

Metro STAR Commander Ellis retreated a few steps, listening to the communication headset he wore. Moments later he turned back to the group. "We have a visual of a motorcycle leaving the area. Two riders. Gender undetermined." Cam, Jackson, Sparks, and Krieger ran toward it had been their cars.

The law enforcement vehicles sped away with squealing tires, sirens sounding. Captain Tibbitts bit off orders into a hand-held radio. Nausea circled in Sophia's stomach as she realized he was directing DMPD cars to join the pursuit with Cam and the others.

She was all too aware that if it was Baxter and Vance on board the motorcycle, both of them were likely armed.

—

"In pursuit of a navy Harley Sportster traveling east on Kingsley Boulevard. Two passengers. License plate Peter Benjamin Lincoln five eight nine," Jackson reported over his radio.

Cam had the Iowa State Patrol Air Wing pilot on speakerphone. "You hear all that?"

"Even better, I've got visual. But the driver just took a right into an alley."

The Polk County sheriff engaged the radio mic again to relay the development. "Driver turned right in an alley off Kingsley between eleven and twelve hundred block. Get a car on A Avenue. Hem him in."

Cam had the Des Moines city map spread across his lap. The pilot's voice was heard. "Vehicle has cleared the alley, turned north on A Avenue."

"Get a cruiser on Frontier, Greenhill Road, K and L Avenues, thirteen hundred block, and north. Trap him." Jackson repeated Cam's order, skidded around a corner, and they had a visual themselves. The motorcycle was several blocks ahead.

Adrenaline was churning in Cam's veins. At the same time he recalled the diversion Vance had arranged in the jail that morning. He hoped like hell they weren't chasing one now.

—

Special Agent in Charge Maria Gonzalez had arrived on scene shortly after Cam left and was being briefed by Franks and Lieutenant Ellis.

Conversation broke off when a Metro STAR team member, clad in black helmet and flak vest, jogged up to confer with Ellis.

"Sergeant Jared Johns," the commander said in an aside to the rest of the group as the man approached.

The SWAT officer stopped, pulling off his helmet to reveal short-cropped blond hair and a lean jaw. "We've located the ambulance at eleven forty-three Front Street in an abandoned warehouse. There's a large stationary object located in the center of the two left quadrants. Dimensions match those of the emergency vehicle."

"Signs of life?" Sophia asked hopefully.

The man turned his blue gaze on her, nodded. His face glistened with perspiration. "Display shows five shapes within one static object. Little movement, all within close proximity. We've got no imaging outside the dimensions of the vehicle. Unless the escapee is lying nearly motionless within that vehicle, he's no longer in there."

"Proceed with the breach," Ellis ordered. Johns nodded, turned, and jogged away, replacing his helmet as he ran.

"Owner of the address is one Emmett Leach," Agent Franks told the SAC, studying his notes on his cell.

"If you have his personal information, make the contact. But I'm not waiting on a warrant. Exigent circumstances."

A horrible sense of comprehension filled Sophia. "Based on what we now know about Vance and Baxter's newly acquired expertise with explosives," she said slowly, "I assume you'll have bomb technicians check out the building before the breach." Her gaze met Ellis's. "Those two aren't known for leaving their victims alive."

⁓

The tires of the sheriff's cruiser screeched as Jackson turned sharply into the alleyway after the motorcycle. The neighborhood had turned more residential, with small homes huddled close together interspersed with the occasional business. "I need a cruiser midway down the fifteen hundred block of Greenhill to block the alley exit. Suspect is westbound and coming fast."

A second cruiser screamed to a halt moments later at the opposite end of the passageway, and the motorcycle driver looked behind him. Then veered off through the bordering yard on their left.

"Shit." The sheriff put the car in gear again.

Cam was in constant contact with the Air Wing pilot, who was guiding their moves. "Cruisers on the sixteen hundred block of Dallas Street," he directed Jackson, who relayed the message to the pursuit team. But on the next block the motorcycle driver reversed course and sped through a group of kids playing baseball in a street before taking to the yards again, temporarily out of sight.

"He can't take residential areas indefinitely." Cam narrowed his gaze on the map, concentrating. "Where the hell is he heading?"

His answer came in the next moment. "You've got swarms of bicyclists eastbound on the MLK Parkway. And on Grand." The pilot's voice sounded over the speakerphone. "If the driver heads north, he's going to run right through them."

Jackson's head swiveled toward Cam. "The RAGBRAI riders were supposed to be rerouted to Hickman."

Foreboding settled like lead in Cam's belly. "And there *will* be thousands more on Hickman. Likely hundreds in between the two roads." Other bikers would have been placed at the fairgrounds, and still more arranged to stay with friends or acquaintances at each stop of the RAGBRAI trip. Inevitably there would be bicyclists who'd failed to hear of the new route. And some motivated by panic, looking for the quickest way out of town.

As if he'd heard the pilot's words, the motorcyclist turned north. "Get cruisers on Leer. Cut him off before he gets to Grand Avenue."

The order came too late. With a burst of speed the cycle roared onto the street in the midst of the bikers. Jackson slowed to a stop. "God almighty, he's going to kill someone."

Traffic was already slow, snarled by the horde of bicyclists trying to make their way out of the city. Vance—because surely he was the driver—was racing across the lanes, disregarding the safety of those around him. Law enforcement didn't have that option, Cam noted grimly. Some of the most effective pursuit maneuvers couldn't be utilized, precisely because of the proximity to citizens.

"Get cars to the streets blocking access to Interstate 235." Jackson radioed the order as he reversed course to find a safer way across Grand. Frustration and urgency warred inside Cam. With the bike ride and the bombings, they didn't have the available manpower to cover all the roads for an effective pursuit. And the longer the chase lasted, the greater the chance of injury to a passerby.

They still had the pilot for visual. He clung to that thought as they pulled to a stop at a red light, watching the bikers go by. Vance couldn't outrun the plane. But given their lack of personnel, they needed to outthink the killers . . .

He frowned. "Is Fifty-Sixth still closed for construction?"

Jackson finished on the radio before answering. "It was last week. Looked like they had weeks of work ahead of them before . . ." Seizing on Cam's meaning, he engaged the radio again. "Attention cars in the vicinity of Grand and Fifty-Sixth. Suspect may enter the construction zone." He turned onto Grand.

Minutes later the pilot's voice sounded. "You must have a crystal ball. The driver took Fifty-Sixth."

Jackson repeated the information. "Tell me someone has the motorcycle in sight."

"He's driving across the Waveland Golf Course, and I am in pursuit. Damn." A disembodied voice sounded moments later, disgusted. "He's reentered Fifty-Sixth headed north, and there is no road. Repeat, pavement is missing for the next mile or so. He's on the shoulder. I've got no entry."

The sheriff released an imaginative string of expletives.

"More bikes on University. Looks like they are being redirected by law enforcement," came the pilot's voice.

"Call off close pursuit," Cam advised. "Just keep the cars in the motorcycle's vicinity. It's too dangerous." The throngs of bike riders and knotted up traffic made a high-speed chase irresponsible. "We've got visual. We're not going to lose him."

"He'll head for Hickman." Jackson's hands gripped the wheel tightly. "He has to. He probably thinks he can get lost in the crowd there."

"But where's he heading after that?" Cam stared sightlessly at the map before him. "None of the motels we've traced to Baxter are on Hickman or in the area. Unless he plans to double back." But somehow he doubted it. Vance would have a destination in mind.

And Cam was all too aware that although they'd found three hotels where Baxter had registered, there could be more.

They'd long since lost sight of the motorcycle. Following the pilot's updates, they drove for a time until the man said, "Vehicle took the Merle Hay exit."

Jackson passed along the information to the pursuit team, but there was a frown on his face. "Where the hell are they headed? To 80/35?"

The muscles in Cam's belly tightened as a sense of certainty filled him. "Maybe. Or maybe he plans to stop before he gets there. Looking at the sheriff, he added, "What better place to get lost in a crowd than at a mall?"

Chapter 10

Sophia had thought it was stressful watching the bomb dog and its handler work. But realizing Jared Johns was assembled with the entry unit of the Metro STAR team and ready to breach the warehouse had her clutching her fingers together in anxiety.

A shiny black tactical truck had rolled up the street from the building housing the ambulance, and a communications officer provided updates to the law enforcement leaders.

Sophia waited next to Franks a couple of blocks away from the site. They all huddled around a laptop sitting on the front of a cruiser. On the screen they had a real-time vantage point from which they could view what was happening at the building.

The warehouse was fronted with three garage doors and one regular entrance that had a piece of plywood over its window. The K-9 dog hadn't alerted more strongly to that entrance than it had to the overhead doors, so it had been chosen for entry.

Two dark-clothed team members wielded a battering ram. The door swung open violently at first contact, and the team members stepped aside for the K-9 handler.

"No verbal response, but there's banging on the inside of the vehicle in response to questions," the liaison reported via the radio wielded by Ellis. "Dog has alerted only on the vehicle, most strongly at the rear." The K-9 handler walked out to meet an individual trudging forward carrying a case and wearing a Kevlar suit that covered him from head to foot.

The man went inside, and the entry team swarmed after him. Moments later the center overhead door rose.

What followed then was the most harrowing scene Sophia had ever witnessed. The tactical team withdrew and the explosives expert approached the vehicle with a long-handled device he'd taken out of the case and assembled. He swept it slowly beneath the undercarriage of the ambulance. And then again. Next he started with the driver's side of the vehicle and ran a handheld device over each of the front doors.

"What's he doing?"

"Bomb-detecting device," Franks explained. "He's trying to figure out a point of entry."

She looked at him. Hesitated. Unsure whether to ask the question that was uppermost on her mind. "What have you heard from Cam?"

"Aerial surveillance is directing the pursuit. Last I heard they were heading for a mall. Merle Hay."

"What—" She broke off when a small robotic machine on wheels went wheeling into the garage, seemingly on its own. The bomb technician on-screen bent down to take something else from the case. Fixed it to one of the robotic claws. Then he walked clumsily to the door and disappeared from view.

Sophia realized she was holding her breath. Expelled it. Whoever was running the robot remotely had it raising its robotic arm to window height. Pressing something against the glass. A few minutes later a large hole appeared in the window of the passenger door. Somewhat jerkily the robot withdrew its robotic arm and laid the tool on the cement. Then it approached the window again, arm reaching up and inside the hole. It withdrew, and the length of the arm shortened while it seemed to search the exterior of the passenger door. A moment later it had the door pulled open.

"R2-D2 should be that handy," she muttered, and Franks turned to grin at her.

"Never thought I'd hear a *Star Wars* reference coming from you."

"You realize Cam has the entire collection. He forced me to sit through viewings of every one of the movies. I learned to murmur appreciative comments at appropriate intervals."

Two bomb technicians returned to the area wearing full body armor. In a few seconds they had the passenger in front extricated from his seat belt and were supporting him out of the building. From what she could see on the screen, the man was limp. Unresponsive. The FBI agent.

"Front passenger not alert. Technician notes three other victims held in the back. All four are bound and gagged. All are alive."

She expelled a long breath of relief. But the sensation was short-lived. The technicians still had to get the rest of the people out. And then dispose of the bomb attached to the back doors.

And if it detonated before they were able to, there would be six victims instead of four.

Vance jumped the curb outside the main mall entrance and they both got off the motorcycle, leaving it and their helmets behind. Inside the lobby Vickie took off the backpack and unzipped it. Pulled out the bag she'd shoved in there and withdrew its remaining balled up contents to hand to Vance. He disappeared inside the mall, heading for a restroom area where his blue T-shirt would be discarded for the yellow one he wore underneath. The cap and false facial hair would pass all but the closest scrutiny. Vickie had made sure of that when she'd purchased them.

She put the backpack into the bag and swiftly she walked through the store and headed to another shop that carried high-end clothing. She picked out several items from the rack, while keeping an eye on the other shoppers in the store. The mall was busier than she would have expected.

That suited her needs exactly.

When a well-dressed woman in her fifties left her friend to head toward the hallway lined with dressing rooms, Vickie grabbed a handful of garments and followed her.

"Can I take these for you?"

Stupid interfering salesclerk. She forced a smile. "Sure. You have such pretty things."

"Oh, we do," the girl agreed enthusiastically as she led the way down the short hallway. "We already have our fall things in, which seems ridiculous, because it's only July. That's why we're running such a super sale." She stopped before a dressing room and handed Vickie a number. "Three items, right?"

"That's right." She went inside the dressing room, keeping the door cracked so she could watch the clerk's progress. When she was out of sight, Vickie walked to the room the other customer had disappeared into and opened the door.

The woman whirled around, her arms clasped over her bra-clad breasts, her mouth an *O* of surprise.

"Oh, I'm so sorry." Vickie backed out quickly. "I'm right next door—I'm so sorry. I got the wrong room." She closed the door and entered the room next to it.

"Oh, don't worry," the woman's voice floated over the partitions. "I've done the same thing before. It's so *embarrassing*."

"It is. I'm just still shook up from almost breaking an axle in the Sears parking lot. There's a hole in the pavement that practically swallowed the front end of my car. I just know it'll be out of alignment now. Did you see it?"

"I didn't, thank God. I parked outside Younkers. Walked right by the display of the *best* purses. Did you see the sale they're having today? I did so much damage there."

Vickie heard the woman's door open. She peeked out and saw her going down the hall to model the top she was trying on for her friend.

She unzipped her backpack and snatched the garments she'd selected before swinging around the corner into the room to lift the woman's purse off the chair and slip it in her pack. Then walked out again into the store.

The salesclerk hurried up to her. "How did those items work for you? Can I get you a different size or color?"

Vickie shoved the hangers at her. "I'll probably be back," she said over her shoulder. Once out in the mall again, she strode to the public restroom and selected a stall. She took a dark shapeless skirt out of the pack and put it on, then pulled out a long black scarf and wrapped it around her head and the lower part of her face. If she avoided close inspection, she just might pass for a Middle Eastern female.

Turning her attention to the coral handbag she'd stolen, she withdrew the keys and wallet found inside. She put the keys in the pocket of her skirt, tossed the wallet in the backpack, and hung the purse on the hook affixed to the back of the door. Pulling out her cell, she texted Mase.

Vickie dropped the cell into the pack and picked up the bag before exiting the stall, nearly running over two elderly women on their way to the sinks.

As she walked out the door, she heard one of them say to the other, "Isn't that disgusting? She didn't even wash her hands."

The walk to the department store seemed to take a century. Below her she could see a throng of people on the next level, milling around the food court. She didn't know what was going on there, but a crowd could only slow down detection.

A security guard was heading her way, and she kept her head bent, gaze averted. She felt him look at her, but she kept walking. Nonchalant. And when she turned the corner, she was able to see that he had continued moving. Every person he passed was given the same scrutiny.

Eat shit, cop, she thought smugly. *You'll never know how close you came.*

Vickie sailed through Younkers, turning the wrong way a couple of times before finding the display of purses. The first sign of trouble came when she saw a store employee locking the doors just ahead of her. Heart beating double time, she continued up to them and futilely pushed on one.

The woman shook her head. "Sorry. You'll have to use the mall exits. Orders of mall security."

"No English." Vickie held up the keys. Shook them. "Go. Now."

"There's some sort of mall security lockdown. We have to . . ."

"No English." Vickie jangled the keys again.

The woman sighed and took a quick look around. "Okay, fine." She unlocked the door again and held it open for Vickie to pass through before resecuring it.

Grinning behind the veil, Vickie walked toward the lot and pressed the car fob. On cue, the lights flashed on a sassy red Toyota in the next row. She slid in, fit the key to the ignition, and cruised up to the doors she'd just exited. Mase wouldn't be coming through them; that was certain. She checked the rearview mirror, her nerves fraying more with each passing minute.

Finally a man exited the mall and approached the car from the rear. She nearly did a double take when she recognized Mase wearing that beard and mustache. Damn, she'd done good. She barely knew him herself.

He got in, slamming the door after him, and she immediately pulled away. "How'd you get out?" There was no one else leaving the mall that she could see.

"Got stopped by a cop. Tased him and yelled for a doctor. Slipped out when some do-gooder came rushing up." He found the lever to move the seat as far back as it would go. "Let's get the fuck out of here."

They'd been inside the mall just under fourteen minutes.

"Nothing so far," the security guard reported as Cam approached him. Frustrated, Cam looked over the railing. Noticed the mob below. "What's going on with the food court?"

"Indoor farmer's market. They're here weekly all summer. I've got a couple officers down there looking. I alerted the anchor stores, and they're stationing someone at each of their exits. Sent along the pictures you sent me, too."

"We got men at the main doors." Jackson was nearby watching the shoppers across from them on the top level. Vance and Baxter would need transportation. Neither would be above carjacking a vehicle, but the Air Wing pilot would notice that kind of activity.

Fists propped on his hips, he tamped down the increasing spike of urgency and tried to predict their actions. He needed to think like Sophie. Consider the killers' past behavior. Use it to foretell their next move.

He arrowed a look at the security guard. "Have you had any reports of a purse being stolen? Or a set of car keys lost?"

The officer dragged a hand over his sandy crew cut. "Sent a guard to Lisette's just a few minutes ago. I know, I know—I said I'd use all personnel on the search. But I still have to do my—"

"Where's Lisette's?"

The man turned and jerked a thumb behind him. "Turn the corner left when you get there. Second shop on the right."

Cam took off at a jog. "Keep looking," he called back to the guard staring after him. He saw the sheriff turning to head his way, so he kept going until he found the store the guard had indicated. Walked up to the first clerk he saw. "Did a security guard just come in here?"

"I . . ." She looked as though she wasn't sure what to reveal, so Cam dug in his pocket to flash his credentials.

She nodded, pointed to a door in the back of the store. "They're in the office. It's Mrs. Newman. She's a really good customer, and this is so bad for business . . ." Her voice trailed off as he strode away.

Cam identified himself to the guard sitting at the side of the desk and filling out a report form attached to a clipboard. He turned to the woman seated near the man. Her carefully made-up face was streaked with tears, and mascara had smudged beneath her eyes. "I'm DCI special agent Cam Prescott, ma'am. Can you tell me if you had car keys in your purse? Did you drive here?"

"Yes." Her expression was startled. "Do they call DCI for stolen purses?"

Ignoring the question, he pressed, "Your car?"

"Yes, yes, I drove. My keys were in my purse. I'll have to call my hus . . ." Her eyes grew large. "She asked me that! The woman in the dressing room next to me. I was just telling the guard, I don't like to accuse anyone, but she barged in my room and . . . and then we had a conversation about the parking lot and I . . . Dear God, I actually *told* her where I parked!"

"And where was that?"

"West of Younkers. The entrance by the purses. I even told her that," she moaned. "Oh my God, how can I be so stupid?"

Manipulation. Sophie had mentioned it several times. Baxter was a master at it. "Do you know the make and model of your car?"

A flare of irritation shone in her eyes. "Well, of course I do. I'm not a complete moron, current evidence to the contrary. It's a red twenty fourteen Toyota Camry. It has a vanity plate. T-A-Z-Z-Y. That's my husband's nickname for me."

He was already on his way to the door, reaching for the cell in his suit coat pocket. "If we find it, someone will contact you."

"Well, I have to say," the woman could be heard telling the guard, "I never would have expected such excellent service over a stolen purse."

———

"I couldn't do anything different. How could I? She took Lisa." Cody Hansen looked from one face to the other. SAC Gonzalez and Agent Franks were stoic. They'd extensively interviewed all the men taken from the ambulance. They'd asked Sophia to speak to the two who had admitted to assisting in Vance's escape. They'd hoped she'd be able to draw out more details. Or at least give an opinion on the veracity of the stories. Hansen had gone over his story again in her presence and seemed unshakable on the specifics.

She allowed the empathy she felt to sound in her voice. "You were worried about your wife. Baxter threatened to kill her. What did you think might have happened if you'd gone to the police? Maybe they could have helped. Or found her before it got to this point."

He shook his head violently. "You don't know. The pictures she sent . . . They're on that phone she gave me to use. She's got Lisa somewhere dark. Underground it looks like. And she lied to us in the garage. Said directions to where she was would be in the office."

He looked at Gonzalez hopelessly. "But you said there was nothing. I haven't gotten a picture since yesterday." His sobs were wrenching. "She went to kill her. I know it. You wouldn't believe the things she said she was going to do to Lisa. What kind of husband would I have been if I had risked that?"

Sophia tried for several more minutes, but at a cue from Gonzalez she stood. "I know they will do everything possible to find your wife, Mr. Hansen."

There was no response. He had his head in his hands, weeping.

They walked a short way down the hallway to stand outside another patient room. "Their stories are nearly identical. But Adams claimed Baxter took his son."

A fist squeezed her heart. Kidnapping women . . . That had been Baxter's MO long enough to be unsurprising. Long enough for Sophia to fear for what might have happened to Lisa Hansen already. But a child . . .

They pushed into the hospital room. Found Daniel Adams gazing straight ahead unblinkingly. At first Sophia worried that the man was catatonic.

She went to his bedside. "Mr. Adams. I'm Dr. Sophia Channing, and I've been working on the Vance case. I'd like to talk to you if I can."

"It was all for nothing." The man's voice was dull. He didn't look at Sophia. Made eye contact with no one. "I risked everything. Everyone. But my boy's still gone." Finally he turned his head to look at Maria. "I wouldn't even care what you did to me. It wouldn't matter. As long as my son . . ." His throat worked, as if choking on the words.

"When did you first know he was missing?"

"Two weeks ago. He was playing outside alone. I was in the garage. Our backyard is fenced in. Safe. When I looked out the garage door and didn't see him, at first I thought he was in the fort part of the swing set. I checked a couple minutes later, but he wasn't playing. He wasn't there."

Shocked, Sophia said, "He disappeared from your backyard in broad daylight?" That was risky. Much riskier behavior than she'd expect from Vickie Baxter.

A dull flush crept up his cheeks. "I . . . I can't be sure. He can work the gate. He could have gone around to the front yard on his own. The garage door was down. I wouldn't have seen him. He's not supposed to, but we live on an acreage and he's sort of used to roaming around it."

In other words, it was a secluded property. "How close are your nearest neighbors?"

"The Tindals are a quarter mile south of us."

Not so risky then, Sophia thought. And Baxter would have scouted the area. Planned how she'd snatch the boy. "Your wife—"

"Died four years ago. Breast cancer."

She glanced at the DCI agents. A person would have to be made of stone to not be moved by the man's plight. It was the most horrific choice imaginable. Help release a vicious killer. Or risk sacrificing your son.

"You don't know where she is." For the first time heat entered his voice, and he directed it at the SAC. "This Baxter. She helped Mason Vance commit the most atrocious murders in the history of the state, and she's still free. Free to take my son. To threaten horrible things." He stopped, clenching his jaw. "How could I put my trust in the police when they didn't know where she was? How could you have found my son?"

"You heard from her yesterday."

He nodded wearily, as if the brief show of anger had exhausted him. "Every few days. She takes a picture with a newspaper propped against him. He was alive yesterday."

A terrible sense of hopelessness filled her, as if transferring from the man before her. She knew from Cam's last message that he hadn't yet caught up with the killers. She didn't want to think about what that might mean for this man's son.

She stayed another fifteen minutes, but Adams said little else. Finally, without waiting for a cue from either of the agents, Sophia rose. Call it a sympathy break, but she couldn't force the man to endure any more today than what he'd already experienced.

Reaching forward, she brushed his hand with hers. "We're going to try to find your son."

He didn't respond until she reached the door, and then his voice was so low she could barely hear him. "She said she wouldn't kill him."

The three of them turned, but it was Sophia who spoke. "Baxter promised she wouldn't?"

"No. She said she'd sell him. To men who use little boys. She described what they'd do to him . . . what kind of life he'd have." His gaze rose then, and his eyes looked like a man enduring the fires of hell. "I would have done anything . . . anything she asked to spare my son that."

Sophia's throat was full. "Your son. What's his name?"

"Henry." He smiled a little, a fleeting curl of the lips. "Henry Sylvester Adams. A big name for such a little guy."

The three of them walked out of the room, down the hallway. "What will happen to him? To both him and Hansen?"

"DA's office will determine whether charges will be brought, but the defense has a pretty solid case for duress." Gonzalez was not unmoved by the interview, Sophia saw now. "I can't see juries finding them guilty for their actions, given what was at stake."

"I wouldn't want to be faced with the choice those two men were presented with," Sophia admitted huskily. She couldn't say with any certainty what decision she would have made in their place.

They headed out the front doors of the hospital toward the parking lot. They'd come in two cars; Maria had driven alone while Sophia had accompanied Franks. "Both of them, Hansen and Adams, are credible. What they described is Baxter's standard procedure. Manipulate. Terrorize. Exploit a vulnerability to bend people to her will." She thought of Cam, on the trail of the two killers, and her voice went husky again. "Our loved ones represent our greatest vulnerability."

"The Polk County sheriff's office are doing an internal investigation into the events leading up to the escape. The inmate they believe started the diversion, Lavontae Cross, had a bundle of fifties hidden inside his mattress. He claimed nearly every time Vance met with the lawyer they shared, he'd fold up a bill and toss it into his cell."

"You suspect the attorney?" Franks reached into his pocket for his sunglasses. Put them on.

"Vance got the money from somewhere, and the attorney was his only visitor. Believe me, we'll be looking at Paulsen hard for unethical behavior, but my point is that Vance isn't above paying for cooperation."

Sophia could see where Maria was going with this. "In my judgment, Hansen and Adams were not paid off. Why waste money when you can leverage a weakness?"

They'd reached the vehicles and stood in front of the two cars, but Maria was still talking. "I have a hard time seeing Baxter doing what it takes to keep not one but two victims alive long enough to pull this off. And the pictures she sent look like both of them are in fair shape."

Although only in her late forties, the SAC was looking every one of her years today, Sophia noted. This case had carved a few more lines in her face. "You think she'd revert to type and engage in torture, as long as she has captives," Sophia said.

The SAC unlocked the car with the remote. "It's who she is. We served warrants on the men's houses, and we already have the cells they claim Baxter gave them, so we'll have definitive answers soon enough. But I can't stop wondering about her kidnapping and keeping the victims relatively unharmed . . . Is that out of character for Vickie Baxter?"

"We don't know what she has planned for them in the end." As Sophia answered, Franks went around to the driver's side of his vehicle and unlocked it, sliding behind the wheel. "Or exactly what she's put them through to date. But Baxter is capable of doing whatever it takes to meet her ends. So, no, this wouldn't be out of character."

She couldn't tell if she'd changed the woman's opinion or not. Probably, like Cam, Maria would wait for the evidence before making up her mind on the veracity of the men's claims. The SAC nodded and walked to her car. Sophia waited until she'd pulled out before using the space to get in the passenger side of the vehicle Franks waited in.

As he left the lot and pulled out into traffic, she inquired, "Are we going back to the ambulance scene?"

His voice when he answered was amused. "You just want to see how it ends."

Sheepishly she nodded. "I do feel like I left in the middle of a movie when we followed the victims to the hospital."

"Bomb disposal is slow work. They'll be at it for hours." He slowed as the light before them turned red. "It's being done remotely. With the robot they were able to diagnose the inner workings of the explosive. Pretty crude, from what I was told. The robot is being used to remove parts of its firing train."

Still a dangerous task. That thought immediately made her think of Cam and wonder how much danger he might be in right at that moment.

Cam met Jackson as he was entering the store. The sheriff immediately turned on his heel to keep pace with him. Cam had already dialed the pilot and was giving the sheriff a condensed version until the pilot answered. Then he broke off to tell him, "They're in a red twenty fourteen Toyota Camry." He spelled the license plate. "It's in the lot on the west side of the mall outside Younkers. If they got to it, it would have had to be in the last five minutes." But he was hoping the duo never got that far. The place was locked down. He'd just been assured of that minutes earlier.

"I'll take a look. And circle around in case they're on the loose." The man seemed upbeat.

Cam disconnected to scroll through his contacts for the next number he needed.

"You doing a BOLO?" the sheriff asked beside him.

"DMPD and Iowa State Patrol. Then I need to update my team."

Jackson picked up the radio mic. "I'll do county and US Marshals." After he'd made the announcement, he glanced over at Cam for a second, his face set in determined lines. "This is it. Has to be."

He didn't answer, but Cam knew exactly what the sheriff meant. There'd been no sightings of the car Baxter had been driving at the gas station. He'd pulled the second Air Wing pilot off that duty when nothing came of it. Baxter hadn't yet returned to any of the motel rooms they had staked out.

If the couple wasn't found in the next hour or two, Cam was beginning to fear that they never would be.

His cell pinged and he glanced down to read the incoming text. Started running. "Officer down," he yelled over his shoulder at Jackson. "It was Vance. Had to be."

Vickie drove around the motel parking lot, looking for a secluded area to leave the car. She found what she was seeking in the portion of the lot reserved for hotel vehicles. After backing into a space between two Econoline vans bearing the motel's logo, the car was as hidden from view as it was going to get.

They wouldn't be staying long, anyway.

"Room one-thirty-two." She reached into the bag to unzip an interior pocket on the backpack and withdrew a packet of motel room cards. She'd written the room numbers on the back, just to keep the damn things straight.

Finding the one she was looking for, she handed it to him. "Give me about ten minutes." She walked away, turned the corner of the motel, and counted windows until she found the one she'd used before. Casting a quick look around and seeing no one, she picked her way through the landscaping and slid the screen and window open.

She leaned in to drop the bag inside. Then backing up to the open window, she braced her hands on the sill and gave a little hop. With legs drawn up, she twirled on her butt until she was facing forward and jumped into the room.

The beds were both made. Empty. She walked swiftly to the bathroom and drew back the shower curtain. He was looking up at her, the tape still secure over his mouth and around his wrists and ankles. Just the way he'd been when she'd moved him last night. She held her finger to her lips and then pulled the curtains closed again as she heard the door opening. Unwrapping the scarf from her head, she dropped it to the floor. Pulled down the skirt and kicked it away. Undoing her jeans, she sat down on the toilet. Jesus, she hadn't pissed all day. Although it had been a near thing the way Mase had driven that fucking motorcycle over curbs and through yards. Her back would be screaming in the morning.

She heard him at the door and hurried to finish. Zipping up, she went to the door and flipped the security latch. He brushed past her to disappear into the bathroom. Shutting the motel door after him, she reengaged the lock.

Exhaustion hit her. She'd been up most of the night getting ready. Not that Mase gave her credit for that. She went to the two new laptops she'd left on the desk and powered them up.

He walked out of the bathroom, minus the cap and facial hair, his jeans still unbuttoned. "Fucking jail food made me fat. This is my size, but they're tighter than shit."

"You'll work it off soon enough."

He leered at her. "That your way of saying you wanna fuck?"

Vickie didn't bother looking up. Like most guys, he was ready all the time. "That'll wait. Let's get this thing done first."

"Jesus, you're greedy."

"I'm practical," she corrected him, looking up. He was right, she realized. He still had his overmuscled physique, but in that shirt he was wearing she could see the start of a gut. While in jail he'd also had to come off the 'roids he'd been taking ever since she'd known him. Which, given the hair-trigger temper he'd developed, didn't seem like such a bad thing.

"First things first." She tried to temper her words with a promising smile, but the truth was she felt an adrenaline crash coming on. The only thing she was planning in the immediate future was eight uninterrupted hours of sleep.

"Fine." He grabbed one of the computers and dropped down on the bed with it. Began typing.

Vickie brought up the URL of the Cayman bank and typed in the account number. Waited for him to do the same.

Bankers in the Cayman Islands must be used to people making strange requests. The one they'd contacted several months ago hadn't even hesitated when they'd asked for a secure account with two codes, each to be entered from a different computer simultaneously. Neither of them could access it alone, because they didn't have the other's code.

"Okay. Ready?"

"Quit looking over here. Jesus."

"Stop your damn stalling. Got it?"

"Yeah."

The account opened on her screen. And the amount . . . Shit, the amount made her so damn happy. Of course, only half of it was hers. She opened the computer calculator and ran some quick numbers. Gave him the amount.

"Already did it in my head."

She snorted. Mase had some fucking evil ideas that rocked, but a mathematician he wasn't. "I'm transferring mine now."

"Just your half." He looked up from the other bed to scowl. "I'm not paying for any of that shit you bought."

Asshole. "Whatever." She did a quick online transfer of precisely half the amount to a second account in her name that had been opened at the same time as this one and left empty save the mandatory deposit. "Got it."

"Gimme a minute." Several moments passed before he looked up. Set the computer aside. "Okay, done."

The task completed, Vickie felt herself relax a bit. "I'll order some room service. We can eat while we discuss where we're going from here. I've been thinking Arizona. What d'you think about that, Mase? We'd never have to be cold again."

"I don't mind the cold." He got up and rummaged around on the desk. Came up with the motel menu. "It's the fucking heat I'm sick of. I'm thinking Colorado. Maybe Idaho."

Idaho? Where the hell would they find rich women in Idaho? They couldn't have more than a couple thousand people in the whole damn state. "Colorado sounds good. Denver maybe. Or live in Boulder, hunt in Denver." Setting the laptop aside, she stretched out on the bed, tucked her hands behind her head, and allowed herself to dream. They could run the same operation, just new geography. The trick might be to move around more. They'd stayed in Iowa too damn long, long enough for the cops to connect the dots.

"You aren't coming with me."

She sat up on the bed. Stared at him. "What?"

He didn't even bother to look up. "Think about it. They're looking for the two of us together. We gotta split up. If I go west, you go east. Doesn't matter where. You just aren't coming with me."

Fucker. Her temper ignited, springing immediately into a full-blown conflagration. "Convenient that you tell me that *after* I bust my ass helping you escape."

He did look up then, and the expression on his face was menacing. "You helped because that was the deal. If either of us got caught, the other planned the escape. You helped because you wanted half of the money. So don't pretend it was any more than that. Fact is, Vick, you need me more than I need you to continue this operation. We had a good run, but it's over. Tomorrow you're giving me the car you've got stashed here, and I'm heading out."

Fuck that shit. But she just lifted a shoulder, laid back down. Mase slept like the dead. She'd be out of there before he even thought about waking up. Let him find his own way to fucking Colorado. She'd done enough.

He got up then, headed toward the bathroom. "I gotta take a shit. Order me a goddamn steak. A rib eye. With a mountain of fries and a six-pack of beer."

Vickie didn't move. He was fucking kidding himself if he thought he'd be hard to replace. Men who liked to rape and torture and watch women suffer were not all that hard to find. She oughta know. She'd been raised by one.

"What the fuck!" When she heard the shower curtain being yanked open, Vickie jumped to her feet. Ran into the bathroom. Mase was standing over the bathtub, fists clenched. The kid looked little. Scared. Lying there tied up in a puddle of piss.

She had a sudden flash of Sonny when he was about the same age. Shaking. Crying. Trying to shit himself so whatever guy was there wouldn't do to him what he knew was coming.

Mase turned on her with a suddenness that was startling. And though she'd never been one to back down from him, Vickie took a step back. And then another.

"What the fuck is he doing still alive?"

"I'm thinking about keeping him."

Vance clasped his head in both hands and bent forward, as if in pain. "Oh, sweet Jesus, the fucking stupidity. You want a pet, get a fucking dog. You shoulda never had the kid you did. After having you for a mother, he was a total loony tune. That's actually worse than death."

She grabbed the heavy makeup mirror off the vanity and swung it at him. He knocked it out of her hand and pulled the weapon out of his waistband in one motion. "You can't do it, that it? Too soft?" He swung the barrel of the gun in the boy's direction. "I'll do it myself."

"You idiot. Think no one will report a gunshot?"

He turned back to her, took two quick steps to press the weapon hard against her forehead. "Then you. Do. It." He pressed the barrel harder against her flesh to punctuate his words. "Figure out a way, but do it now. Jesus. I have to tell you every fucking thing."

"Okay, okay. I got something in my purse. Took it from a vet. It's something they use to put animals down."

"I don't give a shit what it is. Just finish it."

She went to her purse that she'd left in the room that day. Unzipped it and carefully took out the syringe she'd taken from Davis's office. "You need to pick him up."

"Do it yourself." He elbowed his way past her.

"Seriously," she insisted. "Get over and pick him up. I have to give the shot in his ass."

"I'm going to give you something in your ass when this is done. Stupid bitch." But he returned to bend down and kneel over the tub, reaching for the kid.

Vickie rushed forward and knocked him off balance while ramming the length of the needle in his jugular, depressing the plunger. He was quicker than Davis had been. And a helluva lot stronger. He straightened with a roar, his hand gripping hers. They struggled for an instant, while she tried to maintain her pressure on the plunger to shoot as much of the Micotil in as possible before he overpowered her and yanked the needle out.

She turned to run. Her gun was in her purse, and her only chance was to reach it. There was no telling how much of that shit she'd shot into him, but it'd take more to take him down than it had Davis.

His hand grabbed her hair, yanked her backward. She stumbled into him, and he went to his knees. Swayed. "Kill you. Kill you, bi—" As if in slow motion, he fell forward and was still.

His fingers flexed a fraction. Went motionless. She reached up to disentangle her hair from his grip. She turned and looked at his eyes. They were fixed, but there was still awareness in them. "See, that temper of yours, I always said it was a problem," she told him conversationally. Rising, she brought back her foot and kicked him as hard as she could in the ribs. Because she was still pissed, she did it a few more times. He didn't blink. And the awareness that had been there a moment ago was gone.

"Asshole," she muttered. "Always had to have it your own way. Always thought you were so fucking smart. Well, guess what, asshole? Turns out it's not so hard to download spyware that will help me retrieve your new account code. You taught yourself about explosives, and I taught myself a thing or two about computers. Who's the dumbass now?" After one last kick, she'd calmed enough to look at the boy.

And was immediately irritated when he cowered beneath her gaze. "I just saved your ass, kid, so you oughta be grateful."

She reached down and pulled him to his feet, then hoisted him out of the tub and over Vance's body. Wrinkling her nose, she said, "God, you stink. I'm going to cut off the duct tape, and you need to change your clothes. Then we're both taking a nap. I've had a helluva day."

Chapter 11

Cam couldn't let himself think about how close they'd come to grabbing Vance. Thoughts of the near miss were burning a hole in his gut. The triple jolt the killer had given the officer in the mall had landed the man in the hospital. One more thing Vance would pay for.

It'd be easy to let this get personal. Easy to let thoughts of retribution cloud strategy. Instead he focused on how damn close they were. And making sure that the loop he'd set up around the area would eventually tighten around the two escaped killers.

The metro area was the nucleus of the search, but they'd radiate from the hub as needed. Outside Des Moines and its suburbs, they still had Ames and Ankeny, good-size cities in their own rights and within easy driving distance.

State Patrol, police departments from the suburbs, and the US Marshal's fugitive recovery unit had joined the search. Some of the sheriff departments had dispatched officers to assist, as well.

He'd arranged to meet up with Franks and Sophie at the DCI offices to get some of his notes and plan their next step. Then they'd split up again, Sophie riding with him. She'd taken charge of the mapmaking, and had a computer open on her lap, an interactive metro map showing on its screen. She'd highlighted the search area and dotted it with red *X*s to correlate with the motels that offered extended stays. At Cam's direction she'd divided the area into quadrants. Then had partitioned those into smaller sections, with initials attached to each. Cam had assigned an agent to supervise the multiagency team that was combing through each smaller area. He was taking one himself.

It was meticulous work, and he hoped a tight enough net to entrap Vance and Baxter if they had headed back this way. If they had already left . . . He gave a mental shrug. Patrol officers and State Patrol were giving city and state roads the same scrutiny. If the Toyota or Impala were in the open, eventually it'd be found.

Sophie spoke then, and it was as if she'd read his thoughts. "Two vehicles. One for each of them if they decide to split up."

"They have to realize the Toyota was likely reported as stolen." After the events today, he knew better than to underestimate them. "They'd abandon it. Or switch plates, if possible."

She raised a brow. "So you're thinking the Impala is the vehicle they'll take? Baxter can't know we have it identified."

"That's my guess." He pulled into the lot for a motel that was on his list. Cruised slowly past the rows of cars. They'd go inside after checking the vehicles, even after not finding the ones they were looking for. The motel registration still had to be checked for anyone fitting Baxter's description. The one upside to the process was that the motel managers who'd watched the news today were eager to cooperate.

"How many rooms do you think she might have used?" Cam stared at the cars, slowing down when he met one that was the right make and color. Moving on after checking the plates. "Seriously. Paranoia keeps you safe to a point, and then you're just throwing money away. I can't see her wasting cash."

"Well, we can guess it's more than three." Her voice was dry. Baxter hadn't returned to any of the ones they'd discovered. "So at least four. No more than seven. I'd guess four or five. That would allow her to hit one every week, maybe twice a week, move on. It's not a cash thing, since she's using fake cards. It's an exposure issue."

"There you go thinking like a cop again."

She pretended to shudder. "Please. So far today I've seen the bomb squad and SWAT team in action, and watched you tear off after a couple deranged killers. I hardly think I'm in your league. And I don't want to be."

"You're not, Soph." He was deadly serious. "You're in a league of your own."

The parking lot was a bust. Cam pulled under the canopy in front of the motel. She handed his cell back to him. She'd been reading out loud to him the updated texts agents had been sending, then crossing off the areas they'd covered. "Bring your laptop inside in case we get another update." She gave him a mock salute. "Wrong hand, Private. Although"—he got out of the car—"I guess I should be glad you used all your fingers."

Smiling, she slid out her side, laptop under her arm. "Ah, you mean the one-fingered salute. Eloquent in its own right." His cell rang then, the pilot's number showing on the screen. Pulse quickening, Cam answered it.

"You have a motel located between Forest and University?"

"Just a minute." They both went to the hood of the car so Sophie could set the computer atop it. He studied the screen. "Yep. We've got one. It hasn't been checked yet."

"Looks like it's got an Impala matching your description. Maybe not the Toyota. Can't tell, although there's a red car out in the van lot."

Adrenaline fired through his veins. "Stay in the area. We may need eyes."

"You got it."

He peered at the screen for a moment. Then dialed a number. "Jenna. We've got an aerial sighting of the Impala at the motel in your section between Forest and University. I'm on my way, but you and Beckett are closer."

"We're on it," came her response.

They both got back in the Crown Vic, and Cam drove to the driveway of the motel, hesitated. Looked at Sophie.

"Oh no," she said firmly. "You are not even thinking about leaving me behind." Urgency outweighed fear for her safety. He didn't have time to argue with her.

Activating his dash strobe, he pulled out into the street. Accelerated. If the need arose, he told himself grimly, she'd stay put wherever the hell he thought safest.

Because there was no way in hell he was letting Vance or Baxter anywhere near her again.

The monster was still sleeping in the other bed. Henry scooted to sit up and looked at her. After he'd changed his clothes, she'd made him get up on the bed and had taped his arms and ankles together again.

But she hadn't taped him to the bed. Not this time.

He was bored, but he didn't want to wake her up. So he couldn't turn on the TV even if he could reach it. Carefully he swung his legs around so he could slip down the edge of the mattress to stand. Maybe he could just watch the TV without the sound. But first he'd have to get to the remote.

Henry could walk if he took teeny tiny steps, short enough that he didn't trip himself. He could get the remote and be back on the bed, and she wouldn't even know. Maybe she would forget that the TV hadn't been turned on when she'd gone to sleep.

After killing the bad man in the bathroom.

His chest got tight when he thought of the man again. The woman was bad, very bad. The man was worse. Worse than anything he'd ever dreamed of. Henry had thought the woman was going to kill him like the man had wanted. He was glad he wasn't dead.

But it had been horrible watching her kill that man, too. Even though he wasn't a good guy at all.

Henry knew he'd dream about that. About the monster and the bad man screaming about killing him. So he hadn't wanted to take a nap. He never wanted to go to sleep again.

He felt a little bubble of triumph when he reached the dresser. Got the remote. He hadn't made a sound, either, just like when he sneaked up on his dad and scared him. Sometimes his dad knew he was there and just pretended to be scared. Tears stung his eyes at the memory, and Henry tried not to think about his dad anymore. Because then he would worry about seeing him again. And then he would think about what the monster had said about keeping Henry forever.

A movement outside the window caught his eye. The lady had closed the curtains but not tight. He could still see out a little bit. He hopped a bit closer. Then closer until he could push the curtains aside and look out better.

A man and a lady had gotten out of a gray car and were walking to the monster's car. He looked at the woman on the bed. Then out the window again. The man had a brown uniform and wore a gun.

That made him a policeman. He frowned. Except police wore blue uniforms. One had come to their kindergarten class and talked to them. So this man was maybe some other kind of cop. The two

211

people got down and looked at the license plate on the monster's car. Then they got up again and the man looked around. His fingers were touching his gun.

Henry wanted to bang on the window. If the man was a policeman, he would help. He could kill the monster and put her body in the bathroom with that bad guy. Henry raised his hands. He still held the remote. If he made noise, the monster would wake up. But maybe if he waved at the couple . . .

"What the fuck are you doing?"

He whirled around, dropping the remote. His feet got tangled up, and he fell to the floor. Felt himself being lifted up by the back of his shirt and then thrown at the bed. He hit it hard with the back of his knees and then fell forward again.

"What the hell were you doing, you little asshole? Huh?" The monster yanked him up again. "Did you gesture to someone out there? Did they see you? Did they?"

He saw the hand coming and tried to duck, but the stinging slap hit him on the cheek. He shook his head, while the tears ran down his face. "No, they didn't see me. They left."

"Who?" She grabbed the front of his shirt and lifted him up in the air, her face close to his. He squeezed his eyes shut, because he didn't want to see her face, all scrunched up and scary-looking like when she'd kicked the bad guy in the bathroom over and over again even when he'd stopped moving.

"They were looking at your car," he blurted. "The cop and lady."

She released him as suddenly as she'd hauled him up in the air. Strode to the curtains and cracked them a little. "How long ago? How long ago!"

He'd never known anyone who could yell in a whisper before. "Right when you woke up. They only looked for a minute, and then they went away." They'd left before they could see Henry. Before they could help him.

212

He knew it was because no one could help him. Probably not ever.

"Fuck fuck fuck fuck fuck!" She moved away fast, grabbing things that had been lying around and stuffing them into her backpack. Into her purse and another bag. She went into the bathroom, and he turned his head so he wouldn't see the man lying there. Then she was back, putting more stuff in her bag. The computers went in the backpack, and then she looked around.

She looked scared. Maybe the police knew she'd killed the man. Maybe they would catch her and put her in jail.

Maybe when she was in there they would let Henry kick her and kick her through the bars the way she had the bad guy when he was dead.

Because Henry wished that she was killed, too.

She'd put on a blue T-shirt that was on the floor. Then she twisted her hair all up in a knot and pulled a man's cap over it, low on her face. When she put sunglasses on, she almost didn't look like a woman at all.

"We're gonna walk out that door." She shrugged into the backpack. Stuffed her purse in the other big bag and picked it up. "Down the hallway. Out a side door. You're going to talk all the way. Nonstop. And you're going to call me Dad. Dad, can we get something to eat? Dad, are we going to a movie? Shit like that. Make it loud and don't stop talking and calling me Dad."

His lips set, mutinous. He wasn't going to call the monster Dad. She was a mom, but not a very good one because she was mean and her son was dead. She'd told him that. Henry had a dad. Maybe he'd never get to see him again, but he only had one dad and he wasn't going to pretend.

She stopped and looked at him. "This is it, kid. You do this one thing, and I promise you I am going to drive you right to your house. Drop you off. You'll never see me again."

"Really?" Was she lying? She lied all the time. *All* the time. He knew that. But . . . what if this time she was telling the truth?

She came over and pulled out that knife. But this time he knew to hold out his hands so she could cut off the gray tape. Then she squatted down to cut it off his ankles, too. "We got a deal?"

He took a deep breath. Maybe his dad would understand. When he told him how he had to pretend to get taken home. Dad would say that was okay. He would say Henry was smart. Because that's what Dad always told him.

"Okay."

———

"You go inside and check with registration. You have a copy of pictures of Baxter and Vance?"

Jenna Turner nodded. Adrenaline was spiking in her chest. Her pulse was hammering. Cam had said he was minutes away when she'd called him about the plate. She'd update him from the registration desk with what she discovered. If Vance and Baxter were here, something told her they weren't going to go down easy.

Beckett stopped her when she would have opened the door to walk up to the motel. "Just the registration desk." Although she'd often thought she never saw him serious, his expression was serious now. Deadly so. "If she has a room, do not go to it. Do not engage."

Annoyance flickered. "I've been doing my job for at least as long as you've been doing yours."

He looked impatient. "This doesn't have damn thing to do with you doing your job. It's about me wanting you to have the chance to do it again tomorrow. And the next day."

Realization dawned, and her irritation faded to be replaced with a blooming warmth. "Back at ya. If you see one of them leaving the building . . . Hell, go ahead and engage. Shoot first. You're liable to stay alive that way."

She got out of the car, slammed the door, and gave him one last look before he drove off. He'd patrol the lot. Baxter's car was there now. They wanted to keep it there.

There were several people waiting in front of the registration desk, but she had her credentials ready when she strode to the head of the line. "I need to see your manager immediately."

⁓

Vickie looked both ways down the hallway, and then ducked back inside the room until the giggly group of kids in wet swimsuits went past. Then she pulled the kid by the hand and walked swiftly down the hall. There was an exit at the end of it and to the left. It faced the lot that had the car in it, though, so she'd keep moving until she could find a door that led to the opposite side.

The kid was silent beside her. She mentally congratulated herself for keeping him. He was better than a fucking passkey, because no one would be expecting a woman traveling with a little kid.

Or in this case, a man.

Remembering the ruse, she squeezed his hand punishingly. He winced, then seemed to recall their conversation. "Hey, Dad. You want to hear a knock-knock joke?"

Christ. "Sure," she said in her best manly voice. "Let's hear it."

"What's black and white and red all over?"

They passed an older couple in the hallway, and Vickie had to step sideways so her bags didn't bump them. The woman was smiling down at the kid, the way people do who don't know what a pain in the ass they are. "Uh . . . a newspaper?"

She got to the exit, pretended to adjust the bags as she looked out.

"No, Dad, an embarrassed sea lion."

"That's a good one, buddy," she said loudly. Then, taking a deep breath, she pushed open the door and they walked outside.

—

"We've got two possibilities because no one at the front desk could identify her, but only two women are registered for extended-stay rooms. Vanecia Mason and Carly Black."

"Just a minute, Jenna." Cam repeated the names to Sophie.

"Vanecia Mason," she said immediately. "Baxter would have enjoyed the irony."

"I agree." To Jenna he said, "We think Mason is the most likely name, but we'll check them both out. You get room numbers?"

"One-thirty-two for Mason. One-fourteen for Black."

"She sticks to first-floor rooms, did you notice?"

"Because she's always planning for every contingency." They had to keep that in mind, Cam thought grimly. There'd be multiple exits from the rooms.

"We're two blocks away. The rest of the team is ten minutes behind us."

"See you soon." Jenna disconnected.

Since he was getting close, Cam cut the siren. He'd also summoned DMPD Chief of Detectives Lewis and Sheriff Jackson. They needed a tight net around the area, and that would require manpower.

But first they had to make sure their quarry was inside.

—

They'd gotten three-quarters of the way across the lot. If they kept walking, they'd hit a strip mall on the next block. Or behind the

216

motel and across a lot there was a convenience store with a fast-food restaurant. Either would have people. Both would have cars. They just needed to get that far.

From the corner of her eye, Vickie could see the sheriff cruiser coming her way. Slowly. And he was stopping to talk to every fucking body in the lot. Looking them over, probably. The blabbing kid at her side was a good disguise, but she wasn't as sure about her own. She quickened her step.

There was a white fence separating the motel lot from the next properties. There were no nearby driveways, at least. A beaten path on either side of it. If the cop wanted to stop them, it'd have to be on foot.

The gun she'd shoved in the bag she carried was right on top. Handy. If that snoopy sheriff got too close, a bullet in the head might be just the thing to buy them a little time.

The fence was one hundred feet away now. Fifty. "Hey." Vickie heard the voice behind her, walked faster. She was practically dragging the kid now. "Hey, sir? Ma'am? With the little boy? I'd like to talk to you."

Vickie scooped the kid up with one hand. And ran.

~

"You may certainly use my office, Agent." Liz Epsell, the motel manager, hurried ahead of them, showing them into the space.

"We appreciate it."

The woman left, and Cam looked at Sophie. Noted the narrowing of her eyes and knew he needed to talk fast. "I can't worry about your safety and this operation. Tell me you'll stay put—"

"I'm not a child. I realize you're going to clear the area of civilians for the operation." She made a shooing motion. "Go."

Relieved he wasn't going to have to waste valuable seconds arguing with her, he strode to the door. Heard her voice behind him.

"Just do me a favor and come back for me in one piece, okay?"

He shot her a cocky grin over his shoulder. "Haven't you heard? Bullets bounce off me." After closing the door behind him, he walked to the front desk, meeting Jenna halfway across the lobby.

"One of the rooms next to Vanecia Mason's is vacant. I've got a card. Maybe we can hear whether there's anyone in the next—" Her cell rang, and she answered it immediately. Cam automatically followed her when she started walking to the entrance. Increased his pace when she began to run.

"Maxwell's in pursuit," she shouted. "South lot. Adult, gender undetermined, with a small child. A boy. Heading east."

"Shit." He pounded past her. Rounded the corner of the motel to see Beckett disappearing around a white fence. "Take my car out front." Without slowing his pace, he dug in his coat pocket and tossed her the keys. "Try to keep us in sight." Then he began to sprint.

Cam ran for fitness, not for pleasure. He worked on stamina, rather than speed. But he was moving fast now, his legs pumping. Passing the fence where he'd last seen Beckett, he jumped a narrow gully and dodged the garbage strewn in the empty lot. The sheriff was ahead of him, heading for the convenience store.

He was gasping for air when he stopped outside its door. Took a look inside. Beckett was searching the premises, so Cam headed around back. When Jenna pulled up and jumped out of his car, he turned around long enough to motion her toward the fast-food restaurant.

After pulling out his cell with his free hand, he called Franks and apprised him of the situation. Unless Cam called again, the rest of the agents would enter the motel for surveillance of the two rooms. He dropped the phone back in his pocket and swung around a peeling dumpster. Found only empty air. He peeked inside it, careful to keep his exposure brief. There was no one there.

He jogged to the front. Scanned the parking lot. Twelve vehicles. Three occupied at the gas pump. He walked by each of the others, looking at the drivers. Peering in the windows.

An elderly man backed carefully out of a slot and turned, heading for the driveway. Cam trotted toward the vehicle, but he saw no one else inside. Before he reached it, the man had made a cautious turn onto the frontage road.

"Cam! Anything?"

Beckett was exiting the convenience store. To the right Cam saw Jenna coming out of the restaurant. He continued checking out the cars in the lot, but the burn in his gut told him what he didn't want to put into words.

The suspect was gone.

———

"You killed that old man."

Vickie checked the rearview mirror, paranoid as hell. There was no way anyone could be tailing her yet, but she had no idea how they'd gotten the plate on the Impala, either, so she was jumpy.

Her gaze caught the kid's in the backseat. "I didn't kill him. Maybe he had a heart attack or something." The way he clutched his chest when she was tying him up, it was a possibility. "He was still alive when I left him."

"You stuffed him in that pipe. No one will see him to help him."

The drainage culvert had been brilliant, if she did say so herself. The old man's greed had led to his own downfall. She and the kid had crawled around the building to the front, then used the vehicles parked there as cover. When the old geezer had returned to his SUV, she offered him a hundred bucks to take her and her son to the airport. Two hundred if he took the scenic route.

A Good Samaritan the man wasn't. He'd pocketed the two hundred and driven them out of town. Then he'd attempted to give them a guided tour of rural Iowa that was a carbon copy of the area around the Coateses' farm.

Including the miles of desolate gravel. No doubt about it; today she'd been living under a lucky star.

"You said you'd take me home now. Right away, you said, if I helped you at the motel."

"Tomorrow. I promise." Vickie's smile grew wide. "I've got a couple more things I need to finish up first."

———

It took longer than it should have to set up the op on room 132. There had been the nearby rooms to clear, agents to get in place. There were two entrances into the room counting the large sliding window, and it had been found unlocked.

He'd almost suspected a trap, although it was just as likely that it had been unlocked to leave a potential exit. They'd seen one adult with the boy, which left either Vance or Baxter unaccounted for. They'd been able to penetrate the crack between the curtains with a threadlike tactical lens that had given them a wide-angle view into the space.

The lights were off. The curtains closed. Beds empty. There was a glow from the open bathroom door, but their visual didn't allow them to see that far.

Cam drew back, folded up the scope and tucked it inside the heavy armored vest. He looked at the time on his phone, held up three fingers to the men behind him. Two. One.

The window was pulled back, and he hoisted himself up and over as the door to the room crashed in. Agents swarmed in through both entrances, covering the area, clearing the closet, under the bed.

Cam and Tommy ran to the bathroom, weapons drawn, but the man on the floor had ceased to be a threat less than an hour ago. A quick check proved the corpse was the room's only occupant.

Tommy checked for a pulse. "Think Baxter saved us the trouble?"

Holstering his weapon, Cam said, "Who else?"

The other agent rose from his position next to the body. "Why the hell would she take the trouble to break the bastard out of jail, only to kill him hours later?"

"Sophie thinks there was one last thing they had to do. A big score maybe. Something important enough to keep them both together a little while longer."

"A very little while. What's that?"

Cam had bent to look at a couple of garments on the floor. The shorts and shirt were pint-size. Stained. "I'm guessing it's Henry Adams's change of clothes," he said grimly. Nearby were pieces of creased gray duct tape. "It was her. Running out of the lot with the kid." Not that there'd been much doubt. Even as he'd planned the details of the op, he'd been calling the local law enforcement agencies to alert them.

As usual, Tommy was on the same mental wavelength. "We'll hear something. She always leaves a trail."

"Of bodies." Realizing how caustic his voice sounded, he tempered it. It had been a long goddamned frustrating day. And it wasn't over yet. "I've got people going over the interagency crime links. Something will pop. A home invasion, carjacking, stolen vehicle . . . That's her MO, and she'll stay true to type. Whatever fits her agenda, which right now is—"

Franks finished the sentence simultaneously. "Escape."

"It's entirely possible she'll leave the area now." Sophia set a thick sandwich down in front of Cam along with a bottled water and propped her hips against his desk. "Since she killed Vance, I have to believe she had enough time to get whatever it was that she needed from him."

"And she may go ahead with her plan for revenge," he countered. He took half the sandwich and leaned back in his desk chair. It was after midnight. She'd badgered him about going home and he'd eventually done so, just so she could get some sleep. Cam was set up in his home office, running the investigation from there for the time being. He didn't expect to get any sleep.

"Right behind them." The knowledge was like bile churning in his system. "All day long, just minutes behind. She's got the devil's own luck."

"I have a feeling she and the devil have a long-standing personal acquaintance."

She reached forward for the other half of the sandwich and took a bite. "What's showing up on the interagency crime link?"

"Plenty, as usual." Cam returned his gaze to the computer screen and set down the sandwich. "In our area of interest, though, only a few possibilities. Nothing has panned out yet. A stolen car report a couple miles from the motel, but it turned out to be a bunch of wannabe gangbangers out for a joyride. It's a possibility she hitched a ride out of the area, but we've gotten only a few calls since releasing it to the media. And none of them fit."

Each local channel was running the development every half hour. One had suspended regular programming to devote full coverage to the story. Over the course of their run, he thought darkly, the trio of killers had given them plenty of material. The national networks would chime in soon, and then they'd have another whole set of problems when the media descended on the city, full force. It was bad enough dealing with the area networks.

"It's on radio, TV, social media . . ." He finished the rest of the sandwich, chewing reflectively. "I get people can be busy and maybe not catch up with what's happening for several hours. What am I missing? Could she have had another vehicle stashed somewhere? A safe house we overlooked?"

"My guess?" Sophie put down the sandwich and came to stand behind him, her hands going to his shoulders, fingers flexing. "She got a ride. A woman and a child are nonthreatening. And the fact that it hasn't been called in yet means she's either still with the individual, or . . ."

His mouth twisted. "A hostage or dead, is that what you're telling me?"

"I'm afraid so." She rubbed and squeezed the tight muscles in his shoulders. "There's no other answer that makes sense. You've got everything else covered."

"That's what's so damn frustrating." He reached up to cover one of her hands with his. "We can isolate her options, tighten the net around her, but it's the people in her path. How the hell do we prevent them from cracking the door of their lives open, just the fraction of an inch necessary to allow her inside?"

She wrapped her arms around him, hugged him silently. She had no answer. Neither did he. Maybe there wasn't one.

Chapter 12

His phone alarm woke him. Cam's head jerked up at the muted sound, and he fumbled to shut it off before the noise could wake Sophie. Six o'clock. He pushed away from the desk and stretched, not feeling particularly refreshed after the two hours' sleep he'd allotted himself. He checked the crime link again. A couple of stolen car reports since he'd last looked.

He grabbed his cell phone and stood. He needed to check with the officer on both cases, see if he could discern a possible connection. His gaze landed on Sophie, sleeping on the office couch, and he paused.

She'd refused to go to bed without him, but he'd at least convinced her to lie down in here. Once prone, it hadn't taken sleep long to pull her under. He stood for a moment. The sight of her never failed to soothe something inside him, and it was no different now. A strand of blonde hair was covering a portion of that flawless face, but he'd dated attractive women before. It was the endless facets of her that fascinated. Captivated. A tidal wave of emotion surged. He'd walk into a gunfight without a moment's hesitation, but the mere thought of losing this woman undid him.

She moved, restless, and silently he eased away. He could make the necessary calls in the kitchen. Start the coffee, grab a shower and change of clothes before waking her. The urgency of the case was building again. It was never far away. It was lodged there in his gut, constantly churning.

Vickie Baxter was out there somewhere. So were at least two of her victims. He was going to find them all. Hopefully before someone else died.

Fifteen minutes later the coffee was his reward for showering, shaving, and changing in record time. He poured a cup and went through his emails on his phone. There were updates from his agents, a preliminary report from the crime scene team, and photos of Henry Adams and Lisa Hansen. A terse note from Maria informed him that she'd released the pictures to the media.

Cam sipped the coffee, studying the photos. It was the big smiles on both of the victims that bothered him most. Taken in happier times, before some random mishap of fate had brought them to Baxter's attention.

And the kid . . . The caffeine turned bitter in his mouth. Somehow it was even worse contemplating how he was faring in captivity.

He forwarded the report and the photos to Sophie's email for her case files. Was barely finished with the task when the cell rang in his hand. He answered it immediately to avoid waking her. "Prescott."

"Agent Prescott, this is DMPD officer Aaron Sonberg. We had orders to call you about certain types of crimes that come in—"

"What do you have?"

"A missing persons report was just filed on a seventy-nine-year-old Albert Kohler by his daughter. She hasn't been able to reach him since yesterday. She went to his place, let herself in, but says his bed wasn't slept in last night."

Interest sharpening, Cam asked, "Does he drive? Does she know where he was last seen?"

The officer's voice became uncertain. "Yeah, he drives. She says one of the neighbors told her Kohler had said he was going out to get some milk. That was around three p.m. yesterday, he thought. Let's see." There was a pause. "Here it is. Kohler drives a two thousand and six black Durango. Midsize SUV."

Cam flashed to the elderly man backing out of the convenience store parking lot yesterday. Alone. At least, no other people had been upright in the vehicle. So Baxter had been crouched down with the kid. Or else she'd accosted him farther along the route.

But there wasn't a doubt in his mind that this was it. Baxter's getaway.

"Call Kohler's daughter back, get her to her father's house. Tell her not to go inside. Wait for us down the street." He hung up, dialing Franks even as he rummaged in the drawer for something to write on.

Franks answered, sounding as sleep deprived as Cam was. "Meet me at this address." He reeled it off for the man. "I'm going to call it into DMV, get a plate."

"Think this is her?"

"I saw this guy, this vehicle yesterday. Pulling out of the convenience store." He blew out a frustrated breath. "Yeah, I think it's her." After finding a pad and pen, he scribbled a note, left it on the counter. "I'll put a BOLO out on the vehicle as soon as I get the info from DMV."

"Meet you at the address in twenty."

Cam went to the garage entrance door and through it. Pulling it shut after him, he made sure the alarm was engaged again before continuing to his vehicle. Sophie would be safe inside. He'd always had home security, but after both Vance and Sonny Baxter had infiltrated her home, he'd upgraded his own system. It was impenetrable.

And probably the safest place she could be right now.

⌒

Although it was barely seven thirty, Cam was already gone. The realization came with a pang. Sophia hadn't heard him leave, but then she'd slept more soundly than she had in days. Sheer exhaustion could come in handy that way.

She found his note in the kitchen, next to the pot of coffee that would be much too strong.

Got lead. DO NOT leave house w/out calling 1st.

Because it was ridiculous to feel a little left out, she shoved the emotion aside and poured herself some coffee. After the first taste had her grimacing, she liberally added more creamer and stirred. Taking a more cautious taste, she carried it into the bedroom to get ready. There was no way of knowing how long Cam would be chasing this lead, but she would still go to his office. There'd be reports from the crime team that had been called to the motel room. Details from those and any forensic results yielded minute clues that could be used to underscore what she knew about Baxter and assist in predicting her next move.

A profile wasn't a crystal ball. It most closely resembled a road map. And the more landmarks she had in it, the more help it would be.

This was her part of the investigative process. And Sophia was just as committed to it as the agents were to their tasks.

She got ready more quickly than usual, saving time on her hair by putting it up. She was just gathering her things when she heard her cell ring. Picking it up on her way to the sink, she answered while dumping out most of the coffee.

"You still at home?"

"Since you told me not to leave without calling, where else would I be?"

"Yeah." His voice lightened a bit. "You don't always follow directions, so . . . never know. You going in today?"

"I'm on my way out the door, as soon as I give your coffee a decent burial. No amount of creamer could save it."

"You realize this just means you volunteered for coffee detail in the future."

Smiling, she went to transfer the items from one purse to another. "I don't want to enable your learned helplessness, so I'll set up a series of lessons for you on the correct coffee-making process. There will be a quiz."

"Something to look forward to. Listen, I sent you some updates before leaving, but we've got a great lead on Baxter's whereabouts, and I'm assembling the team. Briefing in twenty minutes."

"I'll be there."

He disconnected with his usual abruptness. Coffee making wasn't the only area where his skills could use some improvement, Sophia thought wryly as she dropped her cell into the purse and zipped it. When she headed for the entrance to the garage, there was a noise at the kitchen door.

Mystified, she changed course and went to the peephole. Relaxed a little when she saw the source of the sound. Disengaging the alarm, she unlocked the door and pulled it open. Looked down at the face of the boy who'd been by looking for his cat. Adam.

"Hi there."

He stood solemnly, his lip quivering. He wore a small backpack that looked too big for his frame.

Sophia bent down to his level, the locked screen door between them. "Did you ever find Whiskers?"

He shook his head. Then said, so softly she had to strain to hear, "I have to show you something."

The psychologist in her was torn. She worked mainly with adults but had juveniles on her patient list, and it required no training to sense the boy's distress. But DCI offices were at least twenty-five minutes away, in good traffic. "I'm sorry, honey. I have to go."

"You have to come with me."

"No. I can't." Was he being abused at home? Was he neglected? She noticed for the first time that the backpack was affixed to him with duct tape. Her earlier sense of haste vanished. She'd have to report this to DHS, but first she had to get more information.

"What's your last name, Adam? Do you know your address?"

He turned around then. Slowly. Almost robotically, his arms held slightly away from his body. And then she saw for the first time what he carried in his pack.

The back of it was clear flexible plastic, allowing a view of the bundle of explosives inside. There was a small kitchen timer attached to it with red numbers glowing. Counting backward from 5:53.

"Oh my God!" She turned to run for her phone, thoughts ping-ponging in her head. Would a 911 call get someone here in time? Where was the federal agent who was watching the house? If she could just get his attention . . .

"If you don't come with me, the monster said she'd blow me up."

Sophia whirled around again to look at the boy. *The monster.* A horrible comprehension filled her. "Henry . . . Adams?"

He nodded. Tears ran down his face, but he made no sound. And perhaps that was the most heart wrenching of all. "She can turn it off. She's got a clicker thing. But she can speed it up, too. She said she would if you don't come with me."

A cell rang. It added to the confusion and panic warring inside her. But the boy reached in his pocket and pulled out a black phone.

Handed it to her. "Please," he whispered. "If you don't answer . . . I don't want to get blowed up."

She let out a sob of anguish. Unlocked the screen. And as if watching from a distance saw herself reach for the phone.

"I've been waiting to talk to you for a real long time, Doc."

Sick fear unfurled inside her. She'd heard that voice once before. When Baxter had been pretending to be Rhonda Klaussen. Until that moment Sophia hadn't realized how much she never wanted to hear it again.

"He says you can turn it off. Do it. Then just go. They don't know how you got away yesterday. Head out of state. Find an airport. You're free. You've earned that."

"Always the shrink, huh?" The laugh on the other end was nasty. "I know exactly what they know. Or what they think they do. But I believe in choices, so here's yours. The backpack is wired to blow if taken off, so try that, and you both die. Or you can shut the door on the kid and run and take cover in your bathtub, hoping that will save your ass when I detonate it. It won't, but you can try that. Or you can walk out your door and across the yard with the kid. I had to park a ways away because of the feds watching your place, so you'll have to move your ass. Way I figure it, you got under four minutes."

Sophia couldn't have moved if she tried. Her limbs were frozen, the blood in her veins congealed. *Feds? How can she know about—*

"No purse. No phone. No weapon," the voice in her ear continued. "Better start moving."

The boy gave a loud hiccupping sob, his little shoulders shaking.

Yesterday at the hospital she'd empathized with two men who had been faced with an impossible choice. She realized now that it was no choice at all. Opening the door, she took Henry Adams's hand in hers and started walking across the yard.

"Ring her again," Cam said softly to Jenna Turner, who was seated next to him at the conference table. The female agent nodded grimly. Tapped Sophie's number in to her cell.

It'd been thirty minutes since he'd talked to her. He let Tommy Franks fill in the members of the team collected in the room about the recent update that morning. His mind was too distracted.

Sophie wasn't overly late. He tried to cling to that knowledge and concentrate on what Franks was saying. She'd likely walk in at any moment in one of those two-piece suits of hers that made her look as if she'd stepped out of a glossy women's magazine. There was any number of reasonable explanations for her delay. The battery in her phone went dead. Her cell had fallen out of her purse, and she couldn't reach it when she was driving.

Or Baxter had found a vulnerability in the security system and was even now in his home threatening Sophie.

Jenna caught his eye, gave a slight shake of her head.

". . . the BOLO has been released to all surrounding law enforcement agencies. Fugitive Task Force is on board, State Patrol and an Air Wing plane are currently also . . ."

Cam left the room as Franks was winding down. He wasn't going to sit and wait and worry. Not his style. Outside in the hall-way, he dialed FBI agent Del Harlow's number. When the man answered, he said without preamble, "It's Prescott. Can you contact the agent you have on my place right now and ask if Sophie's left and how long ago?"

"I was just about to call you." At Harlow's response, his gut turned to lead. "My guy just contacted me a few minutes ago and said she did leave the house, but not driving. She was walking hand in hand with some little kid. They went down a side street and got into a black SUV. Then it took off in the other direction. Weird enough that he thought he should call, ask if he should follow them."

A cold blade of fear sliced through him. "Tell me you ordered him to follow them."

The man's voice grew uneasy. "I dispatched another car to the scene, but you know as well as I do the protection detail is for you and your home. But I'm worried, too. If Moreno found a way to get to you through Dr. Channing—"

"It's not Moreno," Cam said bleakly. Disconnecting, he took a moment to lean against the wall as a wave of desolation crashed through him.

Sophie.

She'd said it herself, early on. Sonny Baxter's death had been a trigger for his mother. Whatever Vickie Baxter had gained from Vance's escape, it hadn't diminished her need for revenge.

The door pushed open then, and Jenna walked out, her expression getting concerned when she saw him. He pushed away from the wall and gave voice to the anguish that was gnawing inside him.

"Baxter's got her."

———

She needed to stay awake. Sophia fought against the drug Baxter had injected her with and succeeded in opening her eyes. Black. That was all she could see for an instant until her sluggish brain made sense of the visual image it had received. The backs of car seats. She was lying on her side on a seat. The vehicle was moving.

Unconsciousness approached and receded in a nauseating tide. The backpack was on the floor next to her. The digits on the clock no longer glowed red.

Her eyelids fluttered. She struggled to keep them open. Ordered her mind to focus. She needed to move. To think.

Sophia had been on the phone, hadn't she? Yes. Baxter. Baxter had given her orders. Where to turn. How far to walk. Then to get in the vehicle.

The SUV had seemed empty. The boy . . . Henry. She'd followed him in. Then Baxter had lunged from the back. The flash of the syringe. The prick of the needle.

Trying to think was like clawing cobwebs from her mind. She was in the rear seat, out of reach of the driver. She could sit up. Signal a passing car. Kick out a window. But first she needed to sit up.

A wave of lethargy hit her then, and she could feel herself sinking back into the black hole of nothingness again. Her mind sent a last dim command to move. Then it became as unresponsive as her limbs.

———

"You can't be part of this." Cam stared at Maria unflinchingly without responding. "The hell of it is, you know it, too," the SAC continued. He'd seen her spend all night on a stakeout and never move an eyelash, but she was moving now. Prowling the confines of his home office like a feral cat. "You and Sophia are personally involved. I'd have to be blind not to see it. Dammit, I suspected it weeks ago, but you denied it."

Admitting to it would have gotten him removed from Vance's case in a heartbeat after the man had snatched Sophie. Just like it was now.

He'd raced home with half the team in tow to look for himself. When Vance had held her in captivity, Sophie had managed to embed a message in the new profile she'd written to assuage the man to refute the other one that had been released by the media.

But they'd torn the place apart. There was no note. No hidden message. No secret clues. Nothing but an open back door that acted as a stunning visual rebuke.

He never should have left her alone. Never. And the guilt he felt from doing so had seared itself on his soul.

"Give the lead to Franks," he said finally. "He knows the case about as well as I do. But you aren't taking me off this case. You can't."

The woman threw him a fierce look, but he knew her. The combativeness was a shield for her worry. "Wanna watch me?"

"You've had half of zone one's MCU DCI agents affiliated with this case at one point or another. The other half doesn't know the case at all. It requires every man we've got, but more than that it requires *knowledge*. Not just someone who can read the case file, but someone who has breathed and lived the investigation. Who knows the nuances. The little, seemingly inconsequential details that will suddenly make sense when joined with a newly discovered fact. Added to that there's no one on the team, hell, in the entire division, who doesn't have a personal connection to Sophie. Including you. So are you going to recuse yourself? Call up another SAC to supervise?"

Seeing the answer in her expression, he pressed, "We are the ones who can find her. We're the ones who know Baxter best. And if you sideline any of us—including me—you've reduced our chances. You're not going to do that."

The woman's jaw worked. In a rare show of uncertainty, she smoothed the tight knot she kept her dark hair contained in. He figured it was moments like these that had liberally threaded it with silver.

"On paper Franks will be lead," she finally said. He felt no sense of triumph, no satisfaction at all. Her unspoken acquiescence had been inevitable. "You sent out the BOLO alert. Air Wing and State Patrol are also searching for the vehicle. What else are you planning?"

"The only thing that will lead us to Baxter. I'm going to start thinking the way Sophie would."

He went to her briefcase sitting next to the couch in the office and brought it to his desk. After digging in a drawer for a moment, he took out a letter opener and, without finesse, pried the locked latches open. He took out her laptop and fired it up. This was easier. He knew the password.

While he waited he dug through the file folders she had in the case. Each was color-coded and labeled in her neat handwriting; he found Baxter's file and pulled it out. It was the thickest one in there.

Jenna appeared in the doorway. "Do you want us to go . . ." She came in a few steps. "What are you doing?"

"Go get the rest of the agents. Divide up the file. I'll go through her computerized notes. The answer is in here. Wherever Baxter took Sophie, it's here. We just have to find it."

Gonzalez was already moving. She took the red folder in his hand and turned away to crouch on the floor. Moving quickly, she separated the contents into piles. "Wherever Baxter took her, it wasn't to Kohler's. The house has been cleared, and the man doesn't own any other property."

Jenna had disappeared to return with Franks, Boggs, and Samuels. "Take a portion of the paper copies," Cam said from his seat behind the desk. He had his computer pushed aside and was engrossed in the case files on Sophie's laptop. "Look for any thread, any person or place that ties, even loosely, to this case. Because if it's one thing that Sophie kept saying, it was that Baxter would stay with the familiar. Remember her anchor. Remember her ties."

They worked for an hour, all packed into the office. Instead of taking their assigned sheaf of papers to spread out somewhere else in the condo, agents were on the floor. Leaning against the wall. Or, in the case of Jenna and Patrick, on the couch.

"There's that vet link." Jenna looked up from the page in her hand, a note of excitement sounding in her voice. "Remember? When Vance took Sophie and you found a syringe with the paralytic on the floor of the bathroom? Toxicology report led us to listing vets in the area who had ordered the drugs. We made inquiries."

Cam turned away from Sophie's computer to bring up the case file on his. It took a few minutes to find the information. When he did, he ran a copy. Jenna unfolded her long legs from the couch to go get it. "We were left with a dozen or so names of vets who, when questioned, raised some red flags."

He remembered. And then more pertinent leads had materialized, and the focus of the investigation had shifted. "Okay. Follow up. Concentrate on anything that might have linked them—even in the past—to one of the killers." She went out the door. He knew she'd be headed for her laptop in her car outside.

"Okay, I was on this thing, then off, then on again, so I missed some stuff."

Cam looked at Samuels. They had started with the Department of Public Safety at the same time, but the other man had joined DCI at the beginning, while Cam had first worked for DNE. "But what strikes me as odd is the Coates kids. The son and daughter. Did they ever agree to speak to anyone on the team?"

Cam shook his head. "Sophie called a couple different times, I think. She got nowhere."

"What's up with that?" The man brushed his hand over his blond crew cut. "Maybe they just don't give a shit—out of sight, out of mind and all that—but it's weird. Maybe someone needs to get a face-to-face with those two."

"They both live in California," he said slowly, "but you may be on to something. The Coates place. I understand the ruins of the house are still there, that it was never torn down."

"And that's weird, too," Samuels added.

"Sophie went there." He stilled, searching his memory. "She wanted to get a feel for the place where Baxter spent some of her formative years." Although to his mind, the makings of the killer in the woman had formed much earlier than when she'd gone to live with her relatives. "She spent a lot of time tugging at threads from Baxter's past." He thought best on his feet, so he rose, moving around the chair to grip the back of it. "She talked to old classmates. Neighbors."

Gonzalez was sitting cross-legged on the floor, her gaze on him. "Manipulation. That's what Sophia always said. Baxter would find a weakness. Leverage it."

He went to Sophie's computer again. Scrolled down until he found the information he wanted. "Baxter lied to one guy about her son's paternity. Got several thousand out of him before he shut it off. Sophie talked to several people whose names were also mentioned as possible fathers. Bobby Denholt was dishonest the first time she asked him about it. He only came clean later. Maybe the other guys lied, too."

"That could be a helluva vulnerability to exploit," Maria said. "No one would want their relationship with a serial killer made public. Even the rumor of it."

"Then you can take the other names on that list. The ones she talked to about it. I'll check out the Coates place and the Denholt connection." Sophie had spent a lot of time following up on both. She'd seen something there, with both of the families that maybe he hadn't given enough credence to.

With Sophie in Baxter's custody, he didn't have the luxury of evidence. He was going to go with his gut.

And his gut said to follow Sophie's instincts.

～

Sophia came to slowly, aware of little else aside from the painful ringing in her head. Wherever she was, it was dark. Faintly damp. The wall at her back was cement. The floor, too. Their chill had crept into her bones, settled there.

Her eyes strained, but she could only make out vague shapes in the almost total blanket of black. She tried to open her mouth to yell for help. And for the first time realized she had something across her lips. Tape.

Struggling to her feet, she pulled at her wrists, but they were bound tightly behind her. Her ankles were also secured. She began to inch along the wall.

The barn Vance had held her in had been dark, but when she'd escaped her cell she'd gone on an exploration by touch alone. Eventually she'd found some old tools to help pry open the door. She needed to get an idea of the place she was confined in to better plan an escape from it.

She hadn't gone more than a couple of feet before she tripped over some unseen obstacle and fell. She had nothing to break her landing, so she tried to curl as she went down, taking the brunt of the contact with her hip and shoulder. She lay there gasping for air, the wind driven from her lungs. When her breathing eased, she became aware of one thing about her surroundings.

Wherever she was being held, she wasn't alone.

～

When Tommy Franks pulled into the drive of the old Coates place, Cam was on the phone with the Indianola police department.

"You suspect Dr. Denholt of having something to do with one of the killers?" On the other end of the line, Captain Zirbel sounded skeptical. "I don't mean to make light of a very serious situation, but the doctor . . . He strikes me as someone who'd panic at the sight of a mosquito. He hardly fits the profile of a killer."

"Maybe the profile of a victim. One who can be manipulated by the surviving killer." Cam looked at the ruins of the structure that had been gutted by fire. Why anyone would leave it standing was a mystery. It looked like a litigator's dream. He noted the pickup that had slowed when they'd turned. It paused in the middle of the road, as if the two individuals inside were debating, and then followed them.

He returned his focus to Zirbel. "I've checked with DMV and the Warren County assessor's office. I find only one vehicle and one piece of property in Denholt's name."

"We got your BOLO alert. Have the force watching for it. You want me to double-check on Denholt's car? Monitor his house?"

"Whatever you can do without a warrant. I'll take care of the rest."

A shrug sounded in the other man's voice. "I'll get back to you."

"We've got company," Franks observed.

"Saw that."

The other agent pulled the car around to the back of the farm-house, and the tan pickup pulled in after them.

When they got out, the driver of the truck buzzed down his window. "Don't want to be rude or anything, but this is private property. You guys are trespassing."

Cam went up to the man's window, showed his credentials. "Oh, shit." The man wasn't as young as Cam had thought. Maybe midtwenties. "Sorry, man. Uh, Agent. BJ said we should check it out, but shoulda known." His voice got louder as he turned to look at the other occupant. "BJ doesn't always have the best ideas."

"What do you know about this property?" Maybe the kids' parents had met Baxter when she was living in the area. Even as he had the thought, he realized it was a long shot. And he was well aware with each passing minute that they couldn't afford to waste their time on long shots.

"Our dad rents the land. Has ever since the Coateses died."

Cam and Tommy looked at each other. "Who do they rent it from?"

"The kids, out in California. I mean, I guess they aren't kids anymore, but that's who owns it. BJ here thinks the place is haunted."

"I do not!"

"Yeah, you do." Enjoying a joke on his brother, he leaned out the window and said conspiratorially, "He hears noises and stuff. Screaming."

"That's bullshit, Jake, and you know it." BJ sounded incensed. "But there have been noises lately when I'd come to mow the fence line. Like . . . bumping sounds."

Cam's nape prickled. "Bumping sounds?"

The young man hunched his shoulders. "I heard it about a week ago and again yesterday. I never said it was a ghost. Just . . . sounds."

Cam felt a single thread of hope evaporate. A week ago. The noises would have nothing to do with Sophie's disappearance. "Think your family will mind if we take a look?"

BJ shrugged. "I guess not."

Without a word he and Tommy approached the house. Split up, each taking a side.

Except that Cam never got any farther than the splintered, slanted storm cellar doors on the side of the house. The hinges were rusted, the wood rotting.

But the padlock on the outside was new.

He turned to see the brothers had gotten out of the truck and had trailed him from a distance. "Whose padlock?"

Jake shook his head. "Beats me."

Cam got down on his belly and pressed his ear against the crack in the door. He didn't hear anything, but when he got to his feet he looked at that padlock again. Pointed it out to Franks when he joined him.

"Only one way to find out what's so important it has to be locked up."

Cam went to get a hacksaw and Maglite from the trunk. It took longer than he would have thought to saw through the shackle. When he had, he put the ruined lock aside and grabbed one of the door handles, pulled it open.

Grabbing his flashlight, he went down the surprisingly cobweb-free stone steps. At the base, he shone the light around the area.

It was filled with debris. Timbers that had fallen in from the floor above. It smelled like mold, and there was a faint odor of decomposition, as if a long-ago animal had died in there. He flashed the light upward and saw a huge hole. Wherever the fire had started, Cam surmised, it would have been the hottest area. That's where the flames would have burned through the floor.

He stepped farther into the area, his beam painting wide arcs across the walls and floor. Then he reversed its direction. Until it fell on the bound and gagged body lying in a motionless heap.

He sprang forward, turning the figure over. A woman, he saw, still breathing shallowly, eyes closed.

But he didn't need to bring the light closer to know that it wasn't Sophie.

Chapter 13

The body was too small for an adult, Sophia determined. The boy, probably.

Painfully, she rolled to sit and scooted over so her bound hands were toward Henry. She had some movement in her fingers turned that way, and she used them to discern his position. Seated, legs straight out. That's what she'd tripped over.

She moved backward an inch at a time until she could get a handful of his shirt. Jerk it sideways. If he would lie down on his side, she may be able to get the gag off his face.

Henry whimpered and tried to move away, but Sophia persisted. She reached her arms up as far as they'd go to grasp his shirt by the shoulder. Yanked hard. Off balance, he tumbled over and she immediately shifted again to give her restricted fingers access to his face.

When he felt her touch this time, Henry stilled, as if recognizing what she was trying to do. She loosened an edge of the tape that extended to his cheek and pulled. It took several attempts, but finally he whispered, "You're going to make the monster mad."

Just the sound of another voice was enough to have the strength streaming out of Sophia's limbs for an instant. Then she began again, exploring as well as she could to discover how he was bound. Baxter had simply wound the tape around the boy, kept his hands flat to his sides. But his fingers were free. Sophia nudged his arm with her head, trying to make him understand what she wanted. Then she shifted so that her face was near his fingers.

He didn't move for a minute. Then finally he wiggled his fingers and tried to pry at the tape. Sophia lay still. It took an excruciatingly long time, but at last the tape was partially pulled away.

"Good job, Henry." She took a deep breath, filling her lungs. Having her mouth covered gave her a claustrophobic feeling, even when she could still breathe through her nose.

She supposed she ought to be grateful she was still breathing at all.

"My name is Sophie." She wasn't aware she was going to use Cam's nickname for her until she heard herself say it. "I'm going to move around so my hands are near your fingers. Maybe you can work at the tape around my wrists."

"It won't work," he said in a tone that was much too fatalistic to be coming from a six-year-old boy. "We're locked in here. There are some stairs with a door at the top. She locked it from the outside. I heard her."

She thought about that for a moment, wishing the pounding in her head would fade so that she could concentrate. "Are we in a basement?"

"No. It's like a little house. She said it was a well house. She said there were rats down here, and they'd probably eat us. Do rats eat people?"

"No." She shuddered. She wasn't about to tell him that the animals were capable of gnawing on anything that couldn't get away. Ears straining, she listened, but she didn't hear any rustling or skittering sounds that would have indicated they had rodent company.

"I saw your dad yesterday, Henry." The visit to the hospital seemed far away now. "He's very worried about you."

"You did?" Rather than sounding hopeful, there was a twinge of distrust threading through the words.

"I really did."

He was silent for a minute. "The monster keeps saying she'll take me home if I do what she wants. But she never does."

"No, you can't trust her." A fist squeezed her heart at the thought of everything the boy had been through already at Baxter's hands. "Why did she tie you up?"

"She always does if I'm where she can't watch me. Even when she slept yesterday she put tape on me, but she didn't tape me to the bed that time. Maybe she forgot because she was really tired from killing that bad man."

Oh, God. Sophia squeezed her eyes shut for a moment. What that child had experienced would take extensive therapy to reverse.

But therapy was better than death.

"The bomb . . . It was in your backpack. What happened to it?"

"I don't know. She gave you a shot. Then she took the bag, and she did something to the clock so it wouldn't blow up."

She remembered almost coming to in the backseat. Seeing that the digital numbers were no longer aglow. And Sophia again wondered where Vance and Baxter had gained their familiarity with explosives. It was clear they'd had the escape orchestrated. And explosives had played a major part in the distraction.

"Do you know where she brought us? Have you been here before?"

"Uh-uh. We drove a long time, and I fell asleep. I didn't wake up until we were on a bumpy road with a bunch of trees all over. They were tall and I couldn't see anything else. Then she stopped the car and made me help her—" His voice halted.

"It's okay." Sophia was gentle. "She made you help her tie me up."

"Yeah. I mostly only don't get taped when she needs me to do something."

She could imagine. "When she stopped the car and you got up, could you see the sky? Was it daytime or night?"

"Daytime."

"Did you stop to eat on the way down here? Did you have to stop for gas?"

"No. But she gave me a Gatorade and some donuts before she tied me up again."

So they hadn't driven a great distance. The realization gave Sophia reason to hope. A place an hour or two away, with a lot of trees. If she had a better idea of how long she'd been out, she could more accurately guess their location.

"Could you see the sun when she was driving? Which side of the car was it on?"

"I don't know. It was in the sky." He moved restlessly. "I have to go pee."

"I think we're just going to have to do what we have to do, buddy."

"Yeah, I know. Me and that other lady had to go in our pants lots of times. I heard her."

"Another lady?"

"In that basement. In the burned house. We were there a long time."

The words staggered Sophia. The other lady had to be Lisa Hansen. The ambulance driver's wife.

The kidnapped victims had been kept in the Coateses' house. That thought drummed away inside her head, adding to the din there. Because Vickie Baxter had returned to an area she knew. What she was familiar with.

Which meant that wherever they were being held right now, it had likely been chosen for the same reason.

"Denholt looks clean. I saw his Mazda myself. He even left his practice to follow me to his place, let me do a walk-through. It's empty. I took a look around the property, but there was no sign of visitors." Zirbel's tone said that the findings were no more than he expected. "He swears up and down that he doesn't own other property. Seemed pretty shook-up at the suggestion that Baxter might contact him."

"Thanks." Cam got another alert on his phone and added, "I appreciate you following up." Then he switched to the incoming call. "Prescott."

"This is Officer Recker with DMPD, calling about your BOLO."

A spike of adrenaline stabbed through him, hot and fierce. "You have the vehicle?"

"Well, I don't think so. But I've got the plates."

"This is bullshit! Them ain't my plates, so you had no call to come after me. You can't arrest me on that outstanding warrant, 'cuz you had false . . . false pretenses or something. I know my rights."

"You might want to leave the legalese to your defense attorney," Franks said dryly.

From the looks of his shirt logo, Les Neimann appeared more familiar with racing and beer than with the law. Although given the outstanding assault warrant in his name, the law was more than familiar with him.

Cam let the conversation flow over him as he squatted down by the patrol officer and examined the bent and dented plates on the black Suburban. Wrong make and model to be Kohler's vehicle, but it was a black SUV and that had likely been enough for Baxter's purposes.

Distraction and diversion. That had been her intent. Frustration rose, strong enough to choke him. So far, it was looking as if she'd been pretty damn successful.

Rising, he turned to Neimann, his voice whiplike, cutting through his protests. "Where was this car from yesterday at noon until now?"

"Nowhere much," the bearded man muttered. "Mostly at home until about seven last night, then I was at Stiffy's until it closed. Needed a ride home." Here his voice rose again and he directed the next sentence to Recker. "'Cuz I don't drink and drive. Left the Suburban there overnight, got a ride to get it, and you picked me up before I could drive back home. Like I said, pure bullshit."

"Did you talk to anyone going into the bar?"

"Talked to just about everybody, man. There weren't that many there."

Cam pulled out a folded photo of Baxter and handed it to the man. "Do you know this woman?"

Neimann took a long look. "Everyone in the city who has a TV knows that broad. She's the killer they're looking . . ." His gaze widened. "Are you telling me she did this? She set me up? Holy shit, man, it's lucky I was wasted. If I'da gone out to the car when she was there . . ."

Baxter was likely out cruising for a vehicle to switch plates with long after the bar had closed, Cam thought. Which meant she'd laid low until dark and then started hunting.

"Think she had another motel room to hide out in that we didn't know about?" Franks murmured. His head was down as he texted Agent Boggs an order to change the BOLO alert for all law enforcement agencies.

Cam shook his head. They couldn't know for sure, but it didn't feel right. "She'd be too paranoid to go to one of them after we nearly caught her in one." And the failure to do so still burned. "I think she got spooked by the fact we had tracked down the license plate on the car she'd been driving. Wasn't going to take the chance of it happening again."

He looked at the patrolman. "Good catch on that, Recker. I'll make sure your superior hears about it."

The twentysomething officer flushed a little. "Looks like a twofer. BOLO plate and a warrant to boot."

"It might keep us in the game at least." But he was all too aware that Baxter had succeeded well enough. Wherever the hell she'd gone, she'd traveled there undetected.

Frustration and temper warred, but it was directed inward. This was taking too long, and Sophie's welfare depended on quick action. He could well imagine what Baxter had in store for her victim, but the plan would require time.

Cam needed to make damn sure she didn't get the time she needed.

His cell rang when he and Franks were walking back to the car. When he answered, Jenna's voice was as excited as he'd ever heard it. "I was following that vet lead, right? And lo and behold, I discovered a Greg Davis in Story County was found dead in his office recently. Considered a suspicious death, no suspects. And guess what was up on the perv's computer screen when the body was discovered? Davis liked little boys."

Cam's gut tightened. They were looking for connections, and they'd hit the jackpot. Sonny Baxter had been abused by men for years before being placed in foster care. Davis was on the short list of possible sources for the paralytic Vance had used on his kidnap victims.

"Got a trifecta here, Cam." He could hear the faint sound of a siren in the background of the call. "Because I did a property search on Davis. Ran him through all the counties. And besides his house in Story County, he showed up with a property in Mills County on the Missouri River."

There was a single brief moment when the wave of hope that crashed over him was almost debilitating in its strength. He drew in a breath and expelled it slowly. Too soon to be certain but damn. It fit. It all fit. "You did good, Jenna. Go ahead and call the locals over there and send them to the river property. Give them my number. I want an immediate update when they get there." He hung up, jubilant.

There was a jitter in his chest when he relayed the information to Franks as they walked back to the car. It would be difficult not to be on location when a break like this appeared in the case, but this was no time for ego.

Sophie. Her name scored across his mind like a prayer. He'd know in minutes if they were on the right track.

He wasn't going to let himself consider the alternative.

———

The hinges on the well house door screeched as it opened. Sophia ducked her head and turned her face. The slant of sunshine was a sensory shock after the total darkness they'd been enclosed in. Baxter's figure blocked out most of it. Henry shuddered beside her and shifted closer. The small movement was heartbreaking. Sophia couldn't protect him. She couldn't even protect herself.

"Don't worry, bitch. I'm not quite ready for you." The glee was easy to discern in Baxter's voice when she strode into the space. "You've got a while yet before us two get some quality time." She stopped next to Sophia and gripped her hair, yanked her head back. "Bet you think you got me all figured out. Most of them shrinks did. None of them knew dick. But you're gonna be special. You're going to get a firsthand look at just what makes Vickie Baxter tick."

She released Sophia, then, with a shove, reached down to haul up the boy. Dragged him after her. "You might as well help. We've got lots of arrangements to make so your bitch friend gets everything she's got coming to her."

The door creaked again and shut. The sound of it being secured again had an anguished whimper escaping her. She slumped against the wall, a tidal wave of hopelessness washing over her.

The time she'd spent as Mason Vance's captive had been the most terrifying experience of her life. Escaping him had taken every shred of courage she possessed.

Sophia wasn't certain that she had the fortitude or luck to accomplish it again.

———

"I'm afraid we found the place empty, Agent Prescott."

Cam hadn't even been aware of the level of rising optimism inside him until the sheriff's words shattered it. The Mills County veteran continued. "Property isn't really much more than a fishing cabin, and we have a clear visual through the windows. We had a helluva downpour here last night. There are no tire tracks anywhere close to it."

It took a moment to speak around the hot knot of disappointment in his throat. "I appreciate you checking it out."

"We'll go drive around the whole area, though, and take a close look at all the places there. I'll let you know if anything shows up."

After thanking the man, Cam disconnected. Jenna, Franks, and the other team members in his DCI office were silent.

And it was his imagination that their stillness reverberated with accusation. That feeling, he knew, came from within.

"Fuck."

He blew out a breath in agreement with Jenna's succinct summary of the call. "Yeah." He propped his hands on his desk, took a moment to will away the tendrils of panic. "It was a great lead."

"A great lead would have found Sophia." Jaw visibly clenched, the female agent looked away, pretended rapt attention on her computer screen.

"It was a great lead," he repeated, shoving away from the desk. "I've got everyone pulling at the same types of threads, and sooner or later one of them is going to pan out." *Sooner*, an inner voice sounded. *Let it be sooner.* "Baxter was out of moves. There was no safe house—that's the reason for the motel rooms. I think wherever she took Sophie to, it was on the fly. Like grabbing a ride with Albert Kohler at the convenience store." That had taken no planning, just sheer luck. And an ability to think on her feet. Baxter seemed blessed with both qualities in abundance.

He strode around the desk to pace to the closed door. Back again. "She's not going to go too far. Traveling too great a distance means stopping for breaks. Food. Gas. Every hour she was on the road with two hostages, Baxter increased her exposure. She had a place in mind, and Sophie would say that place played a part in the woman's past."

"There's a big hole in her past that we have no information on," Jenna reminded him morosely.

"So we focus on what we do know." His words sounded far more upbeat than he felt. He glanced at Tommy seated at a table next to Turner, his laptop opened before him. "What was perfect about the lead Jenna found was the location. We need to think of places that would suit Baxter's needs. Remote. Isolated."

"Could be rural," the man said. "Given the years she spent at the Coates house. And the time she spent living in Gladys Stewart's farmhouse, pretending to be her niece while she collected the woman's Social Security and rent checks."

"Stewart." He stopped. "We need to get something on that. Baxter was there nearly two years. Who did she meet during her time there? What areas might be around that farmhouse that might perfectly suit her needs?"

"I'm on it." The older agent grabbed his suit coat and shrugged into it as he went to the door.

To Jenna, Cam continued. "Rivers. Sonny Baxter found a place isolated enough on the bank of the Raccoon River to bury several of the victims. He dumped more into the water. I don't see Vickie staying out in the open, though. She doesn't like exposure. She's a behind-the-scenes multitasker."

He turned his attention to the timeline still tacked to his wall. Willed it to talk to him. "So rivers, lakes, woods—" He broke off as a snippet of memory flashed through his mind. Found it too nebulous to pin down.

"You don't think urban? Like the warehouse they rented to hide the ambulance in?"

"Good thought. I don't think it fits." He tried to channel Sophie, forge an entry into the killer's thought process. "But again, exposure." Half turning, he propped a hip against the desk, folded his arms. "So we're back to our first thought. Who does she have a tie to with access to a property like that?"

Again, a thought niggled. He frowned, concentrating on bringing it to the forefront. Then Jenna spoke, disrupting his focus. "You're going to want to come look at this. Albert Kohler just showed up on the interagency crime link."

She was on the phone even as he sprang over to join her at her computer and read the line she was pointing to. A few minutes later she disconnected and looked at him. "They found the old man tied and half in a drainage pipe. No external injuries, but he requires medical treatment. Possible heart attack. He was conscious when he was discovered, though."

"Head to the hospital. See if you can get a word with him. Maybe he got an indication of where she was headed." The woman was too clever to mention her plans, but she'd also been traveling with the boy. Henry. There was no telling what he might have overheard when she was talking to Vance. The kid could have let something slip.

Wordlessly, Jenna pushed away from the computer, collected her phone and purse, and headed toward the door. With her hand on the doorknob, she turned and looked at him over her shoulder. "Sophia's smart. She's resourceful. And she's studied Baxter. She knows how the woman thinks. That gives her an edge."

Cam stared at the door long after Jenna had closed it behind her. He knew as well as the other agent did that Sophie was going to need a helluva lot more than an edge to get away from Baxter. The woman manipulated. Exploited vulnerabilities. It was how she had gotten cooperation from Hansen and Adams. She'd honed the skill for years, having done the same with Denholt more than a decade earlier.

And he was pretty sure it was how she'd gotten to Sophie, too. He went to his desk, intending to start through her notes again. Sophie wouldn't have been able to turn her back if Baxter had threatened the boy. The woman would have known that. Used the knowledge.

Denholt. His mind reversed course. The impalpable thought he couldn't quite grasp earlier solidified. Something about Sophie's visit with Denholt when Cam had sat across the hall . . .

Comprehension made a belated appearance, and it suddenly clicked. He went to his case files, found the chiropractor's number again. Dialed it.

"Agent Prescott." When the receptionist finally got the man to the phone, his voice vacillated between annoyed and fearful. "I've been thinking about calling you. All this talk with Captain Zirbel this morning about Vickie Baxter . . . Should I be fearful for my mother's safety? Maybe I should bring her to my home for a while."

Cam ignored the question. A persistent notion had taken hold, and his instincts were quivering. "The pictures on your desk in your office. The one taken of the water. Where was it taken?"

"What? Oh, that was snapped years ago. Sundown Lake, near Centerville. My family has a cabin there."

The vise that gripped Cam's chest squeezed so tightly he had to take a breath. Release it. "All day. All day you've been telling us you don't have any other properties."

"I don't. My sisters and I inherited it from our grandparents, but frankly it's much too rustic for my taste. I sold out to them to help finance my business when I—"

"Would Vickie Baxter know about it? Would she ever have been there?"

"I . . ." He sounded uncertain. "I'm not sure. She was never there when I was, but my parents did take the Coates with them on occasion. It's possible."

"Where is it? Exactly."

He quoted an address, then added, "But like I say, it's rustic. The house—and it's not much more than a two-bedroom cabin—sits on eight and a half timbered acres. From the road you wouldn't even know it's there. But back to my mother. Do you think I shou—"

"No. She's fine." Cam hung up abruptly and raced out of his office down to Maria's, already using his phone's web browser to find the number for the Appanoose County sheriff. This was it. It had to be. They couldn't afford to chase down any more dead ends.

Because he had a feeling Sophie's time was running out.

———

The next time the door opened Sophia wasn't taken unaware. She'd heard Baxter approach. She'd spent the time alone moving at a tortuous pace across the entire interior in search of anything that could be used as a weapon. Found the place completely empty.

"Show time, Doc." Baxter strode inside, lighting her way with a cell phone. She crouched down, and there was the flash of a blade. In moments Sophia's ankles were free. The other woman rose. "Get up."

Sophia's feet had gone numb. She tried to rise, almost fell when her legs wouldn't hold her. She felt the back of her suit jacket being grabbed as she was hauled upright again. "Don't have to worry about you making a run for it, huh? Move it." The shove she was given almost sent her sprawling. Regaining her balance, Sophia stumbled out the door of the small stone building and blinked.

With the dense trees hemming them in on three sides, it was difficult to tell how late it was. Dusk, certainly. Or nearly so. "Where's the boy?"

"Taking a rest. He's been a little helper, that kid has." When Sophia tripped over a branch, the woman grabbed her again to steady her. "Just think how bad it'd be if I hadn't taken those fucking shoes off you while you were unconscious. You'd be flat on your face."

The heels on the sandals she'd put on that morning would have made effective weapons, Sophia thought grimly, trying to pick her way through the shadows. She could see water in the distance. A river, perhaps, or maybe a lake. And the low rise of a building several hundred yards in front of it.

It was impossible to tell where they were. And she knew it would be even more difficult for Cam and his team to figure it out.

Desolation mingled with a newfound determination. If Henry and she were to get out of there, it was going to be up to her.

As they walked the short distance to the structure, Sophia scanned the area, looking for possible escape routes. If there were neighbors around, their homes were hidden by the dense trees. A rutted drive sat beside the cabin they were headed for, but it was empty. Where had Baxter put the vehicle? She turned to look for it over her shoulder. There was nothing but woods behind her. Was the SUV hidden there?

"What the fuck are you looking for? There's not going to be a white knight riding to your rescue, bitch. No one knows we're here. Had a helluva time finding the fucking place again myself. It's just you and me. And we've about to become much better acquainted."

There was a note of glee in the woman's voice that sent dread snaking down Sophia's spine. She'd heard it before with Vance. And knew that if something didn't occur to her soon, she was going to die in this place.

Desolation swept through her as she climbed the two steps to the long porch fronting the cabin. There had to be something inside the place she could turn into a weapon. Some way to fashion an escape. She repeated the assurance like a mantra to avoid the panic that was scrambling her nerves.

But when Baxter's hand at her back had her staggering through the doorway, off balance, her first glance around the space made dismay clutch at her throat.

Fresh plywood was nailed over all the windows, including the one in the front door. A few heavy pieces of furniture, upholstered pine. There was a table of similar weight, no matching chairs. No lamps. No overhead light. Two portable spotlights, one on each side of the room provided the only illumination. There were no tools near the fireplace.

Henry sat under the table, looking small and scared. The sight shot Sophia's spine full of steel. The little boy had already experienced more in his short years than most endured in a lifetime. For that reason alone, Vickie Baxter couldn't be allowed to win.

The door slammed behind Sophia. Turning, she watched the woman lock it. "Bet you're wondering if I overlooked anything when I dumped everything from those kitchen drawers and cupboards into the bedroom. Surely there's a knife I left behind. Maybe a heavy skillet to brain her with. Did I leave anything like that, kid?"

The boy beneath the table shook his head. "But you're welcome to look." Baxter waved her arm in an expansive gesture. "Not that you could do a damn thing with a weapon if you had one."

"You don't need the boy anymore," Sophia said quietly. "When this is over, he'll just slow you down. Let him leave now. He doesn't need to be a part of this."

Baxter sauntered into the room, and for the first time Sophia realized the woman was wearing a backpack. Not the pint-size one Henry had worn that morning. Despite Baxter's words, Sophia knew she didn't have to get into the boarded-up bedroom to find a weapon.

Whatever the woman thought she would need to end this with Sophia would be in the bag.

"Yeah, the kid's a pain in the ass, but he comes in handy. Think that old man would have agreed to give me a ride if sweet and innocent over there hadn't been with me? I'm gonna keep him. I can train him. Better than Sonny." The mention of her son seemed to incense her, and she crossed to Sophia in two quick steps and knocked her to the floor. "You remember my son, right? You should. You're. The. Reason. He's. Dead." She punctuated the words with kicks, following Sophia as she tried to roll away.

There was a river of sick horror coursing through her at the suggestion Baxter would try to mold the boy the way she had her son. And Sophia realized that she wouldn't be able to play on the woman's ego as she had with Vance. Given Vickie's long history with therapists, she'd see through de-escalation dialogue. So, deliberately, she chose a different tack. "I do recall your son. You shot him. Maybe you were angry that he brought the police to your door. Or maybe he was trying to kill you. But Sonny's death is on you, Vickie. You're responsible. Just like you're responsible for the way he was abused by men when he was young." She paused, then added in a pitying tone, "Your son *hated* you."

Vickie's face twisted, and she lunged, a snarl on her lips. Sophia was ready for her, drawing her feet close to her torso and then kicking out as hard as she could when the woman got close enough. She caught Baxter in the chest, knocked her away, giving herself enough time to roll and get her feet under her again. She ran for the door, but the dead bolt was placed several inches above the doorknob. Her hands bound behind her, Sophia strained to reach high enough to unlock it, when the other woman charged at her, head lowered.

The impact of Baxter's body drove the breath from her lungs. The woman used both hands to grab her and shove her hard across the room. Off balance, Sophia landed hard against the couch, slamming her head against the pine trim. Her knees buckled. The room was spinning. Her lungs screamed for oxygen.

"Having fun yet? Not so fucking smart now, are ya? Did you ever once ask yourself how I knew when you'd be alone this morning? You haven't. I can tell. Well, my little helper over there planted a bug in your place when he was there the first time. And that's exactly what's going to help me end your fucking boyfriend, too. The explosives I pretended to wire to the kid? They're really being saved for Prescott. How long do you think it will take them to pick up all the pieces of him?"

Fear and rage warred inside Sophia. *Cam.* She couldn't let this monster hurt him. "He's probably found the listening device by now. Cops can sweep for those things, you know." She saw by the other woman's expression that she'd scored a point.

After a moment Baxter shrugged. "I'll figure something out. All I have to do is sit that last pack of explosives next to the condo and boom. One less fucking cop." She slipped out of her pack and put it on top of the counter. Unzipped it. "But don't feel left out. I've got something pretty special planned for you, too."

She opened her eyes. The other woman was unloading objects from the backpack, one by one. Needle-nose pliers. A metal speculum. A sex toy with needles extending along both sides of it.

"We'll start with this, though." Baxter took out a box of cigars. Chose one. "Guess you already know that you're going to be lucky number seventeen." She stilled, the smirk fading from her face.

Nausea circled in Sophia's belly. Slowly, painfully, she stood upright again. Baxter was taller. Heavier. So that meant she'd have to outwit the other woman. Use her brain, because she was no physical match for . . .

And then she realized why the woman had gone silent.

A vehicle was coming down the rutted drive.

In a flash Baxter reached into the pack and brought out a gun. She bent to grab Henry by the arm and haul him out from beneath the table, bringing the weapon up to his head in one smooth motion. "One sound. One move," she whispered nearly soundlessly, "and he's dead."

Car doors slammed. Boots crunched on the gravel. Up the two porch steps. The three of them were unmoving inside, a frozen tableau. Sophia's mind was racing, grasping and discarding ideas frenetically.

She still hadn't decided on one when a knock sounded at the door.

Chapter 14

Cam and Maria Gonzalez sat silently in the Air Wing Cessna 182. It had taken valuable time to fill the SAC in on how he'd arrived at his certainty regarding Sophia's whereabouts. Even longer to wrangle an order for one of the State Patrol aircraft to get him to the Centerville airport, minutes away from Sundown Lake. There had been little conversation on the plane. Both were aware of the enormity of the stakes. Cam had members of his team following up other leads in his absence, but this was the one he'd bet on.

And if he was wrong, the chances of ever finding Sophie alive decreased dramatically.

The knowledge rapped at the base of his skull, a constant, painful reminder. It lay between him and Maria, an unspoken truth too horrible to verbalize.

His cell rang as the pilot began his final descent. Recognizing the number, he answered with a speed fueled by desperation.

It was Herb Wentworth, the Appanoose County sheriff. "Agent Prescott. I just heard from the two deputies I sent out to the address you gave us on the lake. They didn't run into anything like you mentioned."

His gut abruptly hollowed out as he exchanged a glance with Maria. "You're sure they have the right place?"

"I'm not saying they had an easy time finding it, mind you. But there's no vehicle in sight. No sign that the cabin is occupied. Just the opposite. They said the windows appear to have been boarded over from the inside, like the place had been abandoned."

A tiny flicker of hope flared. "From the inside? That's kind of odd, isn't it? Most people would cover the outside, to protect the glass from vandals."

"Guess that's true enough. But they knocked for a couple minutes. Didn't hear anything, so they drove back up to the road, radioed in the report. I'm relaying it on to you."

"Is there another structure on the property where the car could be?" Maria's lips flattened as she listened to his end of the conversation. She'd put a lot on the line in allocating resources toward the Denholt connection. But his instincts still insisted they were on the right track.

Because he needed them to be right. He needed to believe that he was getting closer to where Baxter held Sophie.

"There's no garage. Just some small stone building a ways behind the cabin, and a vehicle wouldn't fit in there."

"Anywhere nearby a vehicle could be hidden?"

The other man sounded rueful. "Agent, that cabin sits on almost ten acres of wooded property. That's a lot of land and a lot of trees. Sure, someone could maybe pull a car far enough into the timber to hide it. We'd have to do a foot search, though, and it's already dark. You might want to wait until morning to come down."

"We're going to land at the Centerville airport in a few minutes," Cam informed him tersely. "If you can spare a car to pick us up, I'd appreciate it. In the meantime, maybe you can have your men go back to the address and start searching for that vehicle. I have a feeling our victim doesn't have a lot of time left. I need to find out for sure whether we can cross this site off our short list."

The man agreed to both requests, and Cam disconnected. Nothing about the report was reassuring, and self-doubt shredded his earlier confidence. What if he'd overlooked something? Maybe he'd seized on Denholt because of finding Lisa Hansen in the cellar of the Coates place. Perhaps he'd neglected some other key piece of information while combing through Sophie's files.

"She's there or she's not," Gonzalez finally spoke. "It's not like we're putting all our eggs in one investigative basket. The team is still at work." She looked at him, her dark gaze unreadable. "Even if it doesn't pan out, this was worth the time spent checking it out."

He didn't respond. Couldn't. Sophie had been taken more than fourteen hours ago. He couldn't afford chasing after leads that didn't pan out.

Time was one thing she no longer had.

———

The strangers at the door had made Baxter paranoid. It wasn't until after the vehicle had pulled away that she put her weapon back into the bag and took out the duct tape instead. She thrust it at Henry. "Tape her ankles together." She watched long enough to ensure he obeyed before disappearing into the open bedroom door. She stayed inside for several minutes, making Sophia wonder if she was checking on the progress of the car that had been outside the house for a few minutes.

The possibility had a ribbon of hope unfurling inside her. Maybe Baxter was checking on the strangers from an unrestricted window. If so, it represented another possible avenue of escape.

If Sophia weren't bound, hands and feet. If she weren't weaponless. Defenseless.

She clenched her jaw against the black well of despondency that formed at the thought. It deepened when Baxter came out of the room. This time carrying a gas can.

"Just in case we have to hurry this party along," the woman said cheerfully. She liberally doused the furniture, splashed the cabin walls and plank flooring. Then made a show of pooling it around and down the front of the door to the porch. "I think you're familiar with my work." Her voice was confidential as she tossed the can aside and returned to lock the door again. "I didn't get to stick around and listen to the screams when dear Aunt Mary and her husband and brat died. Too scared of getting caught. I realized my mistake, though, when Webster was melting before my eyes. I'm going to enjoy listening to you scream. First while I show you a few techniques I learned from Vance. And then again when the flames are eating the flesh off your bones."

Sophia looked for Henry. Found him under the table again, arms wrapped around his knees, his eyes screwed tightly shut. "Have you checked how far it is to the next house?" She saw by the woman's stiffening that the woman hadn't thought of it. "There are probably neighbors in the area. It can be deceptive with all the trees around. Not to mention the fact that sound carries near water."

The other woman's face smoothed. "You're right. So if you get too loud I'll just have to gag you again." She went to her bag and took out the box of cigars. Made a production of drawing one out, holding it up. "I think you know how this is going to start." She set it down to pick up the knife she'd used to cut Sophia's bonds in the well house and approached her. When she tried to scoot frantically around the couch, the woman easily caught up with her. She bent down and sliced open the back of the jacket and blouse Sophia wore. And when the slightly cooler air in the cabin kissed her bare flesh, she shuddered wildly.

Baxter left her for a moment, and Sophia rolled to the couch. Using it for support, she struggled to her feet, still hobbled by the tape. She flexed her ankles frantically, hoping that Henry had left some laxity in the bonds. Baxter watched her from her stance at the table, seeming amused by her actions. Then she picked up the cigar she'd taken out minutes earlier, pulled a lighter from her pocket, and—holding Sophia's gaze—lit the end of it.

She drew on it deeply. Exhaled. Over and over until she had a half-inch ash on the end. And then she stalked toward Sophia.

She began hopping toward the open bedroom door. Baxter got there first, so she turned around, intent on putting the couch between the two of them. She felt a hand on her back and she was shoved off balance, landing painfully on the floor. Her attempt to crawl away was halted by a knee pressed to the base of her spine.

"This is the way my old man would begin." Baxter's voice was still conversational. Sophia could feel the heat from the cigar close to her skin. Hot ashes drifted to her bare shoulder, and she yelped. "He'd draw on the cigar awhile. You want to get it nice and hot. Makes the flesh sizzle when it comes into—"

"Leave her alone."

Both of them stilled at Henry's voice. Sophia craned her neck to look behind her. He had crawled out from beneath the table. And he held the gun from Baxter's bag in two hands. Was pointing it at the woman.

"It's all right. I'm not hurting her. We're just playing." The pressure was gone from Sophia's back. She turned over, struggled to a sitting position.

"You're lying," he said flatly. "You lie all the time. Like when you said you'd take me home and you didn't."

Baxter was on her feet, inching toward him. "Well, I will take you. Promised, didn't I? Just after this last thing."

He backed up a little, the weapon wobbling a bit in his hands. "Uh-uh. 'Cuz you just said you were going to keep me. You hurt the lady in the basement. And you hurt me. You're going to hurt Sophie, too."

Baxter spread her arms out in a gesture of innocence, the lit cigar still held in her fingers. "You don't want me to, I won't. How's that? I'm listening to you. Now you listen. Give me the gun." She inched forward a little more. Henry retreated.

"It's all right. I promise everything will be fine if you just give me . . ." She lurched forward, made a grab with her free hand for the weapon.

The shot was deafening in the small area. Vickie took a couple more steps toward him, and Henry backed up around the table, the weapon still pointed. Then she reached out a hand to grab for the edge of the table. Missed. Fell to her knees. The cigar dropped to the floor. Rolled. "You . . . lil . . . bas . . ." She crumpled, her expression dazed.

For a moment Sophia was frozen. Then she looked from Baxter to the boy. "Henry." Sophia waited for his frightened gaze to meet hers. "It's all right. Come here. Bring the knife."

Blood was pooling around Baxter's body, and her limbs jerked as she tried to move. The boy was watching her body fixedly. "Bring the knife. Come over here. Henry!"

A trail of flame had flared to life beneath the cigar. It raced along the path that Baxter had made with the gasoline, licking along the wood planks. Racing to the door. Up it.

"Now, Henry." Her voice was stern. Baxter was trying to speak. Only gurgling noises came out. "Bring the knife. Stay away from the flames."

Skirting Baxter's body, he set the weapon down and snatched up the knife Baxter had used earlier. Ran to Sophia's side. Smoke was filling the room, stinging her eyes. The boy blinked rapidly, rubbing at his own with his free hand. "Cut the tape on my ankles. Hurry."

It seemed to take an excruciatingly long time to do so, but finally her legs were free and she could get to her feet. "Now my wrists." She turned around to offer her bonds, facing the door. Her stomach plummeted when she saw how fast the flames were spreading. Not only up the doorjamb but in a wide trail that stretched across the length of the space along the front wall.

They wouldn't be leaving the cabin through that door.

—

Cam had probably gotten chillier receptions than the one that met him at the Centerville airport, but he couldn't recall when. Sheriff Wentworth had picked them up himself, and he was clearly miffed about it.

"It's too bad you had to come all the way down here before you let us do a thorough check of the property," he was saying. The headlights of his cruiser speared through the darkness as he expertly handled the curves of the blacktop. "I sent the deputies back to the cabin, like you requested, but I have to tell you, budget's tight and I can't really spare two men to do a vehicle scavenger hunt in the dark, when—"

His radio crackled, and a voice sounded. "Herb, we went back to the cabin like you said."

Wentworth reached for the mic. "Find the SUV?"

"Haven't had time to look for it. We just pulled into the lane and saw smoke."

Cam's heart stopped. Then resumed its beat, thudding so loudly in his chest that it sounded in his ears.

The deputy's voice continued. "When we got closer to the place, we saw the cabin was on fire. We've already got a call in to the fire department."

"They may not be able to wait that long." Cam didn't pause for Wentworth to respond. "Our victim is in that cabin. Possibly with a small boy." Any doubt about that had dissipated as soon as the deputy started talking. "You need to find an entry point."

"Who am I—"

"That's DCI special agent Cam Prescott from Des Moines." Wentworth had the pedal to the floor and flipped on the siren. "He has reason to believe there are people on that property. Do you have access?"

"Negative. The only door is in flames. Fire is worse in the front, but the smoke makes it difficult to get too close."

"How long for the fire department to get there?" His chest felt as if it were being hollowed out by a dull blade.

The sheriff gave him a sympathetic look. "Eight, ten minutes, tops."

Bleakness settled over him like a leaden blanket. He'd followed his instincts down here, and they were screaming at him now.

Sophie didn't have eight more minutes.

"To the bedroom," Sophia shouted, giving the boy a small nudge to get him moving. They ran to the room that hadn't been boarded shut. She tore the pieces of tape Henry had cut off her wrists and pushed him farther into the room, slamming the door behind her. She felt along the wall inside for a light switch, but once she found it she realized that the electricity must be off.

Smoke was curling beneath the door. She coughed as she took Henry by the shoulders, moving him carefully, inch by inch, until they reached the opposite wall. "Stay here for now."

He whimpered. "Are we going to burn up?"

"No. I promise." But she was all too aware that she was making a promise she might not be able to keep. She did a survey of the room through touch alone. The same heavy furniture. Headboard and bedside table. Her fingers explored the mattress. Bedding could be stuffed in the crack of the door. Already Henry was gagging from the smoke.

But there were no sheets or blankets. She grabbed the bare pillows she found and went back to the bedroom door. It was hot to the touch. As best she could, Sophia wedged the pillows in the opening beneath the door. Smoke still wafted in along the sides, but there was an immediate improvement.

Then she went back to her search. One window, boarded, just inches away from where she'd parked Henry. A small closet without doors. Another opening that led to a tiny bath. A metal stall shower. Toilet. A sink hanging on the wall. And nothing else.

For a moment Sophia wanted to drop to the floor in defeat.

"I . . . it's hard . . . to breathe," the boy gasped. Sophia tried the spigots in the sink. No water. Then a thought occurred, and she turned to the toilet. Ran her fingers along the top. Then lifted off the heavy porcelain tank cover. Went back to the bedroom with it.

Setting it on the bed for a moment, she slipped the ruined jacket down her arms, wincing as the movement pulled at the burn on her shoulder. She dropped the material on the bed. The blouse beneath had been slit, too, and she took it off, ripped it into strips. She tied one around Henry's mouth and nose and another around her own. Moving the boy to the doorway of the bathroom, she lifted the tank cover from the bed. Then, with more determination than coordination, she began banging the porcelain against the plywood.

"We need to wait for the fire department," Maria warned. But the car had barely started down the lane before Cam was unfastening his seat belt. They took a bend in the drive, and when they cleared it, he had a full view of the cabin.

It was a scene from hell.

Flames were dancing across the roofline and shooting out a window on the side of the house closest to the road. He opened his door and jumped out as the sheriff pulled to a stop behind another county car. "We need tools. Something. Open the trunk."

Wentworth eased his bulk out of the car and then stood rooted in place, watching the blaze. "Dammit, Prescott. I don't carry equipment for this. The fire truck will be along any—"

"Look for a window that hasn't blown out. That might give us entry inside." Unwilling to wait for the man's acquiescence, he strode to the car and reached in, pulling the keys.

"Don't go off half-cocked. We still don't know if this is even the place."

One of the deputies tore his gaze from the conflagration and said, "We went back and checked after talking to you last time. When we went up the lane toward the road, our headlights reflected off something. We took a closer look, and there's a vehicle parked about thirty yards inside those trees over there."

Cam didn't need the man's words to know that they were at the right place. *Too late. Too damn late.* The refrain was a silent mental taunt. And he knew that if he failed right now, the regret would eat him alive.

He used the fob to open the man's trunk, then stuck his head in and rummaged around. Among the law enforcement equipment inside, Cam found some useful objects. Rags. A car jack. A gallon jug of water. Those he took.

A siren could be heard wailing in the distance. Maria moved over to him. "Prescott, you are not going near that cabin, and that's an order. Wait for the experts."

He unscrewed the lid of the water, drenched three rags, and tied one of them over his face. Shoving the blanket and other two rags toward her, he said, "Follow me." Without waiting to see if she obeyed, he ran toward the house.

The heat from the blaze was scorching. The deputies had said the front was a loss, so he concentrated on the back of the cabin. The fire was at the peak of the roof, slyly slithering down toward the rear. Smoke billowed from it, stinging his eyes, blurring his vision.

But in the pockets between plumes of smoke, the flames provided illumination that the hulking trees and stingy moon did not. Two small windows on this side of the house. Both of them still intact. He went to the nearest one, broke out the glass with the jack, but still hadn't broken through the enclosure.

The windows were boarded from the inside. Recalling the deputy's earlier report, he stepped back and cocked the jack like a bat. Swung it at the wood and heard it splinter.

Forms took shape beside him. He glimpsed a tan uniform and Maria running past. To the other window, he hoped. He swung again and then a third time before the jack broke through the wood.

Before he could wind up again, something flashed in the opening he'd made, smashing more wood to the side. Knocking it away from the window completely.

And then a small shape came flying through it. Cam barely dropped the jack in time to get his hands up to catch a screaming, wiggling body. The boy.

"Sophie!" The rag muffled his voice, and the smoke had turned his throat raw. Her name on his lips felt like a prayer. "Sophie!"

And then she was there, framed in the ruined window, her face darkened with soot. Eyes wide with fear. He saw her place her hands on the sill, try to hoist her body over it. But she was too short. "I can't . . ."

He raced along the back of the house with the child, coughing, his lungs strangling on the smoke. He shoved the boy at the deputy and found Maria. Grabbed a handful of her shirt and tugged her back with him to the window. "Get on my shoulders. Help pull Sophie through the window."

There was an earsplitting crack as something gave in the house. The blaze on the roof rolled down the dry shingles toward them, a crackling tsunami of flame.

He bent down and Maria mounted his shoulders. Rising, he approached the opening where Sophie could still be seen.

"Take my arms," the SAC shouted. "I'll pull you."

Perspiration poured down Cam's face, his muscles quivering as he willed Sophie to move. She made another attempt to hoist herself up, got her head and shoulders out the window. Maria reached forward and grabbed her beneath the arms. Cam backed up slowly and Sophie was pulled from the fiery building one slow inch at a time. Once freed, her weight drove them all backward and he went sprawling, the women landing on top of him.

There was a roar as the roof collapsed. Finding his feet, he scooped Sophie up into his arms and ran side by side with Maria. Away from the wall of fire and toward the road. To safety.

The county cars had retreated to the outer road to allow the emergency vehicles access to the lane. He stopped a distance away from the clanging fire truck, reaching up to claw the damp rag from his face. To pull down the fabric over hers. She twined her arms around his neck, and he lowered his face to hers for a kiss that was far more primitive than tender. All the gut-churning panic from the day poured into it, every bleak moment of despair chugged out of him in a torrent of emotion he was helpless to control.

Sophie accepted the unrestrained fury of feeling. Returned it in kind until the storm inside him calmed. The weight of her in his arms, the press of her body against his gradually healed all the places inside him that had been stripped raw.

He tore his mouth away. Rested his forehead against hers for a moment while his pulse steadied. "You gave me a few bad moments today."

She released a half laugh that turned into a coughing spasm. Concerned, he set her on her feet, one arm keeping her close to his side. "You need to get checked out by the EMTs."

"Henry . . ." Sophie craned her neck, trying to spot the boy in the darkness.

"He's already at the ambulance. We'll contact his dad." Cam could empathize with the hell Adams had gone through with his son kidnapped. He didn't deserve to be kept in the dark any longer. "Where's Baxter?"

Releasing a shuddering breath, she nodded her head in the direction of the cabin. "Her body is in there." Her voice was hoarse, and she had to stop in the telling several times when she was seized by a bout of coughing. "She was describing the torture techniques she was going . . . to use on me. My wrists . . . and ankles were bound. She'd just lit a cigar. She had plans to make me number seventeen. Henry . . . took her gun and shot her."

His gaze jerked to hers. "The kid did that?" To know that her survival had depended on the actions of a six-year-old boy was enough to have bricks of tension returning to his muscles again.

"I'll have Adams notified." He took his cell out and texted the request to Jenna, along with the news of Sophie's safety as they walked to the mouth of the lane where law enforcement had collected. He still had his arm wrapped around her waist. He'd release her later, when the reality of her rescue sank in. After the glacial fear had completely thawed in his veins.

But not yet.

Sophie made a beeline for the boy, who was sitting in the open back door of the ambulance being checked over by an EMT. Soot had collected on his face around the area where the fabric had been, so he looked like a surprised raccoon. When he saw Sophie, his eyes lit up and he pushed away the oxygen mask to speak. "I get to go home now, don't I?"

"Pretty soon, buddy." She reached out to push his hair away from his face. "I'll bet your dad will be calling any minute."

His face sobered. "He might be mad. I shot the monster. Dad always says not to ever touch his guns."

"I'll tell him you had to do it. You were a hero, Henry. If it hadn't been for you, she would have killed me. So thank you." Leaning down, she kissed him lightly on the forehead.

"You're a hero, too." He paused, doubled over to cough before adding, "You pushed me out the window so I didn't get burned up." He thought about that for a moment. "I was really scared."

"Me, too. But we're safe now."

His gaze traveled to the cabin, completely engulfed by flames the firefighters hadn't been able to tame. "I'm glad the monster is dead."

It was a sentiment that Cam could wholeheartedly share. "We're all glad the monster is dead."

—

Cam was completely aware that Sophie wanted to go home. She'd made her wishes clear enough. And God knows, he was anxious to get her back to his condo, too. Just hole up together while they forgot the rest of the world for a few precious hours. Later there'd be briefings with the team, meetings with the DCI administration, and media to dodge. But first he wanted to have her to himself. Long enough to dull the memory of how close he'd come to losing her.

As it was, that wish was delayed by nearly twenty-four hours. Sophie and Henry were treated by the EMTs and taken to the local hospital overnight for further observation. Cam remained at her side throughout, his cell phone silenced, although he answered the barrage of texts and email on it. The wrap-up on a case like this was always substantial. The returned calls waited until the ride home, during which time she drowsed; the feel of her body leaning against his a comforting weight.

She'd given him plenty of grief about the lack of decorating in his condo before. It centered around an enormous TV and sound system and apparently lacked all the little touches a woman would consider homey. But as soon as Sophie walked through the door after the drive from Centerville, he saw the tension stream from her limbs. He felt the same way as he secured the door and reengaged the alarm. The rest of the world could wait for a just a few hours.

She let out a sigh. "Man cave, sweet man cave."

"I figure the first thing you're going to want to do is change." A female Appanoose deputy had loaned her a change of clothes to wear home. The yoga pants, T-shirt, and flip-flops likely belonged to the other woman, who towered over Sophia by at least five inches. He flashed a grin. "I know you've had issues with my decorating style in the past, so I had something brought in to welcome you back."

He led her into the living area from the hallway where she stopped. Blinked. There were flowers everywhere. On the kitchen counter. On the coffee table. The entertainment center. All pink roses with an occasional white one scattered throughout each arrangement.

"I gave Jenna the security code, and she delivered them for me." He shoved his hands in the pockets of his trousers, watching her expression carefully. "It occurred to me that I had no idea what your favorite flower is, but I thought these looked like you. You have a suit this shade, the color of cotton candy. It makes you look . . ." He searched for a word. "Delicate. But you're not, Sophie. What you've been through in the last month . . ." His throat worked, and it took him a moment to continue. When he did his voice was husky. "You're stronger than you look. Thank God."

Her expression aglow, she went to him and stood on tiptoe to brush her lips over his. He took his hands out of his pockets to slide them around her waist. "They're beautiful. And thoughtful. No one has ever given me pink roses before. And there are different kinds of strength. After yesterday I've discovered that I seriously need to start pumping iron."

He didn't want to think about what might have happened yesterday. He knew exactly what her fate would have been if Henry Adams hadn't picked up that gun and killed the woman.

Baxter would have numbered another victim, and Sophie's body would now be buried in the smoking remains of the cabin. With effort, he shoved the thoughts away.

"There *are* different kinds of strength." He stroked up her spine in one smooth movement and then down again. "When it comes to that brain of yours, you're unparalleled. After you were taken, I went over your case notes again to determine a focus for where to start searching."

"My case notes?" The words came out raspy, an aftereffect of the fire.

"We found Lisa Hansen alive in the cellar of the Coates place. You'd focused on Baxter's years there, seemed to think it was important to her formation. I thought it was worth a look."

"Thank God the woman is still alive. So that's what led you to Denholt?" He'd explained the ownership of the cabin on the car ride home.

He nodded. His palm lingered at the base of her spine, his fingers rubbing in little circular motions that had her releasing a contented sigh. "You spent a lot of time trying to predict Baxter's behavior based on people and events from her past. I decided to follow your lead. It paid off. Franks checked with Karen Denholt while I was making the flight arrangements, and she did remember Baxter being at the cabin with the Coates family once. Said she bitched about the amenities the whole time."

"After yesterday, I have a few quibbles with them myself."

He couldn't share her humor. Her situation had been harrowing, and his panic still felt too close. Too real. Cam was acutely aware that the outcome could have been far different.

"The fact that you can even joke about it just underscores what I said before. There are different types of strength." He cupped her jaw in one hand. "I didn't have enough faith in yours. I'm not talking about your mind—that's hard to overlook. Especially since you beat me at Gin nine times out of ten." When she smiled he traced his thumb lightly over the curve of her bottom lip. "But I didn't figure I could trust your emotions when you told me you loved me. First we'd broken up, then Vance's case threw us together again, and after you'd escaped him . . ."

"It was too soon," she began.

"No. Or at least, yeah, I thought that at first. That you couldn't possibly know what you felt because you'd just been through hell." And although she might not have the PTSD diagnosis he'd gotten after the Moreno assignment, she had a lot of the symptoms. "But you told me once that going through a trauma can rearrange priorities. And I get that now. Because during those hours spent searching for you, things got pretty damn clear. Crystal." Emotion thickened his voice. "I love you, Sophie. Life doesn't hand out guarantees, so I guess it's time to stop waiting for one. I'm not going to risk losing you. If you're going to come to your senses and run like hell, this is the one and only chance you get. I'll give you a head start." He paused a beat. "At least to the couch."

The radiant expression on her face gave him her answer even before she went on tiptoe to form the words against his lips. "I'm. Not. Running."

Tension seeped from his body, a fraction at a time. "Wise choice. What I lack in speed I make up for in endurance."

"Good to know." She nipped at his jaw. "Because right now I'm in the mood to put that particular quality to the test."

His arms snaked around her with barely tempered desperation. She probably would have rested better last night had he left her sleeping, but he'd been incapable of leaving the hospital room. Had needed to hold her hand, touch her hair, as if by maintaining that physical contact he could banish the knifelike fear that had carved a hole in his gut.

He tipped his head, found her mouth with his, and threaded his fingers through her hair. His lips moved on hers greedily. The urgency was still there, but now it was elicited by desire rather than panic. And for the first time since she'd been pulled from the burning cabin's window last night, he felt a sliver of peace. She was here. She was safe.

Her tongue found his in a delicate sensual slide. And she was his.

The knowledge completed the transformation from desperation to desire. One of his hands went to the hem of the T-shirt she wore, stripping it up and off her. He lifted his head to look at the picture she made. Smooth creamy skin swelled over the confines of black lace. Considering Sophie's sense of style, he could be assured her panties matched.

A slow primal throb started in his pulse. He was capable of finesse, but that would come later. After hunger had been sated. Greed assuaged. With his thumbs hooked in the waistband of her pants, he peeled them down her silky legs. Felt her balance herself with one hand to his shoulder when he helped her step out of them.

He reversed course with his lips, exploring the jut of her ankle, the feminine curve of her calf. The satiny smoothness of her thigh. He knelt before her, his hands cupping her lace-clad butt. Pressed a kiss against the moist heat dampening the fabric that shielded her cleft. And when her flesh quivered against his lips, any semblance of restraint abruptly eroded.

He straightened, lifted Sophie in his arms, and strode to the bedroom. He laid her on the dark rumpled sheets, a jewel against a velvet backdrop. She drew up one leg languorously and lifted a hand toward him in a gesture of feminine enticement that would tempt a plaster saint. Cam was damn grateful to be a sinner.

He stripped deliberately, his gaze never wavering. Her cheeks tinged pink under his intense regard. Joining her on the bed, he caught both wrists in one of his and drew them slowly, inexorably over her head, watching her expression carefully for any sign of distress. He didn't want the position to trigger a flashback of yesterday's trauma.

But he didn't have to worry. Her neck arched. Her body bowed. And the evidence of her passion incited his own. Cam stretched out beside her, one knee pressing her legs apart as he lifted her breasts from the lace cups. Her nipples were already taut, ready. He rolled one between two fingers while going on a primitive quest for flesh.

The taste of her whipped the fever in his blood to a frenzy. He needed to linger, to savor. Neither was an option. Not with Sophie writhing under him as he feasted. She tugged her wrists from his grip and clutched at his shoulders, her nails scoring his skin not quite painfully. The slight sting called to something savage in him, and he knew control would soon be impossible to summon.

He traced the elastic edge of her panties with one finger, and her hips moved restlessly. Restraint slipped. One hand delving inside the lace, he covered her mound with his fingers. Found the taut bundle of nerves and began the steady rhythmic motion that would drive them both a little crazy.

His name was on her lips, a broken cry. It fed a frenetic craving coursing through him that wouldn't be denied. Reason was receding. His vision graying.

Sweeping the wisp of lace over her hips and down her legs, he settled over her. Almost disgraced himself when her hand reached down to guide him, enclosing him with clever, knowing fingers designed to enflame. Unable to help himself, he plunged deeply inside her slick heat, paused to haul in a shaky breath and summon a measure of logic.

She wouldn't allow it. Sophie set the pace with her hips, demanding and urgent. Her desire fired his own, and he thrust into her wildly, reason gone. There was only the need to take and be taken. To possess and be possessed. She arched beneath him, muscles rigid, a helpless cry on her lips. The sound of her climax ripped through him, demanded his own.

And when the pleasure crashed over him, swallowed him, his mind was wiped clean of everything but her.

Chapter 15

The deluge of media attention was brutal. Her work as a forensic consultant rarely put Sophia in front of a camera. And when it did, her notes were prepared, her remarks brief. She had acquired a newfound empathy for victims who were asked insensitive questions about their ordeals just to provide a reporter with a fresh headline.

As they stepped outside DCI offices, a horde of reporters rushed forward, their shouted questions melding into an earsplitting crescendo. "Agent Prescott, how did Vickie Baxter die?"

His hand at the base of Sophia's spine propelled her forward as he strode across the parking lot to his vehicle. "That matter is still under investigation."

"Dr. Channing, did you see any other victims held at that cabin?"

"Details will be released as the investigation unfolds."

"Good answer," he whispered under his breath as they approached the vehicle. He raised a hand to click the fob and release the lock on the car. As they both got in it, an enterprising reporter sprinted from several yards away to yank open the back door and slide into the backseat. Cam turned around, his expression stony. Unrepentant, the man grinned at him.

"Agent Prescott, can you tell me how many bodies have been linked to Vickie Baxter while Mason Vance was imprisoned?"

"SAC Maria Gonzalez is in charge of media releases. I've got nothing for you outside the details presented at this morning's press conference."

"I think you do. You were there, man." The reporter, sporting a bald head and goatee, leaned forward. "I've got a tip claiming she offed five more people in the last couple weeks. Can you confirm?"

"What I can confirm," Cam said neutrally, "is that you're leaving my car. Whether it's while it's parked or while it's moving is up to you, but you will leave it." To Sophia he said, "Hope he doesn't decide to get out at the Eighty-Sixth Street overpass. That always gets messy."

Her lips quirked. "I can imagine."

"You want me out, just answer the question. Is it true that—"

Cam turned on the ignition, put the car in gear, and headed toward the exit of the parking lot. The reporter looked out the window. "Hey, my car is here. Just stop and answer a few questions, and I'll get out."

Slowing, Cam responded, "Get out now, or get out thirty miles from here. Up to you."

"But—"

He accelerated, nosing the car down the drive to the stop sign. "Where do you want to be dropped off?" he asked Sophia deliberately.

She appreciated his quick thinking. The last thing she wanted was for their relationship to become fodder for local and national news. "The car rental at the airport will be fine."

"All right, all right, you can let me out here." Cam kept driving. The reporter repeated, "I said I'll get out. Just let me out. Jesus, I'm going to have to walk a mile."

Cam cruised to a halt at the stop sign that would allow him to turn into traffic. "Nah. From here it isn't more than a half mile."

The man's muttered response was lost when he got out of the car and slammed the door.

"Honestly, it's like being hounded by a ravenous beast that feeds on fresh sound bites."

He sent her a quick grin. "An apt analogy."

She sent a worried look in the side mirrors. "How can you be sure one of them won't follow you home?"

"There's no point. Gonzalez and Assistant Director Miller control the information dissemination, and we've already discussed what will be released and when. A smart reporter isn't going to waste time on me and miss a chance at her when she leaves the office."

Satisfied with that, Sophia settled back in her seat. "Good. Something tells me she's used to shutting down pushy media types."

"She's the master." His cell rang, and he pulled it out of his pocket to read the screen. His mouth flattened, and his voice went expressionless. "Prescott."

Sophia couldn't hear the caller's words, but she recognized the booming voice. FBI agent Del Harlow. Instantly nausea did a quick spin in her stomach. Turning to her window, she pretended an interest in the scenery that she wasn't feeling.

Sophia knew little about the details of the assignment the FBI agent was planning, but she knew just enough about Cam's last task force assignment involving Moreno to be filled with sick fear. Cam had once revealed that Moreno's lieutenants had conducted frequent "loyalty tests." Which had involved dragging members of Moreno's team off on a regular basis, putting a loaded gun in their mouths, and interrogating them as possible spies.

It didn't bear thinking about what Cam might face returning to that task force.

The phone conversation lasted all the way back to Cam's place. His side of it was terse. At one point he looked her way and said, "You know what it will take." He listened a moment longer, and his mouth twisted. "That's not going to cut it. I'll need it in writing."

When they got into the garage, Sophia got out of the vehicle. Hurried inside. Got to the bathroom and leaned against the counter, fingers gripping the edge. She couldn't face him. Not when her imagination was supplying her in vivid Technicolor detail all the infinite ways this task force assignment could go horribly wrong.

He couldn't share the specifics with her. He didn't need to. She knew enough to realize the mission included using Cam as bait. Pablo Moreno suspected him of being the informant that had nearly brought down his drug distribution network. Cam was walking into a lion's den.

"Soph?" A rap sounded at the door. "You okay?" She closed her eyes. Drew a breath. Then she turned on the spigot and leaned forward to splash water on her face. Dried it.

"I'll be right out." But it was several more minutes before she could steel herself to face him.

He was standing in the living room, his expression watchful as she joined him. "You feel like eating?"

"I can make you something." The task would give her something to concentrate on besides the conversation he'd just shared with Harlow. A sudden thought occurred. "Wait." She hurried to the coffee table in front of the couch, bent down to look at the underside.

"What are you doing?"

"Looking for this." She reached for a small foreign object, peeling it away from the adhesive. Rising, she handed it to him. "Courtesy of Vickie Baxter."

"That's impossible." Turning it over in his fingers, he studied it closely before looking at her. "How'd it get in here?"

Letting out a sigh, she replied simply, "Henry. I let him in that day when he pretended to be looking for his cat. Turned my back for a minute . . ." She nodded toward the object he held. "That's how she knew exactly when you were leaving that morning. She had a narrow window of opportunity to act. She took it."

Cam slipped the transmitter into his pocket. "Sometimes I wish the woman wasn't dead. She got off too easy."

His meaning was clear. She shuddered, headed to the kitchen. "I have no regrets in that regard." Knowing Baxter would never take another victim would enable Sophia to sleep at night. Although, she thought grimly as she took deli meat from the refrigerator, she seriously doubted her ability to do any sleeping until Cam was out of danger for good.

She was adding mayo to his sandwich when she heard him clearing his throat. "That call earlier. It was Harlow."

"I could tell." It took effort to keep her voice steady as she handed him the plate and went in search of a glass. "You're always at your friendliest when talking to him."

Cam settled on a stool at the breakfast bar, but he made no move toward the sandwich. He was too busy watching her. "We have a history."

"I know. That's why it's so hard to figure why you'd put your life in his hands again." She poured milk in a glass. Handed it to him.

"He's a cog in a wheel. He's not making the decisions for the op." He took a drink. Lowered the glass. "He's just the go-between."

She didn't want to have this conversation. To do so would make it far too real. But reality was hurtling toward her on a collision course. There was no avoiding it. She drew a deep breath and met his gaze, her heart hammering in her chest. "So what did your go-between have to say?"

A minute ticked by. Then another. "Soph."

She shut her eyes, as if the action could ward off the rest of his words. "The op is on. Everything's in place. I put him off when he called yesterday . . . but I have to go."

She moistened her lips. Tried to speak. Could barely force the question out. "When?"

"Tonight."

~

There were worse things, Cam decided, then spending a few hours getting reacquainted with a man who—under the worst circumstances—had somehow become a friend. He and Matt Baldwin had formed an unlikely bond when Cam had been undercover. And knowing the odds they faced when they hit Moreno's gated property south of LA made their reacquaintance seem like a moment out of time.

The rest of the team had taken different flights, all heading to LA. He and Baldwin had flown instead to Phoenix, where a car with Iowa rental plates had been waiting for them. Moreno's orders had been for Matt to personally deliver Cam alive. It was a sure bet the cartel boss didn't mean to keep him that way.

Small talk was better than dealing with the adrenaline that spiked every time he considered the enormity of their task. And it was easy enough to fall into the banter that had marked his and Matt's relationship from the beginning.

"The Cubs? Are you still chasing that pipe dream?" Matt chuckled. "You'd have to time travel to find the last time they won the Series."

"Cubs fans are loyal," Cam retorted good-naturedly. "Something you A's fans wouldn't understand." His gaze sharpened when Matt pulled over on the shoulder. And he became a bit more aware of just how deserted this stretch of highway was.

"There's loyalty and then there's insanity. Remind me to teach you the difference some time."

Cam looked at him as the car stopped. He'd been the one to convince Harlow, who in turn had convinced his superiors, that Baldwin could be trusted. But right now every argument they'd lodged against the man came hurtling back to him.

He was all too aware that the biggest risk to this entire operation was the possibility that Matthew Baldwin was playing both sides against the middle. Gaining the feds' trust so he could set them up for his boss.

Tension rapped at the base of Cam's skull. "Run out of gas?"

"No. This is where we start working on our story."

"Which is?"

Baldwin gestured at him. "Moreno isn't going to believe I took you without a scratch on either one of us."

His muscles relaxed a fraction. "You're probably right." He got out of the car, followed Baldwin a short distance from the road. "Just remember you owe me." The words were barely out of his mouth before the other man sent a right hook to Cam's jaw. His head rocked back. Touching his face gingerly, he said, "I saved your life—I didn't kill your dog. Try not to act like you're enjoying this."

"I promise."

It was hard to believe the man's sincerity when he was grinning hugely. "C'mon, he's going to expect me to look like you put up a—" His chin snapped up from the force of Cam's uppercut. "Ah . . ." He spat out blood. "I see you're getting into the spirit of things."

Five minutes of brawling could do a lot of damage, Cam reflected later, after he inspected his face in the mirror clipped to the visor. One eye was already swelling, and blood dribbled steadily from his nose. He eyed the other man balefully. Felt a measure of satisfaction that he looked as bad as Cam did.

Matt was cleaning himself up. Caught Cam's gaze on him and shook his head. "You'll be more convincing appearing like that."

The fact that it was true didn't make Cam any happier about it. He wiped his face on his denim shirt. Figured the smear of blood could be window dressing. Then stopped, aware the other man was staring at him. "What now? If you're thinking knife wound, forget it."

"I'm supposed to be delivering the man accused of being a federal informant to Pablo Moreno in less than an hour. I can't drive up with you seated in the front seat of my car."

Blowing out a breath, Cam got out again. Went to the rear of the vehicle and waited. The other man approached him with a length of rope and made short work of tying his wrists behind his back. Baldwin clicked the fob, and the trunk lid rose. Resignedly Cam climbed in.

The other man stood there looking at him for a moment. "You're taking a helluva risk."

"So are you." The words were true enough. Cam just had to bank on the fact that Moreno wouldn't kill him on sight. After that his odds improved dramatically.

But Matt . . . Moreno held his wife and child. If the mission were successful, the drug kingpin would have a long reach, even from prison. Baldwin and his family would be on the run for the rest of their lives. If it failed, the feds would suspect Baldwin had betrayed them. He'd be the target of every DEA agent in the Western United States.

As the lid of the trunk closed, Cam reflected that he'd still take his odds over Matt's.

An hour and a half later, however, lying on the tile floor of one of Moreno's garages, he was reexamining his earlier assessment.

The drug boss was prowling a slow circle around him. "You did nice work, Matthew. You're sure this is the one?"

Matt was leaning against the trunk he'd just pulled Cam out of. "I'm sure. He's a state agent from the Midwest."

One Italian loafer drew back, and Moreno's foot slammed into Cam's ribs. The oxygen was driven from his body. He gasped and wheezed for air.

"You have his credentials."

"Right here."

There was a moment of silence while Moreno presumably studied Cam's badge. "Hang on to this for now."

"I can give you information." It was a struggle to draw enough air into his tortured lungs to even form words. "I spent a lot of time undercover. I have access to federal informants . . . who feed the feds details about your operation."

"And you will give me all those details. Then I will still kill you. Slowly. And with great pleasure. Because that's what I do to bastards who . . . betray . . . me." His final words were punctuated with more kicks.

As from a great distance he heard the man say, "Secure him. I'll deal with him after tonight's shipment."

Cam was dimly aware that he was being lifted up. Shoved back into the trunk. And when he caught a glimpse of Matt before the lid closed, it was like looking into the face of a stranger.

Sophia used the peephole, then pulled the door open with amused exasperation. "You two don't have to feel like I need a babysitter. Baxter's dead. The danger is over."

Jenna Turner and Beckett Maxwell walked past her into the house. The sheriff was dressed in jeans and a polo shirt and was carrying a pizza large enough to feed a small village. Jenna wore a white denim skirt that showed off her mile-long legs.

Sophia's interest was piqued. She'd never seen the woman in anything other than pants before.

"See, I told her that." Beckett was already setting the box down on the breakfast bar and going to her cupboards to rummage for plates. "But Red insisted. She figured you'd be lonely."

Rolling her eyes, Jenna said, "I made the mistake of mentioning to him that I planned to stop by, and he insisted on tagging along. At least he made himself useful and paid for the pizza."

"See," Beckett said with a wink, "I *am* good for something."

With a wry smile, Sophia reset the alarm and went over to join them for a slice. Any diversion from her constant concern about Cam would be welcome. There would be no word until the mission was over. And the wait was excruciating.

Now she could sympathize with what he had gone through when she'd been taken by Baxter.

The only difference was that he'd been able to do something about it. Sophia was stuck just knowing enough about the details of the mission to agonize over its risks.

After they'd stuffed themselves, she allowed them to bully her into a card game. It was worth it just to watch the dynamics between the two. Sophia had long suspected that the sheriff was more than a little enchanted by the female agent. And after several hours with them, she was fairly certain that Jenna's feelings toward the man had undergone a thaw. The thought made her smile.

It was nearly midnight when Jenna looked up from the cards in her hand. Frowned. "Do you hear something?"

"That's the sound of my heart breaking," Beckett joked. "You're a shark. I'm cleaned out."

"I told you that blackjack's my game." But she slid off her stool, went to the drawn blind on the window in the kitchen, and looked out.

"We're all still a little paranoid." Although, Sophia admitted as she rinsed out the wineglasses and put away Beckett's empty beer bottle, she was a lot less jumpy with company here than she'd been when alone. She'd taken to carrying Cam's letter opener with her wherever she went, even to bed. Which made her feel vaguely ridiculous, if a smidgeon safer.

Clearly unconvinced, Jenna went to the garage entrance, unlocked it, and disappeared through it.

Sophia looked at Beckett, who shrugged. But he got up and followed the path Jenna had taken. Found her on all fours, looking beneath Sophia's rental.

He squatted down next to her. "You won't find me under there."

She swatted at his leg and rose. "I know it's crazy, but I keep hearing noises." Rolling her shoulders impatiently, she turned to go back into the condo. With a quick and sneaky tug on her hand, Beckett pulled her into his arms.

"And I thought you were just trying to lure me out here to take advantage of me."

His embrace was just a little too comfortable, Jenna decided. She was notched between his slightly splayed legs. Hip to hip. Thigh to thigh. "I thought I already had."

He nodded soberly, his face lowering to hers. "So it's only fair that I return the favor." His lips moved over hers persuasively. And Jenna recognized just how much trouble she was in when she slid her hand into his hair and dove into the kiss. Hidden depths. She'd always suspected that Beckett possessed them. As their mouths twisted together, she had the distant thought that she'd like to explore all his secrets. One by—

The rest of the thought was lost as the shrilling of Sophia's security alarm split the air.

Moreno's distribution system was diverse. Each faction of the cartel was responsible for funneling drugs to a different part of the United States. The pipeline of drugs intended for the Midwest depended on a network of tunnels that stretched from the Mexican border to the southern desert of California. Trucks would emerge from the tunnels at varied points, carrying their loads on highways headed to hub areas in Chicago, Kansas City, Omaha, and Des Moines.

The subterranean area was a beehive of activity, especially when a shipment was being dispersed. Workers loaded trucks, interspersing the drugs with more unremarkable cargo.

Along one side of the tunnel were cells, complete with bars and an elaborate security system. The drugs were locked in the cells until they were shipped. Occasionally an employee who got greedy was held in one, too, until Moreno had the time and inclination to make an example of him.

"Are you *loco*? What are you doing bringing him here?"

Matt Baldwin pulled Cam to a stop when they were approached by the security guard. They hadn't expected to go unnoticed. "I'm under Mr. Moreno's orders to find a secure place to hold a high-value guest."

"But not here!" The man gesticulated wildly. "Not in the middle of this!"

"Yeah, well, you want to suggest a more secure place?" Baldwin kept his hand close to his weapon. "Or perhaps you want me to tell Mr. Moreno that you refused to allow me to follow his orders."

The man didn't like it, but neither was he willing to take the chance of displeasing a man who considered beheadings an educational tool. Muttering in two languages, he led them to an empty cell and punched in a code. The door swung open. Cam exploded into action, a man battling to avoid certain death. "Help me with him!" Baldwin shouted at the guard, who stepped in to assist. Together they muscled Cam into the cell, where his struggles forced them all into the corner next to the door. Out of sight of anyone passing by.

Then Matt pulled out a knife and slit the man's throat. When the body went limp, he laid it almost gently in the corner of the cell.

Cam stripped the man of his weapon and peered out into the main area. The bustle of activity continued, the noise level reminiscent of any busy warehouse or dock. Only the cargo differed.

"Okay, let's have them."

Matt dug the wrapped package of tiny GPS transmitters from his pocket. Gave four to Cam and kept three for himself. Baldwin would have used the fourth at Moreno's compound. Then he passed him a set of earplugs, which Cam put in the pocket of his shirt. "Front or back?"

There was more activity at the front entrances and an increased chance of detection. But in the end the decision was a no-brainer. "Front," Cam said. "I'm not sure I recall where all the exits are."

Matt nodded. Turned to precede Cam out of the cell and then hesitated. Looked back. "Remember the stakes. Everything depends on this. Everything."

Everything meant Baldwin's wife and child. Cam could appreciate the sentiment. He knew all too well what it was like to gamble it all for a loved one.

The other man left the cell and disappeared. Cam drew a breath. Followed. When he'd first infiltrated this operation, he'd spent more time than he cared to remember working in this area. There would be perhaps eight people assigned to supervise and another fifty to load the trucks. They would all be strangers to him. The others had been swept up in the raid that his intel had helped make possible.

He was counting on the fact that no one would be that well acquainted with all Moreno's employees. The fact that he was inside the highly secure area would give him a certain degree of latitude.

Until someone noticed that he wasn't working and wondered what the hell he was up to.

Adopting a purposeful stride, he headed for the entrance of tunnel number one. He stepped aside as a truck lumbered in, then slapped a hand beside the huge armored door as it was closing again. Without looking back, he continued to the next entrance. The small GPS transmitter was no bigger than a thumbnail and would affix to any surface. The signal could be detected through stone or steel, giving the feds pinpoint location accuracy.

The rest would be up to them.

Entrances one, two, and three went off without a hitch. It wasn't until he was walking to the fourth entrance that things got totally fucked.

He saw the supervisor's attention shift to him as he went by. Braced himself. The man shouted a command in Spanish. Cam kept walking. Given the noise level throughout the area, the supervisor might believe he hadn't been heard. But Cam didn't fool himself that the man would back off. He just needed to get to a more private area for the confrontation.

He turned a corner filled with rows and rows of boxed blankets that would serve as the decoy cargo on one of the trucks. Felt the expected hand fall on his shoulder and swung around, a big smile on his face, as if in greeting, at the same time extending a hand to tug the other man off balance against a row of stacked boxes.

Cam pulled his weapon and shot him through one of the cartons. One bullet to the heart. Propped the body against the wall and arranged some boxes to hide it, then grabbed a few more of the boxes to carry with him.

The box of blankets had muffled the shot but not completely silenced it. Two men came to investigate, looking around curiously.

Cam held his breath, hoping like hell they didn't start poking around. If the body was discovered, the mission would be compromised.

But someone called to one of the men, and he turned away. The other lingered awhile longer, but he eventually left the area.

The breath hissed out of him, a silent stream of relief. He went to the fourth entrance, affixed the GPS, then continued on to find a spot in between stacks of cargo where he could wait. He dug the earplugs out of his pocket and placed them in his ears.

The dark thought occurred that if the rest of the team failed in their next task, he would be trapped here in the tunnels. And he had a feeling getting out would be a whole lot tougher than getting in had been.

Twenty minutes crawled by. Then there was the sound of voices. A truck moving into the area. Cam muttered a silent obscenity.

The cargo he was hiding behind was about to be loaded. Several workers swarmed over to where he was hidden. One man moved a pile of boxes. Stared straight at him. Opened his mouth to call out.

And then the detonations rocked the area, one at each entrance and exit of the place. Even with the earplugs, the sound was deafening. It was followed by armored trucks crashing through the shredded doors.

Cam removed his earplugs and stayed put. Wading into the middle of the resulting chaos with no way to identify himself as law enforcement was risky. Gunfire filled the area. The supervisors and security guards would be armed.

The task force would be, too.

A familiar figure sidled out of the shadows and fled right by Cam's hiding place, heading down the passageway toward the third tunnel. His face was turned away.

But Cam didn't figure anyone else in the area would be wearing Italian loafers. "Moreno!" Pulling his weapon, he launched himself into the open area to chase after the man. He'd hoped a member of the task force might hear him, but the enclosed space rang with the sound of gunfire. Loud cries. Shouted commands.

Cam saw Matt running toward him from the opposite direction. Moreno halted, swung toward Cam. They fired simultaneously.

He didn't even realize at first that he'd been shot. His arm went numb. His fingers loosened on the weapon. He fumbled to switch the gun to his other hand. Time slowed. Moreno walked toward him, lips curved, with his gun still aimed. Cam saw his death written in the man's smile, and he had a brief moment to mourn the fact that he and Sophie weren't going to have that future after all.

—

"Sorry to freak you out last night," Jenna repeated again as she and Beckett walked to the front door. After the alarm had been triggered, there'd been a visit from a guard from the security company. When even he couldn't come up with a breach in the system, Jenna and Beckett had insisted on spending the night at Sophia's. That is, Jenna had insisted, and Beckett had settled in on the couch, as if his presence was a given. Maybe it was, since the two had arrived together.

"The guard was probably right." Sophia was transferring her things to a different purse. "It could have been something hitting the window."

"Personally, I thought the guy was an idiot." Beckett rubbed at the stubble on his chin. "An owl? You buy that?"

"I don't know." She was hoping that a reasonable explanation would occur to her before nightfall. Cam could talk about her strength all he wanted, but she was very much afraid that it had been nearly depleted.

"If Cam's not back tonight, you can stay with me."

Sophia sent the other woman a grateful look. "I'll let you know."

She waved good-bye, and the two walked toward Jenna's vehicle, which had been parked in the visitor's lot. Sophia closed the front door and crossed to the garage entrance. Today she was going to make a concerted effort to resume her life. She'd go to her office and spend the day preparing to transition her clients back to her schedule.

And maybe, she thought, backing the car out of the drive, if she stayed busy enough she would be able to get through at least an hour without worrying about what was happening with Cam.

She slowed to a stop for the light at the end of the street, behind a car with its windows down, rap music blaring from it. Noticing a rough-looking man loitering on the corner, she double-checked the locks. Paranoia was still alive and well.

The car in front of her turned. There was a flash of movement at the side of the car. As she turned her head, she saw the man she'd noticed looming closer. He had something in his hand that he swung hard at the front passenger window. Sophia screamed, instinctively shielding her face from the flying shards of glass. He used that moment to reach into the opening he'd created, flip the locks, and get in. And then he was over her, one beefy arm around her neck, attempting to drag her from the vehicle.

"Everything you had on your rape list?" His breath was hot against her face. "You and me are gonna add a few things to it."

He was pulling her out the passenger door. Instinct overshot panic. She jammed her hand in her purse, searching, and heard him laugh. "Lady, there's nothing in there you're gonna need where we're going." His laugh turned to a scream when Sophia drove the letter opener into his eye.

Abruptly she was freed. Scrambling over the seat, she attempted to reach the driver's door and felt his hand grip her ankle, pull her back again.

"I'll kill you for that, bitch! I'll fucking kill you." She sliced at his arm, her breath coming in huge racking sobs. Blood covered the man, but still he came. He grasped her shoulders and gave a mighty yank. In a tangle of limbs, she was being pulled through the open door.

"Police! Hands in the air! Right now, right now!"

Relief had her collapsing in the seat, too weak to even lift her head to look at her rescuers. She didn't need to. Their voices made them readily identifiable. Jenna and Beckett. They subdued her attacker, cuffed him, and then split up. Beckett applied first aid, and Jenna checked Sophia for injuries.

"I'm not hurt. I'm not. I just . . ." She shuddered violently, and Jenna slipped a protective arm around her shoulders. "It's never going to stop, is it? How many men did Baxter send after me? A dozen? A hundred? It'll never be over!"

"It's over now," the woman said soothingly. "It is. Right after Leslie attacked you, Cam immediately placed a warning on Craigslist about the ad. Then he filed for an injunction to get the original one pulled. I checked myself this morning. It's gone."

The news didn't alleviate her worry. Adrenaline had faded, leaving her trembling and teary. "I stabbed him in the eye."

Jenna's voice was matter-of-fact. "That's okay. You probably couldn't reach his junk."

Sophia's head jerked up at that; her gaze fixed on her friend for a moment. And then, shaky with shock, she joined her in laughter.

———

"His name is Michael Frasier." Beckett shoved a mug of steaming coffee in her hands, and Sophia accepted it gratefully. They were back at Cam's condo. The DMPD had come and gone, hauling the stranger away.

But not before the man had spilled details to Jenna and Beckett. "His story is shaping up a lot like Leslie's." Jenna sipped from her coffee, her brows raised in approval. "Maxwell. You've got hidden talents."

"That's what I keep saying." The sheriff settled one hip on a stool and drank, then took over the story. "He spoke to Baxter at least a week after the other man, though. He also tripped your alarm last night when he tried to get in through a window."

Jenna's gaze was sharp. "How is that possible? Aren't the feds still watching this place?"

Steadier now, Sophia nodded. "I thought so." And if she'd known the federal agent wasn't out there the first night Cam left, she wouldn't have slept at all. "How long . . . When do you think Cam will be back?"

Jenna and Beckett exchanged a glance. "Don't look at me," Maxwell said. "No one's told me anything."

"I don't have many details," Jenna admitted. "Or none, actually. But he did say it'd be quick."

"If it was over, shouldn't we have heard something by now?" Sophia stopped. Surveyed Jenna. "I'll bet you can get that FBI agent's number. Del Harlow. He's Cam's contact throughout this."

The other woman pulled out her cell, her face a mask of determination. "I'll bet I can, too."

It took nearly an hour and a half a dozen calls, but eventually she had a cell number. Sophia's hands shook so badly she had to redial it twice. Prepared to leave a message, she was surprised to hear the agent answer. "Agent Harlow. This is Dr. Sophia Channing. What can you tell me about Cam? Have you been in contact? Is he safe?"

There was a long pause. And when he spoke, the man's voice was more subdued than usual. "I meant to call you. I'm afraid I have some bad news, Dr. Channing . . ."

Sophia waited in the hospital room, arms wrapped around her middle. Why were these places so cold all the time? That couldn't be good for the patients. Or maybe, she thought, turning to pace, the chill was coming from within her. From the moment Harlow had given her the news, she'd felt frozen from the inside out.

The door opened, and Cam walked through it with a physical therapist at his side. Seeing him standing on his own had all the pent-up anxiety streaming out of her, leaving her limp with relief. "Hey." It was a ridiculously lame greeting, given the wild, unadulterated happiness pumping through her. But her throat was too full to manage more.

He looked tired, cranky, and out of sorts. But when he saw her, his expression flashed to fierce joy. He held out an arm, and she flew to his side, careful to avoid the opposite injured shoulder. Cam buried his face in her hair. "You can't know how much I needed to see you. Did Harlow call you?"

Her head lifted; indignation sounded in her voice. "He did not. I called him after Jenna tracked down his number, and when he told me about your injury, at first I thought . . ." Seeing the frown on Cam's face, she stopped herself, smoothed the furrow from his brow with an unsteady hand. "Let's just say the man knows how to bury a lede."

She'd thought he was dead. The cold, paralyzing fear that had followed Harlow's first words had made it difficult to focus on the rest of his explanation. Cam had been in surgery for the bullet wound to his shoulder. She'd spoken to him once over the phone, when he'd been too groggy from the sedatives to make much sense. She'd taken the first plane out, but it would be a long time before she forgave the FBI agent for not keeping her informed about Cam's condition.

"Another thing he has to answer for," he muttered. Reluctantly he released her long enough for the physical therapist to help him get settled in the uncomfortable-looking recliner next to the hospital bed. "You didn't have to torture me this morning," he told the petite dark-haired woman as Sophia returned to his side. "She's all the therapy I needed."

"He was born under a lucky star," the woman said to Sophia, straightening to tuck her clipboard beneath one arm. "The bullet lodged in his bicep, and by some miracle it avoided bone."

Luck. Sophia squeezed Cam's hand tightly. They'd both had their share of it recently, but only after some sort of trauma. "I'm ready for the kind of luck that leads to winning the lottery."

He slipped his uninjured arm around her waist to pull her close. "I already have. You're a prize I'm hoping to treasure for the next sixty years or so."

Sophia bent down to give him a lingering kiss, one imbued with the promise of hope.

"Aw." The therapist applauded. "Why weren't you that sweet in therapy?"

When Sophia moved away, he looked at the other woman. "Because you're a Nazi, and she's way too good for me. We both know I'm over-chicked, but she's polite enough not to mention it."

The woman laughed on her way out the door. "Gotta admire a man who at least realizes he's outclassed."

Sophia pulled another chair up next to him. "Tell me about Matt. His family."

"Safe." Cam took her hand in both of his. "He saved my life. Moreno was about to finish me off. Matt was behind him. Shot him before he could fire again."

The words had her clutching reflexively at his fingers. "I hope I get to thank him someday."

"Probably not. The task force hit Moreno's compound at the same time they raided the operation. Matt's family was rescued and they reunited. Only to disappear hours later from the hotel they were stashed in by the feds."

Something in his tone alerted her. She reared back to study him. "I know that smug expression. There's more to that story than . . ." Comprehension hit her. "Harlow was right. You were in contact with Matt all along."

He shrugged. "It's always better to be in charge of your own fate. He and I discussed . . . options. I didn't trust the FBI not to keep Baldwin tied up in red tape for weeks. During which time he'd be a sitting duck."

As if in answer to that, the agent walked in, a flicker of wariness on his face when he saw Sophia. "Prescott. I hear you're being released soon. Good to hear."

"Harlow." When Cam strode over to the man, Sophia noted that he made even a hospital robe look sexy. "I've been in touch with my agents back home. Care to explain how someone could try to break into my place if there was an agent watching it?"

Harlow spread his hands. "Cam. You were under a great deal of stress. I understood that. But the surveillance was for your protection. And once you weren't there anymore . . ." The man shrugged. "I'm not the one who makes those kinds of decisions. I don't allocate the resources."

"No, you just allocate lies." Cam's tone was steely. "The paper you gave me that was signed by your superior made me think *his* word was good, even if yours is shit."

The congenial mask dropped, and Harlow flushed. "Fuck that. The task force takes precedence. I did what I had to in order to get your head in the right place. If you were worried about your . . . Dr. Channing . . . your life would be endangered even more. I did it for your peace of mind. You should be fucking thanking me."

Cam's fist slammed into the other man's mouth with enough strength to rock Harlow's head back. The speed and ferocity of the blow made Sophia gasp. "Cam!"

He unballed his fist. Flexed his fingers. "There's your thank-you."

"You goddamned lunatic!" The agent snatched a wad of tissues and pressed them to his mouth to stem the copious flow of blood. "Your superiors will hear about this."

"Yours, too." Cam sauntered back to Sophia's side. "And I still have the paperwork you gave me with the assistant director's forged signature on it."

When the agent stormed out of the room, Cam grinned at Sophia. "That was pretty good therapy, too." He wrapped his good arm around her. "Now. About that future you promised me . . ."

Looping her arms around his waist, she tipped her head back, considered him. "You mentioned sixty years. I should probably tell you, Channing women tend toward longevity."

There was a wicked glint in his eye that had her limbs going weak. "In that case, why don't we plan on eighty years together, with an option on another twenty?"

How many times in the last few days had she despaired of a future with this man? And now everything she'd longed for was just a kiss away. Sophia went on tiptoe to press her lips beneath his ear. "I love a man who knows how to compromise."

Acknowledgments

A special thank-you to Maxine Beckner and Michelle LaCoste, who came up with a very intriguing way to kill off one of my characters. A delightful way to spend a Sunday afternoon. ☺

Thank you, ladies!

About the Author

Kylie Brant is the author of thirty-five romantic suspense novels. A three-time RITA Award nominee, a four-time Romantic Times Award finalist, a two-time Daphne du Maurier Award winner, and a 2008 Romantic Times Career Achievement Award winner (as well as a two-time nominee), Brant has written books that have been published in twenty-nine countries and eighteen languages. Her novel *Undercover Bride* is listed by *Romantic Times* magazine as one of the best romances in the last twenty-five years. She is a member of Romance Writers of America, its Kiss of Death Mystery and Suspense chapter; Novelists, Inc.; and International Thriller Writers. When asked how an elementary special education teacher and mother of five comes up with such twisted plots, her answer is always the same: "I have a dark side." Visit her online at kyliebrant.com.